ROUND UP THE UNUSUAL SUSPECTS

I0846931

ROUND UP THE UNUSUAL SUSPECTS

Elizabeth Crowens

First published by Level Best Books/Historia 2026

Copyright © 2026 by Elizabeth Crowens

All rights reserved. No part of this publication may be reproduced, stored or transmitted in any form or by any means, electronic, mechanical, photocopying, recording, scanning, or otherwise without written permission from the publisher. It is illegal to copy this book, post it to a website, or distribute it by any other means without permission.

This novel is entirely a work of fiction. The names, characters and incidents portrayed in it are the work of the author's imagination. Any resemblance to actual persons, living or dead, events or localities is entirely coincidental.

Elizabeth Crowens asserts the moral right to be identified as the author of this work.

Author Photo Credit: Joey Pauline

First edition

ISBN: 979-8-89820-189-0

Cover art by Level Best Designs

*This book was professionally typeset on Reedsy.
Find out more at reedsy.com*

To Lola, my lucky star

Contents

Praise for Round Up the Unusual Suspects

"Fans of the movie *Casablanca* will love *Round Up the Unusual Suspects!* It was a pleasure to spend time with fictional versions of Bogart and Bergman and imagine what life on the set must have been like. The author has worked on many movies and TV shows, which made the book feel very authentic. Throw in a fun mystery, feisty PIs, some history about the 40s for people who were a little out of the mainstream, and you get an entertaining, thought-provoking read."—**Matt Witten**, bestselling author of *Killer Story* and Emmy-nominated screenwriter for *Pretty Little Liars* and *House*

"A witty, winning mystery that unfolds as a love letter to the golden age of Hollywood. Play it again, Elizabeth!"—**Daniel Stashower**, Edgar Award-winning, *New York Times* bestselling author of *The Hour of Peril* and *American Demon*

"A murdered tech threatens to derail a studio's biggest picture, so newly minted PIs Babs Norman and Guy Brandt are hired to keep the investigation quiet… and the cameras rolling. Navigating diva actors, shady crew members, and a director on the brink, they discover the killer is closer than they think. A zippy, irresistible page-turner, this Hollywood whodunit is pure gold."—**Kelly Oliver**, bestselling author of the Fiona Figg Mysteries and former National President of Sisters in Crime

"*Round Up the Unusual Suspects,* the third installment in Elizabeth Crowens' Babs Norman Golden Age of Hollywood Mysteries, is a fast-paced, delightfully humorous romp through Old Hollywood. Fans of classic Hollywood movies will love spending time with the icons of film history. Cozy mystery fans will enjoy following Babs and Guy as they solve a murder complicated by backstage gossip, Nazi sympathizers, and a couple of wise-cracking parrots."—**Connie Berry**, award-winning writer of the Kate Hamilton Mystery series and Immediate Past President of the Guppies online chapter of Sisters in Crime

"A fun romp through classic Hollywood with plenty of figures that the reader will recognize including some eye-opening facts about the history of the Japanese in California in WWII."—**Clare Broyles** of the Molly Murphy historical mystery series

"If you'd like old movies and solid mysteries, Elizabeth Crowens' *Round Up the Unusual Suspects* will be right up your alley. Fast paced and full of old Hollywood glamour. Set against the backdrop of World War II, Crowens' detailed research shows what it was to toil under the iron fist of both the studio heads and Uncle Sam."—**Dan White**, Telly and Communicator Awards-winning host and creator of *OutWithDan*

"Get ready for a rollicking mystery set in Hollywood's Golden Age! Elizabeth has woven an entertaining tale of intrigue that will give readers plenty to devour."—**Karie Bible**, Film historian, lecturer, co-author of *Location Filming in Los Angeles*, guest on TCM's *Hollywood Hideaways* and *Film Noir Fanatics*, tour guide for Hollywood Forever Cemetery, and host of the *Hollywood Kitchen* podcast

Cast of Major Characters

Babs Norman, former actress, now in her late twenties and a female private investigator, head of B. Norman Investigations. (fictional character)

Guy Brandt, former actor, early thirties, now Babs' investigative partner. (fictional character)

Principal Actors in *Casablanca*

Humphrey Bogart, male lead, plays Rick Blaine. Hired Babs and Guy in *The Maltese Falcon* case. In a stormy marriage to **Mayo Methot**, his third wife

Ingrid Bergman – female lead, Swedish actress who plays Ilsa Lund

Peter Lorre – German-Hungarian character actor who plays Ugarte in *Casablanca*

Sidney Greenstreet – British character actor who plays Señor Ferrari, the black marketeer and owner of the Blue Parrot Café

Claude Rains – British character actor who plays Captain Louis Renault in *Casablanca*

Paul Henreid – Viennese actor who plays the resistance leader, Victor Laszlo

Conrad Veidt – Veteran German actor who plays Major Strasser

* * *

Michael Curtiz – Hungarian director of *Casablanca*

Jack L. Warner, President of Production of Warner Brothers Studio and the most prominent and outspoken of the Warner Brothers. The other brothers involved with the movie studio include Harry, Sam, and Albert.

Hal B. Wallis, Producer on *Casablanca*

Abdul Maljan, Jack L. Warner's Turkish bodyguard and a former boxer.

Abel Wiggins, Irish-born janitor at the office building where B. Norman Investigations is located. Often integral in solving the PI's cases. (fictional character)

Salka Viertel – Former German actress, currently a screenwriter and humanitarian.

Sir Henry of the Baskervilles (Irish Wolfhound mix. Known for search and rescue. Hero dog in the *Asta-Rathbone* case. **Bruno** (bulldog). **Pedro** and **Petunia,** two blue hyacinth macaws the detectives received from a client as payment for a case. Notable pets of the private detectives' menagerie (fictional characters)

Dashiell Hammett – Author of the original novels *The Maltese Falcon* and *The Thin Man*. Friends with Guy and Babs in previous high-profile cases

George Raft, popular actor and former Broadway dancer, well-known for his gangster roles, inspired by real-life acquaintances in the underworld. Friends with known mobsters, **Bugsy Siegel** and **Virginia Hill**

Leon Lewis, local lawyer and social crusader, who ran a network of spies prior to WWII, taking down Nazi sympathizers in the Los Angeles area

Chapter One

"Nobody's allowed to die on one of *my* sets!" hollered Jack L. Warner. "Who's the jackass who wants to halt *my* production?" Flanked by his personal assistant Bill Schaefer, Jack dragged Hal B. Wallis, his head of production, over to the sound stage filming *Yankee Doodle Dandy*, starring James Cagney. He swung open the door as soon as the red warning light turned off and stormed inside.

Michael Curtiz, the film's director, dumped his megaphone and threw down the gauntlet. The parade band on stage accompanied his rage with a drumroll and cymbals.

Warner nabbed Curtiz's discarded megaphone. "Rally the troops—all of them! I have a studio-wide announcement."

Curtiz, turning red, clamped his hands over his ears. The actors and background extras, dressed in woolen military uniforms, stopped marching and sweltered under the hot lights. The live orchestra fell silent.

"Sir, maybe we should check out the dead body first," Schaefer suggested with hesitation.

At Warner's command, an assistant rolled back a piece of movable scenery to reveal a prone figure, an unknown young man wearing bloodied street clothes, but with a swastika carved on his neck.

"Are you sure he's dead?" Warner asked. "He looks like he's just sleeping on the job."

Backing up a few steps, Wallis broke out in a cold sweat. "Has *any-one* been *a-ble* to *i-den-ti-fy* him?"

The assistant director strained to keep self-control but trembled. "Everyone denies knowing him. Our director, however, insisted we ignore the victim and stay on schedule."

Wallis, turning green, gulped down his rising bile but regained his voice. "That's unconscionable. We should secure the set. Everyone will have to swear to secrecy, and under no circumstances is the press to know about it." Schaefer clutched his stomach, and his knees became unsteady. He grabbed a chair to brace himself.

Jack L. strutted the sound stage like Napoleon planning a counterattack and examined the casualty of war with a sense of unnerving calm. He wrinkled his nose and instructed his assistant, "Better call the Burbank PD. Won't take long under these broiling lights for him to stink to high heaven."

The actors, who'd remained in the stance of military attention, were about to wilt. Offstage, on both sides, waited singers and female tap dancers dressed in skimpy satin costumes as a tribute to Uncle Sam.

"At ease!" Warner shouted, accompanied by a round of relieved sighs.

"You think you can direct my film picture?" Curtiz shouted in his choppy version of Hungarian-bastardized English.

"I can and I will," Warner barked. "Don't forget, I sign your paychecks! Furthermore, I still can't understand why you summoned half the musicians' union to play instruments off-camera when you could've used a recording. Money wasted!"

Curtiz glared, with fire in his eyes. "It's because they're featured on camera at the beginning and the end of the scene!" He cursed in his native Hungarian tongue and stormed off the set.

Jimmy Cagney, the star of the show, followed. "You can find me in my dressing room."

Undaunted by his director and lead actor's histrionics, Warner demanded to see the production notes. After a quick glance, he scraped his fingernails through his receding hairline.

"Too much…can't picture it. Summon your editors and set up a projector—somewhere—anywhere, on the damned wall if we must. I'd need to see the dailies and bring me that hot-headed Hungarian *Goulash Gulag Meister* and his la-di-da lead actor."

Wallis broke the point of his pencil by slamming it down on his notepad. "All these delays…I don't want to hear a word from you about going over budget."

"I'm the one who makes the final decisions. Respect your commanding officer!" Warner admonished his confused subordinate.

Wallis gave him a weak salutation, but only out of respect. "Aye! Aye, sir!"

Warner gave one last look at the body. "Go ahead, call the police," he said to Schaefer. "And hire those two private detectives."

Wallis scratched his head with a look as if a screwball comedian had thrown a cream pie in his face. "Who?" he asked.

Warner clenched his jaw. "Babs Norman and Guy Brandt, those young kids who solved the *Blackbird Killer Case* and saved the cast of *The Maltese Falcon*. That was a close call for everyone."

* * *

The phone rang at B. Norman Investigations. Guy picked up and said Jack Warner's assistant was on the line. Babs motioned for him to hand over the receiver.

"The Big Boss desires your company," Schaefer told her.

"If he doesn't mind throwing in two mouth-watering prime-rib dinners at the Smoke House for us," Babs said, who hadn't eaten all day, "we'll consider that his consultation fee."

The two PI partners headed downstairs to their building's garage, where they now had their own assigned adjacent parking spaces instead of playing roulette for empty spots on the street. Babs put her key into the ignition of her ailing Crosley—the *Clown Car*, the brunt of Guy's constant jokes, with a paint job that resembled a motley patchwork. The moment she put her foot on the gas pedal, it made a bone-shaking screech of metal against metal and emitted exhaust that would've choked a triceratops.

"We're taking mine," Guy said after he stopped wheezing. He rolled up his windows to keep out the foul scent. "Can't believe you never had the sense to replace that fossil since it never ran well."

They pulled out of the garage, and he donned his sunglasses. "Now, you're stuck with it since our government stopped new automobile production and only people in *vital* professions, such as doctors and clergymen, qualify to purchase remaining inventories."

"Private eyes don't have priority?"

He shook his head. "Not in your sweet life. Those assembly lines are being converted to produce tanks, aircraft, and weapons for the military. Mark my words. Next thing you know, they'll demand that we ration fuel and rubber for our tires like they do in England. Read the papers if you don't believe me."

Guy flashed his Warner Brothers pass to the gate security guard. Babs panicked as she searched inside her purse. "I must've left mine in my car."

"Try flirting," Guy whispered.

She snorted in defiance. "I will not!"

Much to her surprise, he sweet-talked his way into saying, "She's with me," and pulled into an empty guest parking slot.

When they arrived at the *Yankee Doodle* sound stage, the crime scene investigation was well underway. The Burbank PD sectioned off the area where the deceased lay, but nearby, Curtiz insisted on conducting rehearsals even if it was too noisy to roll sound. He ordered the gaffer and his electrical crew to prep the lights for the next set of shots, but they went berserk, thinking a light was shorting out every time the crime scene photographer's flashbulb went off.

Curtiz insisted his captive cast and crew finish what they started. He'd work around the police, even if it meant yelling and screaming, at the risk of losing his voice, to make sure they kept quiet.

"Isn't Jimmy Cagney your star?" Guy looked around for the missing actor.

Curtiz made an unintelligible grunt and spat into his handkerchief. "We shall work around his crybaby tantrums." He launched a new battle with Wallis. "You complain that clocks ticking means money. Then why does Warner have to be such a stingy fat cat?"

Wallis bit his lip to keep from laughing at the director's deliberate jabs at the English language. "Our detectives-for-hire are here." He pointed out

Babs and Guy. "Jack wants you to perform the entire number, *Yankee Doodle Dandy*, from start to finish."

The director stood his ground. "That's not how we shoot it. We fall behind schedule. Then Jack gets more and more angry."

Warner paced the floor, bellyaching to himself and to any of the cops who would listen. "What if Cagney had been the intended victim? Not that I'm glad this man is an unknown Joe Palooka, but you get where I'm coming from."

The moment Babs saw the corpse, her stomach lurched.

Guy took his handkerchief and covered his nose and mouth. "Did you find any ID?"

"Found a driver's license in his wallet," said one cop. "He's got a German-sounding name: Gerhard Sauer."

Warner, holding a script, muscled in on their conversation. "I want to see this scene played out from start to finish."

Since Cagney left the set, Guy volunteered to stand in and improvise his choreography, but the studio head ignored his suggestion. "If that fussy thespian wants to act like a child, I'll just have to take over and go through the motions."

Babs took her notepad out of her pocketbook. "Did anyone hear any strange noises?" She looked around for reactions but got none. "Did you consider that someone killed Sauer elsewhere and, for whatever reason, dumped his body backstage?"

Babs blew her anger out of her nose. No one seemed to listen.

Wallis gave the PIs an overview to get them up to speed. "The film, *Yankee Doodle Dandy*, is about the life of lyricist and composer George M. Cohan. He performed with his family, and they called themselves The Four Cohans. Playing his father, we've got the famous actor who played the shot-up Captain Jacoby from *The Maltese Falcon*, Walter Huston."

"*Give My Regards to Broadway* is also one of Cohan's famous songs," Guy mentioned.

"We've included that one, along with *Over There*. All patriotic numbers that helped us endure WWI. Just think, we have a song for every star and a star for every stripe."

Wallis stopped and scratched his chin. "You know…I rather like that line. Must insist on using that quote for our trailer. However, what you'll see on screen is a show within a show, as if our cinematographer was shooting a documentary. At the beginning and the end of the scene, the camera will pan, showing an establishing shot of everyone inside the theater. That's where our live orchestra comes in.

"The Cohans perform in a stage production of a show titled *George Washington, Jr.* The song-and-dance medley scene we had been shooting before everything went haywire centers on *Grand Old Flag.* Once edited, it will look like we shot it from start to finish, but since Warner told me you used to be actors, you probably know that most of the time we shoot scenes out of order. We'll stop within sections to film close-ups and from different angles. Everyone's curious to see if there are clues about the killer in the footage we've shot so far."

Babs asked Wallis if he'd drop her a line when the footage was available for viewing.

Jack Warner, however, seemed to have his own agenda. He took over as director and insisted on doing a dry run. "Up with the curtain! Places, please. Stand by, and on with the show of the century. It's the most original thing to hit Broadway. You know why? Cagney…or Cohan, to be more accurate, is the whole darned U.S. of A. squeezed into one pair of pants."

Wallis asked the PIs to follow him and take seats with the extras in the audience.

"How many actors does the scene start off with?" Babs asked.

"Not including the live orchestra and the packed seats filled with the audience, I guess there are about thirty-five, but more join in later."

Lighter on his feet than expected, Warner skipped across the stage and justified substituting for Cagney, who refused to leave his dressing room. "Believe it or not, I've had experience as an entertainer. When my brothers and I started our family business, I used to sing in the aisles in between screenings."

Wallis drew a deep breath and released it. "There he goes again. The boss loves telling everyone the story of his debut in show business. Often, I wonder whether Jack secretly always wanted to be a performer instead of running a studio." He explained the upcoming scene while everyone blocked the action. "Jimmy sings *Grand Old Flag*. Twenty young Boy Scouts stride in from the top of the stairs. Betsy Ross sews the flag, upstage center. Eight more adults, who look like members of a military band, join them in song and advance from upstage right. After that, we cut away to five or six members of a fife and drum corps."

The PIs made every effort to follow Wallis while Warner danced on stage with the hired actors. "Upstage left, a variety of singers march forward, representing the common man and the working class—policemen, bakers, bankers, a nurse, miners, railroad workers—showing their solidarity. Everyone turns toward the flag and breaks into *My Country, 'Tis of Thee* in front of people manning an anti-aircraft gun."

Guy, who had been counting on his fingers, lost track. "How many would that add?"

"Probably another thirty. Central Casting must've broken out bottles of champagne after receiving our requisitions. Then the stage curtains close, and the spotlight falls on Cagney, downstage right. In come the tap-dancing dames, many bearing American flags. This is where we rival MGM's schmaltzy musicals with their elaborate costumes and choreography. Enter Uncle Sam, played by Walter Huston, and the Statue of Liberty. Then Jimmy wows everyone with his signature dance steps. More female flag bearers emerge from behind the rear curtain. Our stage crew has rigged the floor with conveyor belts, giving the illusion that the actors are marching toward the audience while they're actually staying in place."

"Otherwise, they'd march right off the stage," said Babs.

"Correct, but we wouldn't want them to do that," Wallis explained. "As the cinematographer pulls back and widens the focal length of his lens, background curtains continue to open until we see a painted backdrop of the Capitol Building in Washington, D.C. I'm no expert in visual effects, but it gives the audience the feeling there must be well over a hundred people proceeding down the boulevard. Pretty spectacular, don't you think?"

The assistant director leapt onstage and reminded Warner that the soldier actors were still suffering under the scorching lights and waiting for their next order. "Sir, we're not rolling camera. We should dismiss them."

"Tell them it's a wrap until further notice. I won't approve an exorbitant dry-cleaning bill for everyone *schvitzing* in their costumes."

With military precision, the assistants rounded up the various groups of performers and shuttled them toward wardrobe. Curtiz and James Wong Howe, his cinematographer, remained to discuss how they'd execute the rest of that scene.

Warner scribbled a note and handed it to his assistant. "Bill, tell these two to drop everything. I'm calling a meeting to order and want them present."

Schaefer reviewed his memo pad. "Sir, you scheduled one with them already." Then he checked his watch. "They should be there…right now."

Jack pointed to Babs and Guy. "Then you're coming with me and away from the crime scene." In a rush, he sprinted ahead.

Babs shouted loudly enough for him to hear her as he gained distance. "We'll need to sign a contract to make our assignment official!"

"Pick up the pace, you slowpokes, and I'll cut you a check after we get there."

Chapter Two

Jack Warner's massive desk reminded Babs and Guy of a Man O' War battleship, steeled with his oversized blotter, fancy-brand ink pens, and statuette reminders of glorious victories from the past. Captain Jack's crew lined the bulwarks. His personal assistant, Captain's Clerk Bill Schaefer, had his steno pad readied. Joining him was his Acting Lieutenant Hal Wallis, along with an old acquaintance and a new shipmate they didn't recognize.

Warner called their meeting to order by squeezing a circular brass bulb horn, the same kind used in vintage cars and by circus clowns. Even with the windows open, Babs coughed from the accumulated cigar smoke. She grabbed the nearest newspaper to wave it in another direction.

The detectives acknowledged Leon Lewis, also present, who had earned the reputation of being "the most dangerous Jew in Los Angeles." Through his network of spies, he had exposed subversive, antisemitic fifth columnists and had been a crucial ally in their last major case involving the cast and crew of *The Maltese Falcon*. Formerly affiliated with the Anti-Defamation League and a founder of the *B'nai B'rith Magazine*, Lewis had returned to his neglected law practice. He introduced them to Joseph Roos, his former associate, whom they had never met.

Lewis looked like he was on his way to the golf course, wearing his open-collared shirt, baggy trousers, and Argyle sweater vest. Roos, who wore a conservative suit and tie, appeared older with his much fairer, balding hair and glasses. Although unfair to judge a first-time acquaintance, he reminded Babs of a government agent whose sole purpose was to cite her on some obscure violation.

Warner confessed, "I've always been paranoid about the hordes of German immigrants infiltrating America. Warner Brothers declared war on the Nazis back in April 1939 with the film release of *Confessions of a Nazi Spy.*"

He stopped to clear his throat. "Those hateful idiots have plastered our streets with fliers demanding the elimination of all Jews! They even targeted President Roosevelt, accusing him of instituting a *Jew Deal* instead of his New Deal policies! Disgusting, I know. Lewis tells me now the man we found murdered yesterday went by Code Name: 72. He wasn't just a stagehand. He was one of his spies."

"Is that true?" Babs tried to hide her surprised reaction.

"Considering the work we were involved in, I always needed to keep my operatives' identities secret," Lewis explained. "Including my associate, Joseph, who I bet you didn't know existed until today. We always had to take precautions. One of my men had explosives placed in his mailbox and had to move his family out of town until he felt it was safe to return. Now, since it's out in the open, and the United States has declared Germany as an official enemy, we had to reorganize our campaign."

Roos revealed, "We assigned 72 to *Yankee Doodle Dandy* because it promoted American patriotism. In addition, we took a gamble on the assumption that a war film against the Axis Powers could also be a target of German-American Nazi sympathizers. Therefore, we assigned another one of our agents, Rudy Schmitz, known as Number 34, to be on the lookout on *Desperate Journey*, Warner's current Errol Flynn project."

Warner emphasized that Flynn was one of his most bankable stars. Wallis cut in to clarify, "From the production side, Warner Brothers always has a handful of films in the pipeline. Besides *Yankee Doodle Dandy*, we started *Desperate Journey* in mid-January. Then we have two more, both romantic stories, but I can't see how there'd be any threats."

"I disagree," said Babs. "A love story can stir up all sorts of complications, which could lead to murder. Why...my ex-husband can't seem to get it out of his head that—" She cut herself short. Babs didn't want to bring her insane ex-spouse into this situation, which was already grave enough.

Wallis reviewed his production records. "On the last week of February, we'll begin two more films: *The Hard Way*, starring Ida Lupino, and *Across the Pacific*, with familiar friends from your last case involving *The Maltese Falcon*: Humphrey Bogart, Mary Astor, and Sydney Greenstreet, with John Huston directing."

"Any German actors or crew of interest?" Guy asked.

"Perhaps our art director. His name is Robert Haas. Maybe we should conduct a background check. Even so, the enemies in this film are Japanese. Not sure if Jack's assistant told you, but when we received the unexpected news about the dead man, we were in the middle of a production meeting for a film called *Casablanca*, which we plan on starting in April."

"What's *Casablanca* about?" Babs asked.

"It's about love, war, and fighting for a righteous cause. Sometimes one must make tough choices that are for the greater good rather than for personal gain."

Leon interrupted. "However, as far as Joe Roos and I are concerned, let me explain how we've revamped our strategy. Right after the U.S. entered the war, Washington praised our underground organization's contributions to our nation's defense. Going forward, they assigned the FBI, the Immigration and Naturalization Service, and the G-2 Military Intelligence of the Army to operate on many of the issues that we had kept under wraps.

"The LAPD, however, had members of dissident groups within its ranks. They had a Red Squad, more interested in eliminating Communists in Southern California. They refused to believe the Nazis were any sort of threat. Such sentiments don't disappear overnight if they've been simmering since 1933. Therefore, it's reasonable to assume our government won't be able to round up every subversive overnight. One can always discard its shell, like a hermit crab, vacating one's headquarters and resurfacing somewhere else."

"Where does that put us in your plans?" Babs asked.

Jack Warner took over and explained, "Federal agencies will be more concerned about the bigger picture and lassoing entire organizations. Not to pass off a single murder as insignificant, but they'll consider our situation as a job for local authorities. Since there's a good possibility many members of the Burbank Police Department will get drafted, they'll want to hold on tight to their remaining men. That's where you'll come in as our set of eyes…as private eyes. We will pay you well."

Babs didn't want to show the obvious eye roll in front of the big boss, but everyone knew the stranglehold Jack Warner kept on his studio's purse strings.

"Jack, we should let Number 34 finish on your Errol Flynn film and then transfer him closer to activities on the main studio lot." Lewis suggested that was not only where the recent murder occurred, but where their biggest star was located.

"Who's that?" Warner asked.

"Look in the mirror, Jack," said Lewis. "You've contributed to organizations like ours, and you've worked with the War Office making anti-Nazi films. It would be easier for an insurgent to infiltrate Warner Ranch, given its size and landscape, but an attack on your Burbank headquarters would do more damage, given the higher concentration of Jewish stars and producers as potential targets."

Unable to hide his reaction, Warner started to sweat. "Don't you think that assumption is a bit far-fetched? Most of *Yankee Doodle Dandy* is in the can. We've just started Flynn's project."

"Even so," Roos said, cutting in. "I can't picture you, Hal Wallis, or any of your Jewish producers or actors planning on hiding."

"Do you suspect any surprise attacks?" asked Wallis.

"We're not sure what to expect," said Lewis. "That's the problem."

Roos added, "Since the Japanese have allied with the Germans and there has been talk about sending them off to internment camps, we have concerns that antisemitic attacks might come from their quarter."

Wallis referred to his production reports. "What about this alternative? Since we'll be paying to bring these private eyes on board, keep Agent Schmitz on the Flynn film and have Brandt patrol the Warners lot."

"Excuse me," said Guy. "Perhaps you're not aware, but Babs and I have been in between investigations. To supplement my income, I signed up with Central Casting. They brought me on as an extra on *Desperate Journey*. We'll need to consult with someone to ensure there won't be any continuity issues."

"Then once Brandt wraps up his obligations," said Wallis, "we'll reassign him to keep tabs on the Warner Brothers lot, along with the Terrible Turk."

"Who's that?" Roos asked.

"Abdul Maljan, my personal bodyguard," Warner replied. "He's also my masseur and a former professional boxer."

"Jack's got his own private steam room on the lot," Wallis explained. "In any event, Brandt's already got a studio pass and knows his way around."

Babs felt left out. After all, she headed B. Norman Investigations. "Where do I fit in?"

Everyone eyed one another in silence. Babs' growling stomach broke the impasse by making a blatant announcement.

"Not to make it sound trivial, but you'll do what you need to do to follow up with the crime scene investigation team. We also expect you to dig up more on Gerhard Sauer beyond what Leon Lewis and Joseph Roos already have in their files," said Wallis. "Since the FBI has taken over many of their former duties, and they might've uncovered information that we're unaware of, you'll deal with them as well. At least it's a less dangerous option."

Babs asserted her point. "I hope you're aware I can handle a gun."

Guy whispered, "Babs, simmer down. Why don't you follow up with that crime scene photographer? Maybe you didn't pick up on it, but I sensed he liked you, and you never know who he might know."

"It sounds like they want me to stick to more administrative work," she moaned.

Since everyone would split up on separate assignments, Babs insisted she and her partner accompany Rudy for at least one day on *Desperate Journey* to get a feel for the challenges ahead. Not without reservations, Wallis complied but avoided further grilling when Jack Warner's tummy *kvetched* louder than Babs'.

"I guess I promised the little lady to take her and her partner to the Smoke House. Wallis, I don't care if your wife has your favorite pot roast in the oven, you're coming with me." Jack Warner asked Lewis and Roos if they cared to join him for dinner, but they declined.

"As much as I'd love to take you up on the offer, it's best we continue to keep a low profile," said Lewis.

While Wallis and Warner discussed last-minute details and said their goodbyes, Babs turned to Guy. "I want a table at the Smoke House near those pictures of Clark Gable."

Guy asked, "Why?"

"Because I think he's cute."

Making sure they were out of earshot, Guy whispered, "Don't let them know it, but so do I."

Chapter Three

Errol Flynn flashed his million-dollar smile at Babs and asked, "Tell me, gorgeous, what were you doing sneaking around my dressing room?"

"I thought this was Ronald Reagan's." Babs shuddered, but she'd talk her way out of this pickle like she always did.

"Don't believe that for a minute unless your eyesight is as bad as his. My name's posted right outside."

"No, it's not. It's posted under the character's name of Flight Lieutenant Terry Forbes," she argued.

"Then I guess you didn't read the script."

"Jack Warner hired me to protect you." She choked on her words as she eyed the likes of this perfect male specimen—his cleft chin, with a thin, trained mustache, so fine it looked penciled in, which graced his upper lip. Nature had blessed him with a full head of thick, wavy medium-brown hair, and at moments like this, a naughty tendency to raise his left brow.

Flynn laughed so hard that he tipped his chair too far backward and fell onto the dirt floor. Without so much as an apology, he got back on his feet, puffed out his chest, and showed off his six-foot-two-inch strapping frame compared to her dainty stature.

He yanked her out of his closet. She tried to kick him but lost her footing and fell flat on her can. He called for a truce and offered to help her up, but pointed to the chair, as if it was his time to conduct the inquisition.

"Who else sent you to spy on me?" he asked. "I bet Wallis was behind it as well. Am I right? So, they want me off the bug juice?"

She shook her head. "Never came up in conversation. They're worried about political agitators disrupting your film and threatening your life to get to them."

A look of shock wiped away his smug grin. "I have proof I didn't dodge the draft. The studio has done a stupendous job of covering up that I flunked the military health exams."

Curious about why, Babs kept a straight face. "A stagehand, or at least we think he was a stagehand, got murdered on the set of *Yankee Doodle Dandy*."

"Well, I'll be... How come I never heard about that?"

"Hal Wallis used to be a publicity man. He kept the situation under tight wraps between the local PD and the immediate crew and made sure the press stayed out. The contract players knew how to keep their mouths shut. Day players had to sign confidentiality agreements."

"Relax. I promise not to put my mitts on you." Errol insisted he'd behave but begged to know more. "But first, it would help if I knew who you are."

She brushed the dirt off her dress. "This is an awkward introduction and not one I had hoped for. My name is Babs Norman. I'm a private investigator—yes, I'm licensed. My office, B. Norman Investigations, is on Hollywood Boulevard near La Brea." She reached into her purse for one of her cards but came up dry. "Well, anyway, my partner is Guy Brandt, who you might've encountered already. We're working with an outside... consultant who plays one of the Germans, and he's done some stunt work. Warner Brothers hired us to keep an eye out for any suspicious activities—"

"But now, it looks like I'm the one guilty of *unkosher* behavior. Then do me a favor. Mum's the word with our producers about me playing Casanova. Deal?"

* * *

Her hasty exit led to another embarrassment. Not paying attention, Babs turned her ankle after staggering into a gopher hole. Guy offered her a hand. "Didn't I tell you to wear sensible shoes? Wouldn't be to anyone's benefit if we had to wrap up a sprain."

"If that were the case, I could use a cane to my advantage."

"How so?"

"To learn the art of defending myself with one, since I'd never be able to use it to compete with those tap dancers over at MGM. Otherwise, I would've remained an actress. Looking good on a screen test isn't good enough anymore when producers insist you also need to sing and dance."

"Didn't you start your acting career by singing jingles on radio shows in Frisco?"

"Occasional cabaret gigs, as well. Tap dance? Not on your life. During the Depression, we were lucky to put food on the table, though I had always dreamed of becoming a ballerina. There was no way my relatives could groom me to be another Shirley Temple after Daddy was *murrrdurred…*"

Realizing she shouldn't have brought it up, Babs altered her voice just above a whisper and stared him in the eye. "Let's change the topic."

Guy bolstered her to ensure she remained steady. "What caused you to run off in such a hurry? Did Flynn make a move on you?"

Once again, she insisted on shifting their conversation. "You'll have to point out Number 34, or whatever the code name was for the German actor Leon Lewis spoke about."

"Rudy Schmitz? Can't miss him. You'll think we found our *Blond Satan.*"

Babs's forehead wrinkled into a landscape of rolling hills. Guy tested her memory. "Remember Dashiell Hammett's description of Sam Spade in his original novel of *The Maltese Falcon*? He described Sam Spade as a tall, strong-jawed *Blond Satan*. Not even close to what Humphrey Bogart looked like in the movie or the other actors in the two previous attempts Warner Brothers made to adapt that story to screen."

They passed a makeshift tent with a nametag for German #1. Guy announced through the tent flap, "Rudy, are you decent?"

Rudy Schmitz slipped out and straightened up to full height at six-foot-three. A striking performer in his mid-thirties, he could've passed for one of the Teutonic gods of German wartime propaganda. A stray sunbeam broke through the overhead shade trees, highlighting his thick leonine mane.

Aware of her partner's leanings, she still felt uncomfortable asking about his relationships and wondered if anything was developing between them. Even worse, as if there were an unwritten rule that exceptionally good looks equated with insincerity, Babs thought Rudy was too handsome. She didn't trust him.

While everyone got to know each other better, Guy dropped hints that his roommate might give up acting. "He's contemplated moving back home to South Carolina and figures as an able-bodied young man, he's going to get drafted, anyway. I don't want to be stuck with the responsibility of paying the rent by myself."

"What if you get drafted too?" Rudy asked.

"I'll figure a way to get out of it."

"Couldn't handle the rent alone?" she asked.

"You have your Japanese gardener paying a good chunk of your household expenses. If my roommate vacates, I'll need someone to help pay my rent." He glanced at Rudy. No reaction.

When the trio arrived on set, Rudy split to join others in the extras holding area. Wallis introduced the two private investigators to Raoul Walsh, the film's unmistakable director, by being the only one on the set wearing a black eye patch. Wallis gave Walsh an overview for bringing the PIs.

Walsh examined Guy. "Do you mind getting shot?"

"I beg your pardon?"

"Not real bullets, of course. I'm not like some of my contemporaries who've killed a horse or two to get the effect."

"Why, may I ask?"

"I'm short a few extras today," the director explained. "It'll take too long for casting to send more."

Guy turned to Babs after Walsh left. "He must not have remembered that he used me as an extra before."

"So much for your big break on film," she replied.

Errol Flynn, who'd been eavesdropping, cozied up to their conversation.

"I got my start in London playing a dead body in a funeral scene. Now, I'm the headliner. Maybe this'll be the start of a lucrative acting career. Stranger things can happen."

Walsh summoned an assistant to escort Guy over to wardrobe. While the producer went over scheduling with the director and the cinematographer supervised his team for the next setup, Babs took that breather as an opportunity to take in the scenery at Warner Ranch. She had played an extra in *The Adventures of Robin Hood* the last time she was here, and her encounter with Flynn made it obvious he hadn't remembered her. Today, she needed to view this location with a fresh set of eyes and analyze the possibilities of where an unwanted outsider could sneak in, use the natural terrain for cover, and wreak havoc.

Toward the Santa Susana Mountains, she spotted a lone tree and an open field with an aircraft made up to look like a fighter plane. Before she got too close, an authorized, as opposed to an actor mechanic, ran after her and shouted, "Halt!"

She showed him her studio pass. "I'm an official hire." Babs tried to explain why Warner Brothers brought her and her partner on board.

He wasn't buying it. "Run along, or I'll have to report you to my supervisor. Don't need no saboteurs trying to get money from our producers."

Unable to persuade him otherwise, she headed toward the woodsier areas. She got the impression these might've been the Sherwood Forest locations used in *The Adventures of Robin Hood*.

She returned to base camp as the assistant director broke everyone for lunch. Divided by rank, the director, producer, and the top stars sat in a designated location, given extra overhead protection by a canvas sunshade. Below-the-line craftsmen sat elsewhere, and the extras and stuntmen had their own separate section. Unsure where she fit in, Rudy invited Babs to join him and Guy with the extras.

"Too bad they didn't give you special VIP status," Rudy told Babs. "We extras get stuck with a simple boxed lunch. The top brass gets catered to with champagne and caviar."

She swore Rudy was pulling her leg.

Rudy opened his container and took his sandwich apart. "*Mmmm,* baloney and sickening yellow American mustard on white bread. Can't tell you how I miss the hearty mustard from back home."

"I'm impressed with your English. Where was home?" Babs asked.

"Berlin. Born and raised, but as a working actor, I practiced my elocution. On occasion, I'd perform Shakespeare. That's the reason for my slight British accent." Rudy wrinkled his nose at the sandwich before shoving it into his mouth. "Down the hatch, I suppose."

Guy dug into his. "At least it's not liverwurst. I used to slip mine under the table and feed it to the dog."

Armed with a script, Babs wanted to take advantage of the break and skimmed over it. "Considering he's the only Yankee, it looks like Ronald Reagan adds the comic relief."

Guy stopped eating. "How so?"

"They won't be shooting this scene today, because it takes place at the British headquarters shot on a sound stage. He knocks on Flynn's or Lt. Terry Forbes' door to tell them they're needed at a meeting. When Forbes hopes it's for a better transfer, Reagan, who plays Johnny, the American pilot, says, 'Haven't you heard? You're being sent back to Australia to help that intelligence unit out there. You're going to search kangaroos' pouches for fifth columnists.'"

Rudy laughed so hard he had to spit out his mouthful of sandwich into a paper napkin.

Babs flipped to a page farther into the script. "Here's another one. During a scene where a single German soldier holds the Allies at gunpoint on a bridge, Johnny jokes around when it's clear the guy doesn't understand English. He says, 'Come on, you big pickle puss. Just give me a chance to kick you in the middle of your goosestep.'"

While everyone couldn't stop laughing, including others within earshot, another actor wearing a German soldier's uniform pointed to the empty seat beside Rudy. "Mind if I join you?"

"Not at all. Babs, Guy, this is Helmut Dantine. Another official ex-pat who's made it all the way to Hollywood."

"Is that a real German name or your stage name?" asked Guy.

"Many people mock me and say that Helmut Dantine, in German, means I have chewing gum on my hat."

"Ha! As in Dentyne gum?" Guy laughed. "People always accuse me of having gum on my shoe."

Taking that at face value, Dantine poked his head under the picnic table to peer at Guy's boots but looked perplexed. *"Was? Ich verstehe nicht?"*

Rudy translated, "He said, 'What? I don't understand?'"

Babs intervened, trying not to embarrass him. "Of course, he wouldn't. A gumshoe is an American figure of speech or a nickname for a private investigator, or the job Guy and I have and the reason we're here."

Helmut's lips curled into a smile. He chuckled along with everyone else, but Babs suspected he did it to fit in and still didn't comprehend.

"Are you also from Berlin?" Guy asked.

"Vienna."

Babs got curious. "Helmut, did you have a lot of film and theatrical work before you left Germany?"

"I spent too much time getting into trouble. When I led an anti-Nazi youth movement at nineteen, they captured and sent me to a concentration camp. My parents convinced a doctor to get me a medical release. Afterward, they sent me to stay with a family friend in Los Angeles. Then I got interested in acting." He pointed out his German uniform. "Everyone wants to cast me now as an evil Nazi."

"What about you?" she asked Rudy, whom she wanted to know better. She suspected Guy liked him.

"Ah...*The Blue Angel*...Dietrich, Lotte Lenya, Anita Berber, *Three Penny Opera*, Conrad Veidt in *The Cabinet of Dr. Caligari*...those were the days to nourish our muses. I kept company with the avant-gardes—the artistes and the theatrical crowd, which presented its own kind of turmoil. Producers and casting directors at UFA, the premier film production studio in Germany, expressed their interest and wanted me to sign a stringent contract, but I could see...how do you say? The writing was on the wall.

"Everyone was in a financial rut during the Weimar Republic, but my creative life was like...*ein Stück Kuchen mit Schlagsahne*...a piece of pie with whipped cream on top...from '24 until '33 when Hitler took over as Chancellor and shut everything down. I despised those fascists more than they hated me. All I wanted to do was stomp them out...like this!" Startling everyone, he slapped his hands together and caught a buzzing insect mid-flight, crushing it upon impact.

A loud whistle signaled the lunch break was over. Guy, thrilled that Walsh recruited him, was eager to exercise his acting chops even in a minor capacity. So far, all seemed to run as planned, with no threats to their star, nor any antisemitic backlash toward their producer. The only "threats" were when Flynn tried to put a few smooth moves on Babs, but she kept a professional distance.

While Guy accompanied Rudy, figuring he'd show him where to report next, Babs assumed she should reconnect with Hal Wallis. He introduced her to Carl Jules Weyl, the film's art director.

Wallis praised Weyl for some of his other accomplishments. "Besides what he's done for films, Carl is a famous Los Angeles architect. He's the one behind the design of the Brown Derby restaurant and the Hollywood Palace Theatre."

"Here's one of the sets I want to build onstage," Weyl explained. "This one is for the commandant's office. I'll need everyone's approval right away to meet your tight production schedule."

"If the director signed off on it, I'm fine, as well," said Wallis. After Weyl left, he confided to Babs, "Carl is one of my favorites. I insist on assigning him to *Casablanca*, even if I need to pull him off someone else's project to do it."

Wallis gave Babs a tour of the set and explained what they were in for. "Given the recent government-issued curfews and blackouts, our cinematographer has used day-for-night techniques with underexposure and special filters, making his black-and-white film appear like we'd been shooting after dark.

"Warner Ranch's varied topography also lends toward fooling the eye or, in this case, the lens. We've filmed many action films at this location, doubling for the American West, and from merry old England to the Battle of Balaklava in Crimea. Many of these pictures starred Errol Flynn."

"This place must feel like Flynn's second home by now," said Babs.

"Pretty much. The last scene planned for the day," explained Wallis, "involves the heroes discovering a captured British Lockheed Hudson aircraft. They watch as the Germans load it with one of their bombs with the intention of flying it to destroy the Battersea Waterworks. If the Allies spotted it, they'd assume it was one of their planes, allowing them to fly so low that they couldn't miss the target."

Guy caught up with Babs while the crew worked on a new setup. Wearing mechanic's garb and an envelope-shaped cap, he explained his get-up, "Walsh needed more actors playing the German soldiers."

"What sort of part will Rudy play?"

"A stuntman, but I wonder if they're paying him like one. What's in his favor is all the previous scenes took place at night. In one, he drove a motorcycle chasing the heroes' getaway car. He winds up falling from a low bridge into a creek. In others with closeups, he appears as a dark silhouette against fog."

It finally came time to put today's scenes on film. While the Germans hunted for the Allied soldiers on the lam, the remaining three Allied heroes rushed in to steal their plane. Flynn fired up the ignition. Ronald Reagan, the last to board, kicked Rudy in the face, causing him to fall over backward. This was the only time anyone would see his face on screen and only for a few seconds. Guy had his featured moment when Errol Flynn, positioned in a machine gun pit, shot him dead.

After the director approved the final take, Wallis told Guy, "Now, you're needed at the studio. We're not bringing you back to life."

Chapter Four

Jitney buses marked with the Warner Brothers' logo picked up the cast and crew to take them back to the Burbank studio from their remote West Valley location. Once Babs settled in her seat, she reviewed her notes for the day.

"Is this for your report to our employers?" Rudy asked.

"While you gentlemen were pretending to be movie stars, outside of my embarrassment of getting caught in the act, it looks like it's safe to say Errol Flynn doesn't seem to be in any danger."

Guy laughed. "I guess you can call that progress, but we have a long way to go."

"Going forward, all of us should touch base once a day to make sure everyone is well-informed. Especially since we're all going to be working from different locations," she said, closing her notepad and returning it to her purse.

Much of the area had rough roads, scattered orange groves, and farmland; most of it was unpaved and undeveloped. Babs held on to the back of the seat in front of her to keep from bouncing all over the place.

The minute Guy dropped Babs off at home, her stomach howled so loud she thought it would summon her dog. The aroma of ramen soup wafting from the kitchen tempted her to ask her Japanese boarder, Aoi Otake, if he had enough to share.

"*Otake-san?*" Not having to go far, Babs found him in her living room, with his hands wrapped tight around a handleless ceramic cup of steaming *o-cha*, or green tea, and listening to the radio. The moment he saw her, he turned it off.

Babs tossed her purse onto the end table and made herself at home. "Anything interesting?"

"You couldn't understand. Speaking all in Japanese. News...opinions... politics affecting locals. Sometimes entertainment. Tonight spoke of bad news."

Concerned, Babs took a chair. "Tell me."

"They print headlines like: 'Crime and poverty go hand in hand with Asian labor.' They accuse Japanese immigration companies...break laws. Government says we are made citizens illegally. Bad talk about Japanese men are evil menace toward to American women. Accuse Japanese children by crowding out others in the public schools. Big yellow peril! Scared, stupid people claim we steal brains of whites! Now they speak about shipping us out of town now since U.S. is at war with Japan."

"That won't happen, and those accusations are nonsense."

"Miss Babs, don't be so sure. People wanted to do that for a long time."

Sir Henry of the Baskervilles, her dutiful Irish Wolfhound, pattered in from the dining room. Missing his master, he sat at her feet and whimpered. His forlorn face mirrored Otake's dispirited expression.

"No protection for first-generation *Issei* people like me." Otake poured himself more tea. He offered her some if she could find a clean cup.

Babs needed to keep all her Japanese terms straight. *Issei* meant he had been born in Japan. If his parents had come to the U.S. and he had been born here, he would've been *Nisei*, or second-generation.

"But you're telling me no one would protect those people, either. Right?"

"Nobody safe. People also talk of removing Germans and Italians from the West Coast, but there are more Japanese, especially here in California."

"If they force you out of town, where do they expect you to go? Your home and your work are here."

"Our businesses will shut down. Talk of sending us to camps."

"This is the Land of the Free and the Brave," she declared, thinking of *Yankee Doodle Dandy* and *Grand Old Flag*. "You're the most innocent and harmless man I know," said Babs. If she found a spider and wanted to stomp on it, he was the sort of guy who insisted on picking it up and taking it outside.

She tried to place a comforting hand on his shoulder, but he looked offended and jerked away. If she made errors in judgment regarding others' cultural differences, like showing her sympathy by physically touching an older Japanese male, she could only imagine what more ignorant folk would do or think. Out of respect, she made a halfhearted bow and took a few apologetic steps backward.

"I must do as they say. Not a citizen. Am considered a *pri-vir-ledged* guest." Changing the subject, he asked, "You know Charlie Chaplin?"

"We're not friends, but of course, I know of him. Why?"

"His Japanese houseboy…accused of spying."

"No kidding!"

"Also, rumor of Japanese fishermen's boats at Terminal Island being transformed into torpedo boats. Your government people accuse people from my country. Maybe I need to run away."

"This isn't Nazi Germany, and we don't have concentration camps in our country. I know of only one person who's dangerous enough to deserve to be locked up and sent away, and that's my ex-husband Troy, whom I hope is still in jail. For you? That's absurd." She gave it some thought. "Are you listening to American radio stations like I asked to help you learn English?"

"I try…sometimes."

"Maybe you're getting upset about nothing. Sometimes what they print in the papers is nonsense. I'll check what the *Times* says tomorrow. After all, I'm a private detective. I'll handle this."

"You not get in trouble?"

Babs took pause. When she investigated her high-profile case about the celebrity dognappings, she wound up with a police and an FBI record from trespassing on a suspect's property, who had also been under surveillance by the Feds. The second time the police arrested her was during her last major case, when trying to bring the *Blackbird Killer* to justice. She got caught up with Detective Felix Allgood from the Hollywood PD in a few gambling raids over at Ciro's, the swanky nightclub on Sunset. What would happen if she got a third violation added to her list of previous offenses?

"Don't you worry." Like she really knew what she was talking about. Was there a possibility she could lose her PI license after she worked so hard to get it? Despite the doomsayer's chatter in her head, she assured her tenant she'd be fine.

* * *

In the following few days, all was quiet on the Warner Brothers front. Rudy continued his spying assignment on *Desperate Journey*, also doubling as a stuntman. In theory, Wallis assigned Guy to work as a production assistant on *Yankee Doodle Dandy*, but he also expected him to be at his beck and call. Just like Bill Schaefer always being at Warner's command, Hal dragged him into serving as his personal assistant.

Wallis should've sensed trouble when he and Guy walked into Jack Warner's office and had found him dressed in his flashy tennis whites. They were supposed to discuss who they wanted to hire as the director and cinematographer for *Casablanca*. Hal refused to leave such an important decision open-ended and followed his boss over to his private tennis court to play singles against Abdul Maljan. On *normal* days, the big hulk and former Turkish boxer functioned as his masseur and bodyguard. Hal assumed Jack couldn't find one of his regular tennis partners and recruited the *Terrible Turk* instead.

Overheated in his tropical-weight wool business suit, Hal felt foolish jockeying back and forth to conduct business during Jack's game.

"Everyone calls me a raconteur," Warner boasted. "It's because I play a hell of a game of tennis."

Racket...raconteur...there he goes again. Unbuttoning his dampened collar, Hal kept his eye on the ball and wherever his boss navigated the court. Tired of running, he planted himself parallel to the net. He panted and could hardly get the words out.

Being known as a jokester and often earning the moniker of the Clown Prince of Hollywood, Warner served and slammed the ball into his producer's shoe. Wallis leapt in the air like a rabbit under an exploding firecracker. "Darn it, Jack! How do you expect me to replace my Italian brogues if we're at war with them?"

"Payback for interrupting my game." Warner retrieved the ball, this time to execute a proper serve. "Be thankful I didn't garnish your wages."

"That son of a gun," Wallis muttered out of range. He inspected the scuff and tried to rub it out.

"By the way…" Warner hit his ball out of bounds. "Is the Brandt boy your assistant now? Last time I checked, I thought we were paying him to solve a crime."

"We're paying him to do whatever we need him to do," Wallis barked back. "And I'm writing the checks."

"But I'm signing them," Warner replied and turned his attention to Guy. "If that's the case, Sonny, how 'bout you switch places with my bodyguard? You look like you're much lighter on your feet."

Guy was about to retrieve Jack's ball, but Wallis shooed him away toward the sidelines and picked up the ball himself, muttering, "Can't believe he's so cheap that he plays with bald tennis balls."

"Look, we must make our decision…and soon," he said to the big boss before turning to Guy. "Can you hand me my briefcase?"

Guy sprinted with the briefcase over to Wallis. "Don't forget," he whispered, "we need to speak about our investigation."

Wallis replied, "Yeah…yeah." He took out his notes and turned his back on Guy. "Jack, my first choice to direct *Casablanca* is William Wyler. I sent him the script while he was vacationing in Sun Valley. He turned the project down, and I swear he never read the script. Then my secretary sent scripts to Vincent Sherman, Michael Curtiz, and William Keighley to see who might be interested."

"What did Sherman think?" Warner asked, also finding it difficult to speak while following the bouncing ball.

Wallis tried not to laugh at Maljan, who lumbered around the court, contending against his much nimbler employer. "I didn't care for his attitude. He called it 'A marvelous piece of movie junk.' Curtiz wants the project. By the time we'll be ready to go into pre-production, he'll have finished *Yankee Doodle Dandy*. However, he focuses too much on camera movements and might not be the best choice for handling the sensitivity of a love story."

Guy waved his hand, trying to flag him down from the sidelines, but Wallis ignored him. Jack looked at his watch, missing his ball, which bounced out of bounds. He threw a towel around his neck and announced their unfinished game was now over. "The Hungarian always makes money. He stays within his budget and brings in his films on time."

"He wants James Wong Howe to shoot it, the cinematographer he worked with on *Yankee Doodle Dandy*, but he's unavailable," said Wallis.

Jack and Abdul headed back to the studio. "He'll have to accept whoever we assign…and that's that."

Sweaty and out of breath, Guy sprinted over to Wallis. "We never—"

"I know. That's Jack for you." Wallis looked at Guy's exposed face and arms. "Looks like you might wind up with a sunburn. Better put first-aid cream on it."

"But what about—?"

"Later, kid. I need to hire my director first."

Chapter Five

While Rudy and Guy searched for suspects within the more glamorous movie world, Babs felt at a distinct disadvantage without her partner. Already in a testy mood, she had just gotten off the phone with the Medical Examiner's Office. Babs had yet to get Gerhard Sauer's autopsy results. She also knew it was a waste of her time to drive back downtown and demand them in person, because she'd already tried it.

"A dame running a PI agency?" Famous last words. Most men she encountered had their preset notions. Often, Guy would step in when crime investigators refused to acknowledge her credibility. But with him gone and hobnobbing in the world of celluloid and celebrities, someone needed to man the front desk. She no longer had the luxury of sequestering herself in the back office, even if it was to touch up her nail polish when no one was looking.

Even their Irish Wolfhound, Sir Henry of the Baskervilles, and their two blue hyacinth macaws, Pedro and Petunia, knew something was amiss. Out of their office menagerie, only Bruno, their bulldog, slept through her discontent.

The front door opened. Some young kid, armed with a stack of newspapers, asked, "Are you the secretary?"

"I'm the boss." She hated interruptions during her favorite breakfast of coffee and a chocolate eclair. "What do you want?"

"Hey, don't get mad at me. Honest mistake. Didn't expect—"

"A woman to be running a business?" She finished his sentence and put him on the spot. "Aren't you old enough to get drafted?"

Sweat rolled down his neck. "I…only wanted to check to see if you needed a subscription to the *LA Times*."

She pointed to the stack of untouched periodicals and tabloids. "Already got ones for the *Times, Variety, The Hollywood Reporter*, the *Examiner*…you name it, and then some. Tell your office to stop sending its troops over here to bother me. Two of your foot soldiers solicited me yesterday."

"Hey, lady, you don't have to be rude. Got this gig so I can save up for a car."

"Good luck finding one," she said, shooing him away. She was on edge and felt bad that she had treated the poor kid like a rotten egg.

After he left, Babs cleared her breakfast and propped her feet up on top of Guy's desk. Going over her to-do list, she preferred to plan a vacation. Even better? A honeymoon, but who had time to date anymore? Business always had to come first.

She was anxious for updates. Anything from Guy, she could trust. With Rudy, she still had her reservations, but every time the phone rang, often it was a sales call, a wrong number, or an occasional prank from teenagers thinking they're hotshots by pestering a PI agency and making wisecracks that sounded like they were from a Hammett or Chandler novel.

"Babs? Hi. Bill Schaefer, here, Jack Warner's assistant. My boss now requests that you coordinate and turn in a daily report combining your notes along with Guy and Rudy's."

Their conversation was short and sweet. She hung up and sulked that she needed to hire a new assistant. Then the phone rang again.

"Babs, it's Ernie Fischman. The crime scene photographer. We met the other day at Warner Brothers."

That's odd. "Are *you* calling to give me the autopsy report?"

"Uh, no…" he stuttered. "Not quite in my job description. I was wondering if you weren't busy tonight, if you wanted to catch dinner and the new Gary Cooper movie."

Her janitor, Able Wiggins, swung open the office door. Several stamped envelopes stuck out of his back pocket.

"I'm yer handyman. Not yer postal delivery man," he said, after placing his janitorial supplies in the corner and handing her the letters. "Maybe I should start demanding tips."

Unable to handle the two conversations at once, Babs said to Ernie, "Sorry. I'll call you back."

If this is what being a private eye is about, maybe I chose the wrong profession!

With her mind elsewhere, Babs hung up but failed to place the phone receiver back on its cradle. The receiver fell and dangled on its cord. Sir Henry picked it up in his mouth and hung it up properly.

"Too much mail stuffed into yer door slot," continued Wiggins. "Found these on the floor. All it would take is fer a strong enough breeze to come along and blow dem down the hallway. I picked them up and took them downstairs."

She glanced at the postmarks and worried. Some had arrived last week. "Hope the electric company won't cut my power, because I didn't receive my bill in time."

He pulled a note out of his trousers pocket and handed it to her. "You've gotta stop giving out my phone number, or I'll have to charge you as an answering service. What's the deal with the FBI?"

Babs' eyes widened. *They must've called when I was out walking the dogs.* She grabbed the note and shoved it into Guy's top desk drawer.

Meanwhile, Wiggins helped himself to coffee, sat down, and glanced around the room.

"Your office is usually crawling with more critters. Where did the kittens you rescued disappear to?"

"A sympathetic veterinary clinic found homes for them," she replied. "With two dogs and two gigantic birds, I didn't want any curious kitties winding up as somebody's lunch."

"Just wait till another stranger takes you for a sucker and drops off a box in the alleyway."

Both heard a knock on the door, one that sounded polite and almost inaudible.

"It's unlocked." She wiped her mouth with a napkin and scrambled to look ladylike and presentable. Mr. Otake entered with a Japanese newspaper tucked under his arm and a grim look on his face. Bruno opened one eye and went back to his sweet dreams. The parrots, sensing an intruder, emitted two squawks from the back office.

He noticed Wiggins and asked, "Did I interrupt something?"

"My time is yours." Not really, Babs thought, realizing she wasn't making progress on Sauer's case fast enough. All she needed was another distraction.

Mr. Otake unfolded his newspaper with such precision it was like deconstructing origami. He was about to show her an article, but realized she couldn't read it. "Big announcement. Maybe you should turn on the radio to a news station."

She turned the knobs until she tuned into 1070 AM KNX, Los Angeles' All-News Radio.

> "We have breaking news: At the beginning of February, federal intelligence officials began requesting background information on dozens of suspected enemy aliens. Various agencies produced case histories of hundreds of Mexican, Italian, Russian, and Japanese immigrants. Today, on February 19th, President Roosevelt signed Executive Order 9066, starting with Japanese Americans on the West Coast to mandate a case for the internment."

Aware that her friend couldn't follow the newscast in English, after a few minutes, she had had enough and turned it off. She repeated what the radio announcer conveyed, but in simpler language. "This confirms what you were talking about, doesn't it?"

She picked up the phone to call Leon Lewis. "Babs Norman, here. How are you doing? Just turned off the radio. Yes…I know. Disturbing. Is it true?"

"I'm afraid so," Lewis replied. "Joe Roos and I were just discussing it."

"Leon, you're much more hep about what's going on and how the government and its various agencies work. This, of course, is to be confidential. I hope the FBI didn't tap your phone line."

He coughed to clear his throat and followed that with a nervous laugh. "Not the last time I checked. Why are you so worried?"

"A little over two years ago, William Powell's wife—third wife—to make that clear, gave me the keys to her Hollywood Hills cottage after I rescued Asta and kept the *Thin Man* films from disaster. This was a big change, going from paying rent at the decrepit residential hotel where I had stayed near Hollywood and Vine. Since I knew I'd encounter unexpected household expenses, I rented out my extra bedroom to a Japanese tenant. He's clean, courteous, and so unassuming, the best roommate anyone could want, and I want to protect him. But now, with this mandate and executive order from President Roosevelt…"

"Babs, perhaps you should ask how to safeguard your own interests?"

"What do you mean?"

"You need to focus and stick to your investigation. Jack Warner hired you to bring to justice whoever killed Gerhard Sauer and to ensure no one else gets murdered. Don't get sidetracked by trying to help your tenant. Babs Norman versus Uncle Sam? That's a battle you'll never win."

"Leon, you're a lawyer. Don't you have any pull on your end?"

He informed her that the court barred the American Civil Liberties Union from directly challenging the constitutionality of this order and, therefore, he couldn't help her friend.

After she hung up, she gave Mr. Otake a summary of what Lewis had told her.

"What we do now?" he asked.

Babs ran her fingers through her tousled hair. Was there any way she could smuggle him somewhere to prevent his internment? As much as she considered the idea repugnant, could she lie or falsify his papers and say he was Chinese, or would that make much of a difference?

Under normal circumstances, Guy, her right-hand man, would've assisted her in looking into viable options, but now he was busy trying to prevent another murder from happening. She also hated the idea of hiring an outsider, whom she might not trust, but looked at Wiggins.

"Look, I'm a little shorthanded—"

He popped to his feet, grabbed his cleaning supplies, and said, "Be seeing ya."

"No! Wait!"

Mr. Otake exclaimed, "I heard radio shows. I read newspapers. *A-me-ri-can* law people have accused Japanese men as a menace to white women. They say every Japanese immigrant is a Japanese spy. *Hajishirazu!* Shameful!"

Babs and Wiggins flashed looks at each other.

"What a bunch of malarkey!" Wiggins's sonorous brogue upset the two macaws. Pedro uttered a nail-biting screech and flew out of his open cage. He shed one of his tail feathers, which got stuck in Wiggins's thick hair. Seeking her freedom, Petunia followed, leaving a trail of droppings in her wake. Wiggins took Babs' newspaper and swatted at her.

Otake urged him to stop. "Hit bird, and she might bite. Never trust you again."

"How come you know so much?" Wiggins asked.

"He's a gardener and must know something about birds," Babs said, rationalizing.

"I used to raise doves as a child," Otake confessed.

"His English might not be very good, but he's more intelligent than you or me, and these parrots are smart, too. Maybe you should apologize to Petunia. She can probably hear you're sorry by the tone in your voice."

Wiggins gave her the side-eye and put his hands on his hips. "Are you claiming to be a Sigmund Freud for birds?"

Pedro found a nearby perch and startled everybody with a holler that could've put Tarzan to shame. Wiggins stepped aside with his hands over his ears. "All right! You win. You're a smart bird. Now, will you leave me the heck alone?"

Otake suggested she take the macaws back to her place. They had more room to fly and a backyard more like their natural habitat, unlike their small cage and office, where the PIs left them overnight with the dogs.

Wiggins agreed. "Too many complaints from my tenants. Besides your rent payments, which are always late, you don't need to give your landlord another excuse to kick you out."

She still couldn't believe the radio broadcaster was serious.

Wiggins scratched his chin. "Come to think of it, the other night my wifey and I listened to a radio show. The announcer spoke not only about the evacuation of all Japanese people, but proposed to relocate Italian Americans, since Italy had allied with Japan and Germany. The famous baseball player, Joe DiMaggio, raised a big stink. Authorities tried to prevent his father from fishing over at San Francisco's Fisherman's Wharf, because they felt it was a threat to national security!"

"People say immigrants are *un-de-si-rable*. Do not wish to become Americans. My *com-mun-ni-ty* need rescue," Otake pleaded. Petunia landed on his shoulder. She seemed to express her sympathy by butting her feathery blue head against his, like a cat.

Babs urged him to calm down. "One step at a time. We'll concentrate on assisting you first."

Comforting words, but she needed a plan. Guy had a job to do at Warner Brothers. Wiggins? He has his own workload and a family to worry about.

Something had to be done to protect Otake, but what?

Chapter Six

For Babs, listening to the radio was the next best thing to going to the movies. Her favorites were the radio dramas, like *The New Adventures of Sherlock Holmes*. Now, she forced herself to get into the habit of listening to current events.

On February 23rd, Babs was about to pick up the phone and wish her mom happy birthday when she heard the tail end of a radio newscast:

"Not that long ago, the U.S. Navy averted a submarine attack by the Japanese in San Diego, proving not all fears of an invasion were unfounded. California's strategic location made it home to many vulnerable aircraft and munitions manufacturing plants. Cities along the coastline took extra precautions. Residents turned off their lights or blackened their windows at night. Certain radio stations went off the air. Authorities ordered civilian ships to remain docked and grounded commercial air travel. Be aware! This might be the beginning of the Battle of Los Angeles."

"More political muckety-muck," she grumbled. "I'd rather listen to Louella Parsons' scandalous Hollywood gossip than this garbage." Disgusted that the radio announcer interrupted her favorite show, featuring Basil Rathbone and Nigel Bruce, she turned the radio off.

Two days later, an unexpected call at 3:00 a.m. set her heart pounding.

"Hell-o?" Her vocal cords barely functioned.

"Hop in your car! I need you to drive down to Long Beach. They're saying one of the big movie studios is getting the U.S. Air Defense up in arms due to some kind of light show!"

"Jack?" Babs rasped and coughed into her pillow. She reached for the glass of water she had on her nightstand to clear her throat.

"It's all over the radio," Warner shouted.

Still obsessed about keeping up-to-date, Babs had fallen asleep with the radio on, but all she could hear was static. "Who's saying this?"

"Get your *toosh* down there *tout de suite!*"

"I thought you were paying me to solve a murder."

"Someone's going to get murdered if they continue to bash the reputation of my studio!"

"Hold your horses. One dead man is bad enough." She was about to take another sip of water until she noticed a dead fly at the bottom of her glass. "How do you expect to make movies if you're behind bars?"

"I'll find a way!" he hollered. "The show must go on."

Her eyes focused on her alarm clock. "Call Guy. I won't be able to get gasoline at this hour. He probably has a full tank."

"I think his phone is off the hook."

He's smart. She rolled out of bed to tune in a radio station but was out of luck.

"Fill me in," she said, yawning. "Can't seem to get any radio reception."

From the choppy tone of his voice, her boss seemed keyed up. "News of aerial strikes near Long Beach. They also reported a balloon carrying a red flare seen over Santa Monica. Four batteries of anti-aircraft artillery opened fire. Each sighting varied in description and location, and a lot had to do with the fact that the anti-aircraft shell bursts, caught by the searchlights, had been mistaken for enemy planes. Some even assumed the light show was a *Hollywood hoax* and part of an elaborate publicity stunt or a spectacular scene from one of the movie studios."

Does he think he's the only film studio in town? Yeah, he does. Jack Warner believes the Earth and the sun revolve around him.

She needed to wheedle her way out of this. "What's the point? If I drove all the way down there, the military would turn me away. I'm a private eye.

Where's that going to get me? They'll laugh in my face. Even worse, they might think I'm some kind of Commie spy."

Babs was about to ask whether he had considered asking Rudy, but sending a German over there wouldn't be too wise. She stretched and heard her bones pop. "Have you tried contacting the Western Defense Command or someone at the top? They're more likely to speak with you than with an outsider like us."

Babs dragged out their conversation until it ran out of gas, and their words faded. She could only assume he had hung up after the phone fell from her hand, and she conked out.

* * *

Since *Yankee Doodle Dandy* had wrapped, Wallis reassigned Guy to *Across the Pacific.* It starred many of the principal actors he'd worked with on *The Maltese Falcon,* along with the same director, John Huston. Wallis also confided to Guy that he knew from the very beginning he'd cast Humphrey Bogart in *Casablanca.* "Bogie's a hot commodity right now. You're to promise me nothing happens to him."

"I thought Leon Lewis was more concerned about threats against you and Jack Warner?" asked Guy. "And how about his wife, Mayo? Need I remind you of the ongoing saga of the *Battling Bogarts*? Huston had to give him a time-out from filming *The Falcon* after she gave him a shiner in one of their constant marital brawls."

Wallis seemed unfazed. "We'll film all the scenes, even those set on the high seas and Panama Canal, inside our sound stages. What's hard to believe is our screenwriters wrote this before America declared war. It's about a Japanese plot to bomb the Panama Canal and impede the U.S. Navy. Sometimes I wonder when real-life incidents get too close for comfort. Did they cause these disasters, or were these just coincidences?"

* * *

Guy, who looked forward to working with Bogie again, realized the last time he'd seen him was when he'd dropped by his office on December 7th, on that horrible "Day of Infamy." He also remembered that Stu, his bothersome pet myna bird, took to Bogie and wound up going home with him.

Bye, bye, blackbird, Guy thought. Goodbye and good riddance. "So, how's life with a foul-mouthed, wisecracking myna bird?"

"Had to give him away," Bogie said, surprising Guy. "Was afraid Mayo…my wife…would be true to her nickname, 'Sluggy,' and would get into one of her drunken rages and kill him by accident. Couldn't bear to see that."

A production assistant called Bogie back to the set, but he insisted on having one last word with Guy. "Hey, I'd like you to catch me up to speed on why you're here and what you're investigating. How about coming over for dinner?"

"What about Mayo, the volcano?"

"My old lady is more likely to stay out of trouble if she's under the wire. Keepin' her busy does the trick."

"Would you consider a *Maltese Falcon* cast reunion?"

"Sure. Let's make it a pool party. Bring your partner…and your bathing suit. How 'bout it? For old time's sake."

* * *

"Everyone's responsible for being their own bartender!" Bogie announced before cannon-balling into the pool.

Sydney, who was the only guest wearing a three-piece suit, got drenched. Peter, who was already in the pool, skimmed the surface with his hand and splashed even more water in his direction. Sydney flinched, almost causing his lounge chair to topple.

"More water won't hurt you. You're already soaked. Why don't you change and join us?" Peter asked.

"I don't frolic at pool parties," he said in his astute British accent.

"Could it be they don't make jumbo-sized swimwear?" Lorre asked.

Mary Astor snuck from behind Lorre and bounced a beach ball off his head. "Stop taunting the Fat Man. A skilled tailor could custom-make anything."

Household staff brought out trays of finger food, and everyone helped themselves. When Babs doffed her robe, revealing her sexy swimwear, Bogie and Peter whistled in unison. She covered herself back up and was ready to turn tail and run until Mary grabbed her by the arm. "Enjoy the compliments while you're still young enough to get them."

Sydney ordered Peter to take a fallen palm frond and fan him like a slave boy to dry his clothes. While everyone poked fun at him over a fresh round of martinis, Mary stole their attention and upstaged them. She plucked a garden torch from the ground and asked, "Well, isn't anyone going to congratulate me?"

"For what?" Peter asked.

Hamming it up, she clutched the flickering torch like a coveted prize. "For winning the Oscar for Best Supporting Actress in *The Great Lie*."

"I, for one, can't believe *The Maltese Falcon* lost out," Peter said.

"Ain't that the truth," Bogie mumbled.

Drunk enough to be blunt, Mary replied, "Perhaps you're just a sore loser."

"Oh, come on. *The Falcon* deserved to win for the Best Picture," countered Bogie.

Peter chimed in. "Don't forget, our film was also nominated for the Best Adapted Screenplay, and Sydney came up short for the Best Supporting Actor."

At last, Sydney changed the subject and asked the detectives, "So much for the Oscars we deserved but didn't win, especially since we risked our lives with a bird-crazy killer on the loose. I hear Warner Brothers hired you to solve another murder."

"Word travels fast." Everyone barely heard Babs' reply over Bogie's whistling reaction.

"We'll have a third person joining us," explained Guy. "Another actor, and he's a motorcyclist who often works as a stunt double."

Mary relinquished her torch and reached for her pack of cigarettes. "Do you know anything about the victim?"

"He appeared to be a stagehand on the set of *Yankee Doodle Dandy*," said Guy. Neither he nor Babs could disclose he was a spy for Leon Lewis.

"Which is no longer in production, if I got my facts straight," said Bogie. "Have you speculated who, if anybody, might be next?"

Guy stole one of Mary's Chesterfields, despite being used to Camels. "Let's hope there isn't another."

Surrounded by smokers, Babs coughed out her reply, "The investigation… is in its early stages…" She finally snatched Peter's palm frond to waft away the smell. "We each have our assignments."

"You don't suspect any of us are behind it," Peter said with a slightly upturned smile.

Babs strained to keep a straight face. "Should I?"

Peter cackled like one of his villainous characters.

Observing each one and, finally, turning to her partner, Babs said, "Come to think of it, maybe we should recruit them as extra eyes and ears. Unofficially, of course. We need all the help we can get."

Bogie cut in. "Although Sydney and Peter and I…and even Mary…had a bit of experience from helping to solve your last case, how would you describe a routine day on the job?"

"There is no typical day." Babs laughed. "Although I wish there were."

Mary shook her head and protested. "Count me out. I'm still traumatized from our last case and don't have time for this. Remember, I have a daughter to worry about and another film right after we're done with *Across the Pacific*. I need a break."

Being courteous, Guy exhaled his smoke away from his partner. "So far, we don't know a lot. Just pretend nothing's wrong, but if you see anything questionable, please report it."

Chapter Seven

March roared like the MGM Lion. "'Certainly, there's a war, but that's no reason to crawl into a hole and grieve about it,'" said Guy, reading an article from the *Hollywood Reporter*. "'No war was ever won with a chin down and a furrowed brow. So, let's be gay. Let's laugh a bit and spread good cheer.'"

Following that advice, Guy and Rudy planned a much-needed social night out and decided that a double feature of Charlie Chaplin's *The Great Dictator* and Claude Rains' *The Invisible Man* would be right on the money. They figured if they could find an isolated section of the theater, they could share the contents of Guy's whiskey flask and sneak in a few romantic gestures.

"I made a reservation at the *Risqué Café*," Guy whispered to Rudy after the film ended. "They serve German food and have a *Ratskeller*-style cabaret with a farcical review, including those which were big hits in Berlin."

Rudy stiffened. His tenor transformed from gaiety to gloom. "Too *risky* for us, my friend. Call them and cancel. Others can't see us there together. If I craved German cuisine, I could stay at home and cook some of my grandmother's recipes."

Rudy shook his gleaming blond hair like a proud, clean dog after a bath and smoothed it out by hand. "I enjoy the wind blowing through my hair, but I don't trust other drivers," he said before strapping on a helmet and goggles. "After a few drinks, some think they're driving panzers instead of their fancy Packards."

He handed Guy a spare helmet and straddled his motorcycle. "Come, I know a great place with home-cooked meals. It's a bit out of the way, but it's more within our budget. As long as our money is good and we don't have to burn it like *Deutschmarks* to stay warm, no one will talk."

Guy wasn't one-hundred percent sure what that meant, but he couldn't carry on a conversation over the roar of the engine as Rudy steered the bike through unfamiliar streets. He cut his engine in front of the Thumbs Up, a run-down dive. He gestured, mirroring its logo. "Sounds okay, right?"

Save for a few cabbies and blue-collar workers, they had the place to themselves. Guy wanted to hear a song on the jukebox.

"Been busted for a while," the bartender warned him.

Rudy told him to forget it. He was in the mood to play their pinball machine, and the sounds would compete. He challenged Guy, as to who could get the higher score, and let Guy go first, but his coin got stuck.

Rudy gave the machine a hard shove, and it lit up. "My turn," he said, stepping into place and flipping the levers. Every time the steel ball hit the right spot, he'd hear a *ping*! The machine calculated his new score and played a jingle. Just as he thought he'd beaten the score of the last player, the power flickered. The tune sounded like a record being played at a slower speed, and the game came to a halt.

"Kiss it goodbye," said the bartender. "Been wanting to replace it and the old music player, but didn't ya hear? Those War Production Board honchos in D.C. shut down the manufacturing of amusement games. We'll be lucky if they don't force us to turn ours in for scrap metal."

"Stupid Germans… If it weren't for them, there'd be no war," Guy muttered.

"I heard that," Rudy shouted from the bar.

"You're the exception," replied Guy, heading back to his seat and a few cents poorer.

Rudy got defensive. "There are a few decent German souls in town besides the one you're looking at."

Guy leaned in and whispered, "I meant the stupid German war machine. What do you want me to do? Kiss and make up in public?"

The bartender shoved a large bowl of strawberries in front of them. "Free for all my customers. Take as many as you like. My brother-in-law has a small farm, and I've made enough pies to last me an entire season."

Given his aching wallet, Guy ordered a ham sandwich. Rudy chose spaghetti and meatballs and insisted on the strongest drinks in the house.

The boys joked about the funny names Chaplin used for his characters. "Can't believe Charlie played Hynkel, the Dictator of *Tomania*," Guy said. "This bar food better not give us ptomaine poisoning. I'm blaming you if it does."

"I liked the portrayal of the person pretending to be Mussolini as the Dictator of Bacteria, and the fitting name of his aide, *Garbitsch*."

"Tell me," Guy asked. "What was your favorite scene?" He got distracted when he noticed Rudy pick up his fork with his left hand. "You're a lefty?"

Rudy chewed and swallowed before answering. "Are you snooping into my personal politics?"

Guy shook his head and laughed. "I've always assumed you were right-handed."

"I'm ambidextrous, but prefer my left over my right." To prove a point, he kept switching his fork from his left to his right for each successive bite.

Like in the movie, Guy ladled gobs of spicy English mustard onto his plate of strawberries. Rudy overloaded the rest of Guy's uneaten sandwich with the fiery condiment. Both groaned as they rinsed their mouths with their strong alcoholic drinks, since the bartender hadn't given them water.

Rudy grabbed a long strand of overcooked spaghetti. Guy, who swiped his own, shouted, "I'll take the Bacterian people and tear them apart…like this!" Like Chaplin, he tried to pull the pasta apart but couldn't. Instead, it snapped out of his hand like an elastic band and into Rudy's face. The bartender grabbed a hard salami that was hanging from the ceiling and threatened to use it as a truncheon if they didn't quit the horseplay.

"We're actors," Rudy explained. "Rehearsing for a big audition tomorrow…at Warner Brothers."

The bartender snarled. To Guy, it was clear he wasn't familiar with Chaplin's film. "Clean it up, or I call the cops!" He threw a filthy, wet rag right into Rudy's face and refused to serve the two pranksters anything more.

"Too bad we couldn't disappear like the Invisible Man," said Guy. "Think of the shenanigans we could play. Where do you want to go next?"

"My resident manager monitors foot traffic. Wouldn't look good for two drunken sods, like us, ambling in at such a late hour. The last thing I need is to be thrown out on my can. Let's go to your place."

Lucky to have an alternative, the two men delighted in having Guy's apartment to themselves since his roommate had gone back to South Carolina to visit his folks.

They continued to discuss the Chaplin film over cocktails until Rudy confessed how bad it was over in the real and not the cinematic version of Germany.

"You spoke about valueless *Deutschmarks* earlier," Guy said. "Is that what you meant by inflation?"

"Our currency became worthless. Often, we used it as kindling to keep us warm throughout the winter. Everyone had to find ways to earn extra money. Wealthy Americans and European tourists flooded in to take advantage of our decadent nightlife, where their dollars, sterling, francs, or lira went far. After school, I took a job selling dirty postcards for Herr Gutfreund, a Jewish, left-wing political activist and bookseller, who printed secret Marxist literature and…" Rudy lowered his voice. "You never know, in case your walls are thin, if your neighbors can overhear. For all we know, your landlord has his ear to the front door right now."

"Do you want me to check?" Guy started to get up, but was too plastered.

Rudy shook his head and whispered. *"Nein.* I can't believe I'm confessing this to you when I barely know you. I'm probably just being paranoid, but as I was saying…Herr Gutfreund also printed pornography."

Guy refilled their glasses. He had no idea Rudy had been through that. While Guy savored his, Rudy downed his in one gulp.

"Many underground publishers also produced 'Perverted Berlin' guidebooks with directions to the city's lurid nightlife. People could purchase them at any train station, hotel lobby, or downtown kiosk. Besides handselling them to people who looked like obvious tourists, one of my jobs was to distribute them and find new clients."

Guy pulled a book off the shelf. Inside it was a hidden pamphlet written in German with dirty pictures, which he showed Rudy. "Were you referring to something like this?"

"Where did you get that?" Rudy snatched it out of his hand.

"Some flea market…" Guy hesitated but hid it back inside his book. "You don't have to get so upset.

Rudy admitted when business was slow, he learned the ways of his employer's print shop—making black market documents and fake passports. "Also learned the art of retouching photographs. We sold dirty pictures at various levels of censorship, but I used those same techniques to alter passport photos."

Guy took one last sneak peek at the pamphlet before reshelving it. "In Hollywood, you had the Hays Code censoring everything and setting the standard for what they considered appropriate."

"In Berlin, it was no holds barred. Our Girl-Culture cabarets were like the extreme end of the Ziegfeld Follies fantasy. Some of them even had amateur nights where one could win prize money and a free meal if they bested the pros. Believe it or not, some of these subversive clubs survived the beginning of the Nazi takeover—a testament to their warped way of viewing the world."

Guy tried to conceal any signs of shock. He took a feather duster and started tidying the house, already in order, just to burn off a sense of nervousness. He put a record on the phonograph, needing some soothing music. Rudy snapped out of his melodramatic monologue long enough to demand he turn it off.

"I never considered myself a criminal. Working for Herr Gutfreund was the easiest and fastest way to have extra cash. When I came of age, I snuck into those lurid clubs and hung out with the *avant-gardes*—the actors, the artists, and the free-thinkers with their Devil-may-care lifestyles."

After this disclosure, Rudy broke out in a cold sweat—to where it killed their impromptu romance. Even more disappointing was that this was one of the few times Guy had the place to himself. Rudy fetched his keys, making his way to the door, but wasn't too steady on his feet.

Guy got concerned. "Are you sure you're all right to drive? Please leave your motorcycle here and call a cab. How 'bout I pick you up in my car tomorrow?"

Rudy grabbed both helmets and put on his goggles. "If I can tumble off a bridge and into a creek for a film, I think I can handle LA traffic."

Chapter Eight

Torn between pursuing her murder investigation and protecting her tenant, that evening, Babs behaved out of character. She sat alone at her dining room table in the dark and got plastered. With nothing but a blank expression on her face, she refilled her empty glass from a bottle of Kentucky bourbon, part of the stash she got from her divorce settlement.

Her Irish Wolfhound uttered a low woof and pattered in, desiring attention. When she noticed him chewing on something he shouldn't have, she called him over, held out her hand, and demanded he spit it out. It had the size and feel of a business card but was gooey with the dog's saliva.

She realized it was a "Get Out of Jail Free" card from her *Monopoly* game and mumbled, "Warner is going to fire me, and I'm going to lose my PI license." *This had better not be an omen.*

Mr. Otake entered and looked distressed. "Care to join me?" she asked.

Hesitant, he sat down. "I prefer saké, but it's late, and you look…"

"Say it! I don't just look tired. I look drunk."

"You going to bed?"

"Not sleepy. I'm worried and don't even know what takes priority anymore."

Sir Henry toddled over and put his head on Otake's lap.

"What happen now?" he asked.

"Will you please stop asking questions I don't want to answer?" She was about to cry but got cut short when the jumbo-sized macaws dive-bombed after each other in a mock marital battle.

Stepping in a pile of parrot droppings was the last straw. "That's it! They're going outside." Babs flung open the front door. A gust of wind and dead, dry leaves blew in from the canyons. Otake made an about-face and bolted upstairs. She grabbed a broom and swatted at the cackling creatures, who flew to freedom. Then she locked the door and swept the feathers and leaves left behind.

Sir Henry tried to warn Babs with a series of barks, but it was too late. Pedro crashed against the small foyer window, as if proclaiming it was a mistake to lock them out. The dog continued barking while both parrots beat their wings against the glass. She finally pulled down the shade, which she had accidentally left up, closed the curtains, and ran upstairs to find her tenant.

After an exhaustive and futile search, she brushed her hair and teeth with a halfhearted effort, slipped into a nightgown, and went to bed. Sir Henry climbed in with her. While falling asleep, she asked herself why she was risking everything to help her tenant.

A few minutes later, the dog made a low growl. She crept downstairs, where a sliver of light shone through the crack in the pantry door. Babs pulled it open and caught her tenant stealing saltine crackers. She noticed the poor man shaking.

"Mr. Otake, what are you doing?"

"Miss Babs, why don't I turn myself in? I'll get you in trouble."

"No!" She was adamant. "Don't you have any family? Someone who could vouch for you and get you away from the West Coast? Aren't most Japanese men your age married? You mentioned nothing about a wife."

He hung his head. "When my parents passed away in Japan, and I had no more family there, I left the country for America to start a new life. First, I arrived in San Francisco. A local priest introduced me to a Japanese woman whose background was like mine, because her parents were also gone. Two lonely people. We had an arranged marriage."

"Did you love her?"

"We respected each other and fulfilled our duty and obligation. That is the Japanese way."

Babs urged him to get out of the pantry.

"Windows closed?" He asked in a timid voice.

"You mean the shades? No one can look in from outside," she said, and insisted he join her at the kitchen table and explain why he went into hiding.

Babs struggled to focus her eyes on the kitchen clock, aware she'd be a wreck in the morning. Before she could ask anything else, her wall-unit phone rang and cut the silence.

"Helll-ooo?"

Jibber-jabber came from the other end, almost as bad as the yackity-yakking parrots.

"Your birds almost killed my little dog again!" her neighbor clamored. "He's bleeding all over my carpet. Do you have any idea how to bandage a Yorkshire Terrier? I'll never find a vet at this hour."

Mrs. Dietz, oh no, not again. Oh gosh, poor creature…

Otake whispered, "You must have forgotten, Miss Babs. They attack your neighbor's pets. That's why you cannot let them outside. If I try to break up fight, then neighbors know I am here."

This was even worse than what she and Guy had experienced when they gave away Stu, the smart-alecky myna bird they had until recently. Outside of Stu assaulting Basil Rathbone at the movie premiere of *The Maltese Falcon*, he was just an annoyance. "Mrs. Dietz, let me find some shoes, and I'll be right over."

She hung up, took a deep breath, and turned to her tenant. "You're right. I can't be here to mediate, and you need the public to believe you followed internment orders. Leaves us no choice. The parrots must remain inside."

"Unless you can find them new homes."

"Another option, but not my priority."

"What if I am next victim?"

"You stay put."

"That means I am prisoner in your house?"

She slipped her bare feet into the first pair of flats she could find and threw a light topcoat over her nightdress. "We'll discuss this later."

* * *

Babs slept until eleven and woke with a stifling hangover. She called the two FBI agents she was supposed to meet with to reschedule, telling them a white lie—that she had the flu and was still contagious. Unable to find Sir Henry, she assumed Otake must've let him out to do his business. After washing her face and stuffing her hair into a makeshift turban, she threw on a bathrobe. Then she stumbled downstairs to brew strong tea and to settle her angry stomach with saltine crackers, if Otake had left her any.

Once again, she found him cowering inside her pantry. With her curtains still closed, she popped the windows open an inch and cracked open the shades enough to let in some sunlight. She insisted he join her, and no one would spy on them. Both jumped when the giant dog pressed his wet nose against the window screen. She let him in to ensure there'd be no more interruptions.

He asked, "What you do today, Miss Babs?"

"I hate the idea of you retreating into closets. What if Sir Henry scratches against the doors all day until you come out? Got to think of a better option."

"I can switch. Crawl under bed for an hour. Then go someplace else."

Babs scratched her head, needing a solution—and fast. "Go to your room for now. Remember to keep the curtains and shades drawn. Promise?"

* * *

The PI partners had been working on separate assignments and, as of late, had seen little of each other. Since she also had an all-access pass to come and go as she pleased on the Warner's lot, she arrived, unannounced, to where Guy took vigil on the *Across the Pacific* sound stage.

She found him helping himself to a donut. "Hey, maybe you can help me out."

He looked up. "Howdy, stranger. I feel like we never see each other anymore."

She peered over at the lit set to confirm her suspicions. "Didn't you say this film was about a secret Japanese airstrike on the Panama Canal?"

"Yes, but…"

Mary Astor made a straight line for the snack table and wedged between them. She was frantic as she desperately searched for something she couldn't seem to find.

"Are you okay?" Guy asked. "Can I help you?"

Looking green, she clamped her hand to her mouth and forced down a swallow. "Bicarbonate of soda…looks like there isn't any." With one hand, she clutched her stomach. With the other, she pointed toward the set. "If our director insists on rocking the boat again, that'll be the end of me."

Almost unable to converse any further, she acknowledged Babs with a weak wave of hello and sought first aid.

"What was wrong with her?" Babs asked.

"They should be grateful they aren't shooting on location. The art department rigged their studio-built ship on a hydraulic lift so it could rock back and forth to simulate on stage their ship on the high seas. The problem is that it's given the actors a sense of real seasickness. So, Babs, what brought you here to spy on me?"

"Maybe we should discuss this elsewhere."

He led her outside into the blinding sun. When it looked like they were alone, she asked, "Any progress on the case?"

Guy shook his head. "Nope. But I'm curious. Why did you come over? I know you didn't come to get an autograph."

"I wondered if we could get a small part for Mr. Otake in your film. The mandate shut his gardening business down. What if he runs out of money for rent? Isn't *Across the Pacific* about a Japanese military plot?"

Guy toned his voice down to a whisper. "Please don't tell me he's still hiding at your place. Babs, if the Feds find out, you're going to lose your private investigator's license. Since you own the business, I'll lose mine as well. Betcha anything they'll accuse me of being your accomplice."

Babs bit her lip.

"But to answer your question, the actors in the film playing the Japanese parts are Chinese, except for one technical advisor. If you don't believe me, look at today's call sheet and check for yourself. Warner Brothers got special permission to keep him onboard because they hired him before the president's executive order, but I'm sure they'll have to report him once they're done filming. I know this sounds terrible, but many people claim they can't tell the different nationalities apart. Have you been reading *The Hollywood Reporter* and *Variety*?"

"Been busy. What have I missed out on?"

"A recent incident on the set…six Chinese actors, playing Japanese in the film, refused to work until someone from the prop department removed a Japanese flag from a freighter rig. As actors, they knew their roles were playing our enemies, but they objected to the Axis powers' emblem, which the prop department had placed on the boat for accuracy. Our director had no problem taking it down."

If her plan had worked out, at least her tenant wouldn't have had to hide inside closets and crawl into cubbyholes every day. Maybe she'd need to consult with Leon Lewis and Joseph Roos to see what they'd suggest, but she worried that idea might backfire. Disappointed her ingenious idea went south, she asked Guy if it was okay to say hello to Mr. Bogart or any of her old clients before heading home.

Chapter Nine

Jack Warner rang Babs at 6:45 a.m. She forced herself to be civil. For the time being, he paid her bills.

"Have you been enjoying yourself on company time?" he asked, putting her on the spot.

Babs wondered if Jack had anyone spying on her or her partner—the spies being spied on. She stared at her empty coffee pot and wished she had at least one cup inside her before this confrontation. "What's the emergency?"

"While I'm doing my job, running my studio, I'm paying three of you to find out what happened and to make sure any murders don't happen again. Hadn't heard a peep from anyone. Didn't Wallis demand of all of you detectives…and spies…or whatever you call that Kraut, to turn in a daily report so I know I'm getting my money's worth?"

"Sir, it's a challenge to coordinate three people in different locations."

"Miss Norman, what's your plan for this afternoon?"

"If you must know…I intend to visit the FBI agents whom I planned to see the other day but had to reschedule because of a personal emergency."

"*Urgency…smurgency!* Young lady, you need to limit such crises!"

* * *

She met with, of all people, Special Agents William Wright and Sherman Lockwood, the same FBI investigators she knew from the *Asta-Rathbone Dognapping Case*. Wright still wore his black horn-rimmed glasses and had his thinning orange-red hair, only less of it. Lockwood retained his bland visage, slicked-back medium-brown hair, and pasty complexion. Both were clean-shaven and dressed like typical G-men.

After her arrest for trespassing on Countess Velma von Rache's private property, Wright and Lockwood found her possessing WWI German spy equipment. Before turning her back to the mercy of the local police, they questioned her PI credentials and grilled her about being a member of the Communist Party. She couldn't understand why they weren't more concerned about hunting down fascists.

Just like before, Wright lit a cigarette and blew the smoke in her face. "Have you come to confess that all along you've been a card-carrying member of the far left?"

She shook her head in disbelief. "What does it take to convince you we're on the same side?"

"Dame's got an excellent memory."

Lockwood squirmed and began to scratch his arms.

"I'm sorry you got bitten by fleas the last time we worked together. Par for the course if you hang outdoors with dogs long enough, but you aren't fooling me with this fake performance. If you're interested, I can recommend several places for acting lessons."

Caught in the gag, he straightened in his chair and flashed a sheepish smile.

"Gentlemen…you requested I come down here to discuss the corpse on the Warners lot. Do you mind cutting out the juvenile jokes?"

Special Agent Wright repeated his lines from the last time, as if he had a script already memorized. "I'll ask the questions. You give us the answers."

Babs cleared her throat. "This works both ways. My team will help you, and you'll cooperate with us. We both want the same thing."

Lockwood stuck his pinky into his ear, and twirled it around, as if the built-up earwax made him hear things he'd imagined.

"My partner and I have combined efforts with two representatives who used to work covertly with anti-Nazi activists. Your boss in Washington, Mr. Hoover, knows all about them. With cooperation from Jack Warner and his head of production, Hal Wallis, they've assigned one of their former operatives, who is German, on various assignments, including a pro-Allied Forces Errol Flynn picture, which wrapped not too long ago. If there's any information you might've withheld, please tell me so we can solve this case together. Let's start with Gerhard Sauer."

Taken aback that the little lady took the reins out of his hand, Special Agent Wright snuffed his cigarette. He reached for a glass of water, took a few gulps, and replied, "We discovered Sauer kept the books for an underground organization. He had access to their money, which he could use to line his own pockets without raising too much suspicion. Until now."

"Who, what, where, when, and how?" She wondered if Roos and Lewis knew this. Until she had more conclusive evidence, maybe she should keep this to herself.

"The basic establishment seems legit, but a few shady characters have operated on the fringes," Wright explained. "However—"

"You can't release that information until you've verified the details. Yeah, I know the drill. I didn't get my PI license yesterday. The fuzz and the Feds never trust us to keep quiet, and they always accuse us of operating outside of the law." Babs scratched her head with her pencil's eraser. "Well, boys…you're not giving me a lot to chew on. The police accuse me of getting in the way and keep making excuses about giving me anything useful.

"Tell me this: No one heard screams or saw signs of a struggle. This leads me to believe someone killed the victim elsewhere and dumped the body. Maybe even to make a political statement, because the swastika carved on his neck raises a lot of questions. Can you add anything?"

Lockwood poured himself a cup of coffee. Babs licked her lips, craving some herself, but she changed her mind when he spat the bitter stuff back into his cup.

Wright read from one of his reports. "Bruises, broken neck, and multiple stab wounds—some of which, by their angle of incision, looked like a left-handed person had made them."

Babs had noticed Rudy was left-handed. She brushed off the ridiculous thought.

"Makes us think there were at least three people involved in a fight before he died," Lockwood added.

* * *

Once again, she asked herself why she was risking everything to protect her tenant. The Americans might treat the Japanese similarly to how the Germans victimized those they deemed undesirable. For a gardener, who by trade thrived in the outdoors, Otake remained trapped inside her house and in constant fear. He couldn't even step into her backyard or take Sir Henry for a short walk without repercussions.

The wolfhound's job was to serve as an early warning system and bark if intruders were on the prowl, but all it took was for him to poke his nose and pull her curtains aside or to draw undue attention from her neighbors by excessive barking. Maybe she needed to bring him back to the office.

The parrots protested being jailbirds and refused to be caged. The next day, they chased each other throughout the house and crashed into Babs' china cabinet, breaking glass and porcelain given to her by her late great-grandmother. Babs grabbed a broom and, against Otake's warnings, opened the front door and shooed them outside. They transferred their bundled feistiness onto Mrs. Dietz and her Yorkshire Terrier, whom they had already assaulted. She heard yipping and yelling and ran after them. Otake ran after her, but the moment he got within three feet of the open door, he turned tail and went into hiding.

Mrs. Dietz's dog bolted across the street and hid inside someone's hedge. "I'm calling the police...or whoever picks up unruly animals."

Babs grabbed the sheet used to cover their cages at night and bagged the birds one at a time.

"Mr. Otake?" She searched the house but couldn't find him. "Otake-san?"

Babs gave the parrots a few treats to keep them quiet and hunted for her tenant, whom she finally found hidden in her coat closet. "The curtains are closed. Come on out."

"You sure police not coming?" he asked with a mousy voice.

She wrinkled her brow. "No, I'm not."

Taking her chances, she decided it was best to return the colossal and clamorous macaws to the office. Babs grabbed her keys and loaded them into the car. Sir Henry trailed at her heels and squeezed inside.

"Stay put," she whispered to Otake through the closet door. "If the doorbell rings, don't answer it!"

Chapter Ten

With production nearing a close on *Desperate Journey*, Wallis's *big baby* now took priority. Up till now, *Casablanca* had landed on the desks of several screenwriters. Hal preferred to hire the identical twin screenwriters Julius "Julie" and Phillip Epstein, but, at first, they weren't available and had a prior commitment working with the director Frank Capra in the nation's capital. Apart from looking for substitutes, he and Warner had different opinions about who would be best to adapt the stage play to film, and previous attempts didn't click.

By mid-March, the brothers returned to Tinseltown, and Wallis welcomed them to his team. Working at breakneck speed and bouncing fresh ideas off each other, they had a long way to go with only sixty pages of suitable script. Sundays became workdays. Hal invited the screenwriters, along with Curtiz, to his ranch, where they'd spread out the script pages and tried to combine them into a compelling story that everyone could agree on.

* * *

Wallis still contended with the challenge of who they should cast as Casablanca's leading man. He had met with his director to air their grievances, but a messenger interrupted them to deliver a bouquet of carnations. He tipped the kid and asked Curtiz, "Did you send these?"

Curtiz shook his head. "Check the card."

"All it says is, 'April Fools!'" said Wallis. A hidden trigger released, and water squirted into his eyes from a fake flower.

"Someone needs a camera. Make picture." Curtiz pointed at Wallis, laughing. "Show to your grandchildren one day what crazy place you worked at."

Hal wiped his wet face with a handkerchief. "This gag belongs in a Warner Brothers cartoon. You wouldn't think it was so funny if it happened to you."

"No name on the card? Who do you think sent it?"

"Good old Jack Warner," remarked Wallis. "Who else would earn his well-deserved reputation as the *Clown Prince of Hollywood?*"

Looking at his watch, Curtiz switched back to their discussion. "Despite the gossip that he already thinks we're casting him for the part, I'm not buying Bogart for Rick Blaine," he argued. "What about James Cagney? He played many tough guys."

"I think you meant that you're not *sold* on Humphrey Bogart. He's always been my number one pick, but his deal isn't set. Cagney? Never under consideration. Can you believe Big Boss Jack sent me a memo recommending George Raft as Rick Blaine if Bogie isn't available? Raft knows we're gonna film *Casablanca*, and he's already starting a campaign for the leading male part."

"Don't like directing Raft," Curtiz said with a frown. "Pretty face. He can dance, but got no acting talent." On behalf of Bogie, he had his own opinion. "Humphrey Bogart never study, but he is always great."

"It's hard for me to separate Raft from his gangster friends," Wallis confessed. "I wouldn't put it past Bugsy Siegel and his thugs to show up unannounced. Don't need men in black hats pointing gats at my cast and crew, or at me for that matter, if I decide on an actor they don't approve of."

Curtiz laughed. "You watch too many movies."

"Maybe you direct too many."

Another memo from the mogul arrived by messenger. Relieved it wasn't another April Fool's prank, Hal shared select portions. "Jack still favors Raft. He even went so far as to say, 'Who would ever want to kiss Bogart, a guy who, until *The Maltese Falcon*, only played a despicable human being with only occasional, flickering undertones of basic decency? He never gets the girl. Half the time, he's a jailbird or some swine you'd never want to take home to your mother. Bergman would be more terrified of Bogart than attracted to him!'"

Wallis let his boss stew overnight. At last, he informed him that his writers were reworking the script to fit Bogie's persona, and Raft wasn't right for the part.

He had planned to begin production of *Casablanca* on April 10th, but he hadn't yet cast the main characters, and the script was far from finished. Many key crew positions weren't to Curtiz's liking. Delays and setbacks plagued their production all down the line.

Wallis had already assigned Max Steiner to create the musical score and hired Owen Marks as his film editor. The cameraman they wanted, James Wong Howe, had wrapped *Yankee Doodle Dandy* and had already committed to work on an Ida Lupino project. Curtiz, in trying to exercise his power as a director, made his plea to Warner's head of technical services, but he refused to pull him off the other movie. Instead, Wallis offered the position to Arthur Edeson, who proved himself on *The Maltese Falcon*.

* * *

David O. Selznick, Ingrid Bergman's agent, had the gall to call Wallis at home, waking him and his wife on Saturday.

"You're lucky I don't get into the habit of attending synagogue or not answering the phone on the Sabbath." Hungover, Hal scowled at his clock. "Can't a hardworking reformed Jew get any sleep?"

He and Selznick traded jabs back and forth about getting her to play Ilsa.

"She's not enthusiastic about the story," Selznick argued.

"As it is, to satisfy the hungry press, we misled them into thinking Ann Sheridan would play our female lead. Then, when the Epsteins suggested that Rick Blaine's girlfriend would be a better match for Victor Laszlo if she were a foreigner, we considered Hedy Lamarr, but she would've been another loan-out and was unavailable.

"Need I remind you this'll be a genuine star maker? You owe me a favor after we lent you our contract star, Olivia de Havilland, for *Gone With the*

Wind. A smart move, which earned her an Oscar nomination. So, David O… Is that what the O stands for? Oscar?"

"If you really want to know, I have an uncle with the same name. The O means nothing. It just helps differentiate us."

Despite being less than cordial from being woken at an early hour, Wallis's phone manner was far more tactful than Warner's. "Forget her previous successes in Sweden or Germany—film or theatrical. She's still unknown to American audiences, and she won't go anywhere if she's content playing wife and mother back in Rochester, New York."

All it took was a heartfelt interview with Ingrid, and she disclosed her restlessness regarding her marriage to Dr. Petter Lindström. She'd admit she'd only feel alive if working on stage or on screen.

Proud of his recent box office successes, Selznick stood firm. "Do I need to remind you she's set her sights on the role of Maria in Paramount's *For Whom the Bell Tolls*, co-starring with Gary Cooper? She met with the book's author. Hemingway endorsed her and signed a personal copy of his novel."

"Hemingway isn't the one putting her on the payroll, and you're asking more than we can afford. How can Ingrid think she can land that part? It's meant for a Spanish woman. A robust, outdoorsy type. Hope she enjoys climbing rocks."

The following day, the Epstein brothers turned in the first third of their reworked *Casablanca* script—another determining factor. Ingrid couldn't sink her teeth into a part with an unfinished story.

When the give-and-take concessions failed, Wallis tried a new strategy to curry both Selznick and his client's favor. With Jack Warner's approval, Wallis agreed to let the Epstein brothers give it a shot to convince Bergman and Selznick of their project. Since they had put in the most work in adapting the stage play to the screen, they not only forged the role of Ilsa's character, but they could propose how this part could establish her solid career in American cinema.

Having a way with words, both on paper and in person, Julius and Phillip Epstein had easygoing personalities, much more so than the two headstrong producers, and had a distinguished track record. "I'll arrange for your appointment with Selznick," said Wallis. "Say whatever you like about the story and what playing Ilsa Lund could mean, as long as it results in both of them signing a contract."

* * *

Anxious that his progress report of his combined efforts with Rudy Schmitz and Babs Norman's would encounter disapproval and a dismissal, Guy Brandt drove to Warner Brothers and met with Wallis. Hal, however, seemed less concerned with their murder investigation and more overwrought about his casting woes. Their meeting turned out to be more of a one-sided conversation, encumbered by a flurry of phone calls.

"I've got two of the best screenwriters in Hollywood churning out pages around the clock, but with his fussy ego and his damned agent, can't I satisfy anybody?"

"What's the problem now?" Guy asked.

"Paul Henreid has always been my first choice to play Victor Laszlo, the Czech hero and leader of the underground resistance movement, but he feels the script is not worthy of his talents and could set back his career. He might not even be available. Currently, he's co-starring in another Warner's production, *Now, Voyager*, with Bette Davis. So is Claude Rains, who's always been my first pick for Captain Louis Renault, the local French Vichy official. Two actors, who can't be in two places at once! Even worse, *Now, Voyager* is running behind schedule."

"Now, about my report—" Guy couldn't get a word in edgewise.

"No one turns me down, but Henreid did! I told both actors I'd be willing to stall production…to a certain extent, of course, because I also had Ingrid's schedule to worry about. Can you believe he felt the part was too insignificant and could prevent him from trying to get future roles as a leading man? He should be more worried that he's a refugee from the Austro-Hungarian Empire, and now he's considered an enemy alien. You would think accepting a role like Victor Laszlo's would help his reputation rather than hurt it."

***

Already past *Casablanca's* original starting date, Babs sat in Wallis's office with her notebook in hand, ready to give him the insufficient update she received from the FBI on Gerhard Sauer. Her partner had made a previous attempt earlier, but to no avail, and Jack Warner's idea of submitting daily reports never worked out. Now, she had qualms about whether he'd keep her and her partner on the payroll. Wallis focused on his production coups. All else took a backseat.

Lost in his own world, Wallis paced the room. "I had my screenwriters write and rewrite that script. I threw money in their laps to win her over. You can almost say I gave them the task of writing a love letter to get her to commit."

Babs scratched her head. "Who?"

"Bergman…Ingrid Bergman. Her hard-nosed agent, Selznick, has avoided my calls. Would you believe it took a trip to New York to track him down and confront him at his hotel to get him to agree to sign her for *Casablanca*?"

"Didn't I hear she wanted the part in the Hemingway film?"

"Paramount Pictures announced Vera Zorina would play Maria."

"She's not Spanish, and isn't she a ballerina?" asked Babs. "Doesn't seem to fit the bill for how I pictured Maria."

"Ingrid was pretty sore, but her disappointment was my gain. We got her for a reasonable price. Selznick, of course, took his ridiculous chunk out of it as his agent's commission. There was a caveat. We could only have her for a limited time, which meant our production start date would be critical. Every single decision about her hair, makeup, and wardrobe was out of our hands. Selznick wrote it into her contract. He had to approve everything first."

"On top of that, Ingrid had to be provided with a stand-in." He paused and looked at Babs. "Since we're paying you, and you still haven't solved the crime, maybe you should fill that slot."

"Aren't I too short?"

"Maybe, but so is Bogart, and we're going to have to add height to his shoes.

She'd get an exclusive dressing room no matter where the location. Ingrid also needed to be in the main credits and in all advertising and publicity. The list was so long, it was enough to give me a headache."

Although thrilled that Wallis had surmounted a major milestone in casting his female lead, Babs was eager to share what she found out at the FBI, despite the information being inconclusive. Perhaps the producer had an inside scoop the Feds didn't. She was about to take the floor when Wallis's secretary ran in saying Lew Wasserman, Paul Henreid's agent, was on the phone, and it was urgent.

Chapter Eleven

I f they were going to continue seeing each other on a social basis, Rudy and Guy felt it best to attend private parties with open-minded people rather than mingle at men's-only nightclubs, where they could get harassed or arrested. Rudy knew of a friend throwing a more benign get-together that Sunday afternoon at her house in Santa Monica.

Guy insisted on driving. They cruised along Pico Boulevard, dotted with tumble-down bungalows, plant nurseries, filling stations, and vacant lots for sale. Rudy insisted on a slight detour to glimpse the ocean as the last of the morning mist burned off. The scent of eucalyptus mingled with gum trees, cypresses, and sycamores.

They arrived at 165 Mabery Road in Santa Monica Canyon, in front of a large English-inspired house surrounded by a white wooden fence flourishing with ambrosial honeysuckle and pink Portuguese roses. Two pine trees grew on each side of the entrance, along with magnolias.

Rudy knocked, but no one answered. He turned the knob; the door opened. Feeling nostalgic, Rudy said the parties at this address, for the most part, comprised of ex-pats, many, but not all, from the German Weimar Republic. "They turn a blind eye to people like us, because we all come from the same three-ring circus."

The first floor had an oversized living room, full of windows, with a fireplace and a dining area, with French doors that opened to a garden. A polyglot of conversations filled the smoky rooms, but they wouldn't be strangers for long. Rudy took Guy by the hand and led him to the buffet laden with breads, including pumpernickel and rye, ham, sausages, various cheeses, and pickles. "Hope you like *Abendbrot*, or our version of a German dinner. Over here, the beer flows like water. Sadly, we must rely on the American substitutes unless we can get our hands on black-market imports. Who knows what ingredients are in it or how it might taste?"

Guy said he was game to try anything. Rudy wanted to acquaint him with their hostess and continued navigating the crowd. "Looks like we cleaned out Berlin's UFA studios with this party alone. The Film Ministry must wonder if there's any talent left to choose from."

Famished, Guy had no difficulty licking his plate clean. "Up for seconds?"

"Hold off, I spotted the lady of the house." Rudy took Guy to meet Salka Viertel. She greeted him with a kiss on each cheek. Guy gave her a standard American handshake.

Salka wore an unpretentious short gray wool skirt with a slight flare and a simple cream-colored crepe blouse. No jewelry. *"Velcome* to my Sunday salon, otherwise known as Sundays at Salka's." She surprised him by being more talkative and well-versed in the English language than expected. "Consider my abode the *Romanisches Café* of the West Coast."

Guy asked where that was, clueless, having never traveled beyond the United States.

Salka was more than happy to explain. "The *Romanisches Café*, located in Berlin on the *Kurfürstendamm* or *Ku'damm*, for short, was the Mecca, the premier meeting place for free thinkers and artists of all sorts. The Nazis hated the place because it attracted left-wing intellectuals. Many of its impoverished patrons came straight from the soup kitchen. They'd linger in the café for hours over a cup of coffee and a game of chess."

"How long have you been in the States?" asked Guy.

"My husband and I left Europe in '28, long before…" Then she paused and muttered something unintelligible in German with a stern scowl. Finishing her sentence, she said, "Before '33…that dreadful year when…you-know-who…we don't like to utter his name in here…upended so many lives. Berthold, my spouse, started out writing and directing at Fox. I, essentially, became a bored and anxious *film-wife* with too much time on my hands.

"Greta Garbo became my savior. Since she knew I had a thriving career as a theater actress before I arrived in the States, she got me a few small parts here and there, but my star burned out before it had a chance to shine. However, I used my skills as a translator, often with German songs and lyrics, and that led to opportunities to write for the studios."

She must've been downplaying her accomplishments, Guy thought. He'd dig into his clippings collection of entertainment magazines and newspapers to see where she was selling herself short.

"Yet, according to many, my greatest accomplishment," she said, "is that of being a cultural ambassador, bringing so many artists together."

Guy couldn't help but notice her gold wedding band, but with the lack of an accompanying engagement ring with a diamond. He wondered if she had hocked it to flee Germany in a hurry—so common and so sad. "Where is your husband? I'd be pleased to meet him."

She gave him a half-smile. "He couldn't handle Hollywood life and, for certain, couldn't handle any sort of failure or disappointment. Now, he follows his muse between New York and London."

"You must miss each other, I'd think."

She sighed. "Here, I have my international family."

Rudy shifted the topic. "Salka, I was telling my friend, who was concerned he doesn't speak German, that you invite folk from everywhere."

"Viennese, Czechs…of course, they speak German, but we also have French, Italians…and Greta Garbo…she's Swedish."

Guy's pulse raced. "Do you expect her this afternoon?"

Salka gave a quick look around and shook her head. "Greta is a private person. She hates being bothered with crowds, especially by those who ask her for favors. Since she lives in the neighborhood, she prefers to visit on her own terms, but getting back to your question, an American or two will arrive with their European friends. The Brits who come here…Christopher Isherwood, Aldous Huxley and his wife…Oona and Charlie Chaplin—"

"Charlie Chaplin?" Guy asked. "He's one of the richest men in Hollywood and, why…I don't know, but he's always kept his British citizenship when so many ex-pats tried to sever their ties with the past."

"People worship him here," she explained. "I've even heard others philosophize that his tramp character reminds them of the proverbial Wandering Jew, a transient, never quite being accepted and roaming from one difficult situation to the next, trying to get by in his own bumbling way—something many of us relate to, Jewish or not. We want an abundant and peaceful life, and all of us yearn for acceptance."

Rudy interjected, "Don't you also attract quite a few musicians?"

"We do…even scientists. Would you believe I've had the pleasure of meeting Albert Einstein? Many were lucky and arrived in California before the *problems*…on a university assignment like Einstein at Caltech back in the early thirties, or the musicians and composers on concert tours. When the political situation became too dangerous, they turned their backs on the life they knew and remained here. Others fled with whatever they could stuff in a suitcase, often stopping in several countries along the way. Once they realized they weren't secure no matter where they traveled in Europe, they bought a one-way ticket across the Atlantic."

Shaking his head in disbelief, Guy couldn't imagine the turmoil these people must've gone through.

"Were you born in California?" Salka asked. "I don't think I've met a person yet who has."

"I guess you can say I'm an émigré from the Midwestern part of the United States, bored, with limited opportunities, and looking for adventure," Guy joked. "Silly me. I had hoped to get rich and famous in Hollywood…as an actor, no less."

"Didn't we all?" Her joviality seemed to be mixed with pathos. "I had performed in Europe, but few seemed interested in me over here. Greta gave me a helping hand and has been more than generous. But you and Rudy should mingle and get to know others, and don't feel offended if someone comes around and asks you for money, or should I say charity, which is more apropos. My husband and I have supported the European Film Fund since it's imperative we all help each other."

This was all new to Guy. Rudy explained, "Leisel Frank, the daughter of the musical comedy star Fritzy Massari and wife of the scenarist and author, Bruno Frank, partnered with Charlotte Deiterle, wife of William Deiterle, a film director you might've heard of. They, along with others, established the European Film Fund. Refugee film workers have pledged one percent of their weekly earnings to support their unemployed brethren. These women also helped bring to Hollywood the last batch of refugee writers to leave Marseille and Lisbon. Paul Kohner, an agent, became their studio liaison. He appealed to people like Jack Warner and Louis B. Mayer, figuring they'd be sympathetic to the plight of Jews. The Hollywood film studios agreed to employ many refugee writers at $100 per week, but that's not to say they didn't have a tough time adjusting."

After Salka had parted, Rudy explained to Guy that she offered a refuge for those newcomers down on their luck. "Her home is a haven for the homeless. Many of us, and by *us* I mean recent émigrés…others have accused us of leaning a bit too far to the left of what Washington deems as acceptable politics. Some gifted artists have been fortunate to find mediocre assignments and have often needed sponsors. For actors, directors, and writers, it was much easier for their predecessors, the earlier ex-pats in the '20s, who didn't have to overcome language barriers when films were still silent. Once the talkies took over, that changed everything."

"How does Salka afford to throw these parties?" asked Guy.

"*Was ist das?* Are you all work and no play?"

"A murder investigation never sleeps."

Rudy raised one eyebrow. "Her acting career never quite transferred into anything lucrative over here, but she was being modest, perhaps in never having met you before. With Garbo's influence, I guess, Salka established herself as a respectable writer in a world dominated by men. She's written a couple of screenplays, along with getting small parts in at least two of them, and it doesn't appear Garbo's popularity is going away soon."

After second helpings at the buffet, Guy and Rudy checked out the rest of the party. Among the attendees, Rudy noticed Conrad Veidt, an actor who had made an impact in Europe with such films as *The Cabinet of Dr. Caligari*, where he played the haunting somnambulist.

"Seems like I might've found my *doppelgänger*," said Conrad, who looked Rudy up and down. Despite their vast differences in hair color, they stood almost head-to-head, and both sported an uncannily long and slender frame.

He asked if Rudy was an actor. "Perhaps you should play my stand-in or stuntman. I'd be willing to refer you to the casting director where I'm under contract."

Rudy hesitated, but Guy took the initiative. "I'll take your card, if you have one. My friend is shy."

Suggesting they step aside, Rudy disclosed that Veidt had made it clear to the public he was anti-Nazi. He also mentioned Veidt's wife is Jewish. "That's why he finally left Germany. Now, everyone talks of casting him as the person he most despises.

"Not sure how familiar you are with German cinema, but early in his career Conrad starred in a silent film directed by Richard Oswald called *Anders als die Andern*, or *Different from the Others*, about the angst of a homosexual musician. In the story, a blackmailer spots Veidt's character being too overt in public with his protégé lover and forces him to his ruin."

The two men heard someone pontificating from his soapbox. "One year they praise our work, the next year they burn our books!"

Rudy pointed out that he was the playwright and poet Bertolt Brecht. "Revered in Germany until the Nazis banned it, he wrote *Three Penny Opera*."

Guy thought he recognized someone. "Is that?"

"Billy Wilder, born Samuel, but nicknamed Billy after Buffalo Bill's Wild West Shows. A Jewish screenwriter from the Austro-Hungarian Empire who refused to go into his family's bakery business—"

"Sounds like we have something in common," said Guy. "I refused to accept a ready-made career managing my father's general store."

"He didn't have it easy at first," Rudy explained. "Worked as a taxi dancer in Berlin before he got established. That's when I first heard of him. But I had to scrounge for equally disgusting jobs before I escaped."

"I can't imagine anything worse than getting kicked, punched, or shot at like they did to you while filming *Desperate Journey*," said Guy. "God forbid you didn't wind up in the hospital after falling off your motorcycle!"

"Perhaps not, if your life is at risk, but on a moral level, what I did back in Germany—"

"Tell me. I want to know."

Rudy lowered his voice and stopped Guy cold with a firm stare. "Enough about me. As I was saying about Wilder, I heard rumors it wasn't much easier for him here in California, at first. One story was that a producer offered him eighty dollars, on a dare at a party, if he'd jump naked into his swimming pool."

Guy spat out his beer and grabbed a napkin. "Did he really?"

"Whether it's true? Who knows? He redeemed himself by the time he wrote *Ninotchka*, starring Garbo. Most likely, that's how he and Salka know each other."

"Who's the broad?" Guy referred to the statuesque woman who seemed to follow Wilder.

"Birgit Müller," Rudy murmured. "She's of no interest."

For whatever reason, Rudy struck Guy as in no mood to associate with Wilder nor his companion, and all of a sudden Rudy's carefree comportment took a downturn. "Are you alright? You look a bit peaked."

"Could've been the pickles." Rudy placed his hand on his stomach; his face paled. He maneuvered him to Salka's backyard garden, where he seemed content to avoid the other guests. Guy felt compelled to break the silence.

Rudy appeared to get lost in thought, paying more attention to the birds and flowers. Unable to read his mind, Guy took that as a cue to refill his glass and give him some distance. Despite the language barriers, he reminded himself he was still working on a murder investigation. Even if he couldn't depend on his ears, he could still observe anything out of the ordinary.

Upon his return, he overheard a boisterous conversation in English, which wavered between attempting to sound refined to coming off as crude, uneducated, and with the telltale twang of a Southern accent. It came from an overdressed redhead, the only flagrant showoff flaunting furs. He eased in her direction with an uncertain gut feeling. At last, she turned around.

Virginia Hill! She didn't know Guy personally, but he sure as heck didn't want her to recognize him as a private eye. All he could think of was that she was Bugsy Siegel's gal. Despite fabrications that her parents came from a titled background, she wasn't an ex-pat. Not by a long shot, and the truth was more likely she was a hick from Alabama.

He also swore that somewhere in his clippings collection, he had read an article where the police had accused Miss Hill of stealing jewelry, but he couldn't believe that was the reason for her being here. Almost no one had any. Those who had probably pawned it to pay their passage over to California. Money? Extortion? Not from a crowd donating a portion of their paychecks to fund other refugees. He had heard that before she aligned with Siegel, she had become a self-made woman with the Chicago mob.

His thoughts jumped back to his recent frustration over trying to play a broken pinball machine on his first date with Rudy. The bartender told him that the War Production Board had forced factories to make substantial quantities of metals available for war production. Refusing to believe it at the time, later on Guy found an article stating that thirty companies, mostly in Chicago, were affected. Could the mob have a monopoly on this business? They seemed to have their hands in everyone's pockets.

Whether it was the wise guys from the Windy City or the riffraff on the West Coast, he and his partner had to contend with Bugsy Siegel and his gang from the *Blackbird Case*. Those thoughts alone made him woozy. He sought Rudy, and they left shortly thereafter.

Chapter Twelve

As her sputtering Crosley gave one last belch of revolting exhaust, Babs parked in the office garage. Sir Henry accompanied her as she snuck in the first macaw, hoping to bypass Wiggins. What she didn't expect to find was her partner and his paramour inside the anteroom with the radio on. Beer in hand, Rudy had buried his nose in a newspaper. Guy drank an orange-flavored Nehi soda and appeared to be reading a script.

She rushed inside, locked the door, and asked Guy, "Aren't you supposed to be working?"

"My show wrapped. Two days before, John Huston jumped ship and accepted a commission with the Army Signal Corps. Vincent Sherman took over as director. Warner wanted to get his money's worth out of me. He had Wallis send a messenger with the most recent draft of *Casablanca*. Wallis reassigned us to that project. That includes you."

Babs grunted. Guy asked, "Do you have a problem?"

"I really thought we would've resolved this case by now…found Sauer's killer and why he or she did it."

"Why? Do you think it'll look bad on our record?"

She couldn't even make eye contact. "We have so many other things on our plates. It would be helpful if this were all over."

Her moans of self-pity wouldn't last long. Babs' smuggled parrot let out a shuddering squawk, loud enough to alert passersby.

"Aren't the birds supposed to be at home?" he asked. "We're not an animal refuge. What about Wiggins's warning about them bothering the nearby tenants?"

Babs realized she had left the other bird in the car. She excused herself and said she'd be right back.

Upon her return, Guy asked, "What's the deal?"

"My next-door neighbor threatened to call the police after they attacked her dog."

"Shouldn't have been a problem if you kept them inside."

"Too destructive, and they drove us nuts."

"*Us?*" He pointed to himself. "*We* are supposed to be solving a murder. Please don't tell me you're still protecting Mr. Otake."

Guilt radiated from her face.

"Babs, I assumed you complied with the relocation orders after we last spoke."

Rudy placed his paper aside. "Maybe I can help. What's the problem?"

She pointed to Guy's script. "In *Casablanca*, from what I've overheard, everyone wants to get their hands on letters of transit to escape from war-torn Europe and North Africa to a new world of freedom."

Rudy and Guy looked at each other with raised eyebrows in unison.

"In Mr. Otake's case, his need isn't the product of a bunch of clever screenwriters. He's in an impossible situation." Out of breath, Babs plopped into a chair.

"I've had a bit of experience avoiding red tape," said Rudy. "Otherwise, I would've never made it out of Berlin. I also know others who've been in similar situations. Give me a chance and let me ask around. Perhaps I can find a solution."

* * *

In a room smoky with tension and cigarette ashes piling in ashtrays, Michael Curtiz and Hal Wallis went through a stack of headshots with Jack Warner in his office.

"What about Sam?" asked Wallis. "Here's a character, created by our playwrights, who is an entertainer and a close friend of Rick Blaine, a man who's pretty much a loner, who plays by his own rules and doesn't allow many into his inner circle. This guy, Sam, knows Rick better than Ilsa."

Warner held up photos of popular Negro actors, William Gillespie, Napoleon Simpson, Fred Skinner, Eddie Rochester, and Elliott Carpenter, but Wallis shook his head. "These guys are used to playing stereotypes. Sam might be Rick's employee, but he's a respected entertainer in his own right. In a certain sense, he's Rick's right-hand man, not a 'Yes, sir…No, sir,' subordinate like most Negros on screen."

Curtiz looked at the two producers. "Didn't you want to cast a woman at first?"

"Yes. My personal favorite was Lena Horne," said Wallis. "We also bandied about using two other female vocalists, Ella Fitzgerald and Hazel Scott, but decided against it. Those we had in mind all sang, but none played the piano.

"If romantic scenes between Rick and Ilsa were to take place by the piano, having a woman come between them could pose problems. That's when we stuck with the original male character from *Everybody Comes to Rick's*. Besides singing, being a musician became a more important factor along with proven acting experience."

The choice boiled down to Clarence Muse and Dooley Wilson. Muse seemed like too much of a caricature in his screen tests, and the scenes featuring Sam needed to emphasize the irreproachable friendship between Rick Blaine and Sam, not comedy.

"Dooley came from a theatrical background," said Wallis. "However, he was a professional drummer and couldn't play the piano. I'd seen him in *Cabin in the Sky*, MGM's all-black musical, liked his performance as Little Joe, and tested him. He might've lacked skills in one area, but he had the personality."

"Why is he called Dooley?" Curtiz asked.

"His real name is Arthur, but once he sang a popular song called *Mr. Dooley*, and everyone called him Dooley afterward," Wallis explained. "Did you know the man had actual experience performing in a band in Casablanca? The real country, not the movie."

Curtiz and Warner gave him disbelieving stares.

"No joke. Believe it or not, he also performed for the real Lawrence of Arabia during the '20s."

After experimenting with dubbing someone else's voice, they let Dooley sing on his own, finger the piano, and have the music of a professional play in the background. The next hurdle: Paramount Pictures, who had him under contract, had loaned him to MGM for a film called *Cairo*. With *Casablanca* already delayed, Wallis took a chance and scheduled Dooley's scenes for the day following *Cairo's* completion.

* * *

Lew Wasserman, Paul Henreid's agent, called Wallis. "You can thank Bette Davis for getting my client to agree to star in your film."

"Star?"

"Oh, that's right. We need to talk about where you place his name on all the publicity campaigns."

"Getting back to Davis, she can drive a hard bargain. What sort of persuasion did she put into his head?" Wallis asked.

"As you're already aware, they're working together right now on your film, *Now, Voyager*. They've become close friends. Nothing romantic, mind you, like their roles on screen, but he's always valued her opinions and confided he felt the part of Laszlo would hurt his career.

"Without hesitation, Bette said, 'You're wrong, wrong, wrong! It's a wildly good part for you, and you could bring a great deal to it. I know you can. He is not only what you see written in the script. This part of Laszlo is much better than you think it is.' She complimented you."

"Me?" Wallis laughed. "She's always threatened to sue good ole Jack, demanding to get out of her contract."

"I'm conveying this secondhand, but she said, 'Laszlo defined Ilsa's character. Ingrid Bergman is a wonderful actress. You will enjoy working with her, and with Bogie, too. I've also worked with him.' Paul knew Bette had good instincts and would never steer him wrong. Taking that into account, she's the one who convinced him, not me, to be part of your team."

* * *

All along, Wallis knew that the veteran German actor, Conrad Veidt, would be the perfect choice to play the evil Nazi, Major Heinrich Strasser. Warner got uneasy about the outrageous salary he had to pay to convince him to play the part, which he thought was too insignificant. Because of their similar stature, Wallis assigned Rudy Schmitz to be Conrad's stand-in and stuntman, also justifying his "spy presence" on the set.

Other parts fell into place. Everyone agreed on casting Claude Rains as the two-faced and crooked Captain Louis Renault. They chose Peter Lorre to play Ugarte, the shifty trader of illegitimate documents. Curtiz was close friends with fellow Hungarian expatriate, S. Z. "Cuddles" Sakal, whom he cast as a waiter in Rick's Café, but only after asking for a much higher salary than Warner wanted.

Wallis agreed to pay Sydney Greenstreet the exorbitant sum of $3,750 a week for two weeks' worth of work for the small but pivotal part of Señor Ferrari, the black marketeer and owner of the Blue Parrot Café. Now a big screen star after his film debut in *The Maltese Falcon*, he had also initially turned the part down.

Considering all the hurdles they'd surpassed with more to come, everyone involved in *Casablanca*, whether it was within the inner circles or on the perimeter, put on a veneer of confidence. Notwithstanding the unsolved murder in the background, few believed they'd pull off this project.

Chapter Thirteen

The camera started rolling for *Casablanca* on May 25th. Over the next three days, Michael Curtiz had planned the Paris flashback sequences on Stage 12A. The production team shot the script out of order because various sets remained unfinished, and actors, like Paul Henreid, weren't available. He was still filming *Now, Voyager*.

The principals needed for the first day were Humphrey Bogart as Rick Blaine, Ingrid Bergman as Ilsa Lund, and Dooley Wilson as Sam. The rest were background extras, with little to no dialogue. Meanwhile, stagehands made sure they were a few steps ahead and prepared the additional sets for the other scenes to take place in Paris. But no one expected any unusual drama.

The studio's policy on attendance and punctuality expected all employees to show at call time, which, in this case, was 8:30 a.m. Production would have to end earlier than usual, so those who lived farther away could get home in time for curfew.

Jack Warner, who would've given everyone a case of first-day anxiety, had taken the train to New York to be present on the 29th for the premiere of *Yankee Doodle Dandy*; a big deal, because he had promised ticket sales would go toward the purchase of war bonds.

In Jack's absence, Curtiz became the king of his domain. He'd sneer at anyone who put in their two cents, and if they persisted, he'd order them off the set. Not to be intrusive, Babs and Guy observed the hubbub away from the camera. Meanwhile, since Warner was in New York, accompanied by his bodyguard, he didn't require additional security detail. Therefore,

Rudy volunteered to check on alternatives for Mr. Otake.

Inside Rick Blaine's Paris apartment, during a rehearsal for Bogie's first intimate scene with Ingrid, Bogie felt his entire approach was like having two left hands. "I don't like love scenes. Maybe because I don't do them very well. It isn't possible to shoot a love scene without having a hairy-chested grip standing four feet away from you, chewing tobacco. I'll handle that in the privacy of my bedroom."

"I watched some of your films two or three times to feel prepared," Ingrid replied.

"Considering the characters I've played," he said out of the side of his mouth, "betcha you thought you were kissing a convicted criminal versus a romantic hero."

"Rumors from the trades, I guess…" She held back a laugh to veil her uneasiness. "The only thing I know about you are the awful stories about your wife."

"Mayo? No worries today. I assure you she's still sleeping off last night's bender."

Curtiz butted in on their banter. "No chitchat bar stories. Back to grinding."

Babs' mouth dropped. Others suppressed their giggles at the innuendo.

Edeson, his lensman, offered to reinterpret, so it didn't sound like he was referring to sex. "I think he means back to the grind." Then he turned to his assistant. "Let's go for another take."

Bergman, who wore only a minimal application of makeup, remained restless. "Are you sure you angled on my good side?"

Bogie mugged for the camera. "Don't think I have any good sides. In fact, being around you…I confess, I'm a bit intimidated by your beauty."

Still insecure, she blushed. "Next to you, I feel rather tall. Don't you feel self-conscious?"

"Do I have a choice?"

After lunch, the crew ran into technical problems after they moved to the interior of La Belle Aurore Café. Curtiz, always a perfectionist, insisted on doing more rehearsals than expected. Inside the café, the dialogue and action centered on Rick, Ilsa, and Sam, save for a few waiters, a bartender, and a table or two with customers in the background. Discussions focused on the impending German occupation of Paris. Rick knows he's already on the enemy's blacklist.

They planned for a medium shot with Sam at the piano playing *As Time Goes By* for Ilsa. Rick enters holding a bottle of champagne. He pours and hands the glasses to Ilsa and Sam. Then Rick and Ilsa react to people shouting in the street.

Full of conflicted emotions, Ilsa kisses Rick. "Kiss me. Kiss me as though… as though it were the last time."

In the background, Sam continued to play their favorite song until stopped by the director. The sudden shift made his accompanist miss a note and slam his fist on the keyboard.

"No, no, no! Do it again!" Curtiz pointed at Bergman. "Do it more with your eyes!"

"If I stare into these bright lights any longer," Ingrid protested, "you'll see they're bloodshot."

Guy, who had been observing the rehearsals with his partner from behind the camera, whispered to Babs during their dispute. "Wallis has had me on a short leash since Warner's been out of town. That's why I never gave you any updates on our investigation."

"That doesn't excuse Rudy. He's avoided me. I know you don't want to hear it, but he gave me a bad feeling from the very beginning."

"Who dares to have a conversation when I'm trying to make a movie?" Curtiz's voice boomed and echoed throughout the stage like the Wizard of Oz behind his trumped-up facade.

Guy argued, "The camera and the sound weren't rolling."

"Let's hire new private investigators. I don't care. Find another murder to solve elsewhere."

Unapologetic, Curtiz told them this was their one and only warning. He stormed off the set to give his cinematographer the next hour and a half for lighting. When filming resumed, the sound mixer complained the set's ceiling caused problems. To add to those acoustical complications,

Sam fingered his piano. Instead of having the music pre-recorded, Elliott Carpenter played *As Time Goes By* live, offstage, where the actor could mimic his hand movements.

"I need to put a mic in there," interrupted Francis Scheid, who supervised the sound.

In his usual discourteous manner, Curtiz yammered, "Oh, shut up, you dumb soundman."

"Hey, I didn't ask to work with you," Scheid clamored. "In fact, I hate you. No, I despise you. I'd tell you what I really think of you, except there are ladies present."

The rehearsal stopped, and it became a shouting match between Scheid and Curtiz, with fists ready to fly and no one willing to referee.

Needing someone else to pick on, Curtiz targeted Scheid's boom operator. "Who are you to stand there and say nothing? What is your name?"

"Coblenz, sir. Manfred…Manfred Coblenz," he uttered.

Curtiz derided the innocent man. "Another Kraut fleeing the mess over in Europe to cash in on Hollywood paychecks? Somebody should send him to hair and makeup, so my eyes don't get sore from looking at him."

Having had enough, Scheid rose to his feet. "Look, you miserable bastard! Warner assigned him to me like they stuck me with you. We've never worked together before, but as far as I'm concerned, he's doing a swell job. It's you who's causing the problem by not letting me prep the set. Background noise caused the interference."

"Shut your mouth, you peasant!" Curtiz not only ostracized Scheid for interfering, but he selected several other crew members, at random, to cut down to size.

After a dozen rehearsals and four takes, Scheid had enough and turned off his recorder. "To hell with you!" he said and stormed off the set.

From the peanut gallery, Babs and Guy looked at each other.

"Shouldn't we do or say something?" she asked.

Guy shook his head. "It's not our place to interfere. Unless someone threatens murder."

Chapter Fourteen

The frustrated soundman went home, drank a pitcher of Tom Collins, and told his wife he expected Warner Brothers would fire him for insubordination. Since no one called to give him the bad news, he drove to the set the next morning.

Wallis had seen the dailies and called his boss, who was still in New York. "Despite the soundman complaining about the low ceilings and with placing his microphones, I heard buzzing on the soundtrack from the arc lamps. How come no one noticed that?"

Jack Warner chewed out Wallis. "Don't forget. We were first, the pioneers of the Sound Age with *The Jazz Singer*. Of all the studios, others expect us to set an example. Our *talkies* must sound better."

Everyone pointed fingers at each other as to who was at fault.

"We must ensure this sort of oversight doesn't happen again," said Wallis. "Even if we have to punch a hole in the ceiling to put in a microphone and record this properly."

Production fell behind schedule, which meant wasted money. Curtiz continued to pass the blame on Scheid. When Wallis refused to replace him, the director still wanted someone to take the fall and insisted this would be his boom operator's last day.

Scheid protested, "Coblenz? He did nothing wrong. Replace your pig-headed director who wouldn't let me do my job."

Wallis stepped in as a referee. "None of us wants to reshoot those scenes, but you have no choice." He calmed down Scheid and Curtiz but pulled Coblenz aside. "Sorry, son," he said, apologizing. "Report to personnel. I'll guarantee they expedite your final paycheck."

* * *

For the time being, they'd stick with their original Day Two schedule and would juggle their scenes for reshoots after conferring with their art director. Babs and Guy observed the melee from the sidelines, but not for long. When rehearsals were about to start, Ingrid asked, "Where is my stand-in? She was here yesterday."

"How did that get overlooked?" Wallis pointed at Babs. "You! Come here so she can study her lines while they do a relight."

"She's so much shorter," said Edeson.

"Put her in heels," insisted Wallis. "Wardrobe will figure out something."

Babs protested, "I was on my way out of here for an appointment to meet with the Burbank PD. They're finally giving me access to the crime scene photos."

"Let it wait!" blasted Curtiz, insisting an assistant escort Babs offstage. When she returned, the highest heels were still far from sufficient. A grip had to tape a bunch of wooden wedges under her flats to get her close to Ingrid's height. Such a rigging made walking awkward.

"I feel like the Frankenstein monster," she said, walking like Boris Karloff.

Curtiz tried blocking a scene, recruiting Guy to stand in for Bogart, because his stand-in hadn't showed either. Jokes circulated. Perhaps they eloped.

Babs hobbled on the wooden wedges. She also found it impossible to do her private investigative work monitoring Bergman if she was off in her dressing room on a break, rehearsing her lines, while Babs had to be available for blocking the scene and lighting.

Finally, Babs tripped over a cable and took a tumble. "How do you expect me to do my job—any job—whether it's standing in or doing my investigation if I have a twisted ankle?" A production assistant fetched her an icepack, and she elevated it on top of one of the grip's wooden apple boxes.

Right before the cast and crew broke for lunch, a trio of visitors crashed the set. Bugsy Siegel, with his gal, Virginia Hill, confronted the production team, accompanied by the Warner's contract actor, George Raft. The soundman shouted, "Cut! Your noisy clodhoppers just got recorded!"

Wallis raised his hand and insisted the incensed soundman stay put. Then he approached the intruders with the intent of diplomacy. "This is a closed set. How did you get in?"

Siegel took out a wad of cash and shuffled it, letting the high-value bills float midair from one hand to the other. Raft replied for everyone, "I was curious to drop by the set because they rejected me for the part."

"You were never in the running." Wallis forced himself to be calm. "I think you've got it confused with a few other parts you turned down that we offered to Humphrey Bogart, like *The Maltese Falcon*. Guess you were wrong about thinking it wasn't an important film."

"That's not what I heard from J.L.," Raft replied.

Wallis shifted his eyes to take a quick glance around the stage. He'd have to choose his words with caution. "Look, we've got talent that's never worked together. New crew members in the mix. Ruined sound from yesterday's footage that we'll have to reshoot. Script revisions arrived this morning, which means my actors haven't had time to study their new dialogue, and I could use two aspirin right now. Is there anything else I can help you with?"

Raft looked at Siegel. "Come to think of it, there is. My friends have wanted to break into showbiz. Any way of getting them a screen test? You've got a camera and lighting crew. How 'bout giving them one now?"

Curtiz marched in and shouted, "Schedule to keep! Schedule to keep! Who's asleep on their feet?" He wanted to know what was causing more delays.

Siegel pointed to the idle crew. "Your cameraman is just standing around waitin' for instructions, right?"

The producer wouldn't argue. Not if Siegel had a hidden firearm. "Send them over to wardrobe," he told the assistant director. "Tell them I need a few well-dressed Frenchmen for the nightclub."

"My lady and I aren't changing into any costumes," insisted Siegel. "We had these glad rags custom-made, and they're fine as they are."

Wallis kept his masked facade and pulled Curtiz aside.

"Parisians don't dress like that, and only French whores wear that much makeup!" the director contended.

"Tell Edeson to make sure they are off-camera as much as possible. Our editor will cut them from the footage," Wallis instructed. "The screenwriters haven't even drafted the ending yet, and I won't ask them to create extra lines for these thugs."

"What's my other choice?" asked Curtiz, loud enough for Siegel to overhear him.

"Are you willing to take a bullet?" Siegel asked.

Wallis wished Curtiz good luck.

* * *

"Let's see what we can rearrange," the assistant director said to Curtiz. Both tried not to show they were sweating bullets and went over the list of scenes to see where the gangsters could fit in.

"While we're having lunch, a whole slew of extras will arrive for the Paris nightclub scene. Casting instructed them to arrive in costume and makeup, using their own formal attire. Of course, the wardrobe department will have last looks and approval, in case someone was way off the mark. We'll film the establishing shots until the camera comes in for an intimate closeup of Rick and Ilsa dancing. The entire scene is a quick clip. Less than twenty-five seconds on screen but filmed from various angles and focal lengths."

Curtiz gave him a wicked stare.

"I take that back. You will have *final* approval."

"Unless J.L. or Wallis insists on stepping in my mud," said Curtiz, while his assistant had to reinterpret his jargon. "These nightclub people… Will they look French? Where is casting finding them?"

"Remember Warner's commitment to help refugees from Nazi Germany? He works with organizations that help people from all persecuted countries. I'm sure there'll be no lack of Frenchmen, but regarding Siegel's demands, the Paris nightclub would be the perfect place to hide him. Dark room. Dim lighting. Men wearing black tuxedos. Long shots of a whole dance floor with an orchestra in the background. Can't ask for anything better. Even projected on a large screen in a theater, no one will recognize Bugsy and his girlfriend."

"I don't like anyone interfering with my directing."

"Michael, I understand, but this is the perfect way to do it. If Jack Warner insisted on dancing the tango while everyone else was doing the rumba in that scene, we'd have to let him have his way. Come on. Let's get this over with."

"What about his demand for a screen test?" asked Curtiz.

"Have Edeson set it up during lunch. Someone will bring him a plate of food, and he can eat it while the crew sets the lights. Tell him they'll have to improvise the dialogue. Warner would hang all of us if we loaned them a script from this project. How 'bout it?"

* * *

Bogie, not feeling too social, disappeared into his dressing room and requested his meal be brought to him. Ingrid asked for the same, but she insisted she needed to study her lines with her dialogue coach. Betty Brooks and Russ Lewellyn, the two stand-ins for Bergman and Bogart, reported to the assistant director while everyone else was still on their break. Her hair was messy. He had a slight cut on his swollen lips.

The AD, already under pressure from having Siegel and his clan crash the set, chewed them out. "Where were you at call time?"

Miss Brooks had difficulty putting her words together. "On the way over…we got into a wreck."

"We meant to get here on time and were running ahead of schedule, but some hotshot, who looked like the actor George Raft driving a fancy convertible, was in so much of a hurry that he ran us off the road. My car hit a tree," explained Russ. "While we had our car towed, the cops had us hop in theirs to get checked out at the hospital."

"The docs said we were more shaken up than anything else," she added.

"Once they said we were good to go, we had to take three buses to get here. Couldn't afford a cab before our first paycheck, sir."

The AD marked in his report their adjusted call time and told them to grab a bite to eat. "Look in the mirror while you're at it. You'll need to clean up. Unless Curtiz or Wallis doesn't buy your excuse and fires you."

Edeson and a skeleton crew set up for Bugsy's screen test. "Let's make this simple. Put him against a blank wall with a standard key light and a fill. Throw a spotlight behind him to set him apart. Don't want it to look too flat."

"What are you gonna have me read?" Bugsy asked.

"Sorry, we don't have a script, and you'll have to wing it. Your pal George knows the routine. He'll stand right beside me. Your eyeline will be on him. He'll respond to you with lines he'll make up from off-camera. You know…if you want to come back another day, we can find another camera guy and do this the right way. Not a lunchtime rush job."

Siegel opened his jacket, enough for Edeson to see the pistol shoved into his waistband.

"Sir…didn't mean to offend you…"

Raft interrupted. "None taken. Were you trying to tell him you weren't expecting us?"

"Yeah, but you said it better than I could've. It's your choice if you want to do it the right way and reschedule. Meanwhile, we might be able to rustle up a script with lines you could memorize."

"This way is the right way," Bugsy uttered. "Right now!"

"Not arguing. Just letting you know we'll have to improvise. We're under the gun for time. That's all."

Miss Hill, who had been sitting in a director's chair on the sidelines, asked, "What's his motivation?"

"I know it's not in your job description," Edeson said in hushed tones to his assistant, "But do you mind grabbing a small table and a chair for Mr. Siegel to sit down? The prop guys are at lunch, and I need a clean, empty glass and a bottle of booze. Screw the rationing. Bring a bottle of the genuine stuff to calm him down. If you can't find any, Bogie should have some in his dressing room."

Then Edeson addressed Siegel. "Guess I'm the temporary director, too. You're going to play a man who is upset because you saw a girl you were in love with but never thought you'd see again."

"I don't get this improvisation thing. Who am I supposed to be talking to?" Siegel asked.

"I suspect that's where I come in," replied Raft. "Nobody wants to see me on film. They already know what I look like. The whole point of the screen test is to see your reactions, Benny."

Raft bent over and whispered into Edeson's ear, "Whatever you do, don't call him Bugsy. If you noticed just now, I called him Benny. Benjamin Siegel is his real name. The one he was born with. People nicknamed him Bugsy 'cause of his temper. Ya don't want to set him off."

Edeson nodded.

"Benny, think about Virginia," said George. "You…I mean your character was in love with a girl, but don't look at her. You can think about her but look at me. All right?"

"Yeah, I think I got it."

Edeson advised his assistant to mark a slate with today's date, saying, "Benjamin Siegel: Screen test."

Then his camera assistant called to get his attention. "Sir, we don't have the sound guy here."

Edeson slapped his hand against his forehead. "Bring Scheid over here. On the double! The rest of the gang will get an extra-long lunch break, despite J.L. getting outraged about that…and the cost of the extra film we're using."

While his assistant fetched the two guys from the sound department, Edeson wolfed down his already cold meal, dripping gravy on his shirt.

Once the soundman gave the okay, Edeson's assistant ran out with the slate. "All right. Benjamin Siegel: Screen test. Take One."

Siegel stuttered. Edeson yelled, "Cut! Do that over. This time, do it with more emotion. This woman ruined your evening."

"Who?" blurted Virginia. "Is there another woman involved?"

"Not you, honey," replied Raft. "The character in our make-believe movie."

Virginia uttered a sigh of relief. "How was I going to know that?"

Not used to wearing so many hats, Edeson shouted, "Camera and sound are still rolling. Do it again, or we're going to run out of film."

While he repeated his lines, Curtiz approached and asked, "Got enough?"

When Edeson got the thumbs up from the soundman, Curtiz said he needed them to prepare for this afternoon's shots.

"You gonna give us a part in *Casablanca*?" Siegel asked, with Hill looking on.

Curtiz replied, "We will work you into the nightclub scene. Can you dance?"

"My buddy, Georgie, can. He was the pride of Broadway before he moved out West."

"Guess we'll work him in, too," said Curtiz with reluctance. "Just make sure you don't upstage our stars."

* * *

After lunch, everyone performed their duties, setting up for the nightclub scene. While the stand-ins made themselves available for lighting and blocking, a choreographer pulled Bogie and Bergman aside to teach them the proper way to do the rumba. Clashes ensued between the producer and the sound department about whether they should try to save time and money by recording the live orchestra or to let them play for the actors and dub it with better quality sound later. Guy wanted to jump in and dance with Babs to prove he could show off moves as good as Raft's, but she insisted on sitting it out. Her ankle still hurt after wearing those "stumbling blocks" to boost her height until the real stand-ins arrived.

Every time the camera crew had to set up for another angle, Siegel and Hill complained.

"Whadda ya mean now you have to do an overhead shot?" he shouted.

Raft did his best to calm his temperamental friend and offered him a drink from his flask. "Better get used to it, Benny. You'll find you'll do more waiting around than actual acting."

"What if I get tired, or my feet ache from all the dancing?"

"That's what you're getting paid for."

"Georgie, you mean we're getting paid to be here today?"

"Here, probably not, but in other cases…yeah, but I'll look into it."

* * *

When the assistant director announced the official wrap for Day Two, Siegel reapproached the director. "So that's it? What about tomorrow? I can wear a tux if ya need me to."

Curtiz tried to find the best words. "You'll drink all our real whiskey. We'll have none left for Humphrey Bogart."

Raft, realizing the director needed to be let off the hook, stepped in and wrapped his arm around Siegel's shoulder. "Come on. None of the cheap stuff they're givin' us here. Let's go to Ciro's. Celebrate on my tab. All right? You got your screen test."

Siegel asked, "When do we see it?"

"Someone will contact you," said Curtiz. "Got to get the film processed, and the sound synced. Casting needs to see it, too."

Siegel leaned in head-to-head with Curtiz, like two prizefighters getting ready for a match. "You better see to it. I intend to become a big star."

Raft refereed. "Now, now, gentlemen. Let's act civil. Can't afford to kill off one of Warner Brothers' best directors." He looked at his friend. "So, you want to earn your keep like the working-class, instead of bumming from me all the time?"

"Since when don't I earn my keep, Georgie Boy? Besides, I thought I was your boss, eh?"

"Your track losses outweigh your income. Maybe tomorrow you'll bet on a lucky horse at Santa Anita."

* * *

Despite Siegel's love for placing high-stakes bets at the racetrack, the real world, beyond Hollywood, forced him and his friends into alternate plans. While the three had been out of touch and taking advantage of the Hollywood nightclubs and gambling within their own private circles, the local mandate with the Japanese resident aliens shifted from voluntary to involuntary evacuation. One of the first assembly centers closest to Los Angeles included the Santa Anita Racetrack in the City of Arcadia, just east of Pasadena.

Immigration enforcement agents excluded close to 18,000 Issei and Nisei without trial. Evacuees stayed in horse stalls until the War Relocation Authority and the U.S. Army could finish building permanent internment camps away from the coast and in government-owned wastelands farther into the interior. Armed guards confronted Siegel, Hill, and Raft and made them turn around.

* * *

On Day Three, Babs turned to Guy as they pulled up to the Warner Brothers gate to present their passes. "So far, no one has said a word about Gerhard Sauer."

"I think everyone was more concerned about joining the body count after Bugsy Siegel's arrival. By the way, were you able to reschedule your appointment to review those crime scene photos?"

"Would you believe that person took off on vacation? If I'd been able to see him yesterday, as planned—"

"Why not try calling the crime scene photographer and see if he could get you access to those files?"

"*The Woodpecker?*"

Guy gave her a funny look. "Why did you call him that?"

"He's constantly pecking at me and asking me for a date."

On stage, the PI partners noticed a few new faces. Curtiz continued to belittle Scheid, but Wallis carried out his promise and brought in a new boom operator. German-born art director Carl Jules Weyl arrived at

Warner Brothers armed with sketches and a miniature-scale model of the set planned for the interior of the Aurora Café. No stranger to working with Michael Curtiz, since he had worked with him before on *Yankee Doodle Dandy* and *The Adventures of Robin Hood*, he sat down with both the producer and the director and made his case about the hardships of building suitable sets with wartime restrictions.

Weyl explained, "In April, the War Production Board announced we had to cut our costs by nearly seventy-five percent, and some of our basic supplies were no longer available."

He further elaborated that his construction crew was refurbishing several sets from productions like *The Desert Song* and tweaking them just enough to make them suitable for Rick's Café, the Blue Parrot, and streets in Morocco. He also had his team transform the Paris train station from *Now, Voyager*. "We were lucky. We only needed to install new railing and add a sign."

To drive the point home, later in the day, Hal Wallis called an emergency meeting for the cast and crew. In his hand, he held a copy of one of the entertainment trades.

"Taking into consideration our first-day incident with the sound department, which caused the waste of valuable film stock, I want to read you a memo that Harry Warner, Jack's older brother, posted in a recent issue of *Variety* magazine."

Everyone grew silent, and he continued, "The article starts out, 'One hundred feet of wasted film may cost the life of an American soldier, who may be your own son or brother. Every foot of lumber, every nail, and every bit of material is vital. Therefore, it is up to every individual to save, save, and save so that our war machinery will have the materials to forge into munitions, ships, guns, tanks, and planes.'"

Wallis paused and stared to make sure everyone paid attention before resuming his monologue. "Hey, Scheid," he called out to the soundman. "This one's for you. 'A take is ruined because a mic shadow was cast upon the face of a player…or the player missed his lines. Multiply the wasted takes throughout the industry, and we have a staggering total of film material lost.'"

He fingered his way down the page to skip to some of the more important parts. "'It isn't enough that we buy defense bonds, act as air raid wardens, help in civilian defense, or have our sons go off to camp. Everyone must learn to practice wartime economy—'"

Suddenly, a loud yawn interrupted his wearisome harangue. "Who did that?"

Ingrid weakly raised her hand amid another yawn, even more presumptuous than the first. She rubbed her eyes and apologized.

Curtiz spoke up. "We need to be filming, not listening to speeches."

Wallis scanned the exhausted crowd. "Okay, I made my point. From now on, work out your issues. Don't waste any more of our time or money. Agreed?"

With groans kept to a minimum out of respect, everyone agreed so they could get back to work. Curtiz barked at everyone to pick up the pace.

Chapter Fifteen

For Babs and Guy, their first tempestuous week of production was about to take a different turn. On Friday morning, he phoned her at home earlier than usual. "Can't go to Warner's today. Gotta get my butt down to the Army recruiting center."

"You what—? Why?" Sir Henry barked in the background. "Shush, you'll wake Otake-san."

"Who are you tellin' to shush?"

"Not you, the dog. He'll rouse the entire neighborhood. Yeah, I know. I should've left him at the office with Bruno and the parrots, but I stopped to check if Wiggins had neglected them last night. Don't even get into it about the curfew. For whatever reason, he acted up yesterday, so I took him…and just him, home afterward."

"Remember back in November, before Pearl Harbor, I had to register down at the recruiting center? Well, I got the dreaded summons in the mail. Babs, I can't get out of it. You'll have to patrol the set by yourself today and explain to everybody what happened. There's a war going on. They'll understand I had no choice."

"Like heck you don't! I'll claim you as my dependent, because I depend upon you for my business to survive!"

"Babs, I think you have that backwards. Besides, the dependents' exemption works if you can prove you have kids. They'll ask for their birth certificates."

"Maybe we should get married, and I'll pretend I'm pregnant."

"What if they expect a doctor's note?"

"Then act crazy. Start a fight. No, I take that back. You'd get beaten to a pulp."

"Babs, you're an intelligent broad. Otherwise, I wouldn't have put up with your antics and strange logic for so long. Right away, they'll probably spot me as a homo and reject me, anyway."

She sighed. "That won't help your public record…or mine, for that matter, for employing you."

"Now, you're worried about how it's gonna affect you?"

She cleared her throat. "Stop thinking like an idiot. That's not what I meant, and you know it."

"So, I'm an idiot now?"

"You're the one who woke me before I had a cup of coffee and should know I don't act civil when I'm in this predicament." With the collar of her chenille pink bathrobe, she wiped the sleep from her eyes.

"Babs, arrive on time. The studio expects it. Everyone will take my excuse in stride. Moreover, Rudy will keep you company."

"Warner assigned Rudy to survey the lot. Jack's bodyguard, Abdul, has been on extra alert, but for his boss only. Rudy needs access to other stages, like the Crafts Department, where the sets are being constructed…you know the drill."

"Babs, you have a murder to solve. Be thankful you're not stuck in the office making phone calls to people who don't want to talk to you." Guy hung up, took one last sip of his coffee, and headed to his car, but realized he had to double back because he left his draft summons on the kitchen counter.

* * *

Down at the induction center, Guy wondered what all the hurry was about, only to get stuck waiting in a long queue. "Reminds me of those long, ridiculous lines people stood in while looking for work during the Depression. Hate being reminded of tough times."

"Rough times now, but different," said the youth behind him, who looked like he must've lied about his age. "Might as well get used to it."

Guy pulled a case out of his jacket pocket, took out a pair of fake prop glasses with clear lenses, and put them on. He moved forward but stepped on the foot of the brawny bully in front of him. "Hey, four-eyes, you ain't gonna last five minutes in bootcamp."

The kid formed a fist, but the teen in front of him held him back. "You had the gall to enlist?"

"Drafted," said Guy.

"You're too scrawny anyway," the bully blurted. "Those Krauts would put you in your place in no time."

No one expected this budding brawl to be broken up by a gal. When they were almost to the front door, heads turned as Babs dashed in to start a grievance of her own. A few wolf whistles hailed from the crowd. She pushed one aggressor aside and grabbed Guy by the collar.

"You're coming with me!" she said, paying no heed to the consequences.

The surrounding browbeaters doubled over with laughter.

"Who's this babe? The sore loser you left behind at the USO dance?"

"Ah yeah, your sweetheart felt abandoned, 'cause you ditched her to join the Army."

One dude grabbed her by the arm and gave her a forceful kiss on the chops.

"Leave her alone, bro," Guy contested. "Let me handle this. Save my place in line."

Guy pulled her aside. "What's the deal?"

She wiped the bully's saliva from her mouth. "You can't go through with this."

"Go home and stop embarrassing me. I've quit your agency before, and I can do it again." Guy resumed his place in line, but she trailed at his heels.

"Hey, skinny boy!" The first punk taunted Guy again. "You would've never made it out of the trenches in the last war. If you weren't wearing suspenders, your pants would hang around your ankles. They're going to reject you."

Once everyone stepped inside, the desk sergeant handed each a small bag on a lanyard.

"What's the bag for?" asked Guy.

"It's for putting your money around your neck so you don't lose it. Keep moving. Don't ask questions."

One uniform commanded, "All right, men. Drop your drawers. Down to your skivvies."

The doc shouted, "Hey, miss. You can't go in here!"

Babs skidded to a stop on the slick linoleum floor, almost falling on her can. "I'm looking for my friend. Oops! I had no idea…"

Guy turned around in shock.

"Guard! Someone! Get her out of here," cried the doctor.

"What should I do with her?" the MP asked. "Recruitment for the Women's Army Auxiliary Corps is in another building. This place is for men only."

Babs kicked up a fuss. "I won't leave until I speak with the officer in charge!"

"You're talkin' to him." The doc looked at the MP. "Take her away and call the police. I got better things to do than to deal with her disciplinary action."

* * *

While the military police apprehended Babs, the recruitment team subjected the inductees to a battery of tests.

"Listen up!" one of the noncoms said. "We're going to give each of you a container. You're to go to the men's lavatory and return with a urine sample."

"Relax," said the man next to Guy. "Leave your embarrassment at the door. You might as well take it in stride."

Feeling like he was a calf being led to slaughter, Guy's variety of tests included X-rays, a thorough dental examination, ears, nose, and blood tests. The doc realized his prop eyeglasses were fake right away.

Next, he sat down for a one-on-one interview with a psychologist.

"We need to know how well you'll adjust to Army life," he prefaced. "Your name is Gary Brandt? Sounds like the famous actor—"

"Yes, sir, it does. That's why I have everyone call me Guy. The running joke is, 'He's the *guy* with the name that sounds like Cary Grant.'"

"Well, Mr. Brandt, are you married?"

"No, sir." *Although my boss thinks that might get me out of this mess.*

"I need to know if you've got what it takes to make a soldier. Do you enjoy going around with girls?"

"Pardon me? Are you asking me if I have anything against them?"

"Do you?"

Guy felt on the spot. Maybe his hesitancy would work in his favor. Now he had to figure the best response. "Girls are fine. I enjoy a sneak peek at a girlie magazine, like the rest of my friends. In fact, one of my girlfriends was so upset about me getting drafted, she followed me here."

When the man nodded and check-marked a box on his form, Guy realized he might've sabotaged his efforts if he wanted to get rejected for being homosexual.

"Do you think you'll take to the Army as well as anyone else?" the shrink asked.

"Some recruits in the hallway thought I was too skinny to fit in, but…sir, is that all?" Guy looked at his watch. His insides did flip-flops. "Got a boss who expects me at work. When are you going to let me know?"

"We're done for now. We'll inform you if we classify you for general service, limited service, or reject your application."

"What's the next step?" He hoped there wouldn't be one.

"Wait until your local draft board notifies you. Then you'll report back to the induction station for the rest of the works."

"One more thing, sir, if you don't mind."

"What's that, son?"

"A close gal pal of mine…the one who followed me and caused a scene…" He didn't dare admit Babs was his boss. "Can you tell me what they did with her?"

"Ask one of the MPs on the way out. If he doesn't know, he'll be able to steer you in the right direction."

"Thank you, sir," Guy said, giving him a weak salute.

"No need to salute me while you're still a civilian. All right. Scoot along."

* * *

Guy bailed her out at the police station. Babs wished she had salvaged the "Get Out of Jail Free" card she had found Sir Henry chewing on not too long ago.

"Are you in the Army now?" she asked.

"They'll need to assess my medical exams. Should take a week, and then they'll get back to me. Kinda spoils everything between us, but it's too bad the draft wouldn't be a reasonable option for Mr. Otake."

Babs appeared nonplussed. "How can he—?"

"He can't. Too old, and he's *Issei*, a first-generation Japanese in our country."

"But I—?"

"Didn't know anything about it? Same here. When they instituted the draft, anticipating a war with Japan or Germany, the military recognized the need for soldiers with enough knowledge of Japanese to serve as translators and interpreters. Many Nisei, or second-generation Japanese Americans, had to register for the draft like I did."

"Doesn't that contradict Roosevelt's mandate?"

"You would think, but I guess there were others who convinced the president that a Nisei fighting unit could counter Japanese claims of American prejudice. It sounded like a plausible solution for your tenant at first, but he's too old, and being first generation, he'd never qualify."

Chapter Sixteen

Everyone needed a break after the first week of *Casablanca* chaos. When the weekend arrived, Humphrey Bogart hoped to weigh anchor and cruise over to Catalina Island on Sluggy with Sluggy— both his wife, Mayo, and the boat shared the same name. He loved telling everyone he also named one of their dogs Sluggy, and they nicknamed their Shoreham Road residence Sluggy Hollow. The PIs were aware of Mayo's alcoholic rages from when they worked with them during *The Maltese Falcon* case. By now, Babs wanted to have faith that Mayo believed nothing had or would happen between her and Bogie. So did Ingrid, but Mayo begged to differ.

Contrary to her rival's accusations, Ingrid desired quiet days at home with her husband, Petter, and her daughter, Pia, who were in town and would soon return to their home in Rochester, New York. Her constant complaint was, "If only you'd give me final script pages."

Her dialogue coach became one of her most dependable friends and an unofficial member of her family since she moved to Los Angeles. Ingrid had hoped to use her spare time to make headway in polishing her character. Family had its importance, but work, for Bergman, always came first.

Elliott Carpenter, assigned to do the actual off-camera musical accompaniment, offered to give Dooley Wilson piano lessons on his first day off. Michael Curtiz invited Hal Wallis over to his San Fernando Valley ranch to go skeet shooting, while Jack Warner was on his way back to Los Angeles from New York.

Soon, new faces hopped onboard, including those with significant supporting roles such as Conrad Veidt, Claude Rains, Sydney Greenstreet, and Peter Lorre. Still finishing his obligations on the film *Now, Voyager*, Paul Henreid would join them later. Everyone expected a flood of extras through Warner's revolving doors. Rumor had it many of these background players would come from Salka Viertel's Sunday afternoon salons.

* * *

On Saturday morning, between Babs and Guy, it became a battle of wills over who would be the first to put their key in their office's front door.

"After you, mademoiselle," he said with a slight bow.

In case any of the building's tenants or Wiggins were present, she kept her voice low so as not to rouse the animals. "Thanks, by the way."

"For what?"

"For bailing me out yesterday."

He laughed. "You caused quite a stir at the induction center."

Her cheeks bloomed with a rosy blush. "It won't happen again."

"Knowing you, that's doubtful." He cried, "Ouch!" after she gave him a playful jab in the side.

She encountered resistance trying to open the door. Enlisting his help, they gave it a shove and discovered Bruno taking his morning nap.

"You would've fooled me, but I thought some of Hollywood's top animal handlers trained you," Guy said, pushing the bulldog aside, who seemed to double as a doorstop. He fetched Bruno's leash and announced, "Time to go out, you lazy lug."

Babs promised the coffee would be ready by the time he returned. Once she was alone, she turned to the parrots. "Did Pedro and Petunia behave while we were gone? Otherwise, I hope you understand your days are numbered."

Pedro tried flattery to summon her sympathy. "Pretty girl...pretty girl!" he replied. Then he whistled, "*Whoo! Whoo!*" like a lustful sailor.

Babs chuckled. "You're going to have to do better than that to gain my favor." She put fresh water in their cage. "What about you, Petunia? Can you one-up your playmate?"

"*O sole mio!*"

"Italian? Are you siding with our enemies? Betcha you don't even know what that means."

Babs let the birds be and tackled the pile of delinquent mail. Then the phone rang.

"Who?" she asked, yawning.

"Ernie... Ernie Fischman. Remember? I'm the one who always shows when there's a corpse to be captured."

"What? Who died and where?"

"To be captured on film. I'm your friendly neighborhood crime scene photographer."

Paying partial attention, she reached for her coffee. Half of it missed her mouth. She blotted the spill on her desk using discarded envelopes instead of wipe-up rags. "Of course, how can I help you? Did anyone else croak?"

"Well, that's a heck of a way to react to someone who's about to ask you out."

She scrunched her brows. "For a date?"

"Don't tell me you're working weekends."

"What if there's another murder?"

"The murderer can take the weekend off."

"If I don't make a dent in these bills, someone's liable to turn off my electricity."

"Nonsense. Wait one more day. You need to get out and have some fun. How 'bout it?"

"*Uh...*" She yawned again. "What did you have in mind?"

"Griffith Park? The planetarium, perhaps? I hear Venus and Mars will be visible tonight."

Just what I need when I barely know this fellow...the planets of love and sex!

Before she had to give Ernie a yay or a nay, Guy returned with Bruno and an armful of newspapers.

"Gotta go. My partner's here."

"Is something going on between the two of you I should know?"

Babs laughed so hard she could feel it in her stomach. "That should be the least of your worries."

"Promise you'll call me back?"

"You've got my word." Relieved to hang up, she turned to Guy.

Curious, he asked, "Anything I should know about?"

"That pushy crime scene shutterbug wants to ask me out on a date."

"Why not?"

"I should spend my time here in the office. What about you?"

"We won't have to worry about threats to the Warners. Jack assured me his bodyguard will spend the weekend with his family. Rudy will be free. We plan on spending time together. You deserve a break, too. Why don't you give him a chance?"

Pedro kept squawking, "Pretty girl! Pretty girl!" Bruno wagged his pipsqueak-sized tail in rapid succession, as if he agreed. Guy fed the bulldog and gathered his belongings.

She shouted, "Not so fast. Leaving so soon?"

"Unlike you, I don't plan on making this my home this weekend." Halfway out the door, he said, "I guess it's your turn to lock up."

"Wait!" Babs called out.

"What now?"

"Would you mind asking Rudy if he'd take the parrots? I'll throw in a cash incentive."

Guy raised one eyebrow, as if to convey, "You've got to be kidding," and with that, he left.

Babs started to call Fischman back, but stopped and put the phone down. Giving herself a few moments longer to think it over, that's when she heard an ear-piercing squeal. She rushed over to the parrot cage and found Pedro attacking Petunia.

Risking getting thrashed herself, Babs separated the birds by wadding up the towel she'd placed over their cage at night. She shoved him into a corner while she shooed Petunia out of the cage, using a feather duster. Once she freed the bird, she locked the cage with Pedro inside and took a deep breath.

Babs noticed a raw spot where he had plucked feathers off Petunia's neck.

She wanted to kick the large cage with Pedro inside, but what good would that serve?

The phone rang again. She answered with a harsh, "Yes!"

"Is that any way to treat your date?"

"Oh, Eric… Sorry, I'm in the middle of an unexpected crisis, and—"

"So, I guess our date is off?"

"Got an urgent matter on my hands."

"Maybe I can help."

"Can you handle birds? Rather large ones."

"I've refereed cockfights at my uncle's farm. Why?"

Babs withheld the urge to argue. She considered such sports cruel and abhorrent. "These are Amazonian parrots," she said, examining her arms for bite marks or scratches.

"You're talkin' *big* birds. Expensive ones, too. I bet."

"I need to run the wounded one to the vet right away, and it can't wait. But I could use some help. Injured animals sometimes attack their rescuers."

"I'll be right over."

Babs hung up, surprised Ernie was so eager to volunteer. Half an hour later, it took everything Ernie had to stop laughing when Babs' hair looked like a bird's nest. Together, they secured Petunia and hopped into his car while he drove to the vet's, who wanted to keep the bird overnight for observation.

Ernie hinted, "There's still time to go out and have fun this afternoon."

Babs took a quick look at the tiny mirror in her compact. "I'm not going anywhere until I shower and change my clothes."

"Understandable. Let me take you home."

After accepting his help, she wondered what she had gotten herself into. With the bird crisis under wraps, she also had her concerns about Mr. Otake, whom she had left alone in the house with the other dog. Then she found a note tacked to her front door, along with visible signs that someone had attempted to jimmy the lock.

We've had complaints from neighbors sighting a possible Japanese resident alien hiding in your residence and not in compliance with recent evacuation orders. Contact us immediately. Signed by Mr. John Reilly, Field Officer for the Immigration and Naturalization Service, Special Agent William Wright and Special Agent Sherman Lockwood, FBI.

"Oh, brother! What next?"

Since Babs had already dealt with the FBI agents, she pulled their business card from her wallet and called them from her kitchen extension while Sir Henry sat at her feet.

"Got the note. For what do I owe the pleasure of your surprise visit while I was out?"

Lockwood answered, "The U.S. is at war with the Japs, and one of your neighbors reported seeing one hiding in your house."

"I live alone with a gargantuan Irish Wolfhound. He stands close to six feet tall. From afar, if he poked his head under my curtains or shades, it would be easy to mistake him for a human. Just that he's awfully hairy unless he's some kind of Sasquatch, but no one's sighted those in the Hollywood Hills for a while."

"Not our department. Anyway, it's too late to call today, and the INS office is closed on Sunday, but you'll need to call Field Rep Reilly and drop by on Monday. He must've been in a good mood. Otherwise, he would've ordered the police to break down your door."

Without a search warrant? After the call, she went to the fridge, let Sir Henry gnaw on a knucklebone, and realized she'd promised to touch base with Ernie.

First, she had to take a shower. With both her hair and body wrapped in damp towels, she went over to her closet to find fresh clothes. Otake startled her when she discovered him hiding in her closet. He clamped his hand over her mouth the moment she screamed.

"You said not to make sudden noise," he warned her, but the wolfhound went into hysterics and started barking downstairs.

Otake took his hand away. Her heart raced, but she willed herself to remain calm. *He'd have to pick my closet at a time like this. No place was safe.*

She showed Mr. Otake the note but then realized he might not be capable of reading it.

"When was this?"

"Maybe hour…hour and a half ago. Why?"

She shook her head in disbelief. "Bad news, I'm afraid. Did Sir Henry bark up a storm while I was gone?"

"Bark up a storm?"

"That's right…I need to avoid using idioms around you that you can't translate. Did the dog make a lot of noise?"

"Yes. Much noise."

Her thoughts flashed back to when Mr. Otake approached her a year and a half ago. He was desperate for a place to stay after so many others refused to rent rooms in their homes to Orientals from any nation. He offered to work her yard for free to live in a house surrounded by flowers and with the opportunity to plant a vegetable garden. To enjoy the shade trees, rather than live in a tenement boarding house downtown in Little Tokyo, with barely a blade of grass springing up between the blistering asphalt.

She felt more sympathetic toward him than she did toward Eric Fischman, whom she was supposed to see later. They drew all the shades and closed the curtains before sitting down at the kitchen table.

"You know, I can get in a heap of trouble helping you," she said.

Otake humbly lowered his head.

"From what I read in the papers, weren't you to register with some kind of agency? Like the War Relocation Authority?"

"At first I refused, but my former employer at the gardening company had to register along with all his employees, so I had no choice. My boss warned me people would've found out anyway from my bank account."

"If this drags on, how do you expect to pay your rent?"

"My bank account…now it's frozen. The money I hid in my room it's almost gone."

"That's what I thought." She wouldn't be able to cover his expenses forever. "Did you mention anything to anyone about your intention to avoid being sent away?"

"I told my coworkers to spread the word I had committed suicide rather than get taken to an assembly center. They should think I am dead."

"Who do you mean by *they?*"

"Anyone connected with immigration, the police, or the government."

"Looks like your plan backfired. An INS agent and the FBI summoned me down to their offices. I'll have no choice but to take time away from my case and take care of it. Furthermore, if they can't find any funeral records or a death certificate, they'll prove you were lying. Mr. Otake, is there any other way Japanese residents have avoided going to these detention centers?"

"If we have money and a place to go…far, far away from the West Coast, there are other options. If we had relatives or a sponsor—"

"Too bad my relatives are in the San Francisco area, another evacuation area. Otherwise, I'd have my mom let you stay in her guest room. So, you're saying if I had a cousin in Missouri willing to be your guarantor that you'd be safe?"

"Yes, I think. Maybe…"

Babs sighed. "My partner isn't on good terms with his pop. Otherwise, that could've been an option. He lives in the Midwest."

"Not sure where all your states are located."

"Doesn't matter. It would never work. We've got a big country compared to the one you came from. I think the entire country of Japan would fit within the size of California. In the Midwest, you could get lost. Blend in with the scenery."

"Blend in? Scenery?"

"Sorry, I'm talking slang again, and you have a limited knowledge of English. All the same, I hate that you need to hide all day and night. I'm worried about the dog. We'll have problems if we keep him at the office, and by having him here, it appears his barking might've given you away. Later, I promised a friend we'd get together. Will you be alright if I leave you alone with Sir Henry?"

"I try."

Babs realized it might not have been his fault regarding her neighbor's spying. Anyone could've mistaken the dog for him. In fact, she did once or twice. She warned Mr. Otake to be extra careful and then realized she had misplaced Ernie's phone number.

* * *

To play it safe, Babs changed her mind and took Sir Henry with her on her date with Ernie at Griffith Park. If he made a sudden affectionate move toward Babs, the dog got protective, as if he tried to convey, "Hands off!"

Much to Ernie's dismay, personnel at the Griffith Park Observatory refused to let the dog inside the planetarium, but they were fine if he remained outside. Babs got annoyed when he had to jockey back and forth to pay phones to check in for assignments.

He provided a convenient excuse. "Just when I'd rather be with a hot dame having fun, everyone seems to like to die on the weekends. Had to give some of my work away to competitors."

Their date started on a sour note and continued like a brass band out of tune. Babs didn't expect a gourmet spread, but she'd hoped for picnic lunch a step up from peanut butter and jelly. Sir Henry begged for a bite, and Babs realized, for the first time, the comical effect of dogs and peanut butter. The dog cracked them up when the peanut butter got stuck to the roof of his mouth, and he kept sticking his tongue in and out like a snake.

Throughout their date, Ernie revealed he held the old-school attitude (like her ex-husband Troy) that men were smarter and deserved higher pay than women. He also clarified that he had major issues with Babs running her own business, often making her unavailable when he had time off. To make matters worse, they both had erratic and unpredictable schedules. He was also against the "Rosie the Riveter" attitude of women replacing the men in the factories who had gone off to serve in the war.

Babs asked, "Any chance you might get called for the draft?"

Ernie seemed smug. "They won't get their mitts on me. Got excused as a conscientious objector. Said it was against my religion to kill the Krauts or the Japs."

She tried to contain her disgust of such derogatory language. "Over at Warner's, there's been talk about the shortage of labor and women stepping into traditional men's roles. People might have to train ladies to work as camera assistants or set painters. Others want them to remain only in secretarial jobs. Personally, I feel if a woman has the talent, nothing should stop her."

Sir Henry perked up his ears, as if he was also eager to hear the answer.

"Call me old-fashioned, but a woman's place should be in the home," Ernie replied.

That was enough to make her shudder. "You're as bad as my mother! She's always putting me down for being a career girl and not opting for a more traditional lifestyle like hers. The problem is…she had no choice. I'm a modern-day gal, and these are different times."

Babs argued that she'd rather be unmarried and struggle on her own than be trapped with a cad like her ex in an abusive relationship. Before making a slip of the tongue, she stopped before mentioning that she had a roommate and didn't live alone. No one was supposed to know, except Rudy and Guy, that she was still concealing Mr. Otake.

"What would your father have thought?"

"Have no idea," she replied. "It's because of my dad, Cliff Norman, that I fought for justice and became a private investigator. He got murdered when I was only nine or ten…*oops!*" She had no intention of blurting that out, but there was no backing out of it now.

"Did I hear that right?"

She dropped her head to her chest. He scooted over and tried to put his arm around her to show he cared, but she inched away, showing she wanted to be left alone.

Nothing he was going to do would salvage their date now. And here, Guy, her partner, was making headway in his new relationship with Rudy. She, however, hit a dead end.

Chapter Seventeen

For Rudy and Guy, the weekend felt like a whirlwind of unanticipated social get-togethers. After Guy left the office on Saturday, oblivious to the impending developments involving Babs, the two rode by motorcycle to the decadent residential hotel, the Garden of Allah, where they had invitations as guests to a private party.

"Long before my time, the LAPD hired two undercover detectives, who became mercenaries, getting paid top dollar to arrest social vagrants in public places," he warned Rudy. "If we tangled with the police, given the Garden's long-standing reputation, that could cost me my hard-earned private investigator's license."

Rudy felt confident that cops wouldn't be present, and it was doubtful either of them would get recognized. "Perhaps the owner, former silent screen star Alla Nazimova, and her manager regularly paid them off. Aren't you forgetting about my own concerns regarding my previous affiliation with Leon Lewis? I used to make regular trips to the Friends of New Germany's Aryan bookstore. I had witnessed money change hands to fund subversive activities and had passed on that disgusting literature after translating it. It wouldn't have surprised me if they had their members keeping me under watch, and those whom the FBI hadn't rounded up might still be out there waiting to retaliate."

The Garden of Allah, however, had its own unique persona. Guy had heard stories about their pool, constructed in the shape of the Black Sea, where Nazimova was from. Famous people, often intoxicated, fell in fully clothed. Marlene Dietrich enjoyed swimming *au naturel*.

"Wasn't there a famous line about this pool in a Mae West film?" Guy asked.

"Indeed, there was. The humorist, screenwriter, and actor, Robert Benchley, once remarked after someone tossed him into the drink, 'Get me out of these wet clothes and into a dry martini.' That made its way into the script of *Every Day's a Holiday*."

Rudy also mentioned, "The actress, Tallulah Bankhead, fell into the pool late one night wearing a beaded evening gown. After struggling under its weight, she ditched the dress, swam to the surface, and emerged from the water wearing nothing but her diamond jewelry. When given strange looks, she replied, 'Everyone's been dying to see my body. Now they can see it.'"

A bit overwhelmed by the free-wheeling atmosphere, even though he brought swim trunks, Guy got stricken with a wave of modesty and refused to change out of his street clothes. Instead, he felt content to sit on the sidelines.

"Rudy, I couldn't convince you to take a couple of talking parrots."

"The ones in your office?"

Guy nodded.

"Obligating myself to pets would be like tying myself down with a child. Why do you ask?"

"Tenants have complained in our office building, and neither Babs nor I can keep them at home. I feel sorry for them and would hate to dump them at the city pound."

"In the script of *Casablanca*, I seem to recall a location…the Blue Parrot Café, am I right? Maybe you should talk to the art director or whoever's in charge and see if they need real blue parrots, even if the film's going to be in black and white. Every time I've seen it mentioned, it kind of reminds me of a famous, depraved nightclub in Berlin."

Guy lost all interest in the men frolicking in the pool. "You must tell me more."

"This westside burlesque nightspot was famous—the *Kakadu* or Cockatoo Bar with live parrots. Free admission for the well-dressed. Open till 3:00 a.m. The queers snuck in and mixed with the heteros. The wide range of patrons consisted of bankers, musicians, painters, tourists, and foreign news correspondents. Police officials loved these *nachtlokal,* which is the German word for nightclub. The more *erotic* ones," he said, lowering his voice from eavesdroppers, "were near the Alex, or Berlin's Police Headquarters."

"The police turned a blind eye?"

"They often took part in the fun. What's more, the *Kakadu* had faux-Tahitian décor with red lighting and fireplaces, and an enormous blue and gold bar. Ha! Blue and gold—just like your parrots. Over every dining table was a parrot in a cage, which was also the club's emblem. When a customer wished to leave, he tapped his water glass with a knife. This signaled the bird to squawk and say, 'The bill! The bill!'"

Guy laughed, "That's hilarious."

"As amusing as it was, the parrots…I guess they couldn't help themselves, but they let their droppings fall on the plates of unwary patrons if they weren't careful. Yet I wonder if *Casablanca's* art director had something like that in mind."

"What a brilliant idea! Someone might pay us to get these pests off our hands."

Rudy swirled his cocktail before taking a sip and sighed. "I wish I'd be so brilliant as to figure out who murdered Gerhard Sauer and why?"

"Did you know him?"

"Gerry had always been a secretive man. I was aware he was queer and wondered if that had something to do with it."

Guy's face hardened. "What else have you been withholding?"

Rudy's acting skills failed him when his face turned the color of the bottom of an ashtray. Telltale droplets of cold sweat appeared on his neck and forehead like a sudden outbreak of measles.

"We've been running in circles this entire time. Tell me, Rudy, did you kill him, even if it was by accident?"

As if his neck joints had rusted stiff like the Tin Man's from *The Wizard of Oz,* Rudy could barely gesture a negative reply.

"Then what?" Guy demanded.

"There was something between us."

Although Guy would never be satisfied without a further explanation, he spotted Dashiell Hammett, clothed in a work shirt, buttoned the wrong way, and baggy khaki trousers. Guy assumed he must've left his bungalow to see for himself the poolside frolic. Hammett also recognized Guy and headed toward him and Rudy, swinging a bottle of booze.

"Hey, if it isn't my non-fictional sleuthhound? My Sam Spade in the flesh," said Hammett, whose messy hair looked like he had just woken from an all-nighter. He pulled out a lounge chair and sat down. "I haven't seen you since you, your gal partner, and Humphrey Bogart came to me for advice during the filming of *The Maltese Falcon*."

"Me, Sam Spade?" Guy pointed to Rudy. "Here is your Blond Satan."

Hammett gave him the once-over. "*Hmmm*. Much taller than I imagined, and the devilish part is yet to be seen."

Guy wryly curled his lip. "Believe me. He fits the part. Bogie fit the character but was way off from Spade's original physical description in your book."

Hammett looked at Guy. "I know you're a private eye." Then he faced Rudy. "But what about you?"

Noticing Hammett was alone, Guy changed the subject. "Is Lillian around?" referring to his famous playwright girlfriend and often his caretaker, Lillian Hellman.

"She's off in New York on one of her playwright adventures."

"Dash, why are you here?" asked Guy.

"In LA? Drinking away my loneliness…and despair. If you really want to know, the studios got the bum steer when they thought they could still milk a few scripts out of me. As far as the *voyeuristic aquacade* is concerned," he said, snickering, "I thought I could cop a free lunch while no one was looking."

"What drew you back to the Garden?" asked Guy.

"This joint changes like the seasons, but it was convenient since they're amenable to temporary rentals. I'm sure the studio will let my contract expire when they realize my creative inspiration took an extended holiday."

"About this party? Didn't know you were into this kind of scene."

"Nothing wrong with enjoying the view from afar, is there? Besides, it might give me an idea for a new story unless the censors who bow to the Hays Office kill it."

"As long as you weren't planning on calling the police."

Hammett suppressed another hiccup. "Or being coerced to join in. What about you? I don't see you splashing around in the buff?"

Guy demurred. His cheeks turned a rosy hue. "This is a novel experience for me. Best to sit it out, I guess."

"Go, have your fun. Join your friends," Hammett said, waving him off.

* * *

Rudy took Guy back to Salka Viertel's the following afternoon.

"You seem to be drawn to this place," Guy commented.

"It's a gut feeling," Rudy replied. "One I can't put into words. I also believe I'm going to find the solution for Babs' Japanese friend from being around all these ex-pats."

This time, the food seemed to be a potluck hodgepodge, and the bar wasn't too well-stocked. Guy, in trying to decide what was safe to eat, commented, "One never knows these days what one is eating unless they cook it themselves. People often add potato starch to bread, sometimes extending it with sawdust." Rudy eyed the desserts, and Guy went on to add, "People also get creative with sugar substitutes. I've heard of those using grated carrots to make foods taste sweeter."

"I can tell you one thing," said Rudy. "The beer is nowhere near the quality we had back in Berlin."

Despite apprehensions, the men piled their plates. Rudy, being so long in the limb and able to see heads above the others, looked around for their hostess and finally nodded in her direction. Guy said he'd catch up and lingered by the buffet. That's when he spotted an old client, one who was unmistakable by his short and pudgy stature, thick lips, and bulging eyes. Even while speaking German, his voice stood out among the rest—Peter Lorre, with whom he worked on his *Maltese Falcon* case. He had a much smaller but vital role in *Casablanca.*

"So, we meet again," Peter said with an air of levity. "Sometimes I wonder if you're stalking me."

"I thought you were already one of the established Hollywood elites," Guy said. "What are you doing among a bunch of recent émigrés?"

"I should ask you the same question." Lorre, who had been dangling an unlit cigarette in his mouth, offered one to Guy and lit both.

"A friend brought me here. What about you?"

"Maybe you forgot that I'm a German-Hungarian Jew and was lucky to arrive with the early wave. I had a flourishing acting career in both film and theater in Germany before the Nazi takeover. Goebbels praised my performances until he found out I was Jewish. Then he banned my films."

Guy dived into his wartime lunch of spam-based staples, home-grown vegetables from victory gardens, and cornflake peanut butter cookies. He almost felt guilty and tried not to make it obvious he was famished.

"Those who took over the new German government condemned everyone who didn't fit into their ideal. The one thing they couldn't accuse me of was being a Marxist. They loathed them, too."

"That, I never quite understood, 'cause I'm not quite savvy with politics. Why would they consider Marxists offensive? They're both totalitarian governments."

"The only Marxist views I support…are those from the Marx Brothers." Peter chuckled to himself, trying not to let it show. "Anyway, acting is a ridiculous profession unless it is a part of your very soul, and I couldn't toss my soul away that easily."

Guy tried not to spit out his food while laughing.

"After I left Germany," Peter said, "I considered Vienna, but it wasn't safe there, either. Here I was on the run, battling drug addiction, and prospects for work were dismal. My wife and I fled to Paris and almost starved. Alfred Hitchcock saved both my life and my career when he sponsored me to come to England to film *The Man Who Knew Too Much.* My next challenge was to learn how to speak English!"

Guy finished the last of his beer. "I suspect your Mr. Moto films aren't too popular anymore since Pearl Harbor."

"That's the way the cookie crumbles. Although I prefer mine with chocolate chips." Peter bit into the one he had hoarded for dessert, but winced and stuck out his tongue. "Can't tell if whoever baked this used real chocolate or swapped it like they do with everything else these days."

Guy giggled, recalling Peter's sardonic humor. "I'm sure you no longer walk around with a pair of glasses in your pocket to imitate Mr. Moto if asked for autographs."

"I think not, but as you know from our previous time spent together, for years people tarnished my good nature by confusing me with the madman I played in the movie *M*. Now, they'll despise me, because they'll think I'm Japanese. Can't seem to win, I guess."

"Come and meet my friend. He'll think I've abandoned him." Guy led Peter out to the backyard. He introduced him to Rudy, and they immediately started speaking German.

Guy cleared his throat. "Aren't you forgetting that I only understand English…and maybe a few French *bon mots* here and there?"

"Sorry. It's one of those natural instincts," Rudy replied.

During their conversation, Peter admitted giving contributions to the European Film Fund, despite having his own personal creditors hounding him for loans he hadn't paid back.

"It's always a problem when you spend more than you earn, and I'm a sucker for helping others less fortunate than me, because I've been there myself. However, unlike actors such as George Raft and Paul Muni, who turned down parts that wound up in Bogie's lap because they didn't want to die at the end of the script, I enjoy collecting my paychecks. I don't care what I do, but people love to cast me in the oddest roles. In *Casablanca*, I play a shady wheeler and dealer who kills two German couriers for irrevocable letters of transit—a coveted commodity."

He leaned in closer and lowered his voice to a whisper. "Hate to let you down, but I got a little secret for you boys."

"What's that?" Guy asked.

"There are no such things as letters of transit."

"How did you escape Germany?" Guy asked.

"I got out with the help of a few friends, sheer luck, and perseverance." Peter looked at Rudy. "What about you?"

"Similar to the movie we're working on. In '33, when Hitler wanted to cleanse Germany of what he considered *undesirables*. At my first chance, I left Berlin for Switzerland. Took a few roundabout routes and landed in *Casablanca*."

Rudy took out cigarettes and offered one to each of his friends. "Changing the subject," he asked Peter, "you wouldn't happen to know a German ex-pat named Gerhard Sauer?"

"No, but he better not ask me for money, 'cause I don't have any to spare."

"I'm afraid he can't. He's dead," Rudy said with a bittersweet reply.

Peter apologized for his inappropriate reaction. "That was callous of me to assume that. Was he an actor? I've never heard of him."

"A stagehand." He kept quiet about Sauer's history of spying for Leon Lewis.

"Were you close?"

"Casual acquaintances."

Another lie.

Peter noticed their glasses were empty. "Everyone says I'm an excellent bartender. I also make a surefire hangover cure, although it's disgusting. Why don't I surprise you? Let me refill your glasses."

With Peter out of earshot, Guy had a few burning questions for Rudy. "Smart move for sneaking in the inquiry about Sauer. Did you say you spotted someone of interest?"

"Maybe it was my imagination. Whoever it was, we never caught up. I thought it was the man who got fired from the sound department during the first few days of production. If he didn't land another gig, he might've come here to speak to somebody about a loan from the Film Fund. LA's a tough town without money."

"At least that option exists for those in need. Rudy, I'm curious. I didn't want to ask you in front of Peter, but since you aren't Jewish, what motivated you to team up with Leon Lewis?"

"You really want to know?"

"Come on. I'm a PI. Eventually, I'd squeeze it out of you."

Rudy lit a fresh cigarette. He started to blow a smoke ring but stopped. "My best friend from childhood was a Jewish kid named Levi Bernstein. As he grew into adulthood, he became a brilliant medical student but hid a secret double life. In the evenings, far away from his colleagues and university professors, he liked to be called Leia. He'd restyle his hair, put on makeup, and wear a dress. Never bothered me, since I had many eccentric friends within my avant-garde social circles.

"We went to one of Berlin's bawdy halls one night. *Leia* decided to take out *her* yarmulke, with a prominent gold Star of David embroidered on it, and wore it like a woman's fashionable half-beret to make some kind of socio-political statement. A few brownshirts in the crowd didn't find it amusing, and that's when the melee began. I tried to intervene, but I was drunk and outnumbered."

"I hope you were alright afterward. What happened to your friend?" Guy asked.

"The last I heard, they sent Levi or Leia to a concentration camp where he or she, depending on your fancy, got killed in a riot. That's why men like Leon Lewis and his associates have my sympathies."

Peter returned with their drinks and proposed a toast. "There's a line in the script of *Casablanca* where Rick Blaine says to Ilsa, 'We'll always have Paris.' Rudy, my new friend, we will always have our cherished memories before the hardships. Let's raise our glasses, because we'll always have Berlin."

Chapter Eighteen

After delays the previous week, on Monday, *Casablanca* filmed the scenes with Bogart and Bergman in Ilsa's Paris apartment. Babs had her mandatory meeting with John Reilly, the INS representative. Guy and Rudy monitored the set in her absence.

While the set dressers were making their final touches and the hair and makeup crew did their last looks, Rudy whispered to Guy, "This place doesn't remind me much of Paris. Have you ever been there?"

"Sorry." Guy shrugged. "I have nothing to compare it to."

"I'd imagine the heaven-sent smell of fresh croissants wafting through the window from the bakery below. The tune of a beggar playing his accordion, cut short by a police whistle. Motor cars passing by. A woman's voice shouting from her window to another neighbor…"

"Hate to cut short your nostalgic musings. Except for the baked goods, those would be sounds the Foley artists would create in post-production editing," said Guy. "We already witnessed what sort of sound challenges could arise simply from the layout of the sets alone."

Curtiz demanded another rehearsal. "I want to see the words on your faces. Skip to Rick's line, 'I was just wondering.'"

Ingrid and Bogie got into their positions and began reciting their dialogue in a scene that ended with a kiss.

"Cut! Cut! Cut!" hollered Michael Curtiz when she leaned in to kiss him. "Ingrid, you looked like you were trying to kiss a horse!"

Bogie mimicked a neighing sound. *"Whoa, Nelly!* I resent the equine reference. Unless you're hinting I'm a stud about to win the Triple Crown."

Curtiz, always one to dish out the insults, cut Bergman down to size.

"You're nothing. Nobody knows who you are in America. Hedy Lamarr would've done better if cast in the part, but Louis B. Mayer refused to loan her to me. Maybe her agent can change his mind."

Ingrid's nostrils flared as she spouted vitriol. "So, you're saying no one has heard of *Dr. Jekyll and Mr. Hyde* or *Intermezzo?* My agent, David O. Selznick, would beg to differ."

In her defense, she objected that the Epstein brothers had written a new draft of the script, but it still wasn't the final approved version.

"From one moment to the next, neither I nor Humphrey know what we're supposed to be thinking or saying, and you give us little time to memorize our new lines. How can you not think it'll affect our performance?"

She tried to remain polite and professional, but Curtiz had his own agenda.

"Then try harder. We'll do it again and work during lunch if necessary. Lunch is for lazy bums. Start from the top. Put it on film this time." He pointed at Francis Scheid and said, "Roll sound, you stupid soundman!"

* * *

Babs had her mandatory meeting at the INS office. She sat in the hot seat in front of Reilly's desk, which had an American flag to its left, one too large for the room. Photos of him at awards and ribbon-cutting ceremonies, along with certificates of merit, adorned his walls. The one good thing she could say about him was she didn't see a single ashtray, and his office smelled like the cut chrysanthemums he had on an end table. However, she couldn't figure out why the FBI agents were also present. They sat at the back of the room on either side of the exit with notepads in their laps.

Reilly sifted through several folders on his desktop and began the inquiry. "Miss Barbara Norman—"

"Please, call me Babs."

"Babs, as a private investigator, I'd like to assume you keep abreast of the news and take for granted that you're aware of Executive Order 9066. Correct?"

"Yes, sir. I am."

"Are you also aware, as of this date, that the evacuation of Japanese residents from the West Coast of the United States is no longer voluntary, but mandatory?"

Babs nodded.

"Speak up, lady. I want to hear it in your own words."

That was abrupt, she thought. "I'm aware."

"A woman named Mrs. Doris Dietz filed several complaints at my office; she claimed—no, swore—she had seen a Japanese man, in his fifties or sixties, in your backyard or peering through your windows. Is there any truth to that?"

Can't believe she's finally taking her revenge for my parrots attacking her Yorkshire terrier! Better give my best Oscar performance.

Babs took a deep and slow breath without letting it show. "None whatsoever." *You're doing great, Babsy. Keep up the good work.*

She started perspiring. He resumed questioning. "So, are you aware if you're not telling us the truth, both of you can land in jail?'

"Sir, I wasn't, but I assure you that's not an issue. I currently live alone with a mammoth dog who, when he stands on his hind legs, is as tall as a human. Once, from far away, I thought he was a burglar when I saw him through the window."

Babs expected a few laughs but noticed everyone was eerily silent.

"That doesn't account for someone being spotted in your backyard," said Reilly.

"Look, I've never bothered to get my fence repaired, nor have I found the need to plant privacy hedges, but I have kids chasing their balls, and laborers from all over, the meter man from the gas company, telephone workers, even the milkman, cutting across my yard all the time. Mrs. Dietz complained he looked Japanese. How close was she? My plumber is Mexican. People have mistaken him for Chinese."

Doing good, Babs. Keep it up.

Reilly took out a pack of Black Jack chewing gum. He asked if anyone wanted some, but everyone declined. She strained to maintain a straight face. Because of its black color, actors often used the gum to pretend they were missing some of their teeth. From far away, one couldn't tell the difference.

"Congress also passed Public Law 503. Violations of the president's executive order would be misdemeanors punishable up to one year in prison with a five-thousand-dollar fine—"

Special Agent Wright whistled in reaction.

"There were others that insisted the length of imprisonment should be for five years," Reilly said while chomping on his gum. "But they kept it at one."

"In a hypothetical situation," Babs said, trying to appear savvy, "if I were involved in such a case, wouldn't you agree this executive order violates a lot of fundamental freedoms such as civil rights and the right to due process? This would put a Japanese American in a contradictory situation. People accused them of lawbreaking, no matter if they stayed or left their homes. Those internment camps you're sending them to are just prisons in disguise."

She turned to the FBI agents for a second opinion. Lockwood avoided eye contact and looked toward the ceiling. Wright said it wasn't his doing.

Babs glanced at Reilly's clock. If she could tire everyone out to where they'd be glad to get rid of her, she could congratulate herself on making headway, or at least for the time being. Before she left, however, Reilly handed her a piece of paper, which looked like an invoice for one hundred dollars.

"What's this?" she asked.

"A fine."

She examined the flimsy document. The paper lacked a logo or insignia from a government agency and looked like someone had typed it at the last minute on borrowed onionskin stationery.

"For what?"

"Every time I have to waste my time by calling in a violation, we…our agency needs compensation for our time…and manpower." He appeared to struggle with that explanation, as if making it up on the fly.

This sounds like one of those scare tactics used by thugs who extort protection money from poor, mom-and-pop business owners!

"I've never heard of such nonsense. You can't expect me to walk around with that amount of cash or a checkbook."

Who could she ask whether he was telling the truth? These intimidation tactics reeked of rotten fish, but she'd have to bolt past the two special agents if she tried to make a run for the door.

Reilly picked up a pair of scissors. He opened and closed them in rapid succession. "To make this minor issue…let's say…go away… How 'bout rounding it to three hundred? I'll shred the document, and we'll call it a day."

Unsure at first how to react, Babs opened her purse, pulled out her wallet, and dumped two pennies on Reilly's desk.

"Take it or leave it. I'm giving you my two cents."

* * *

After spending Sunday afternoon with Rudy at Salka's, Guy regretted he hadn't asked Peter for his famous hangover recipe. Everyone from craft services to the set medic tried to comfort him with their miracle cures, none of which worked.

Curtiz lambasted Babs for arriving late and enjoyed making a spectacle of her in front of his captive cast and crew. "You playing bookie?"

Babs scratched her head, a bit confused by his malapropisms. She had just been through the wringer with government agents, and it had nothing to do with gambling.

"You mean hooky…like skipping school, right? Not bookie."

"Oh, I guess I mean hooky."

"Are you the school principal? What are you going to do? Keep me for detention afterward?"

He smirked, and she regretted having said that. Known to make his moves on attractive ladies, she hoped she hadn't left him an opening by exercising her smart mouth. Doing her best to remedy the mess, she replied, "Took care of legal matters. If you want to exchange places and handle those for me, be my guest."

Curtiz's assistant director intervened with a memo from Wallis, taking her off the hook. When she joined her partners, Guy said she had missed a lot of stud and racehorse innuendo.

"Speaking of racehorses…" Rudy rose and offered Babs his chair. "I have to go somewhere related to your friend."

Babs was about to ask who, but Rudy put his finger to his lips. No one should mention Otake's name.

* * *

While they filmed the street scenes of the Parisians reacting to the German army advancing into the city, along with Rick and Ilsa's dialogue, as they looked out the window, the crew prepared the set for the Paris train station. The art director, Carl Weyl, had mentioned earlier, he had recycled a set from *Now, Voyager,* adding a railing and making a few tweaks here and there.

Following that, they blocked and filmed the two-shot with Rick and Ilsa, discussing that nothing would stop the Germans now, and by Wednesday or Thursday, they'll take over Paris. Ilsa, frightened they'll uncover the records of Rick's activities against the Reich, fears for his safety. Rick knows he's on their blacklist already.

* * *

Curtiz despised people hanging around the set without an obvious function and demanded Babs and Guy work as extras in the Gare de Leon scene where Rick, Ilsa, and Sam planned to catch the last train from Paris to Marseille. An assistant escorted them over to wardrobe. They handed Guy a hat and trench coat.

The props assistant, instead of giving Babs an umbrella, insisted she carry a suitcase in each hand. Convinced this was the director's way of punishing her for arriving late, she complained, "He's doing it on purpose. Curtiz wants to see us get drenched."

Not that they'd be an exception, because everyone in front of the camera had to experience the same discomfort with the studio's rainmaking machine. She kept trying to read from the director's expression whether he was enjoying a private joke.

After the first rehearsal, she told Guy, "Someone should give us a bump. Don't they call that hazard pay?"

"Keep your eyes on the crowd," Guy said, keeping in character. "Here, while you're whining about a fake downpour on a movie set, there could be a killer lurking among these extras, ready to pull a knife."

She gave him a dirty look but realized he was right.

Chapter Nineteen

At the director's request, hairdressers dyed Rudy's hair to match Major Strasser's, but at least with black-and-white film, they allowed him to keep a few streaks of his original blond to double for gray.

"Why didn't they have you wear a wig?" Guy asked.

"They were concerned about the scene at the end when the major gets shot. Remember, I'm also doubling as Conrad's stuntman, not just as his stand-in. They worried a hairpiece might fall off."

Guy touched his hair to see if it had ruined its silken texture. Rudy jerked away as if he had stuck a wet finger in an electric socket.

"What's the problem?" Guy asked, surprised at his adverse reaction.

"I'm trying to get into character," Rudy replied, but Guy didn't interpret it that way. Ever since Rudy had confessed there had been a relationship between him and Sauer, he sensed a growing detachment between them.

A loose strand of Rudy's dyed hair had stuck to Guy's fingers. He examined it closer in the light. "Hope this comes out after the movie is over. If you had to shave it all off to get rid of it…you'd resemble—"

"A concentration camp detainee," Rudy said, finishing his sentence. "Let's talk about something more pleasant."

* * *

Meanwhile, Babs visited the stage where they were constructing the Moroccan streets and exteriors. Since no one had asked for her ID at the door, she figured she'd take a quick look. She wandered through the narrow, jumbled passageways, as intricate as an Arabian mosaic, which she imagined must've led to cavernous residences, retreats for illegal trade, or even houses of ill repute.

She closed her eyes, trying to fantasize about the thrill of being there. Taking a few steps forward, she stumbled, realizing the Art Department made the sets so realistic that the ground under her feet was uneven. Knowing these structures led to nothing backstage, she ambled over to where the construction crew and set painters had set up the bazaar.

The stalls consisted of tents or tent poles with fabric canopies providing shade from the relentless desert sun, but in this case, powerful arc lamps. Yet, it seemed to miss the smells of exotic spices unknown to her normal palate, and the chirping of birds. Perhaps a stray monkey or two scurrying by.

Despite the industrial fans trying to cool the hot sound stage, Guy caught up. He wiped the beads of sweat with his handkerchief and worried about where she had gone. "What in heaven's name brought you to Casablanca?"

Babs giggled, knowing he had stolen Captain Renault's line right from the script, but she got serious right away. "Isn't our job to be on the lookout for any suspicious activity? Our investigation has been more like quicksand than desert sand. After all, Gerhard Sauer was a stagehand, or at least everyone thought he was until Leon Lewis disclosed he was also one of his former operatives. Since I knew you were with Rudy, I wandered over here to get a preview of coming attractions. How's he doing?"

"Promise me you won't laugh, but Curtiz wanted him done up more like Conrad."

One of the set painters approached the detectives and asked who they were and what they were doing there. The PIs flashed their IDs and explained they were on assignment from the big guys on top, Warner and Wallis.

Babs asked him, "Is it true they recycled this set from another Warner Brothers film?"

"Correct, *The Desert Song.* These days, because of government restrictions on the usage of raw materials, they've got a stranglehold on our budget. We can stretch the rules by stealing from stuff already built."

Guy looked around like a fascinated kid in an amusement park. "I must admit, I'm impressed. Never been to Casablanca myself but, right now, I feel like I'm there. Except it might need the aroma of Turkish coffee and incense perfuming the marketplace."

"You'll smell plenty of camels…and donkey dung if our animal handlers aren't on the ball," the worker replied.

The two detectives headed back to Rick's Café on Stage 9, choosing seats close enough to the action but far enough away not to invoke the wrath of the director. Before they settled in, Babs looked around for a discarded newspaper.

"Taking up housekeeping?" Guy joked.

"Trying to get up to speed on current events. It's easy when you're entrenched in the film world to block or forget about everything, like it didn't exist."

"Heads up!" Curtiz's assistant director made a crew-wide announcement. "Before we start, I've got to read this memo from our producer."

Since he said he was going to forgo using a megaphone, he urged everyone to gather closer. Babs tossed her newspaper aside and joined the others.

"We'll wrap at 6:30 p.m., so everybody can get home before dark," said the AD, who flashed a special glance at Curtiz, who had a reputation for working his actors overtime. "Otherwise, some of us, like Claude and Paul, who live in Brentwood, can't drive home after curfew."

The speech was brief, but upon hearing his name, Claude Rains strutted onstage wearing the kepi hat and the prim uniform of the Vichy prefect, Captain Louis Renault.

"He's not as tall as I had imagined," Babs whispered to Guy.

"Probably head-to-head with me."

"Guess he'd have the same problem if paired with a leading lady like Ingrid."

"Around her, I guess, wearing elevated shoes and standing on platforms for the cinematographer will be the norm."

Curtiz poked fun at Bogart, who was having trouble getting used to the lifts in his shoes. "Grow a few inches…and devil up!"

Once again, Curtiz baffled his cast and crew. He often used his own vernacular that only he would understand. It also became clear to the detectives that he had a beef with actors. Babs had observed Curtiz for only a short time, but being a man, he favored women over men, often toning down his impropriety. That also applied to her, compared to Guy, whom he'd berate at any opportunity.

In the past, when she worked with Bogie on *The Maltese Falcon*, she remembered he could get testy when he lacked sleep or had been drinking. Bogie withdrew during breaks and drank alone in his dressing room, but, for the most part, his astute insistence on professionalism forced him to hide it.

Working around the fact that Paul Henreid was sick in bed, Curtiz chopped up the scenes, flustering the actors. At one point, the director confused himself and called for a break.

Babs asked the soundman what was happening.

"Curtiz is probably phoning home and conferring with his wife. He can't seem to decide anything without her. I'm surprised you've never heard of Bess Meredyth," Scheid replied. "She used to be a silent film actress, but now she's his secret guardian angel."

Babs scratched her head. "Are you saying the *Great Dictator* has a weak spot?"

Scheid nodded. "He sees light and shadows and camera movements through a crowd. That's why Warner loves to hire him on action films like *The Adventures of Robin Hood* or *The Charge of the Light Brigade*. Remember, he started with silent pictures, and English is his second language. If he could make a film without actors, he'd do it in a heartbeat."

She asked, "How do you know so much?"

Scheid pointed to his sound equipment. "I always wear my earpiece. For better or for worse, I overhear lots of conversations…and fights…that people are unaware of. After the talkies came into play, Bess left acting and became a successful screenwriter under Irving Thalberg at MGM. Gotcha a great little piece of trivia, if you promise to keep it a secret."

"What's that?"

"People hear less about screenwriters than they do about actors or directors, but you'd be surprised how many credits Bess has accumulated. Anyhow, the title of one of her more forgettable films is called *Pass the Prunes.*"

Babs bit her lip to keep from laughing out loud.

"Like many women in this business, she took a backseat to her husband. She also had a son from a previous marriage, so now she fulfills the role of being more of a wife and mother. Since she possessed the understanding of dialogue and what the actors needed to convey on screen…or the vital skills he lacked, he often calls her several times a day for advice."

Babs thanked Scheid for the tidbit and strolled over to Ingrid, who seemed to be writing something in a notepad.

"A diary?" Babs asked.

Bergman blushed. "Perhaps."

Babs leaned in closer. "Mind if I look?"

"As a matter of fact, I do," she said, pulling it away. "It's mostly an acting diary. I enjoy when our director gives me critiques. Every day is a learning experience."

"There are others, like your male co-star, who'd have a different opinion."

"I suppose, but there's one thing I can never understand about Michael Curtiz."

"And what's that?"

"My birthday's at the end of August, and he always calls me Christmas Baby. I have a dialogue coach to help me with my lack of English, but why he calls me that? I don't know."

The director came back from his *secret phone call.* He blamed his hardships on his team of screenwriters, and his assistant director demanded quiet on the set. To compensate for the shortened hours, Curtiz worked right through the designated lunch break. Rains anticipated trouble. Having worked with Curtiz before, he snuck in an alarm clock and set the timer to ring when they were to break for lunch.

The infuriated soundman yanked off his headset. Curtiz looked like he was ready to explode. One idiot had the gall to shout, "Someone planted a bomb!" as the cast and crew searched for the source of the noise. Rains, alone in knowing the clock's hiding place, let the crisis continue before revealing what caused the commotion.

Finally, Claude exclaimed, "Good Lord! It must be lunchtime," and gave a sly wink to the detectives.

Chapter Twenty

While Guy, Rudy, and Babs worked their case behind the scenes, the core *Casablanca* team aired their grievances. Bogie, who had kept a lid on complaints until now, blew his top. "Great! More revised script pages in every color of the rainbow, and new dialogue to memorize. Can't anyone make up their minds?"

Shortly thereafter, Wallis, who had been visiting the set, confronted Warner in person in his office rather than writing another one of his countless memos. "We're already two weeks into production and don't have a finalized script."

Warner countered. "Need I remind you that every time we switch schedules, we continue to pay a handful of overpriced actors to sit around and do nothing!"

Even before he hired the Epsteins, Hal Wallis had issues with the story. He and his story editor, Irene Lee, submitted the material to Robert Brucker, who felt it wasn't believable, and the writing team of Aeneas MacKenzie and Wally Kline, who worried the love triangle issue would never get past the morality censors. Once Wallis decided on "The Boys," one of the Epsteins' affectionate nicknames, he brought in an additional screenwriter, Howard Koch.

The Epsteins proceeded first, and Koch would tail behind with revisions. Rather than collaborating, they worked independently. Each wrote scenes and presented them to Wallis for approval. Koch had constant clashes with Curtiz.

Often, the brothers felt like they were passing along their own vital letters of transit. At one point, Julius Epstein let loose his frustration. "Respect for one's craft? Forget the glory of signing a studio contract except when you take your check to the bank! Working at Warner Brothers is like laboring on an automobile plant assembly line. The studio assigns you a script. When you finish it, the producer hands it over to another writer to polish."

On Friday, June 5th, Wallis released Howard Koch from the screenplay. One week later, he let the Epstein brothers go.

Wallis called Warner with another of his many predicaments. "There was one scene in the script in which Ilsa comes into the cafe and asks Rick if he's taking care of everything and covered up for Laszlo. Can you believe Curtiz failed to shoot the scene? I asked him about it, and he told me he had simply forgotten!"

* * *

As the following week progressed, the art department had to adjust certain sections of the interior of Rick's Café, which gave the cast a few days off. Rudy remained at the studio and patrolled the area for any potential incidents, of which there were none. However, he and Babs constantly butted heads. He often failed to disclose his reports to keep her up to date.

Meanwhile, she and Guy spent some of that time catching up in their office. Babs finally received Gerhard Sauer's long-awaited autopsy and police reports. Neither told her anything beyond what the FBI agents had confirmed earlier and did little to ease the constant pressure. Warner badgered her with constant calls and would reprimand her, saying things like, "I'm paying you to cooperate, and if I don't see any progress soon, I'll fire you!"

One afternoon, a sudden draft blew loose papers from Babs' office, out her open door, and into Guy's front reception area. As she rushed in a panic to retrieve them, Sir Henry, who was closest to the phone, picked up the receiver in his mouth when it rang.

"Hello, this is Sergeant York from the U.S. Army Induction Center. Is Cary Grant…sorry, I mean is Guy Brandt there?"

"Sergeant York?" Guy said to Babs as he retrieved the phone. "Gary Cooper just won the Oscar for Best Actor in the film called *Sergeant York*, but whoever this is sounds nothing like him."

Babs, only able to hear Guy's side of the conversation, tried to interpret her partner's facial expressions but to no avail.

When he finally returned the receiver to its cradle, another breeze whooshed in from the other room. "Speaking of *drafts*…they summoned me back. I guess I get my verdict today, whether I'm innocent or guilty."

"Don't they usually send you a letter?"

"Dunno, but you might be right. A call seems unusual." He grabbed his hat and jacket, gave the dogs each a pat on the head, and told Babs he'd be back later.

* * *

Stuck in another long line, this time, however, there seemed to be a more somber tone among those waiting to get into the induction center. Guy wondered if these men were "call backs" for their "army audition." Like the last time, the military personnel asked everyone to remove their clothes, a relief since it was a sultry day in summer. They shuttled them to yet another waiting room where the young men sat shirtless and in their boxers, reading discarded newspapers, with windows open and fans blowing. It was short-sleeve weather for the recruiters.

Guy, who kept bouncing his leg from agitation, turned to the freckle-faced redhead to his left. "D'ya have any idea why they made us strip again? Felt like they gave us every test in the world the last time." Since they had taken his watch along with his street clothes, he looked for a clock, but all he saw on the wall was a photo of President Roosevelt in a snappy recruitment poster.

"Maybe they want to see if you got out of shape since the last time," Red remarked.

A corporal with an envelope cap entered the room holding a clipboard. "When I call your name, sound off and weigh in. Adams, Thomas…"

Some kid in the back stood and raised his hand as if he were a schoolboy being summoned to the principal's office. "Right here, sir!"

"Line up along the right wall."

"Appleby, Roy…"

"Aye, aye, sir."

"You're not in the Navy yet. Line up behind Adams. Single file."

"Brandt, Gary…"

Guy stood and headed over behind Appleby.

"Halt! You're going over there." He pointed to the left.

Bemused, Guy did an about-face. The corporal continued to go down his list. Guy felt self-conscious, standing by himself, half-naked.

Another non-com arrived and took the inductees on the right to another location. The corporal remained, reviewing his notes, until it appeared he was going to walk out of the waiting room and leave Guy behind.

"Excuse me, but where am I supposed to go?" Guy asked.

The corporal looked up. "Sorry, I forgot. Follow me."

He led Guy down a hallway in the opposite direction. He knocked on a door with a pebbled-glass window. When told to enter, he opened the door for Guy but remained in the hallway. Guy entered, and the doctor in the lab coat over his Army uniform told him to take a seat.

"Did your pop serve in the First World War?" the Army doctor asked.

"Yes, sir. He gave me his trench watch to prove it. Survived the Battle of the Somme."

"Then God was on his side. Many didn't make it. If it wasn't enemy fire, it was the disease and filth that did them in. Hope you weren't dead set on making him proud."

"Sorry, sir, but I don't understand."

"They weren't too happy with your medical examinations."

"I can always gain ten pounds."

"Being underweight has nothing to do with it. Did anyone approach you about being a conscientious objector?"

"Excuse me, but what is a *con-see*-whatever, anyway?"

"Heard rumors there were a few anti-war protesters infiltrating our centers, trying to plant anti-American thoughts into men's heads. Wouldn't affect your profile, at any rate."

Forcing himself not to show his nerves, Guy waited for the gavel to fall.

The doctor stood and said, "Step closer, son. I want to find out for myself." He took out his stethoscope, placed the cold metal diaphragm against his chest, and listened. When done, he removed his earpieces, went over to Guy's paperwork, and stamped it with a 4F.

"How come I didn't make the cut?" Guy was more surprised than anything else.

"We detected a slight heart murmur. The first examiner suggested getting a second opinion, but I just confirmed it. You should see your personal physician and check that out. Might be nothing to phone home about, but the Army didn't want to take a chance in an emergency on the battlefield."

Somewhat relieved they hadn't rejected him because of his sexual preferences, he worried about a new concern. Was this going to mean he was going to die young?

Chapter Twenty-One

If Guy really got drafted, who could I find to replace him? What if he got killed in combat and never came back? While he was down at the induction center, Babs' worries got the best of her. She swallowed two aspirins with Nehi orange soda from their vending machine and burped out the fizz afterward.

Just as her headache began to subside, two men she had never seen, identifying themselves as Mr. Miller and Mr. Plante from the INS, walked into her office. After accusing her of hiding a fugitive, they turned her office inside out. She tried to prevent them from ransacking her storage closet, but they shoved her aside and continued to rifle through both hers and her partner's desks.

"According to our records," Miller said, "Mr. A-o-i...Aye-o..." He had trouble pronouncing his tongue-twister first name, just like she did, and wiped the excess saliva on his lips. "Mr. Otake, I'll call him that from now on, registered as a Japanese non-citizen resident. After cross-referencing, no one could find his name on any of the rosters for relocation camps."

Plante warned Babs about the severe fines and imprisonment she might face.

Just when the situation started to calm down, the phone rang. *Where's my assistant? That's right...getting drafted!*

"Hold those thoughts," she said as she answered it. "Central Casting? Oh, are you calling to announce you're going to compensate my partner and me after getting deluged the other day? Did you want to put us on the payroll for even more embarrassing scenes?"

On the other end, the person had difficulty articulating. "I'm sorry to say, but a German couple, who were to play background extras in Rick's Café… Your associate, Rudy Schmitz, he found their bodies."

"Murdered?" Babs blabbed that way too loudly in front of the wrong people. Maybe she should tell a white lie and say it was Mr. Otake. "I suppose you want me over there to identify the body?"

After she hung up, she told the agents, "Look, I'm in the middle of a murder investigation, and two others just died. Next time, if there's a next time, which I hope there isn't, call first before wrecking my office."

Babs tried to speed over to Warner Brothers in her floundering Crosley but hit traffic. By the time she stopped for gas and found guest parking, Rudy had gone elsewhere. What she encountered didn't even seem like a crime scene. Ernie Fischman was there with his photographic equipment, but instead of taking pictures of the deceased, he was taking glamour shots of Ingrid Bergman.

Babs examined Ernie's lighting setup with a leery eye and felt like everyone had given her the runaround. "Where's the director and the cast?"

"Curtiz had a problem with the script. He gave the other actors the afternoon off."

That still didn't answer her question, and she hated being out of the loop. "Central Casting called to tell me there was a murder. I cut a meeting short with government officials to run over here. Did somebody die, or is this a practical joke?"

"No one told me anything," said Ernie. "Publicity hired me to snap a few photos of the leading lady."

Babs asked, "Where did the Burbank PD go?"

"Never saw any cops." Ernie turned to Ingrid. "Did you?"

"None at all," she replied, shaking her head. Her hair and makeup assistants, who had been on the sidelines, agreed.

"Now, I'm really confused," Babs said, looking around the stage in all directions.

"Whatever happened didn't happen here," Ingrid added, appearing tranquil, but a bead of sweat rolled down her neck. Right on it, her makeup assistant patted her with a tissue and stepped out of the frame.

Babs, full of disdain, looked at Ernie. "How come you're over here and not over there? Isn't that your job to photograph dead bodies?"

"Can't earn a living simply shooting corpses. The living look better anyway."

Ingrid and her assistants gave him icy stares.

"Babs, to answer your question," said Ernie, "no one ever called me, but while I've got your attention, are you doing anything this evening?"

Babs reran the scenario in her head from the last time they were together. *All right. I had an injured parrot. Not the most romantic start to an afternoon, but he had the nerve to admit that women shouldn't be running their own businesses.* She also remembered blurting out, by accident, that she had become a PI because of her daddy's murder. In short, their date had sunk like an anchor. She felt her excuse for bowing out was a good one. "Ernie, I'd better call Central Casting."

When Babs got on the phone with Central Casting, she received shocking news. "A double suicide?" *That ruling was quick. Too quick. Were Rudy or Guy aware of this? Maybe Rudy knew them. Did either already inform Wallis or Warner?* "Has anyone else had other thoughts?"

"The cops found a note," said the casting rep. "The deceased were distraught about being forced out of their homeland and into a country where they didn't speak the language and who condemned them as…I think the English translation from the German meant…*perpetual enemy.*

"Then they worried Hitler would win the war, and they'd never return home to Vienna. Back there, they hadn't been famous, but they had enjoyed a semblance of prosperity and respect as working actors. Now, they were outcasts, 'spit upon like vagabonds, and treated like stray and diseased dogs.' The translation was sketchy, but I think you might get the point. The couple, although in love, felt forced to marry at the last minute for visa reasons—"

That last sentence rang in Babs' head. She loathed the idea of anyone being coerced into an action to avoid political or legal repercussions.

"Landlords had evicted this couple several times," the casting rep explained. "They felt they were 'without a country' and 'only heaven awaited them with open arms.' Someone told me they quoted a famous German poet, but I wasn't familiar with him."

Babs returned but discovered Ingrid Bergman and her assistants had already left. Ernie was packing his equipment. He asked her, "Any thoughts on where you might want to go tonight?"

* * *

Even though Rudy and Guy ran into him recently at Salka's, Babs, Bogie, and Guy welcomed Peter Lorre when he arrived to film *Casablanca*.

"Too bad Sydney and I," he said, referring to Greenstreet, "have such small parts and don't have scenes together this time."

"It's not like you haven't seen the fellow in the last decade," said Bogie, cutting in.

"Perhaps Warner will see us as a winning combination like they did in *The Maltese Falcon* and pair us together more often," remarked Peter.

Bogie raised his convenient glass of tap water instead of something stronger. "May we share many happy hours together!"

Peter, having nothing in his hand, cupped his fingers and pretended. "I'll drink to that," he said and downed his imaginary libation.

While Peter headed to wardrobe and makeup, Curtiz and his lensman blocked the action with stand-ins and lit the set.

Babs, who had watched the men make their mock toast from the sidelines, went to check on Ingrid but discovered her dressing room was empty.

The assistant director dispelled her panic and explained, "Maybe you should reread the script! By the time Ilsa and Laszlo arrive, they look all over for Ugarte. He has the irrevocable letters of transit they desire, but they never find him. Therefore, if Peter is on call, Ingrid would have the day off."

Embarrassed because she should've known better from her brief time spent as an actress, Babs still couldn't wrap her head around the fact that films always shot their scenes out of order. Instead of heading straight for a phone, she told a production assistant, "In case anyone needs me, you'll find me at the commissary."

* * *

After ordering a glass of lemonade, Babs took the production diary out of her purse and started reviewing her notes. *Too full of personal memos.* If requested, she'd never be able to show it as is to Jack or Hal.

Ernie! What was she going to do about the *Woodpecker*? She got so caught up in the milieu that she left him hanging. Why did she always allow her immediate predicament to overshadow her personal ones?

Save the business! Solve the case! She could hear Pedro and Petunia's voices ridiculing her in their typical parrot fashion. So far, Ernie hadn't proved to be "the one," but everything else prevented her from finding out or seeking an alternative. In that respect, she'd do her darnedest to find Sauer's killer and prevent anyone else from getting hurt, but was she victimizing herself by denying her own needs? Was that going to be the ultimate sacrifice she'd have to make for her business to thrive?

What if she followed her mother's advice and gave it all up for a man? Then she thought of Troy, her insane and pugnacious ex-husband. Enough said. She slurped the last drop of lemonade from her glass and returned to Stage 9.

Curtiz started with Scene 37, the first scene introducing Ugarte. The wardrobe department dressed Peter, like Bogie, in a white tuxedo jacket.

"Whose idea was this? If this really were the desert and I got caught in a sandstorm," Peter cracked, "wouldn't I get dusty wearing white?"

His remark received a few snickers, but not from the on-set wardrobe crew.

When Curtiz wanted to change the camera's position, Peter kept teasing Curtiz during the break and extinguished his cigarette, using a tiny eyedropper, which he kept hidden in his pocket. He was so subtle at first that Curtiz hadn't noticed. Finally, in frustration, Curtiz shouted, "Who's making me look like a fool?" Everyone feigned innocence.

After the juicers readjusted the lights and everyone had their last looks, they finished filming the scene where Ugarte produces the stolen letters of transit from his pocket and asks Rick to hide them. Ugarte told a server he's expecting someone and excused himself to try his luck at roulette.

At the end of the day, Guy confided to Babs, "It won't be a spin at the wheel with Peter. He's grateful to have a lucrative career here in America. He's given Rudy and me his word he'll cooperate the best he can to help find Sauer's killer. All of us suspect this person is within the German ex-pat community."

Chapter Twenty-Two

Up to his pranks again, Peter Lorre targeted Claude instead of Curtiz. After constant remarks that he seemed far too serious, Peter pulled a few other cast members in on the gag and wrote an additional scene, which they rehearsed and memorized. When Rains arrived that morning and saw them rehearsing, he became panic-stricken.

"Peter, I can't be going senile yet. I'm still a healthy fifty-three-year-old man. But my memory…it's drawing a blank. I just watched you rehearse that scene, and I can't recall a single line of it!"

Everyone doubled over laughing. Claude realized it had all been a practical joke. He took it in stride and was more relieved his memory hadn't gone to pot.

The next uproar involved the props department. The assistant director and the prop master announced, "People are stealing items. Now, the letters of transit have gone missing!"

"Recent scenes involved a lot of extras," Peter said, murmuring to Bogie. "Anyone could've done it."

Bogie couldn't figure out what the big deal was. "Can't someone fold a few pieces of typewriter paper and position the camera, so you'd never see the writing on the inside?"

"*Pssst*…I've got a little secret," said Peter.

Leery that he'd be the butt of the next practical joke, Bogie hesitated before replying, "And what's that?"

"There are no such things as letters of transit," Peter replied.

While Bogie argued with Peter that if there were no such things, then why would the screenwriters write it into the script, the eager detectives finally had their chance to jump into action. Babs and Guy demanded a behind-the-scenes tour of the Warner Brothers Prop House, not realizing their warehouse took up more square footage than a city block. One big whiff of its smell reminded Babs of a massive church rummage sale. The two pulled aside two chairs, complete with identifying inventory tags. Guy sat on a medieval-like dragon throne. She chose a Rococo Louis XIV reproduction.

"Peter informed me there are no such things as letters of transit. If you don't believe me, maybe we should interrogate our screenwriters," said Guy.

"Weren't there letters of transit in the original stage play?" she asked.

"Yes, but they're literary devices…objects of desire everyone is after. Alfred Hitchcock calls them MacGuffins…in a sense, like the Maltese Falcon. Nobody ever challenged them about the existence of such documents in Casablanca or any other Axis-controlled territory."

"What if these missing papers weren't props, but coded spy documents in disguise?"

"I can imagine it now…if this had been *The Falcon* script, someone would be after two hollowed-out copies of Hammett's book. One had a loaded gun. The other had a hidden treasure."

Babs scratched her head and confessed she didn't follow his logic.

"That's because there isn't any! I'm playing with you."

She took a deep breath and let it out. "Everyone needs to be considered a suspect. Even your friend, Rudy. Don't you think it's a little hard for you to be objective?"

"You're jealous because I've found a love interest, and you haven't. Maybe you don't trust me."

A stagehand barged in before the showdown started and told Guy he needed his chair. Babs thought she saw several overhead racks of chairs, attached by hooks and using a pulley system. "Follow me."

Leading him to the far corner, they passed a variety of odd objects, including a gigantic fake birthday cake, big enough to hide a full-grown human.

"I always wanted to surprise somebody with one of those," Guy laughed.

"Maybe Warners will lend me one for Rudy's next birthday."

Babs pointed to several black statuettes inside a glass case. "Well, look what we have here. The leftover props from *The Maltese Falcon*. You know, we never got to meet Frank Sexton, the prop maker who created it."

"It's too bad our Blackbird Killer didn't steal these instead of murdering all those people—" Guy cut himself short.

"Could've been easy to take a mold and remake a bunch. Those people weren't so easily replaced," she replied. "All the same, what an auspicious place to plant our butts."

Guy pulled on a rope, and the chairs wheeled around on an overhead track. They each chose one to their liking and resumed free-associating. Soon, a sudden whirring sound startled them when the chairs started moving in a clockwise motion.

"Looks like there's a motorized option for this contraption." He shoved her over just in time, so she wouldn't get hit by the suspended moving objects.

Another warehouse technician stopped the machine and made his selection. "Guess you've never seen anything like this before. Happens all the time to those not supposed to be in here. Mind if I see your IDs?"

They showed them their all-access passes and explained they were working directly for Jack Warner, the Boss of all Bosses.

"Better watch yourself. At night, when we turn off the lights, the objects in our prop house come alive."

Babs gave him a dirty look and ducked as he swung around a heavy chair and walked off laughing. After her close call, she smoothed down her hair, readjusted her barrette, and stared at her partner. "So, as we were saying…anyone can be guilty."

"Honey, you sure do like to round up some *unusual* suspects."

"Honey? I'm your employer. Not your doll baby."

"Babs, we're on the same side."

"Well, maybe Rudy isn't. That's all I'm saying, and you…No, *we* need to be more objective. Half the time, he disappears, and we don't even know what he's up to. He also hasn't been too cooperative in giving me his progress reports. Such behavior won't reflect well on any of us."

The floor rumbled as the aerial tramway buzzed into action again. Not wanting to get hit, the detectives grabbed their chairs and scuttled to a safer spot. Once they settled, she suggested, "Warner has been breathing down my neck about cracking this case, and I don't blame him. All I'm suggesting is that Gerhard Sauer's killer might've been hiding in plain sight the entire time, and everyone needs to be considered a suspect."

Guy reached for his last cigarette but accidentally broke it in half upon noticing the No Smoking sign. "The least likely to be considered would be Ingrid, and I refuse to believe it would be Bogie. Are you insinuating it could be Conrad, Claude, or Peter?"

Babs brushed her sweat-dampened hair out of her eyes. "Peter? We've had no proof of whether he still struggles with his former addictions. Veidt? I must admit I'm jaded, since he resembles a former foe in a previous case. Rains? It's hard to differentiate him from his smarmy character, Renault."

Another stagehand told Guy he needed his chair.

"Again? I feel like there's some kind of conspiracy against us finding out who murdered Gerhard Sauer," he whispered.

They continued their discussion as they headed back to Stage 9. She took out her production diary to make a list. "Maybe we need a neutral party to help us with our investigation. Someone with nothing to lose and who doesn't have a vested interest in *Casablanca*. You've mentioned that Rudy knows a German woman who throws parties for the international residents. What about her?"

"Salka Viertel? Too well-known in the ex-pat community, she also has her own personal interests to protect."

"Guy, how about Dashiell Hammett? He's been a surprising source of advice and a willing ally in our two previous high-profile cases."

"His insobriety could cause our plan to backfire."

"Come to think of it, his leanings toward leftist politics might raise suspicions with the FBI. Would you believe they've had their eye on me for a while? You've known me longer than anyone in Los Angeles. Since when did I give you the impression I was a Commie? Seems like every time someone acts in a manner they disapprove of, they accuse them of being Communist."

As they rounded a corner, making their way back through the maze of sound stages, they found themselves on a collision course with a bicycle messenger, delivering dailies to editors.

Guy picked Babs off the ground and told him to watch where he was going. "Speaking about film, what about the photographer you always call *The Woodpecker?*"

"Ernie? I think I'd stake my fate on Errol Flynn before Fischman." She justified her decision not to get him involved. They only had casual dates and not with the most propitious results. "While we're coming up with left-field options, why not ask Manny, my miracle dry cleaner?"

"Who?"

"The guy who always bails me out in a pinch and lends me gowns and cocktail dresses for last-minute occasions." Babs admitted she was kidding. "Hey, he's unaffiliated and fits the criteria."

Knowing they needed help but unsure where it would come from, the PIs cornered Bogie and begged for his cooperation.

"We need all eyes and ears on set," insisted Guy

"Ask Sydney or Peter. Wallis and Warner keep complaining they're sitting around and getting paid to do nothing because the script keeps changing from day to day, but I'm not playing Sam Spade this time," Bogie replied. "That's what you're getting paid for. Nowadays, since I'm playing Rick Blaine, I'm adopting his attitude of 'I stick my neck out for nobody.'

"Maybe you forgot from the last time we worked together. Every time I'm away, my wife accuses me of philandering." He unbuttoned his shirt cuff and rolled up his sleeve. "See these scratches? Mayo could jeopardize our entire production."

* * *

Discord reigned supreme. Wallis sent out what was supposed to be a final script. Jack Warner disapproved and recalled it. Babs felt like she had reached an impasse and summoned Rudy to a meeting. "There are five murders in *Casablanca*." She counted them on her fingers. "The first and second involve the two German couriers carrying the letters of transit."

"I apologize, but I'm less familiar with the script. Number three?" Rudy asked.

Guy said, "The gendarmes found out about the random stranger on the street, who didn't have the correct papers, and the ones he possessed had expired."

Babs added, "Then the Vichy police shoot Ugarte while trying to escape."

"At the end of the film, Rick Blaine shoots Major Strasser," said Guy, "although we haven't shot that scene yet."

"In self-defense or on purpose?" Rudy asked.

"Who knows? They change the script all the time," said Guy. "Why are you so worried?"

"Just wondering whether I might need extra protection and should demand hazard pay as a stuntman. Someone could still get killed if shot with blanks at close range."

Bogie's wife became a regular fixture. Mayo insisted on keeping an eye on her husband. Curtiz went so far as to call her a wild animal. Once, she tried to throw her empty liquor flask at him but missed. Curtiz screamed for security. Next, he astonished everyone by proclaiming, "Better sleep with a sober cannibal than a drunken Christian."

Guy raised his eyebrow. "Where have I heard that before?"

"Sounds like Herman Melville…the guy who wrote *Moby Dick*," said Bogie. "It's surprising what can come out of Curtiz's mouth." Then he requested everyone leave Mayo alone and keep her at arm's length.

Paul Henreid, no longer ill, joined the cast, but he still had his qualms about playing Victor Laszlo. "Since when does a leader of the Underground wear a fancy white suit in a desert climate? It almost glows in the dark. I feel so stiff. There isn't a single wrinkle in my pants. Laszlo would be a walking advertisement to get caught by the Nazis. You'd only see such a scene in a musical comedy."

Rudy interrogated many of the extras, whose English language skills were sketchy. Ingrid remained discreet. She refrained from voicing any harsh opinions and positioned herself out of Mayo's eyeline. Claude seemed to take a liking to Babs. He felt the private detectives were a necessity rather than an annoyance and confided, "Bogart is allowed to complain. He's paid his dues and put up with a lot since he left the stage in New York and moved out here. Henreid, on the other hand, is such a prima donna that I gave him my private nickname, Paul Hemorrhoid!"

Wallis, who exclaimed *Casablanca* was turning into a never-ending disaster, didn't want to tread on Curtiz's territory unless there was no other way. Behind his back, he called and complained to his boss that he felt like a referee.

"Jack, the cast keeps on saying they didn't know what they were doing. We still have no ending. We don't know whether Rick or Victor Laszlo would get the girl. Both insisted they had better be the one. Ingrid has complained she didn't know who she should be in love with and how to react to the other. Curtiz told her to play it down the middle. She's still got her heart set on abandoning ship and replacing the actress they hired on *For Whom the Bell Tolls*."

Warner rubbed it in that Wallis had interrupted his manicure. "I've paid four key screenwriters, not to mention the others I hired and fired on the side, to revise this script—the Epstein brothers, who finish each other's sentences so often that it scares me, and Casey Robinson, the love scene script doctor. Casey made a romantic hero of Errol Flynn in *Captain Blood*. He made Bette Davis so alluring that, despite her trying to sue me to get out of her contract, I wanted to take her for a romp in the hay.

"Then you hired that junior writer, Phillip Koch, who won't even work in the same room as the twins. Can't figure how that threesome pulled it off. They're all *schmucks* with Underwoods! Every one of them! I should cancel their studio contracts and have them wait on tables."

Wallis let him finish his rant. "Do you still hire people to put their ears to the doors in the Writers Building to make sure they're working?"

* * *

For Babs, that scene sparked other meanings. Lost in thought, the *what-ifs* flashed through her mind. What if the INS caught her hiding Otake? What if they threw the book at her? Could she lose her private investigator's license for being a humanitarian? She bit her lip, trying to repress her panic.

Before they rolled the camera for the next scene, a production assistant delivered a note for Babs, who read it and frowned. In her mind, she wanted to plead, "Hide me, Guy. You must help me!" Forcing herself to remain calm, she turned to her partner and said, "It's from *The Woodpecker*. He's got two tickets to a show tonight and wants to ask me out."

Chapter Twenty-Three

Inside Stage 9, Guy held a cup of coffee in each hand. He poised a chocolate éclair, wrapped in a paper napkin, in his mouth. Moaning, like trying to communicate with his dentist when he's got an array of tools in his mouth, he caught Babs' attention, forcing her to look away from her notebook. She plucked the pastry from its perch, grabbed the lighter of the two beverages, and assumed it was hers.

"Next time, either I find a tray, or you can get it yourself." He tried to spit out the last piece of soggy paper napkin.

He inspected his shirt to confirm that none of the coffee had splashed on it, then took a sip of his. "Yours was the last éclair. On another note, how was your date last night?"

Babs, who had already sunk her teeth into the pastry's cream filling, scowled. "*Grrr...*"

"Oh? That bad?"

"*Uh hum.*" Babs wouldn't scoff it down just to answer. Cream filling got all over her mouth and chin. She panicked when she couldn't find a clean paper napkin or handkerchief. She was about to find something to wipe it off, but froze when the assistant director yelled, "Quiet on the set! Roll sound!"

Scheid confirmed. "Speed!"

"Roll camera!" said the AD.

"Speed!" said Edeson.

"Scene 70. Interior of Rick's Café. Major Strasser's table. Take 2. Marker!" said the camera assistant as he hit the slate.

The director called out, "Action!" Edeson pointed out that Claude missed his mark, and Curtiz insisted they start again and get it right.

Before the camera started rolling, Babs bounded for the ladies' washroom. She nearly had a stroke when she saw Mayo Methot's reflection in the mirror. Still jaundiced regarding Ingrid, Mayo's predictable new ploy was to show up boozy and often belligerent. She insisted on monitoring her husband, whom she believed was cheating.

Ingrid insisted on summoning security to escort her out. Bogie stopped her and explained, "As long as she keeps quiet, it's better she sees for herself that nothing's happening."

Any attractive young woman was a potential target, which meant Mayo could lash out at Babs if provoked. Avoiding direct eye contact, Babs spoke to the mirror while she powdered her nose and reapplied her lipstick. "How's your husband's chess game going?"

Since production started, many knew Bogie set up a game in his dressing room. During breaks, he'd play by himself. Mayo took out a brush and fixed her hair. She seemed to ignore her.

"Big day today." Babs forced herself to engage in conversation. "They're using a large cast to fill the restaurant. Including a band and performers. Maybe they'll let you take part." She stopped herself before saying, "Better than just sitting and giving everyone the evil eye all day." Knowing the woman's reputation, such banter might've sparked a riot.

* * *

Perhaps prompted by Babs' earlier comment, Mayo took her husband's chess game out of the dressing room and into the stage area. In a public demonstration, she flipped the board, scattering the pieces on the floor. Bogie picked them up, forcing himself to remain calm.

"Maybe you need a simpler game to play, like a crossword puzzle, without so many pieces," Henreid suggested.

"I've always preferred chess. This helps my concentration, and no luck is involved." Bogie kissed Mayo on the forehead. "She gets dramatic at

154

times. When she doesn't get the attention she's after, she'll give up and go elsewhere."

Insiders within the movie colony had been privy to plenty of scuttlebutt about the *battling Bogarts*. Babs satirized her last name by adding a "d" at the end. "She's employing the *Mayo Method* again." She also reminded Guy about the tantrum Mayo had when they first met during their previous case, and when she flung porcelain plates at them like an Olympic discus thrower.

"But I don't remember Bogie being so passionate about chess when he did *The Maltese Falcon*," said Babs.

Claude mentioned, "The rumors I heard were that she stabbed Bogie in the back with a butcher's knife, but I couldn't believe there was any truth to that."

Bergman chimed in, "When my agent informed me I would play his leading lady, I think he mentioned that once, Mayo faked a suicide attempt by firing a few shots into her bedroom ceiling."

Bogie approached them and set the record straight. "She's always pressuring me to get Warner to give me a chance to play better roles in better pictures." He raised his chin, pointing in Curtiz's direction. "And with better directors."

Rains seemed confused. "Am I wrong, but I thought they considered Curtiz as one of their best?"

Everyone went in separate directions for lunch. Except for Claude, they headed to their dressing rooms.

Babs, who remained behind, turned to Guy. "When you saw Bogie clean up, did you notice any chess pieces missing?"

"Why? Are you getting superstitious and assigning them special meanings?"

"Haven't you suspected all along that Gerhard Sauer, in a certain sense, was a pawn? Those are the pieces that are the easiest to sacrifice. Correct?"

"Well, but—"

"Not that I'm an expert, but when I was little, I'd watch my father play chess. In real life, a bishop judges morality. From what I remember, in chess, the bishop can move diagonally in all directions if the squares are free. The queen can move in any direction. It's the most powerful piece, because it combines the powers of the bishop and the rook."

"Who'd you suggest is the bishop? Bogie? And what about the queen? Mayo?" Guy suddenly lowered his voice. "Or maybe…"

"Who?"

"You haven't met her yet, but maybe Salka Viertel. She's a queen, of sorts. A mother of men, nourishing the masses—"

Curtiz took the detectives by surprise. "Toil is man's allotment; toil of brain, or toil of hands, or a grief that's more than either, the grief and sin of idleness."

"Who? Me?" Babs pointed to herself and then to her partner. "Us?"

The director reverted from the eloquence of Herman Melville back to his slaughtered comic book English. "All you do is talk. Who knows what you say behind my back? I want to see action."

Babs looked at her watch. "This is our meal break." Although she wasn't hungry after eating the éclair, she glanced at Claude, off in a far corner, munching on an apple. He had been brown-bagging his lunches to avoid conflicts and politics.

"I don't see you eating. Lunch is for sissies, and we pay too many security guards. You'll work for your paycheck."

Curtiz never liked the idea of two idle detectives, but now, with Mayo on the prowl, he ordered Babs and Guy over to the wardrobe department to get dressed as patrons at Rick's Café.

* * *

When they returned, they looked almost unrecognizable. One hairdresser fitted Babs with a bushy blonde wig, recycled from another period piece, but had updated it to a more contemporary style. When Babs complained it looked ridiculous, her hairdresser shared a wild story.

"A Hollywood producer's wife from another studio, not ours, traveled to Germany. Because the Nazis fired her Jewish friends from their jobs and confiscated their businesses, they had no way anymore of earning a living. So, she smuggled in diamonds, hidden in her mounds of hair, and cashed them in."

Wardrobe assistants put Babs in a simple black gown, something not to detract from the major talent. Always fashion-conscious, she worried she looked dowdy.

"Our director wanted to use some of the refugee actors' actual experiences to make *Casablanca* more realistic," the assistant explained. "Many of these people encountered pickpockets, like you read about in the script, and they traded their jewelry for next to nothing to get exit visas."

For Guy, a male hairstylist had slicked back his hair, Valentino-style. Using a grease pencil, the makeup artist created a thin mustache and reshaped his eyebrows. To further disguise him, they gave him a clear glass monocle as a costume prop. Despite being seated most of the time, a wardrobe handler made Guy wear lifts, since the trousers were too long, and they didn't want to pin them. In contrast with the featured players, who all wore white tuxes, Guy wore black.

"Now the shoe is on the other foot." Babs pardoned herself for the terrible pun and remarked that now he'd understand what she had gone through wearing makeshift lifts, while standing in for Ingrid.

"Looks like the *queen* has arrived," said Guy, who pointed out Salka Viertel, walking toward Michael Curtiz with a clipboard in hand. Acting as a provisional casting coordinator, behind her was her congregation of extras, dressed to be cast as patrons of Rick's Café. Curtiz inspected her ensemble and handpicked the ones he wanted for today's filming.

They looked restless, and almost desperate, as if they were about to be given a free pass to an all-you-could-eat buffet after being starved for a week. Little did they know, the studio followed wartime restrictions. Now, to avoid waste, most food to be eaten on set would be artificial.

"These people appear to be genuine European refugees," said Guy. "Especially if Salka's involved, they would know firsthand what it was like to flee the Nazis…which is what this entire film's about."

"Whomever they choose, I'd like to see a list." Babs kept her voice just above a whisper. "Sauer's murderer could be among them."

Using a megaphone, the assistant director cut everyone short to make a company-wide announcement. When he said it came from the top brass, Curtiz, who was the one not to be upstaged, and Salka Viertel stepped aside so he could have the floor.

"Warner Brothers is not a charity. The job of our properties staff is to keep a detailed inventory of everything from spoons to cigarette cases. Between them and the wardrobe personnel, they need to account for everything from fake eyeglasses to costume jewelry. Our hair and makeup department must also keep tabs on all wigs, hairpieces, and fake mustaches. For continuity's sake, any missing items can cause major problems for our editors in the cutting room.

"We've also received complaints about missing personal items. People have accused others of sneaking into their dressing rooms. Others swore items had vanished from their street clothes and personal effects. Regardless, we won't tolerate petty thievery and will prosecute offenders to the full extent of the law. If you see something, speak up. Don't be shy and hold back. Am I clear?"

While accusations buzzed through the crowd, Rudy observed how Viertel looked after her flock. "In a sense, you and she are alike."

Babs couldn't imagine what he was talking about. "How so?"

"You both rescue strays. In your case, it's animals. With her, she saves souls."

"You need to tell me more. It seems like you know a lot that I don't."

"Sounds like part of you prays for a mishap to jumpstart this stalled case," Guy said with sarcasm.

"The Feds informed me our victim, Sauer, was skimming off the top of someone, somewhere, and somehow," said Babs. "Anyone with the gall to commit those crimes could be capable of something more, don't you think?"

"You might be confusing the thieves with those who killed Sauer," said Guy. "Maybe they're not connected."

Other than the tense start with the assistant director's warning speech, the rest of the day's shooting schedule focused on scenes with Rick's house band, a female chanteuse, and Sam playing the piano.

Despite the earlier speech, at wrap, not only did people report more items disappearing from the set, but Ingrid, not knowing who she should turn to, ran to the detectives in a panic and choked up with tears. She continued to sob as she hunted through her pocketbook.

"This week, last week…I don't remember. Maybe I was stupid, but one day I wore a pair of pearl earrings in a setting with tiny diamonds. Given to me by my grandmother. Curtiz told me to take them off. He wanted me to wear gold clips with my costume. At first, I put mine inside my purse for safekeeping, but I got worried. If any thieves lurked around while our backs were turned, the first place they'd look would be in my purse. Then I remembered searching for a hatbox or an inconspicuous object. Hate to say it, but I can't remember where I hid them. I've turned my dressing room inside out, but they're gone."

"Why didn't you report it?" Babs asked.

"I guess I had too much to think about and forgot. It's bad enough we keep getting revised script pages and must memorize new dialogue."

"And you can't remember when or who was on set that day?"

Ingrid shook her head.

"You wouldn't happen to have a photo of them by any chance?" Guy asked.

"Not sure. If I do, it might be back in Rochester with my husband. Right now, I'm living in a temporary place here in Beverly Hills."

"Would you be able to sketch a picture of them?"

"I'm no artist, but I'll try."

Curtiz, acting more like a commandant than Conrad Veidt, demanded everyone who remained empty their pockets.

While he and his assistant conducted a military-like inspection, Babs and Guy got out of their costumes. She returned her wig, and both had their makeup removed.

When they returned to bid their last goodbyes and to see if Ingrid's earrings turned up, Curtiz stopped her. "Not so fast. Join me in the screening room. Watch footage from yesterday. Maybe you'll notice somebody stealing."

Babs scowled. Guy's eyes met hers, and he spoke up. "We'll miss curfew if we don't hit the road."

"How do you think I have time to watch dailies after wrap? I sleep here."

He's got to have a cot in his office or something, Babs thought. But we don't. What does he expect us to do?

***

The next morning, Babs woke from a fitful sleep with a stiff neck, given that she had nodded off in the passenger seat of Guy's car. "Reminds me of my salad days when I got evicted from my Hollywood apartment, and I had to grab a bit of shut-eye in the office."

He choked on his yawn and grimaced from the horrible taste of yesterday's cigarettes. "Could use some Dentyne gum right now. Did you sleep well?"

"Kept having Captain Renault's dialogue rebounding in my head…all night long," she moaned and rubbed her eyes.

"From which scene?"

"*There is no hurry. We already know who the murderer is. Tonight, he will come to Rick's. Everybody comes to Rick's.*"

"Well, I wish we knew who the murderer was and had solved this case already." Guy tried to stretch but slammed his knee into the underside of the dashboard. Babs clamped her hand over his mouth the second he yelped. "Quiet! You'll alert the graveyard shift security guards."

"Who do they expect to find if they're sending everyone home before dark?"

"Maybe they're worried some enemy of whoever will sneak onto the lot and plant a bomb."

Guy sniffed under his armpits. "*Whew!* Glad I have a spare shirt in my trunk, but I need to find a washroom first."

"Got an extra outfit for me?" Babs joked.

"Hope you brought perfume. At least we'll have our costumes to change into."

They were groggy and grumpy by the time they could snag breakfast.

Rudy, however, bounced onstage and seemed energetic and chipper. He wondered why Babs was wearing the same clothes as yesterday. "Where were you last night?"

"Blame Curtiz!" she replied.

He continued to give her the third degree. Guy confessed Curtiz forced them to stay late and watch dailies after wrap to see if they spotted any suspicious activity on the film footage.

"Stuff we wouldn't have noticed during filming. Can't always see everyone when you're stuck in one place."

Babs cut in. "He kept us after curfew. We slept in Guy's car."

"What about Curtiz? Does he think he's above the law?"

"I suspect he's got a bed somewhere on the lot…and a clean wardrobe in his closet."

* * *

In a memo to Jack Warner, Wallis wrote, "We were still dealing with a headstrong director, a cast who hated a good deal of their dialogue, and actors, like Sydney Greenstreet and Peter Lorre, being overpaid to sit around for weeks doing nothing, because we weren't sure we would need them again. Both had much smaller parts than they wanted, but we still didn't have a finished script and were never sure when we'd film their scenes.

"On top of those headaches, Ingrid was desperate to be free to star in *For Whom the Bell Tolls*, despite being rejected. She kept insisting the woman they cast was wrong for the role. I couldn't understand her reasoning. Both women are Swedish, and Hemingway wrote it for a Spaniard. Regarding Curtiz and Bogie, they argued so often that I had to come to the set and intervene. Not to mention the issue of Bogie's wife. Can you believe he had the *chutzpah* to tell *me, yes*, me, to mind my own beeswax?

"Steiner, our film's composer, made it clear from the beginning he disliked *As Time Goes By*. We also argued about which music to use for the scene when the German soldiers and the supporters of the Free French have a showdown at Rick's nightclub. He wanted the Germans to sing the *Horst*

Wessel Song while the French sang *La Marseillaise*. I pointed out *Horst Wessel* wouldn't be an appropriate number for high-ranking officers, and we'd also run into copyright issues. Instead, I found an alternative. He wasn't pleased."

* * *

After constant goading, Babs got her list. Not only did it include the background extras, but whoever compiled it added others who worked in significant positions behind the camera. In addition, the casting office at Warner Brothers provided resumes that seemed more like biographies or the sagas of all involved.

"From Germany, we have Conrad Veidt, of course, Curt Bois, and Trudy Berliner…not sure who she is. Manfred Coblenz—"

Guy interrupted, "Wasn't he the fella Curtiz fired?"

Ignoring him, Babs continued reading the names. "There are the Austrians, Paul Henreid, Ludwig Stössel, Max Steiner, our film's composer, oh…and the guy we met on the set of *Dangerous Journey* who made the joke about chewing gum on his hat—"

"Helmut Dantine?" Guy asked.

"He's got a bigger role this time. He plays the Bulgarian husband trying to get an exit visa for him and his wife, but who's gambling away his life savings. Let's see… We have a few Russians…Leonid Kinsky, who plays the bartender, and Dina Smirnova." She skimmed down the list. "Can't forget the Brits, Claude Rains, and Sydney Greenstreet, and it says here something about the prop man, *Limey* Plews. I think his real first name is Herbert."

"When I heard people complain about props disappearing, I was wondering who was being called Limey," said Guy. "We also have an Aussie, Orry-Kelly, the costume designer. Didn't I hear we have a husband-wife team from France in the cast?"

Babs nodded. "Marcel Dalio, who plays the croupier. He's married to Madeline Lebeau, who plays Rick's dejected and *rejected* sweetheart."

She counted on her fingers. "If you include people in other positions, who may or may not be in that scene, it appears we have representatives of thirty-four nationalities among the cast and crew."

"Sounds like we're going to have to round up twice the usual suspects," Guy remarked.

"More like unusual suspects," Babs countered.

A production team member cut their conversation short. "Everyone's to take their places, and that means you, too."

The argument between Rick Blaine and Victor Laszlo about purchasing the two letters of transit preceded the scene needing the large cast. Laszlo kept upping the ante and couldn't understand why Rick wouldn't accept his outrageous offer of two hundred thousand francs.

They're interrupted by loud singing. Downstairs in the café, a group of German soldiers have taken over Sam's piano and chant the *Watch on the Rhine,* or *Deutschland Über Alles,* with great enthusiasm. Captain Renault, observing from the bar, shoots Rick a wary glance.

Laszlo intervenes. He storms down the stairs. Ilsa notices. He approaches the house band and demands they play *La Marseillaise.* Blaine nods and gives them the go-ahead. It is song versus song as Laszlo, looking proud and strong in his stark-white suit, belts out the lyrics to the French national anthem. But Major Strasser realizes Laszlo and the French Resistance outnumber him. He's losing the battle.

Curtiz framed a close-up of Yvonne, Rick Blaine's mistress. In tears, she churned out the heartfelt lyrics. Then the camera cut to Laszlo, leading his supporters in triumph. Ilsa looks on with devotion. At the end of the song, Yvonne shouts, *"Viva La France!"* The Allies cheer. Strasser is livid. He struts toward Renault and insists he shut down the café at once.

Renault blows the whistle and announces the place is closed until further notice. "I'm shocked, shocked, to find that gambling is going on in here."

Then the croupier hands him his winnings. Renault, a hypocrite, stuffs the bills in his pocket, turns to the crowd and orders, "Everybody out! At once!"

Satisfied with the take, Curtiz snatched the whistle from Claude and blew it as hard as he could, watching with glee as people jumped and covered their ears.

Then he yelled, "Cut!" His assistant announced, "That's a wrap! Everyone out!"

A production assistant rushed to Guy and gave him a message. "Someone named Abel Wiggins is on the phone. He says it's urgent."

Babs insisted on accompanying him to the production office.

"I was caring for your birds and your bees," Wiggins said in jest, but Guy knew he was serious, "when the phone wouldn't stop ringing. At first, I ignored it. But someone was insistent. Figgering it might've been the cops or the FBI…who knows? I answered it, and…it was your pa.

"He rode in on a train from Kansas, or wherever you said you're from. Stayin' in some cheap hotel off the boulevard. Has no idea that's where the hookers hang out, but he'll find out soon enough if the cops don't nab him first, thinking he's one of their clients—"

"Did he say why he came? Hope it's not about Mom."

"He raised a stink and asked me if I knew the real answer to why the military rejected you. He thinks it's 'cause you're…you know what…"

"Queer."

"Your words, not mine, but I lied and played dumb. That's a conversation between you and your father. I'm not one to intervene."

"Can't make it any worse than it already is."

Chapter Twenty-Four

On Friday, July 3rd, the *Casablanca* producers, cast, and crew threw a party for Michael Curtiz to celebrate his 15th anniversary at Warner Brothers. In the background, the crowd sang a chorus of *For He's a Jolly Good Fellow*. For the hungry masses, the commissary had set a buffet. Warner's Publicity Department hired *The Woodpecker*, Ernie Fischman, not only as a photographer, but they doubled up his duties to work as a roving reporter.

Curtiz asked, "Why you not have a light show like when I first come to this country?"

"Fireworks? Our food staff worried BBQ smoke might set off air raid sirens, and everyone will think the Japanese attacked the West Coast," replied Wallis, grousing about the cold fare on the menu. "Otherwise, we would've had a weenie roast."

"Weenie?" The words went right over his head. Snickers circulated among the crowd as Curtiz examined the inseam of his trousers, thinking he might've interpreted it as something else. "How can the Japanese see us if they're in submarines?"

"Maybe they have their periscopes up," Wallis replied.

"Let me tell you a funny story." Jack Warner grabbed a megaphone and cut them short. "When Mike first arrived in the States, my older brother Harry promised him a press conference and a spectacular reception. When his ocean liner docked in the New York harbor, fireboats spouted streams of water high into the air.

"On shore, we heard blaring patriotic music from a military band. Roman candles…bursting rockets…fireworks lit up the sky! Mikey, here…" he said, flinging his arm around his shoulder, "he was so *verklempt*, he cried like a baby."

"Jack's brother expected me to memorize a quick speech," Curtiz added. "But I couldn't speak English very well."

Jack, who loved teasing him, said, "Still can't."

"Ah, theese America! Vot a vunderful velcome for the great Mihály Kertész… My real Hungarian name. Und theese Varner Brothers. I love all five at once."

"Harry corrected you about the proper number of brothers in our family," Jack Warner remarked. "There are only four. Yet he never had the heart to tell him the truth—that the fireworks weren't for him."

Curtiz raised an eyebrow. "You mean you didn't do this in my honor?"

"All a matter of timing, my dear friend. It just so happened your ship pulled into port at the same time as our country's Fourth of July celebration."

"Why? You piggyback to save money. You—"

Warner slapped his hand over Curtiz's mouth. "In any event, Mikey proved himself to be a man who always does his homework."

"I wanted to learn the American way."

"How 'bout interpreting that to mean he'd think nothing of getting into the trenches if it meant getting the subject right? Early on, we assigned him to a gangster film. Would you believe this boy from Budapest posed as a criminal and spent a week behind bars to portray the realism? Now, that's what I call *chutzpah*!"

"Or *meshuga*. Crazy, if you didn't understand Jack's Yiddish," Wallis explained to the audience.

Curtiz grinned with pride, enjoying every moment of his accolades. "I just got finished directing *Yankee Doodle Dandy*, a film about the *American* dream…"

"And a movie with an unsolved murder," Babs murmured from ten feet away.

"Maybe it's because I've been through so much hell over there and seen so many people without liberties that I love to do the *American* story," Curtiz emphasized. "But Jack, there's one thing I don't understand."

"Besides our language?" Jack gulped his champagne by accident. "What's that?"

"In Europe, if an actor or director established himself, he lived forever."

Warner flashed his wide smile to the audience. "What's wrong with that? If there wasn't a war, I'd move my *toosh* over there if it meant immortality. I hate funerals. Especially if they're mine."

Curtiz gave him the rare courtesy of getting a few chuckles from the audience before saying, "I signed a contract here at Warner Brothers, and it ruined me."

Jack laughed it off. "How so?"

"Here, if I don't make dough, you'll kick me out. Hollywood is money, money, money, and the nuts with everything else."

Errol Flynn, who was present with director Raoul Walsh and the major stars from the recently wrapped film, *Desperate Journey*, stepped forward and took over. "Now, about this guy's language… Could you believe he always called me *Earl Flint*? Another time, he told me, 'You are thrilled and excited. Let me see the little *tinkle* in your eye.' Half the time, we never understood his instructions and had to improvise."

"All right, *Flint*," Warner said, on purpose. He snatched the megaphone out of Flynn's hand and ushered a young man into the spotlight. "If it weren't for the fine taste of Stephen Karnot, whom I'm sure most of you have never seen nor heard of, *Casablanca* might've been the baby thrown out with the bathwater."

"History, in many ways, started on Monday morning, December 8th," said Wallis. "Workers on our sound stages, editing, and makeup rooms, scenery docks, and our administrative offices joined their fellow Americans, listening to the radio broadcast of the President of the United States in his address to Congress. The Japs had stabbed us in the back the previous day, and now it was war! America became a country unified as never before. Now, Stephen, here—"

Fischman, wanting to capture the moment on film, rushed to the front and blinded everyone with his flashbulb.

Wallis blinked several times and rubbed his eyes. "Couldn't this have waited? We would've been happy to pose afterward."

Fischman made a sheepish shrug. "Just doing what they're paying me for."

Wallis complained he still saw spots from those bright lights.

"As I was saying, Karnot was one of several readers in our story department. From the pile of screenplays, novels, and short stories agents send us, hoping they'd get made into films, one particular play caught his attention. Its title: *Everybody Comes to Rick's.*"

Warner grabbed the kid by the arm so hard it looked like it hurt. "You thought pretty much of it, didn't you?" When Jack tried to put the words in Karnot's mouth, Wallis intervened.

"Why don't you let him speak for himself?" He plucked the megaphone out of his boss's hand and gave it to Karnot. "When I finished the manuscript. I thought it was pretty good. So, I passed on my report, and—"

"The rest is history," shouted Jack.

"Enough of your jabbering, Jack," said Wallis. "These people are here to eat, drink, and be merry."

* * *

Ingrid turned to her co-star, Paul Henreid, and asked for a cigarette. "Is it true you caused a sensation while filming *Now, Voyager*, that you lit two cigarettes at once? I think I read something about it in the gossip magazines."

"Ah, yes. With Bette Davis. They asked me to offer her a cigarette, but I felt the need to make it more intimate. Instead of handing her a single cigarette, I'd take out two, putting them close together between my lips."

"Show me, Paul," Ingrid said. "I could use a smoke."

Henreid took his gold cigarette case out of his pocket. His name engraved on it with an image of a family crest.

"No one can accuse you of stealing props," she noted.

"It would be easy to spot if somebody took mine. I heard you had your grandmother's earrings disappear. Did you ever find them?"

Ingrid lowered her head. "No, and they're irreplaceable."

"I'm sorry I brought it up. Did you still want me to do my cigarette trick?"

"Please. Perhaps that will lighten my mood."

"I'd light them both at the same time." He had a little trouble talking while trying to demonstrate. "Then I'd hand her one of them already lit."

Ingrid took it and smiled.

"To me, it signified a special moment with a gesture, like a secret kiss."

She took a puff with a prolonged exhale.

The Woodpecker barged in on their intimate moment, becoming even more butterfingered as he juggled a notepad and pencil with his clunky press camera. "How 'bout a big smooch for the camera?"

"Smooch?" Ingrid wrinkled the flawless skin on her forehead. "I don't always understand your silly American jargon."

"He means an obvious kiss for his photograph," Henreid whispered.

"Why should we?" Ingrid got defiant.

Ernie stuffed the notepad into his back pocket. "Aren't you husband and wife on screen? You're some of the film's top-drawer talent."

"Perhaps later." Henreid handled it with diplomacy. "Come. Let's fill our plates."

As they walked away, Wallis said to Warner, "Saw the dailies. Those scenes with Babs and Guy in Rick's Café will wind up on the cutting room floor. You're not to bellyache about money, and I don't care if Curtiz blows his top regarding reshoots. The final cuts will be without them."

"No reshoots," said Warner. "It's bad enough we had that skirmish between Curtiz and his sound mixer. Then his boom operator had to take the fall and get fired."

"Can't believe you're getting soft over some poor stranger."

"I'm not, but mistakes cost me money."

"Regardless, we have talented editors. They'll make sure no one recognizes our private detectives. Same deal with the worthless footage featuring George Raft's gangster pals dancing in the Paris nightclub. Poof! They'll be gone!"

* * *

Claude pulled Babs aside when he saw her giving Bogie's wife the eye. "Looks like she and her hubby are making friends with the bartender. If you stay out of the line of fire, you'll be fine."

"Are you so sure?"

"I've always admired Bogart. Like me, he did serious stage work on Broadway. Sometimes after hours we'd drink together, but I've noticed during filming, he'd also indulge. At first, discreetly. Later, not so much."

"But now?"

"While we've been filming *Casablanca*, he's shown no obvious effects."

"Unlike his wife," said Babs.

"You can say that again," said Claude.

Fischman nearly collided with them with his Speed Graphic. "How 'bout a shot of the two of you for the trades?"

Without even waiting for their permission, he fired his flashbulb. Babs yanked his camera out of his hand. She threatened to pull the dark slide from its film holder, exposing his film.

"Hey, what gives?"

"Use your brains. I can't have my pictures in print. Not as a PI to the stars."

He gave her a look like a puppy who piddled on the floor and still didn't get what he did wrong.

Rains took over. "Unlike me, who thrives on publicity, she can't show her face if she has to go undercover."

"I'll make up for the mistake if you're up for seeing me later," Ernie told her. "Would you mind returning my camera?"

She gave him a glare as she handed it back.

"Glad this camera only uses single sheets," he said. "If I had been shooting roll film, you would've ruined everything I had shot so far."

Neither apologized. Both remained angry. Ernie skipped off to see who else he could badger.

"Something going on between you?" Rains asked.

"I'm not so sure. We never agree on anything. Sometimes, I'd wish he'd *fade-out* of my life."

CHAPTER TWENTY-FOUR

"Didn't smell any alcohol on his breath. At least he doesn't drink."

"Like my ex-husband, but that's not everything."

"You were married before?"

"That's a conversation for another time," Babs replied.

"Getting back to Bogie, you must realize I'm inches away from him during scenes. Even if I take a nip or two, and I do from time to time, I laugh off any criticism. Mark my words. He can get confrontational over the most trivial of matters. I've seen it firsthand and have heard about it from others. I don't know everything that goes on behind closed doors, but you missed out on an amusing confrontation between him and our director one day when you and your partner were away."

"Tell me."

"Bogie had another altercation with Mayo and couldn't convince her he had a hands-off policy regarding his leading lady. Both drank a bit too much, but she kept drinking while he hit the sack. She woke him at dawn to resume arguing. Mind you, I wasn't there, but I heard he threw a coat over his pajamas and drove to the studio."

"I'm scared to think where this is leading," said Babs.

"Since he wasn't needed until eleven, Curtiz, upon learning from the gate guard that Bogie had checked in hours earlier, sent his assistant director to find him. He found Bogie completely hammered and riding his bicycle on the studio lot, crashing into things."

Babs almost spat out her lemonade. "Gosh! Did he get hurt?"

"Warner intervened and made sure he didn't. Don't hang me if I don't repeat his exact words, but he said something like, 'Listen, I don't care if you bust your ugly face, but there are hundreds of people depending on you in this picture, and some of them get a paycheck that wouldn't handle your liquor bill for two days.'"

"What happened next?"

"Bogie swore it would never happen again." Claude lit a cigarette and made certain he'd blow the smoke in another direction. "On a different note, I heard you and the two other guys you associate with are in the middle of a murder investigation."

Babs took a nibble from her plate. "Since you play a police officer on screen, maybe you can enlighten our case."

He laughed. "I know little about solving crimes, but I guess I play quite a convincing Vichy prefect if asked for my advice."

"Any thoughts?"

"Stagehands discovered the body on the set of *Yankee Doodle Dandy*, correct? That means Bogie's wife couldn't have done it."

"True, but—"

He stood straight and assumed his authoritative air as Captain Renault. "Realizing the importance of this case, is *your team* rounding up twice the usual number of suspects? You've checked out all the refugee extras in Rick's Café, have you not?"

"It's a tricky process," Babs said. "Especially since Curtiz expects us to act in the same scenes, but I've had other theories. Ones which were unpopular with my partner." Babs bit her lip. She toyed with the possibility that the killer had been hiding in plain sight the entire time. *Imagine if it were Rudy.* But she couldn't share it in mixed company.

***

Not everyone who came to Curtiz's party received the red-carpet treatment. Joseph Breen's presence was never a welcome sight. Known as the Censorship Czar of the Hays Office, the place where all Pre-Code cinema creativity came to a halt at the whims of the moralistic watchdogs, Breen wanted to further censor *Casablanca*'s script. To Babs, who listened in, a storm was brewing between the Hays Office and the screenwriters.

"That bit in Scene 48," said Breen, "when Renaut says to Rick Blaine after he rejects his girlfriend, 'How extravagant you are—throwing away women like that. Someday they might be rationed.' That has got to go."

Defending his stance, Phillip Epstein meant business. "Quit whitewashing our storylines!"

"We're trying to be realistic," said Jules. "Changing it to, 'Someday they may be very scarce,' is ridiculous."

"You must make it less obvious that people were trading exit visas for sexual favors," Breen asserted.

Phillip was fuming. "Then how do you expect the audience to get the point if it's too inconclusive?"

Breen remained resolute. "I also object to the line Renault says to Major Strasser, 'You enjoy war. I enjoy women. We are both very good at our jobs.'"

Jules barked back, "Stop being such a stuffed shirt! Renault is such a vital character. His dialogue reveals so much about the plot."

Claude, who had abandoned Babs when he sensed this conversation was about him, stepped in to intervene. Bogie barricaded himself between Breen and the twins to stop the argument from going further. Wallis assisted Bogie and split up the twins as Breen tramped off in another direction.

As if the do-gooder's presence wasn't enough, Special Agents Wright and Lockwood from the FBI showed their unbidden faces. Babs took it as a personal affront, assuming they were there to hassle her. To her surprise, they disregarded her and went straight for the buffet. Wright helped himself to a whopping portion of cherry Jell-O. By then, the heat had caused it to become runny. The rainbow-red, jiggly dessert dripped over the side of his serving spoon and stained the cuff of his jacket.

Guy couldn't help being sarcastic and made a terrible joke about Communists. "If you're hunting for Reds, it looks like the Red Scare came to you."

Babs wondered what else could go wrong, but at least it wouldn't come from their corner. Apparently, Jack Warner had invited Leon Lewis and Joseph Roos, whom they met with at the start of their case, and who brought Rudy onboard. Making a rare public appearance, they pulled the special agents aside for a private conference.

Her reprieve, however, was brief. Now it seemed to be her turn to receive an urgent phone call. Praying it didn't involve Mr. Otake, Guy escorted her to the production office.

While she was on the line, Guy kept cutting in and wanting to know what was happening.

At last, Babs looked at her watch. "It's almost curfew. Do you mind if I come down to the station to straighten this out tomorrow morning?"

After she hung up, Guy asked, "Police station?"

"Troy's at it again."

"Your ex-husband is out of jail and trying to kidnap you back to San Francisco?"

Babs lowered her head, barely able to give him a nod. "Mrs. Dietz, my nosy neighbor, who always complained about the parrots, phoned the cops when he tried to break into my house. Troy knows how to pick a lock. What if the police got in? What if they found Mr. Otake? If they did, he and I are both going down."

"Let's hope you're just jumping to conclusions and assuming the worst. Where's Troy now?"

"At large. He skedaddled before the cops arrived. Probably staying close to Hollywood. But Otake..."

"He can't stay at your place any longer."

"Any suggestions?"

The door opened. Rudy asked, "Did I barge in on something?"

"Yes," she replied. Guy said, "No," but voicing it at the same time came off comedic.

"Not sure who to believe," Rudy said, trying to make light of it. "Care to fill me in?"

Babs kept her voice low and summarized the predicament.

"If Salka Viertel hasn't gone home, I'll talk to her now and take him to her place in Santa Monica. She's got more experience than any of us, bailing out others when they've been down on their luck."

Rudy excused himself and left the two detectives alone.

"Even without Otake's worries, what are you going to do about Troy?" asked Guy.

"I wish I could just shoot him. Then he'd leave me alone once and for all."

"You really don't mean that, Babs."

"Of course, I don't. But what are you going to do about your dad?"

"Wiggins has been so good at keeping him busy; maybe we should consider him as an unofficial partner."

Babs wiped the tears from her eyes and burst out laughing. "Don't tell me he's got him working his trusty mop and pail. Never met your old man, but I can't imagine your pop on cleanup duty. Whatever Wiggins uses to sanitize our floors—reeks."

"So far, he's stayed out of my hair, and Wiggins made sure we were never at the same place at the same time. You know what's a crime? That my father would look for an excuse to put me in jail for my sexuality. That a bunch of roughhouses would try to beat me up because of their preconceived notions about what a man is supposed to look or act like. Or some innocent man, like Mr. Otake, was born of a certain nationality and, therefore, he's guilty of wrongdoing. These acts line up right behind that of murder, because they kill one's humanity."

Babs scratched her head and hadn't expected a soliloquy. She sat behind the production office desk and stared at the walls, cluttered with blueprints, headshots, and location stills the production designer had taken of sets on the other sound stages.

Suddenly, a thought came to mind. "Do you remember when they summoned you to the Army induction center, and we brainstormed ways for you to avoid the draft?"

"How can I forget?"

"But do you recall when I dropped the foolish hint about pretending we could be a couple, and maybe that would get you off the hook? Well, I just came up with a wild idea."

"Hope it's not something that'll get you arrested. Your nutty plans have landed you in jail twice, maybe more."

"Will you please listen? Look, I'm getting swiped from both angles. Troy needs to get off my back once and for all. I also got to keep this pushy photographer at a distance and can't deal with him either. You must get your parents, or at least your dad, to leave you alone."

"What do you suggest?"

"We need to get married."

Chapter Twenty-Five

Guy blanched. "What am I going to tell Rudy?"

"If society won't allow the two of you to tie the knot, we might as well do it to get out of our jam."

"Babs—"

"It won't be a real marriage, of course. Queer and lesbian stars do these all the time to save face from bad publicity. Don't ask me why, but I think they're called *lavender* marriages."

"Are you confessing you like women?"

"I'd always desired a wonderful marriage like the one my parents had before my pop's life got cut short. Not with a jailbird like my ex. Troy will finally give up trying to kidnap me back to San Francisco, thinking I'm his runaway bride, and your father will leave you alone once and for all if we make it official. Besides, I think I read somewhere we can get an easy annulment if we don't consummate it by a certain time. Why don't you go down to the County Clerk's office and see how we can expedite our marriage license?"

* * *

Babs returned home to inspect the damage, most of which was cosmetic. From another room, she heard whimpering but couldn't yet determine where it was coming from. "Mr. Otake!" she called out. She made the rounds of his routine hiding places, trying to detect where she kept hearing babble in unintelligible Japanese.

Then she realized she had forgotten to check the laundry room. Babs found him contorted and hiding inside her front-loading clothes dryer. She was probably the only one on her block to own one of these newfangled contraptions.

"I couldn't take breaths," Otake said, panting hard. He tried to disentangle himself as she pulled him out, trying not to cause more discomfort.

"Thank God. You're okay now." She explained that her friends would have to relocate him to a more reliable place this evening.

While Rudy made temporary arrangements with Salka, Guy got permission to borrow the fake birthday cake he'd seen in the Warner's Prop House. The Wardrobe Department provided the men with deliveryman uniforms. They arrived at Babs' house in separate vehicles and explained their plan to smuggle Otake out of the house.

Rudy clarified Otake's instructions. "If you curl up as small as possible, you should have no trouble climbing inside the cake."

"No!" he yelled and dashed upstairs.

Babs ran after him. "It's the perfect disguise in case a neighbor is watching. Why not?"

"Cake like your dryer. What if I get trapped?"

"It's made of cardboard. A few powerful punches would destroy it. If you still need help, you won't be alone."

She escorted him downstairs and offered to warm him a cup of saké.

Guy said, "No more suitcases than you can carry."

Babs assured him, "Whatever you can't take with you, I'll keep it here until you return to Los Angeles."

"Can I come back?"

"This war…soon it will all blow over. Our government will realize how stupid they were to vacate the Japanese from the West Coast…how they ruined the businesses and livelihoods by uprooting so many innocent people."

Rudy followed Otake to help him pack only his essentials. They returned ten minutes later, and the men donned their uniforms. Everyone laughed when Rudy's sleeves ended four inches above his wrists, and his pants landed five inches above his ankles.

"We'll take Guy's car," said Rudy, going over the logistics. "He'll drive. I'll sit in the backseat to steady the cake with Otake inside, so it doesn't slide or tip over. Lots of sharp curves in the Hollywood Hills."

* * *

Over the next week, everyone got their affairs in order. Even though Salka was doing Rudy and Mr. Otake a major favor, he had put her in a precarious position and promised he'd find an alternate arrangement.

To pull off their harebrained wedding plans, Babs and Guy needed to determine the soonest day in *Casablanca's* shooting schedule using a minimal number of actors. One without crowds. They decided on Friday, July 10th. Curtiz planned on making a company move to the Metropolitan Airport to shoot the scenes involving Major Strasser's arrival. The chief talent would be Conrad Veidt and Claude Rains. The rest of the cast had minor actors playing German and Italian Nazi officials and French police officers.

This would also be the only location for *Casablanca* away from the Warner Brothers lot. Humphrey Bogart, Ingrid Bergman, Dooley Wilson, and Paul Henreid had the day off. Once the detectives disclosed their secret, everyone except Paul, for reasons unknown, offered to attend the civil ceremony.

The proposed wedding party agreed to meet beforehand for coffee at the Warner Brothers commissary to go over the details. Ingrid insisted Babs let her be her maid of honor. "My husband would *kill* me if I lent you my ring—"

Dooley and Bogie gave each other a conspiring look. "Are you so sure, Miss Ingrid?" asked Dooley.

"What I meant is he wouldn't forgive me. He'd never kill me, and right now he's on the East Coast with our daughter."

"That wouldn't stop anyone if their intention was strong enough," said Bogie. "He could always hire somebody to do it for him."

"He wouldn't dare!" Ingrid got so incensed from Bogie's badgering that she balled up her dirty paper napkin and threw it in his face.

Dooley held up his hands like a referee. "Hold on. Both of you. No need to start a brawl."

Bogie agreed, "Just yankin' your chain. Don't get to cut up like I usually do around Curtiz compared to other directors. Sometimes I try, but often my antics go over the mad Hungarian's head. Guess mine went over yours, too."

Ingrid stopped to catch her breath and turned toward Babs, trying to ignore them. "I'll provide the bouquet and style your hair. That's the least I could do."

"Don't want to volunteer her services," Bogie said, "but you've probably already noticed that Ingrid likes to bring her cameras to the set. She's a real shutterbug."

"My fondest memories of my father were when he always took photos of me," she explained. "I guess that's why I'm so much at ease in front of the camera. When I'm around my family, I'm always taking snapshots and home movies with my tiny handheld motion picture camera."

"Said and done," Bogie declared.

* * *

Curtiz gave Rudy the day off for the wedding. Rudy, however, refused to be Guy's best man and confronted him with strong opinions. "If you go through with it, you'll be stuck with each other and will always have to convince the public you're a couple," he argued.

Guy fought back. "After my roommate joined the Army, I couldn't afford our apartment on my own. When you refused to take his place, it made sense to move into Mr. Otake's guestroom. At least, behind closed doors, the public will assume Babs and I are an actual couple living together."

Rudy set forth the facts. "It's not that I declined your invitation. Even if I had to pretend I was your new roommate and nothing beyond, I'd already warned you about repercussions from my past involvement with Lewis's organization. I couldn't expose you to that kind of danger."

"Like I don't risk my neck in my line of business? Up till this point, I've never even carried a gun, but that doesn't mean someone won't point one at me."

"My first task is to find Sauer's killer. Perhaps that comes from helping so many flee that wretched regime in Germany, but I also feel it's my duty to guarantee the safety of Babs' tenant. Beyond your obligation to Warner Brothers, yours is to stand up for yourself. To put your father in his place and tell him about your heart murmur. That's the real reason the Army rejected you. There'll be a lot I'll have to do to get Otake better situated. I just can't understand why you thought marrying her would solve your problems. If you want to know my opinion, I think it'll create more complications than you ever imagined."

"I'm marrying Babs because in this world, you and I can't get married! Furthermore, I trust her. Otherwise, I wouldn't be her partner, and her ex-husband's threats are real. Once, he threw me across the room like a helpless rag doll! Troy keeps insisting she never annulled their marriage. If we got hitched, this would be a surefire way to keep that beast at bay. We've tried everything before. Nothing worked."

Guy's father and Babs' mom would be the hardest people to convince their marriage was real. Dorothy Norman, known to everyone as Dot, had always goaded Babs into getting remarried. She'd even recommend that Babs return to her ex-husband and overlook that once he almost killed her by his abusive behavior. Babs, knowing she'd never be able to keep her marriage to Guy a secret, braced herself on how to approach her busybody mom.

Dot's reaction: "Goody gumdrop! I'll take the train to LA from San Francisco."

Exactly what Babs dreaded. Since Babs' father was no longer alive to give her away, Dot insisted on being there for the wedding. Meanwhile, acting as an intermediary, Wiggins took Guy's father to the beach and distracted him with local tourist attractions to keep him out of his son's hair.

While Rudy munched on his sour grapes, Bogie volunteered to serve as Guy's best man. He also mentioned that being away from the set for a couple of days might give the Epstein twins time to finally finish the script.

CHAPTER TWENTY-FIVE

Babs couldn't believe her ears. "It's still not completed?"

"Halfway done, if we're lucky," Bogie replied. "Why do you think we're always in such a bad mood?"

"I thought that had to do with your congenial director," Babs joked.

"He does his best to pour salt into our wounds. Not having a clue which man Ilsa Lund trots off with in the end makes our job as actors that much more difficult. Could you imagine dating somebody and falling in love, but with an uncertain future?"

Babs thought of *The Woodpecker*. She had never fallen for him, but she was glad she didn't have to deal with him, and Ingrid volunteered to take the wedding photos.

Dooley chipped in. "Ya'll figgered out by now, I can't play the piano worth nunthin', and I doubt they'd have a keyboard down at the County Clerk's office, anyway. But there's nothing stoppin' me from humming a tune. How 'bout the wedding march? Or I can always sing *As Time Goes By*. Whatcha think, Miss Babs?"

"You'll have to call me Mrs. Babs none too soon." She thanked him for his offer and said she was glad she'd have the support of her friends.

Fame had its mighty muscle. Bogie arranged with city officials to ensure their security team would also be on guard. He also convinced Jack Warner to release his bodyguard, Abdul Maljan, and assured Babs, "The Turk, he's a former boxer, a professional. If your crazy ex-husband dared to show his mug, he'd turn him into mincemeat."

Chapter Twenty-Six

Guy knew a visit from his pop wouldn't be without an incident. At one point, he found himself alone with him at Babs' place. Mr. Brandt poked him so hard in the chest that he nearly fell over backward. "When the Army wouldn't take you, I came so close to disinheriting you!"

To defend himself, Guy grabbed an empty ashtray and put it in front of his torso like a shield.

Pops Brandt narrowed his eyes and inched closer. "Glad you straightened up and decided to marry a gal like a normal man. After I'm gone, the two of you can get the heck out of this filthy, degraded town and take over my store. Bring home a steady and respectable income. Instead of hustling from client to client and going after criminals."

Guy set the record straight. "Pop, you've got to stop treating me like a child! The Army wouldn't take me because I had a heart murmur! It had nothing to do with any preconceived notions you had about me. Like it or not, my roots are here, and other than seeing Ma, I'd be content if I never set foot in my hometown again."

* * *

Other than the showdown between Guy and his pop, the week passed quicker than a pinch. Babs met her mom at Union Station when her train arrived from San Francisco.

Babs stopped and opened the door of her Crosley. Dot reacted without thinking. "Is that a wind-up toy, or does it actually drive like a normal car?"

Babs shoved her luggage into the backseat. "Get in unless you feel like walking."

The car backfired when she started the engine.

"Now, if your father were here, he would've sold you a decent car—"

"Please don't remind me of him. It'll get me upset." Babs needed to keep a level head and keep this from blowing out of proportion. "Mom, hate to tell you, but you're going to have to sleep on the living room couch."

"Honey, don't you have a guest bedroom?"

"Guy's got a bad habit and decided to sleep in there."

"All men have peculiarities. Why, your father—"

"Didn't I tell you not to bring him up?" Babs made a sharp turn and swerved through traffic on purpose, and her mom slid across the front seat. "As I was saying, Guy decided it was best to sleep separately."

"Guess that means I won't be changing diapers soon."

"Mom! We're doing it because Guy snores! I need my beauty sleep, and you'll have to make do. You'll hang your dresses in the front coat closet. There's a washroom with a toilet and sink by the living room. That'll be fine for your hair and makeup, but there's a full bathroom with a shower off the laundry room."

"Don't you have a monster-sized dog?"

"Sometimes he's here. Other times, I leave him at the office. I've taught him to sleep on the floor."

* * *

Los Angeles surprised everyone with cooler temperatures and an un-expected drizzle on the wedding day. Before heading downtown, the detectives made a detour and stopped at their office. Guy wanted to retrieve his trench coat and favorite fedora in case it rained harder.

Taking her chances, Babs left hers at home. She expected the weather would let up later and wore a smart gray linen suit. Underneath, she wore a white rayon crepe blouse with a pointed collar. She determined that her wide-brimmed hat would suffice as an umbrella, if necessary.

Since Wiggins had family commitments that afternoon, it was up to them to feed and walk the dogs. Babs refreshed the water in their bowls. "Guy, what did you decide about our rings?"

He unlocked his top desk drawer. "Would you believe I had to purchase half a dozen boxes of Cracker Jack before I could find two toy ones? For the most part, I came across baseball cards, whistles, and tiny figurines of dogs and horses."

She broke into song, "Buy me some peanuts and Cracker Jack… Well, anyway. You'd better not strike out."

"If I must stuff my face with any more of that candy-coated popcorn and peanuts for another prize, I think I'll… Never mind."

Guy found the two rings tucked away in the far reaches of his drawer. But as soon as he pulled them out to show them to Babs, Pedro swooped down and stole the bands from out of his hand. It became a tug-of-war when Guy tried to yank them from his beak. Pedro thrashed his wings in Guy's face and deposited them for him and Petunia inside of their cage.

Pointless to contend with two feisty birds, he took a quick look at the objects on his desk and asked, "What else could we use on such short notice?"

Noticing a ball of red yarn, which she used for playing with kittens when they had them in the office, she snipped two short lengths. "Have you ever tied a string around your finger?" she said, demonstrating.

"To help me remember to do something I might otherwise forget?"

She nodded. "This might have to suffice."

* * *

When they arrived at the County Clerk's office, Babs' nose twitched.

Guy noticed. "What's wrong now?"

Wiping it with a handkerchief proved futile. "It's the institutional smell of government buildings—"

"What did you expect? Orchids and roses? Like a church wedding with all the trimmings? Will you be able to stomach it long enough until we get

184

out of here?"

"Can't wait to bury my nose in the flower arrangement Ingrid brought me."

Once they found the right location within the municipal maze, Babs wanted to rush to her mom, but Abdul Maljan held her back with one hand.

"Lucky you arrived when you did," he explained, "'Cause you missed the action earlier."

The couple froze.

"Your pop ranted about setting you on a straight path. I warned him I didn't care, but if he stepped out of line, he might as well add a hospital bill to his trip expenses."

"You didn't!"

"Pops Brandt tried to convince the justice of the peace that this wedding was an elaborate ploy for his son to avoid the draft. I grabbed him by the collar and paired him with Babs' ma. Told them to stay put. Not worried about her, but I warned him I wouldn't hesitate to dislocate a limb or two if he misbehaved. It wasn't until I instructed one of the guards to handcuff the two of them together that he shut his trap."

Guy's mouth dropped to form a big round "O." The detectives glanced at their folk from a distance. Babs' mom smiled, pretending nothing was out of order. Mr. Brandt's grin looked forced. Both struggled to hide their handcuffed wrists within the excess folds of their overcoats.

When the justice of the peace asked if the couple was ready, Guy was so nervous he couldn't stop shaking. Babs confessed, despite her embarrassment, the story of how her parrots stole their rings and how they'd have to pretend, substituting them with the string *forget-me-nots*.

"This'll be over in a jiffy," their officiator told them. When he got strange looks from the parents, he clarified, "The ceremony. Not your marriage."

He verified the couple's full names. Babs cringed when he addressed her as Barbara Ann Norman. She loathed her legal name and preferred Babs, which is also what she used for her stage name as an actress.

Soon, her thoughts went elsewhere. "Is this my imagination, or did anyone else hear footsteps?"

"Come on, Babs," Bogie replied. "You've been watching too many movies where a jerk disrupts the ceremony at the last minute."

The words almost got stuck in her throat as she yelled, "Troy!"

Breaking past security, he shouted, "I object!" Even though they hadn't gotten to that point in the ceremony yet.

Despite his size and bellicosity, he was no match for Maljan. With moves almost too smooth to follow, the Turk secured his ham hock-like arm around Troy's neck. With three rapid, powerful punches, Troy wouldn't have known what hit him. One security guard picked him up by his legs. The other braced his shoulders, and they removed him posthaste.

"Shall we resume?" the officiator asked. "Or do you expect more drama?"

When they got to the actual part where the justice of the peace asked if there was anyone who objected to the couple being man and wife, the ceremony came to a halt with a riotous shriek. Mayo barged past security. Under the cockeyed impression her husband was committing bigamy and getting married to Babs instead of Guy, she swung her purse, weighted with a brick, at the justice of the peace.

A battery of guards wrestled with her, trying to keep her at a safe distance. In the scuffle, Mayo's gold wedding band slipped off her finger. All eyes fixated as it rolled, and rolled, and rolled like a loose wagon wheel, finally settling in front of Babs' feet.

Bogie retrieved it and gave it to Babs. "Here. At least that'll compensate for the rings your parrots stole. I guess Polly wanted more than a cracker."

"More like Cracker Jack," Guy said.

At last, the justice of the peace asked the groom to kiss the bride. Guy puckered his lips but stopped. He shot a glance over to Ingrid, as if needing last-minute, nonpartisan advice. Then he whispered to Babs, "Betcha my pop's been waiting for this, but…I've…never kissed a woman before. Well… except for my mom, but that's a different kind of kiss."

With an audience awaiting this expected moment, Babs tried not to show her surprise.

Dooley stopped humming. "Come on, whatcha waitin' for?"

"Are you going to plant your lips on your gal or what?" Bogie asked.

"I guess you'll have to stick your neck out for somebody. Even if it's only your business partner," Babs whispered to Guy.

Guy gulped, took one last look for everyone's approval, and said to Babs, "Here goes nothing, kid."

Being better actors than credited for, the private eyes went through the motions while Ingrid captured those rare moments on film. Babs whispered, "See! That wasn't so bad."

"I guess there's always a first," he snickered. Then he turned to the rest and gave them a wink.

Ingrid insisted on posing them for additional photos. "After I process the film, do you mind if I show these to Orry-Kelly, our costume designer? If he hasn't chosen our wardrobe for the finale yet, I'd love to see Rick and Ilsa wear similar outfits."

Bogie wanted to make an announcement. "Ladies, gentlemen, since we were already downtown, I was going to treat everyone to an early supper at the Biltmore Hotel. Now, however, I feel obligated to spring my wife from jail."

Handing Dooley a crisp one-hundred-dollar bill, he said, "This should cover the tab and then some. After they tip the waitstaff, the merry couple can use the rest as their wedding present."

* * *

On Sunday, Babs and Guy's pleased parents boarded their respective trains at Union Station. The "married" couple celebrated their departure by finishing a bottle of champagne Dooley Wilson had given them as a wedding present.

Upon their arrival on Monday morning, with obvious hangovers, Jack Warner greeted the detectives. His flashy smile suddenly became evil.

"You're fired! Both of you."

"For what?" Babs had yet to drink her coffee, and she could smell it off in the distance.

Warner asked, "Are you going to run out on company time for a honeymoon? I was still paying you to scout behind the scenes, even though most of our major stars had the day off. Explain to me why you couldn't have been reviewing police reports rather than getting married."

Guy intervened. "What about Rudy?"

Wallis, who had accompanied his boss but kept two steps behind, explained, "We'll keep him on the payroll. He can continue standing in and doing stunts for Conrad Veidt."

Was there any way they could talk them out of it? Both producers were obviously unaware of the real reason behind their marriage. Babs argued, "We've hardly made headway with the long list of refugees playing extras in Rick's Café."

"That'll be Rudy's job from now on," said Wallis.

"He can't possibly do everything he needs to do as Conrad's stuntman and stand-in and query all the extras you'll need between now and the end of the—"

Guy dragged her off to the side before she could say the word "film," and kept on walking her in the opposite direction until they were out of earshot.

She fought to break free. "Hey, what's the deal?"

"They had their minds made up. We'll need to take a different approach." He led her toward the snack table with a steady hold on her arm. "Look! There's an éclair. Grab it before it's gone."

She shoved the end into her mouth and munched on it out of discontent. With her still in his grasp, he let her chew and swallow before going further.

"Babs, you've played your cards and lost. Being confrontational won't work."

She gulped and wiped her mouth with a napkin. "What do *you* suggest?"

"Remember how we dropped hints at Bogie's pool party about recruiting the actors to expand our investigations team? Maybe it's time to take action and start with Bogie, since we've already built his trust as a previous client. With his help, he'll convince Sydney Greenstreet and Peter Lorre, since we all worked together on *The Maltese Falcon* affair.

"Between our persuasiveness and their cooperation, I'm sure we can rope in Rains, Bergman, and maybe Henreid, if we're lucky. Rudy would be the best person to convince Conrad Veidt. They're always scheduled together."

Guy helped himself to a cup of coffee and offered to pour one for her.

"You've got to remember that on most days, many members of the main cast have shown up and watched everyone else's performances. They're contending with the fact their script still isn't finished, and nearly every scene is shot out of sequence.

"Sydney wears a white suit with a red fez and might have difficulty muscling in and out of the crowd without attracting attention. Peter, however, can be a slippery little weasel if he wants to—just like his character Ugarte. That's why he's perfect to play such a…" he searched for the right word, "…rapscallion."

Babs' harshness dissolved into laughter. "*Rapscallion*... Your choice of words sounds like we're working on an Errol Flynn pirate movie."

"In a sense, we're going to have to be sneaky and underhanded and operate like a bunch of buccaneers." He joined her in the humor. "We'll get our stars to continue in our footsteps, and the producers will never know the difference."

Over coffee, the detectives went over the details, but their fun came to a halt.

"The bosses gave me instructions to collect your studio passes," said a production assistant.

"Oh boy, they're playin' hard ball," Guy grumbled. "Tell them we'll turn them in on the way out. First, we'd like to say goodbye. Otherwise, we'll get hounded later with questions about why we disappeared so suddenly."

The kid agreed, but he'd escort them out. Once he was out of range, Guy turned to Babs. "Do you still have that list?"

"Of extras?" She opened her pocketbook. "It's right here."

"Rip out a few pages of your notepad. Divide the names onto the separate sheets of paper. We'll break up the tasks for everyone who's willing to cooperate. After all, people like Bogie and Rains are in almost every scene and work pretty much all the time."

When the cast and crew broke for lunch, the PIs set off to conspire with the other actors to do their legwork and agreed to meet at the Craft Service table.

"Since Warner fired you, are you going to be all right for money?" Ingrid asked, ironically reaching for a Payday candy bar in her purse.

"Looks like Tightwad Warner asked you to *ration* your paychecks," Bogie remarked. "He pulled that number on a lot of us earlier, and you don't have to blame it all on contributing to Uncle Sam."

"He made you support the war effort?" asked Guy, who made himself a sandwich piled high with sliced Spam and pickles. Others stared as he could barely open his mouth wide enough to shove it in.

"Jack figured a way to skim our paychecks any way he could," Bogie explained. "Warner Brothers had high hopes for *The Maltese Falcon*. Even though they'd already purchased the rights to the story from Dashiell Hammett, they took an enormous risk producing it for a third time."

"Kinda like three strikes and you're out, *heh, heh, heh*," cackled Lorre.

"You might word it that way," Bogie replied. "However, with *Casablanca*, I don't think any of us thought it would amount to a hill of beans—"

"Here he goes *refrying* us with that *hill of beans* speech again," Lorre said, interrupting.

Bogie raised his eyebrow.

"Like refried beans. The popular Mexican dish. Can't believe this German-Hungarian guy…" Peter said, pointing to himself, "who barely spoke a word of English until he had to work on his first movie for Alfred Hitchcock, made a joke that went over *your* American-born, *Yankee Doodle Dandy* head."

Bogie curled up the side of his mouth into one of his typical wry smiles and pretended to go along with the joke. "As I was saying before Peter's interruption, none of us here, except the producers, think anything is going to come of this film, and they got us at bargain basement prices."

"For *Casablanca*?" Guy asked.

"We're just here, going through the motions, collecting our paychecks, and are hungry for a better project down the line."

Ingrid elaborated. "We still don't know what's happening to the script. Some of us don't even like each other, and I won't mention who. If we had our first choices, speaking for myself, I'd rather be co-starring with Gary

Cooper on *For Whom the Bell Tolls*. By now, I'm sure that's not much of a secret."

"For me," said Bogie, "I'd rather be out in the harbor sailing on my Sluggy." After a few stares, he clarified, "Sluggy…my sailboat. Not my wife, Mayo… nor my dog, or any of the other things I call by that nickname."

"Since you just brought up Hammett," Guy said, interrupting, "maybe we should recruit him on our team. He used to be a Pinkerton detective."

Babs called everyone to order. "If we don't finish this meeting, you'll have to go back to work, and Guy and I will get kicked out. In a nutshell, we're going to have to hasten the resolution. My partner and I are going to be broke if we finish this case on our own dime."

"Why would you want to do that?" Bogie asked.

"'Cause Warner Brothers *had* been a well-paying client…until now. I'd like to redeem my firm's reputation and remain in their good graces."

Ingrid reached into her purse again, but this time pulled out her billfold and handed Babs a twenty. "It's not much, but it's all I've got on me. My dialogue coach will drop off a check at your office. This should keep you afloat for now."

Babs' eyes widened. She was about to take it but resisted. "Oh, I can't."

With a stare so intense, it would bore holes through Hades, Ingrid couldn't have looked more serious. "I insist."

Babs hesitated a second too long. Ingrid opened Babs' purse and stuffed the bill inside.

Lorre volunteered to stick around, even after his filming was over. "I'd be delighted to play Peck's Bad Boy or a Puckish rogue, able to cheat, lie, and steal like Ugarte if I have to."

"I'll make sure nothing gets past my watch," said Sydney.

Bogie agreed to take on the role of the vigilante. "Whatever doesn't kill me will make me even more determined to bring this case to a close. Don't mind lighting a few firecrackers, unless Mayo or someone else does it first."

"What's in it for me?" Henreid asked, lighting a cigarette. He refused to acknowledge the benefit of getting involved. When he noticed Babs wagging her hand to blow away the smoke, he excused himself from their conclave and said he was going outside.

Lorre smirked. "I guess he doesn't want to stick his neck out for nobody or somebody or anybody."

Rains, still in his Vichy uniform, placed his police whistle in his mouth and blew, as if to rally backup. "And I'll promise to stir up a bit of action and round up twice the number of *unusual* suspects."

Curtiz, hearing the shrill echo across the sound stage, charged in and broke up their get-together. "I wondered where all my stars had disappeared! What's going on that's so important?"

The actors got him to swear to secrecy. Bogie threatened him if he didn't cooperate. "I'll give you such a headache, you'll walk off the set—screaming and regretting you ever stepped foot on this stage."

In the end, the director sided with the detectives. He surprised everybody by chipping in a token amount of financial assistance to add to Ingrid's.

Chapter Twenty-Seven

After a harrowing week, on Sunday, Rudy insisted on going to Salka's with business in mind. Guy picked him up and looked forward to making a detour by the beach on the way over. Surprising Rudy, he galloped across the sand to the water's edge and kicked off his shoes. Taking a deep breath, he flung out his arms and, with all his might, yelled, *"Olly, Olly, oxen free!"*

Rudy, who had trotted behind, cocked his head and held open his palms in want of an explanation. Guy took another lungful of the salty, fresh ocean air. He noticed the dumbfounded look on his friend's face and doubled over, laughing. "Heavens! I need to do that more often."

"Do what?" Rudy asked, still clueless.

"Remind myself there's a beach and an ocean, instead of roasting under lights on a smoky sound stage and pretending I'm in a North African country."

"What's this *Olly* thing?" Rudy asked.

"It's an expression from a kid's game. Anyone who's hiding can come out in the open. I'm saying it because I'm thrilled to be here."

"Perfect weather. Perfect day, eh?"

"You betcha!" Guy wrapped his arm over Rudy's shoulder and gave him a slight hug. Rudy jerked with eyes widened.

"What's wrong?" Guy continued to lead him back toward the car.

"You're a married man!"

Guy pointed to the vacant stretch of beach they had all to themselves. "You think a few seagulls will report our kiss and tell? Come on, I'm starved.

The party has started without us."

Ten minutes later, they arrived at Salka's. Guy surveyed the Sunday crowd. He cringed, and his gay mood dampened. "Someone invited a Gypsy fortuneteller."

Rudy pulled him toward the kitchen. Giving Guy a curious look, he asked, "Since when did the Romani do you wrong?"

Guy reached for an "Economize with Victory" quart of Acme Beer. Having to wash two glasses from the steep pile in the sink, he poured one for himself and one for Rudy.

"Babs and I had a case when we both first started our business involving those scoundrels. Out of town in the Moreno Valley. They probably couldn't find a local shamus dumb enough to fall for their bait. We, being newcomers and desperate for a gig, regretted every darned minute. Would you believe the cash they paid us was counterfeit?"

"Most have no scruples whatsoever," said Rudy. "I guess they grow up believing such behavior is normal. In Germany and in occupied Europe, the Nazis threw them into camps, just like anyone else they deemed undesirable."

Guy took a sip of his beer and squinted to make out her features. "She's no Gypsy. Under all that garish costume jewelry and pretense, she's the Filipino woman I saw the first time I visited the Santa Monica Pier."

A sign on her table showed donations were welcome. Guy sneezed from the frankincense belching from her brazier. Rudy tossed a fifty-cent piece into her brass bowl and said, "My treat, since Warner just fired you. If she's not Romani, she's harmless, right? I'd like to know what the future will bring."

Guy said he felt skittish and insisted Rudy get his cards read instead. The woman shuffled and laid them out in a geometric configuration. "Pick one," she said. "Your choice."

Rudy chose one near the middle. She laid it face up. "The Six of Cups. You're involved with a friend. Someone you've already known. Choose another."

Next, he chose the Hanged Man. "This card has several interpretations," she said. "Many consider it the card of sacrifice. Others view it as a world turned upside down, forcing one to think of alternatives. Especially in a crisis, where surrendering to circumstances might be your best course of action."

This time, Rudy picked the card of Death. He glanced at Guy and sprang to his feet. "That's it. I've had enough."

"No, wait!" she cried out. "The card means change. You and your friend will encounter a big trans-for-ma-tion in your lives. Nobody dies, but there's no going back."

Too spooked to pick up where they left off, Rudy thanked her for her time, threw in an extra dime for a tip, and scooted from the room in a hurry. Guy found him standing in a deserted hallway with his back to the wall, scraping his fingernails on the surface of Salka's wallpaper.

"It's nonsense," Guy said, attempting to calm him down. "She's a performer, and this is all an act. The card means nothing. You hear? Nothing."

Once he slowed his breathing, Rudy admitted he was more ashamed than frightened. Guy suggested they head back to the kitchen. They refilled their glasses and grabbed a plateful of pickles and Vienna sausages.

* * *

Rudy mentioned he had something urgent to discuss with Salka. They found her in her backyard garden, accompanied by a buxom, overly perfumed woman with a Germanic accent, who fawned over the lilacs and hibiscus. "So beautiful and fragrant! A nirvana to the nose, and to think I can hear the ocean all the way from here!"

Salka reacted. "You've never seen such an outdoor arrangement?"

"Near Munich, we had a family house in the countryside. Nothing like being so near the ocean, but we had rivers and streams, and the men loved their fishing," the woman said.

Salka seemed hesitant to ask, "What's of it now?"

"Alas, the Nazis forced us to flee and are using our old estate as their local headquarters."

"Enjoy mine while you're here." Salka offered the lady her handkerchief to wipe her misted eyes. She acknowledged Rudy and Guy's presence with a wink.

Rudy took this as his cue to approach her in private. He suggested to Guy that he circulate and assured him he'd be fine in his absence.

"I can't tell you how grateful I am for your generosity," Rudy said to Salka.

"Think nothing of it. My home is a port of call for those who need sanctuary," she replied, checking to make sure no one was eavesdropping. She led him over to a shade tree, which everyone else seemed to ignore. "Of course, you know *he* can't remain here. The U.S. government guard dogs know my place too well. It's ridiculous, but they think I'm helping the Communists with my film fund."

"Because you are friends with Bertolt Brecht?"

"He won't shut his mouth about his Marxist ideology and wants to bring all his Commie cronies over here. Sometimes, I get so paranoid that I assume every English-speaking American who comes to my parties must work for the FBI. I hope your male friend doesn't."

"Guy Brandt?" Rudy made a nervous laugh. "Not on your life. But about our *Japanese friend*, you know that Guy and I went to great lengths to smuggle him inside a fake birthday cake we borrowed from Warner Brothers."

Salka laughed. "Yes, I thought that was clever of you, but about your Japanese friend…he's hiding in plain sight. He's quite useful and insists on earning his room and board, but we're taking a substantial risk. Have you found him other accommodations?"

Rudy made a quick look over his shoulder to make sure no one was eavesdropping. "I'd rather not name names, but Guy and I have a few acquaintances at the Garden of Allah and hope one of them will be cooperative. Residents come and go all the time. The hotel's transient nature provides a reasonable cover."

"Considering the parties and the place's reputation. Well, you know…it's fair game for the gossip columnists. What about cops? Don't they like to drop by on a frequent basis, and who's going to pay for it?"

Rudy lowered his voice even more. "I am, for now. Do you think the *film fund* can lend me a hand? Who manages that for you?"

Salka gave him a blank stare, halting their conversation, and made a convenient excuse that someone needed her elsewhere. "Call me. During the week. We'll discuss matters later."

Rudy noticed a strip of yard on the side of her house. He spotted a smallish man, swathed like a beekeeper in protective garb from the sun and insects, pulling weeds. Before he had time to check him out, Guy intersected his path.

"Rudy, it might be my imagination, but I think I saw Manfred Coblenz among the guests."

"Who?" Rudy tested his memory.

"The soundman… Sorry, I mean the boom operator who got fired in front of everyone at the beginning of production."

"Really?"

"Come to think of it, Babs mentioned she saw his name on the list of background extras inside Rick's Café. Darn it! I wish Jack Warner hadn't let us go."

Rudy put his hand on Guy's shoulder. "Don't worry. If Conrad's on call, I'll be there. Most of those scenes also involve Bogie and Bergman…Rains, and others who've vowed to be cooperative. Even if Henreid doesn't…as you say…give a hoot, we'll cover everything in your absence."

"What about Mr. Otake?"

"Salka confided he can't remain here much longer. Too many government agents are aware of this place. Maybe you can convince your famous writer friend to co-sign for a place to let in the Garden of Allah. That way, no one will suspect us, and he'll be a stone's throw from Babs."

"Hammett?" Guy rubbed his chin. "He looked pretty tight…and broke the last time we saw him. The booze must've affected his sense of money management. He's bailed Babs and me out in the past, but I'm not sure how trustworthy he'd be now."

"If you can think of a better option, let me know. Come. I'm concerned about your friend," Rudy said. "I'd like to speak with him further."

Mr. Otake remained where they last discovered him. Not to raise his alarm, Rudy whispered low enough to keep their discussion private. "Where has she been hiding you? I can't imagine it's the guesthouse. That's too out in the open."

Surprised he had visitors, Mr. Otake lost his balance from his squatting position and fell over backward. Guy and Rudy helped steady him. "I stay in basement."

"I didn't think most houses had basements in Los Angeles."

"Here in Santa Monica, some have partial ones with crawl spaces. She… Salka says I'm safe for now, but maybe not for long."

Guy asked, "Isn't it dark and damp, being so close to the ocean? What about bugs?"

"Better than Babs' closets or hiding under her beds. She never dusts. Your big dog…he sheds a lot. Spiders don't bother me. They are my friends."

Rudy couldn't understand. "I'd like to see this place where you stay for myself. How do we access it?"

"A door. Off the kitchen area," Otake explained.

Rudy nodded and gestured for Guy to follow. "For now," he told Otake, "you have nothing to worry about."

They pushed past the crowd, headed into the house, and opened the door to Salka's cellar, carefully negotiating its wooden stairs and almost overcome by the musty odor. The only light came from a single window. Rudy regretted they hadn't the foresight to ask Otake where they could've found a flashlight.

Guy swore he had heard footsteps. "I think someone else might be down there." Rudy put his finger to his lips as they proceeded with caution. They recognized Otake's luggage and discovered several bedrolls and eating utensils, and what appeared to be a safe house.

Rudy headed back upstairs. Guy followed, closing the cellar door. "Maybe we should leave," Rudy said through gritted teeth. Beads of sweat broke out on his forehead like a sudden rash. His thoughts were elsewhere as he peered toward the far entrance to the kitchen, as if he were trying to pick someone out of the crowd.

"One of Major Strasser or Conrad Veidt's lines keeps playing in my head," Guy remarked. "The one where he says, 'Don't be in such a hurry. We have all the time in the world.'"

"Don't we all have bitter memories…haunting our present happiness?" Rudy muttered.

Guy wasn't sure how to interpret that and couldn't figure out why Rudy seemed drawn toward the exit. The one thing he understood, however, was they didn't have all the time in the world. They needed a surefire solution and pretty darned quick.

Chapter Twenty-Eight

On their drive back to Hollywood, Rudy and Guy differed in their opinions. "I approached Salka about a loan from her film fund to get Otake situated," Rudy said. "Something's wrong. She abruptly changed the subject."

"Perhaps this relates back to our case. Since you were intimate with Gerhard Sauer, you were in a better position to know whether he really had his hands in the cookie jar. Maybe Salka discovered a significant amount depleted, and now she's extra cautious. Did you ever see any of that money? Did Sauer ever give you any?"

"No! Of course not, and, in case you were going to ask, we made sure Leon Lewis and his associates were unaware of our relationship."

Guy observed Rudy's muscles tighten and the veins emerge on his neck. "Have you considered his killer might've wanted to help himself to the pot? Regardless of whether Gerhard pocketed some for himself, if the killer acted more like an informant and had ratted him out, the police would've tied up the donations during the investigation."

"Which would mean Salka and her partners running the charity wouldn't be able to access it," said Rudy. "Corrupt cops could also *conveniently* misplace a large portion of it and keep it for themselves."

"What do you suggest we do next? Maybe Salka is worried about her own neck."

"Let's worry about Mr. Otake. I don't need to remind you there are too many restrictions for me to bring a guest where I'm staying. That's why I always had to meet at your place instead of mine."

"Which you can't even go to anymore, now since I'm living with Babs."

Guy failed to pay attention to who had the right of way at a four-way stop and slammed his foot on the brake. He took a deep breath and allowed the other driver to pass. They drove a few more blocks in silence before Rudy made a fuss. "Looks like I have no other choice but to dig into my own pockets to get her Japanese friend settled."

Guy waited a beat. "Can you afford it?"

"You can't without a steady stream of income, and neither can Babs. I guess that makes me responsible."

"Rudy, you owe him nothing."

"He reminds me of so many who were desperate to leave Germany. I have stories. Ones you've never heard of. About helping strangers. Friends of friends who needed to escape those monsters. What he is going through isn't much different."

Guy rounded the corner. He took an alternate route to Rudy's, using side streets, avoiding more trafficked thoroughfares. One thing he didn't want was to get involved in a tense conversation about karmic reckoning.

"If I wind up as his benefactor, it needs to be kept a secret," said Rudy. "We can't put the apartment under my name."

"We can't put it under Otake's."

"Guy, you don't have a job, and the hotel management will want to check someone's references. But your writer friend has a reputation here in Hollywood."

Guy stopped short again. This time at a red light. The two lurched forward.

Rudy glanced at him with concern. "Do you want me to drive?"

Guy shook his head. "No, I'll be fine, but Hammett? I'm not so sure. He was three sheets to the wind when I introduced you."

"*The Thin Man* and *The Maltese Falcon* were hits at the box office. Assuming he's paying his rent on time, his rep will hold more weight than mine. Besides, he's more than qualified. Before he earned his living as a writer, he worked as a Pinkerton detective."

"What's in it for him? asked Guy.

"If he needs an incentive. Offer him a fine bottle of Scotch."

"Are you buying?"

"That'll be your contribution."

* * *

After he and Rudy parted ways, Guy tried to piece together the best strategy. Should he call Dashiell Hammett first, or should he drop by unannounced? He wasn't familiar with Hammett's favorite bars, where he could just wander in as a customer. A surprise visit at the writing room? He wasn't even sure which studio Hammett was under contract with, and he'd need a front gate pass. What if it were Warner Brothers? Even though his writer friend loved to bet on the ponies and that was one of the usual places to find him, Guy knew for certain the Santa Anita Racetrack was out. Immigration officials had converted it into a Japanese holding center.

Should he let Babs in on his plan? Maybe not, but the Scotch was the deciding factor. In her divorce settlement, Babs wound up with her ex-husband's impressive liquor collection, along with the fancy carved wooden cabinet he stored it in. To her, it meant little. She rarely drank, but the judge deemed it something of value, since Troy had little else to offer. If she knew his Scotch might be Mr. Otake's passport toward freedom, Guy thought, she wouldn't mind relinquishing it.

Outside their brief encounter at the pool party, Guy and Dash hadn't spent significant time together since they wrapped the *Blackbird Killer Case* involving the cast of *The Maltese Falcon*. After all, Warner released the film just one month before the Japs bombed Pearl Harbor.

The trickier situation would be to transfer Mr. Otake out of the Viertel household. He'd have to check him into one of the Garden of Allah's bungalows, one as far away as possible from either the pool or the bar, where tattletales couldn't blow his cover. Someone would have to sneak in essentials like food and medicine because they'd have to prevent him from leaving the place and getting them himself. Otake would remain a prisoner of circumstances.

* * *

The next challenge: to convince Dash to go along with it. Otake suggested Guy bribe him with some of his saké. Babs had it hidden in her attic. He thanked him for his offer but said it was an acquired taste. "Save it for yourself when this whole mess blows over."

When he finally approached Dash in person, Guy tried to paint a picture of all the advantages he'd have by taking Mr. Otake under his wing. "The studios are hot for WWII scripts right now. Think of the edge you'll have over your competition."

"What competition?" Hammett opened a fresh pack of cigarettes and offered one to Guy. "Could you believe my bosses just asked me to work on a romantic comedy? Considering all the grim, hard-edged, *she-done-him-wrongs* with no pretty picture in sight, I wrote for *Black Mask* and those other detective pulps, whoever thought I could master the happily-ever-after must've turned the corner and backed into the wrong alleyway—"

"Only to stare into the barrel of a .38 Special," said Guy, thinking he was clever by finishing his sentence.

They both laughed when Dash formed his fingers into the shape of a let's pretend gun and pointed right at him, saying, "You betcha!"

Guy did his darnedest to turn this conversation around and persuade him otherwise. "Just think. Mr. Otake could be a great resource for you to write about his culture. He could help you get the facts straight. Make things realistic."

Dash seemed unimpressed and undecided. He gazed at his typewriter with a blank sheet of paper held in place against its carriage. A warm breeze caused it to flutter and blew a balled-up discard across his desk like a tumbleweed and into his wastebin.

"I *donnn't* know." Already soused at ten in the morning, he slurred his words. "Since I can't seem to commit any words on paper, I was kinda thinkin' of heading to the East Coast. To New York."

"To get back together with your girlfriend? Lillian Hellman?"

"More like my partner in crime."

"Must be a challenge keeping up your relationship and being so far away."

"She's doing well writing for the theater these days with *The Children's Hour* and *The Little Foxes*."

"She has you to thank for your mentorship," said Guy, paying him a compliment. He wasn't sure if Hammett was blushing or whether he was getting a whiskey nose from excessive drinking. Women... Men... Guy didn't know which way was up with relations with women or men anymore. He pulled a flask from his jacket pocket. Took a swig and watched Dash lick his lips. He sealed the deal when he asked, "Care for some? In the car, I got an entire bottle."

Chapter Twenty-Nine

Back at Warner Brothers, the secret cabal of actors, substituting for Babs and Guy, didn't have all the time in the world. Even though Bogie, Bergman, and Claude Rains were rehearsing or on camera most of the time, Sydney Greenstreet and Peter Lorre needed to pick up the slack, and everyone needed to take advantage of the scenes when groups of extras populated the set. Their brief moments of opportunity would arise from within Rick's Café, in the streets, in the Black Market, and inside the Blue Parrot. Of course, this would all depend upon Michael Curtiz's cooperation, and Wallis and Warner not finding out.

After they wrapped filming one night, Bogie offered to pay for the first two rounds at a local bar. He presumed if he could loosen everyone up, people were more likely to talk. For his next ploy, knowing he always had a chessboard set up in his dressing room, he started a group match. It would be the gang against him, and for each move, he'd throw in a quarter. Once people got involved, they were more inclined to divulge information. Whoever he felt came up with the cleverest play at the end of the game would win the entire pot.

"What if an attractive lady decides she wants in?" Claude asked. "Wouldn't that cause your wife to declare war?"

Bogie pulled a pair of handcuffs out of the box, holding his chess pieces. "The cops gave me this as a souvenir from her last arrest. A little reminder in case she misbehaves again."

Claude asked whether the police had given him the key.

"If she raises a stink, I'll cuff her to her chair, and if she persists, I guess we'll be taking home an extra one."

***

Ingrid had the wedding film processed and printed. She had shown Orry-Kelly, *Casablanca's* costume designer, the striking outfits that the PIs had put together at the last minute. Right away, he had members of his wardrobe department shop for fabric and create replicas, so they'd be ready in time for Rick Blaine and Ilsa Lund to wear in the final airport sequence.

During a fitting session, she confided in him about her new role in the murder investigation and begged for his cooperation.

"I thought they were doing a splendid job, but Warner fired them," she said. "It's too bad he thought they were taking too long."

"Isn't that a matter for the police?"

"What good have they done so far? Meanwhile, Babs and Guy requested that I and the major cast members ask around in their absence. Anyone who came to America from another country would be a suspect."

"That would include you, since you're from Sweden, and me," he said. "I came from Australia, the Land Down Under, before coming to Hollywood. Rains, he's English. Henreid, he's Austrian… That would be a majority of our cast."

"There's nothing to say you couldn't pitch in and help."

"I have enough on my plate," he said, getting upset.

Looking in the mirror, Ingrid tried on her hat to see how it would complement the overall look. "How would you feel if there were a murderer right under your nose?"

"Uncomfortable, to say the least."

As she turned to see a fuller view, the designer tightened the fabric at her waistline but accidentally stabbed her with a pin. "Ouch! Be more careful."

He apologized but admitted that her insistent questioning had distracted him.

"What about the thefts happening on set?" she asked. "Have you or your assistants noticed any missing inventory of late?"

He poised a sharp needle in his hand. "Come to think of it…I have received a few complaints."

Ingrid turned on the waterworks. "Someone stole a precious pair of heirloom pearl earrings, ones my grandmother gave me. They still haven't turned up."

"I'm so sorry." He offered her his handkerchief.

At that point, the tears had done their job, and she had already swayed him with her charms. Ingrid handed him a copy of the list of extras. He promised his wardrobe department would give her full cooperation and would keep an eye and ear out for anything out of the norm.

* * *

Despite being asked to make themselves available, production kept postponing Peter Lorre and Sydney Greenstreet's remaining scenes for one reason or another. Wallis kicked up a fuss about paying their salaries if they weren't working. Sydney, although a veteran stage actor, insisted his time on set was educational. He was new to the nuances of film, and *The Maltese Falcon* had been his first time on screen. He and Peter would give Bogie's wife the evil eye if she got out of line but, otherwise, they had time to kill.

One of the director's assistants forwarded a short script to Greenstreet for a publicity trailer for *Background to Danger*, slated to be his and Peter's next project. Sydney reminded the boy that he needed his own durable upholstered chair, one that was sturdier than the standard director's chair, to support his weight.

"I've destroyed two of the other kind already," Sydney explained. "Heaven forbid I injure myself in another mishap."

While the young man went to fetch the proper seat, Sydney reviewed the material standing up. Peter prepared him a cup of tea but put in six teaspoons of sugar as a practical joke. He kept his eyes on Sydney, waiting for his reaction.

"Ah, life is sweet." Sydney smiled without flinching. Instead, he giggled while reading his dialogue.

"What's so amusing?" Peter asked. "Care to let me in on the joke?"

Sydney explained it must've been Warner's doing. "He insinuated that if I had nothing better to do, then I should memorize it."

Peter plucked it out of his hands and read it out loud with a booming voice, imitating his friend's. "I want to tell you of a story more mysterious than *The Maltese Falcon*. It's an amazing tale of desperate people clashing against a background to danger—"

Sydney snatched it back. "It's my narration to memorize, not yours. So where were we? Ah, yes…"

Peter lit a cigarette and peered over his shoulder, and Sydney chuckled again.

"What's so funny?" asked Peter.

"There's a note referring to me as the sinister master of espionage." He mumbled a few lines until he got to the part where he described himself.

"What else?" Peter asked.

"They continue to call me the Fat Man. I guess I'm branded for life."

"Isn't it obvious?" Peter quipped.

"They call you dangerous because you're dynamite."

"Guess I am a bit of a firecracker," Peter cackled. "Speaking of espionage, how do you plan to interrogate the café patrons to see if there's a bad actor among them?"

"If they weren't such bad actors, they wouldn't be playing background extras."

Peter gave him a look that could kill. "That's not what I meant, and you know it."

"Just pulling your leg. I enjoy getting the last laugh."

Bogie barged in on the two crackpots. "Is this what the boss is paying you for?"

"Why should you care?" asked Peter. "It's not coming out of your pocket."

"I'm just thinking, instead of sitting around, maybe you could do something more useful."

Sydney asked, "What did you have in mind?"

"What about interviewing the extras since Warner banned our private detectives from the studio?"

"There's only so much we can do when Curtiz is using them."

Their argument went nowhere. A production assistant informed Bogie that they needed him back on the set. Sydney assured him they'd see what they could do during lunch.

* * *

Everyone liked to make fun of the director's dismantling of the English language. Today, being no exception, Claude put him on the spot. "Did I hear you say, 'Casa Blanket?'"

The look on Curtiz's face was priceless, and Claude wished Ingrid had been there to capture the moment with the camera she often brought to the set. Claude exchanged jabs with Curtiz, whom he'd worked with on frequent occasions. He would also take great pains to dispel the tension between them and everyone else on the set. On the previous day, after Curtiz demanded that he enter the scene with *more energy*, he responded by bursting through the scene on a bicycle.

Silliness aside, the erstwhile private detectives had delegated to Claude a serious task. Starting first with those who had speaking parts, he targeted Austrian émigré Helmut Dantine. In the script, Captain Renault would proposition a young Bulgarian bride to exchange favors for a visa for her and her husband. The actress who played her was an American and Jack Warner's stepdaughter. Why would she need to steal jewelry? She had no apparent motive for the murder. Dantine? Maybe.

During break one day, Claude had stepped outside for a smoke. He noticed Dantine in a panic, patting down his pockets as if looking for a cigarette, so he offered him one of his. "I heard rumors you spent time in jail. Is that true? What sort of crime did you commit?"

For lack of a match, Claude offered him a light.

"Not what you'd expect, but I guess it became more commonplace as the war progressed."

Claude gave him the side-eye. "Did you kill a Kraut?"

Dantine shook his head. "Political dissidence. Protests. Distributing flyers and anti-Nazi propaganda they didn't approve of. I was young, strong-willed, and hard-headed. Wasn't even out of my teens."

Claude choked on his laughter. "At that age, you feel you can revolutionize the world."

"Pretty much," Dantine replied. *"Kinder werden es auf die harte Tour lernen,* or children will learn the hard way."

* * *

Peter Lorre was eager to stir up mischief. He capitalized on his squirrelly nature to make friends with the foreign extras in between takes and would sell single cigarettes to them at a discount to get them talking.

Since he was fluent in multiple languages, including French, he endeared himself to Marcel Dalio, who played Rick's casino's croupier, and Madeleine Lebeau, who played Yvonne, Rick Blaine's rejected mistress. In real life, she was Dalio's wife. In *Casablanca,* when Rick refused her affection, she drank too much and flirted with Nazi soldiers.

Dalio told Lorre his hard-luck story. "My birth name was Moshe Blaushild. My wife and I fled Paris before the occupation. Just like the dreams of the people in our film, we found ourselves in Lisbon, hoping to get visas to travel to America.

"The Nazis did something reprehensible. They took photographs of me and used them in antisemitic propaganda, perhaps because I had been such a popular actor in France. They used these pictures to illustrate what the insidious Jewish suspect looked like."

"That's terrible," said Lorre, offering to light Dalio's cigarette. "You? You're a refined-looking gent. How do I say? With a pleasing aesthetic. I'm surprised they didn't use my ugly face to illustrate their imaginary enemy. People all over would recognize me. I had played enough monstrous men on film. Especially back in Germany."

"The story of how we came to Los Angeles," said Dalio, "very similar to what your screenwriters tried to portray in this movie."

"How so?" asked Peter.

"In Marseilles, my wife and I obtained visas to go to Chile…in South America, but officials discovered they were forgeries and detained us in Mexico, our first port of call."

"That must've been terrifying," said Peter.

"It was," said his wife. "We didn't speak any Spanish and thought we'd never get to America. Some passengers didn't. However, we were fortunate not only to make it to Hollywood, but to continue performing in the profession we knew and loved."

"Sort of like playing roulette," Peter remarked. "Here in our film, you fix games in Rick Blaine's casino. There, it was like taking chances and gambling with your lives. Sometimes one wonders if it is luck or whether you're dealing with fate."

Chapter Thirty

Babs quickly discovered that sharing an office with Guy wasn't the same as living together. She had gotten used to Mr. Otake's obsession with cleanliness. One afternoon, she came home with her arms full of groceries. Staring at the bottles of his Nehi soda, taking up every inch of space in the fridge, she noticed Guy had entered the kitchen. "Do you need to keep so much on ice? What about a little common courtesy?"

He reached inside and grabbed one with each hand and placed them on top of her kitchen table. "Babs, you sound like my mother."

"I'm your wife... Well, not really."

He reached into her grocery bag and stole one of her carrots. Her overstuffed paper bag broke, and its contents fell through the bottom. The dogs gamboled over to lap up her broken eggs.

She shook her head and was beside herself. *So much for rationing!* "I hope you like oatmeal, because you're not getting scrambled eggs."

Babs pointed to his accumulated collection of empty bottles in the corner. "See what happens when you don't rinse them? Flies everywhere! The least you could do is return them and get back your bottle deposits."

"You're the one who insists we keep food out during warm weather. Can't tell you how many times I've found ants crawling in the dogs' bowls and on your dirty dishes in the sink."

"That's because both of us have been gone all day trying to solve a murder."

Their disputes weren't getting them anywhere. Babs got on her hands and knees to salvage her groceries while he munched on the stolen carrot like Bugs Bunny. "Ever since we rushed into this marriage to get your father off your back and my ex-husband off mine, we've done nothing but quarrel. Whatever happened to the good old days when we were the best of friends?"

Guy handed her his second bottle of Nehi as a peace offering. "When we first met…"

Babs snapped her fingers. "It was an audition, wasn't it?" she mused. "Over at Paramount Studios. Neither of us got a callback for our dream role."

"Actually, I think there had been a mix-up," he recalled. "The casting assistant took the list of rejects and called those actors back by accident. We were lucky to afford one meal a day back then and were so disappointed that we didn't get the parts."

"Remember what happened after we left?"

"I noticed prop food being thrown out from another film," Guy said with a sly smile. "It was actual food from a banquet scene, not the artificial stuff they use now because of wartime rationing, and I insisted we steal it."

"A pretty bold move, don't you think?"

He closed the refrigerator door and sat on the floor next to her. She continued to test her memory. "We didn't want to get caught with the loot, so we walked over to the cemetery adjacent to the movie lot."

"Right! Hollywood Memorial Park…the perfect place to enjoy our pilfered picnic."

"Didn't I also rescue a bouquet from the trash?"

"You placed the flowers on the grave of an unknown soldier."

"Guy, he had a name on his plaque. We just didn't know him."

Sir Henry placed his furry giant face in Babs' lap and eyed a lineup of ants marching one by one. "If anyone gave us funny looks, we pretended to mourn over the gravestones while we dined on one of the park benches."

"We soon realized each other looked familiar." Guy began counting on his fingers some of their recent auditions and humiliating experiences they had picking up work as extras.

"I confessed to you about the modeling jobs I did on the side, but those were slim pickings," said Babs. "Had always done a miserable job at waiting on tables, and secretarial work was out of the question. I didn't take steno and always did the two-finger, hunt-and-peck on a typewriter."

"We were both disheartened with acting and needed a change."

"Can't tell you how many of my auditions turned into casting couch disasters."

"Babs, remember what happened after lunch?"

"When we caught that tramp stealing fancy wreaths left on gravesites?"

Guy nodded. "Then we discovered him reselling them to a vendor around the corner. We reported him to the ground's caretakers, who gave us a reward for our efforts."

Bruno had waddled over to Guy and melted his piggy-like bulldog body into his lap. "It helped me pay my rent for the next month. Then, as I offered to walk you back to your car, I said, 'Hey, maybe we have a talent for this.'"

Babs threw back her head and laughed. "Except I didn't own a car because I couldn't afford one and was too embarrassed to admit it. I took two buses to get to our audition."

"So, I drove you home. Along the way, we brainstormed."

"We came up with the most ridiculous ideas until I found a discarded newspaper in the backseat. That's when I found a listing in the classified ads section about obtaining a private investigator's license."

"One without a prior law enforcement background, right?"

Sir Henry woofed and agreed. "Then I asked you, 'Guy, wanna go into business together?'"

"And I replied, 'With a woman?' I argued potential clients seeking the services of a private investigator might not trust a woman in charge, and there might be times when I'd have to pose as the head of the agency to make us appear more legit. When we finally set our minds to it, we had to go to Perris."

Babs scrunched her brows. "I've never been to Paris."

"Your memory's rusty. Not in France. In Perris, California. Part of this was a correspondence course, and the other portion had to be completed in a classroom in Perris, California."

"Oh…right! The town didn't seem to be much more than a train depot, but wasn't that where… Didn't we have our first big case involving those

Gypsy con artists?"

Guy rolled his eyes. "Don't even remind me. Regardless of what we went through, we obtained bona fide PI licenses in the end—thus the dawn of our new careers."

"Are you sure you still don't have a secret desire to get back to acting?"

Suddenly, Pedro and Petunia started one of their constant marital squabbles, halting the detective's reverie down memory lane.

"You need to track down an animal trainer…like one of those we met on the *Rathbone-Asta Case*," said Babs. "Someone who understands large birds and can train them to behave properly."

Guy got up and let the battling birds out of their cage.

"Why did you let them go free?" She pointed to the broken glass, still in disrepair, on her grandmother's breakfront. "They're going to destroy my house."

Somehow, their disagreement about the parrots circled back to the tension within their artificial union. "You know, I was just beginning a relationship with Rudy before your ex-husband resurfaced. This was the first serious one I'd had since I'd moved to LA."

"Don't tell me you plan on seeing him while we're *married*? People will talk, and I still don't trust him."

"You're just jealous! Why don't you take time off and see that *Woodpecker*-photographer fellow?"

"You won't want to hear this, but I think Rudy is hiding something from us."

Simmering down, her thoughts turned inward. She had always struggled with men and still suffered from the fallout of her rotten marriage with Troy. Every time she thought it was over, he would come back to haunt her, and she never seemed to make any headway with newcomers. She had never fallen in love with Detective Felix Allgood from the *Falcon* case, but it was all for the best that she didn't. Not only had he lied to her about being single and available, but he despised private eyes and ultimately planned on ruining her.

Regarding the *Woodpecker*, his values were too old-fashioned. It was much easier and more productive to bury her nose in her work and hope her career success would compensate for her shortcomings in love. Now, she feared that by marrying Guy, if the right man came along, she'd screwed up all hope for a genuine relationship.

After Guy left the kitchen, she muttered something about wasting her time arguing and removed all the Nehi out of the fridge, except for two.

* * *

If he didn't play his cards right, Rudy dreaded that Mr. Otake might suffer the same fate as his German friends—the ones who didn't measure up to the Nazi party's standards. Just like when he worked undercover for Leon Lewis, ferreting out fascist fifth columnists, the American bureaucrats in charge of Japanese relocation did a fine job of concealing information from the press and making sure the average citizen was in the dark.

Over the next few days, Curtiz planned to film inside Rick's Café with scenes pretty much devoid of any stunts, so Rudy pulled a few strings to get time off. After he squared away all of Mr. Otake's immediate needs, Rudy stuffed a change of clothing and provisions for a few days into a saddlebag, got ahold of a California road map, and sped off on his motorcycle to Manzanar, the nearest Japanese internment camp, hidden in the Mojave Desert.

Unlike anything he had ever experienced, the unforgiving dry desert winds blew with such force that often when he rode against them, he felt like the Hand of God was pushing him back, as if to say, "Go home! Turn around! Don't fight it. It's no use."

After a few detours and false turns, at last, he spotted a tall watchtower, manned by armed guards. Hemmed in on the far side were the foreboding mountains with ancient peaks kissed by bursts of clouds against a clear cerulean sky. Barbed wire separated the compound from the main road.

From a distance, Rudy observed a group of detainees exit a caravan of cars. After the soldiers ordered the prisoners to relinquish their keys, they forced them to unload their suitcases and throw them into a pile. It reminded him of the Nazi book burnings.

The main driveway led to a gate, marked with a wooden sign mounted between two poles: Manzanar War Relocation Center. Rudy rolled his motorcycle up to the guardhouse, a fortress made of stones.

"Halt! No civilians allowed!" said the young recruit, pointing his rifle at Rudy. "You better not be a nosy journalist or some kind of spy!"

Spy? Yes! Journalist—no. Rudy soon realized his native German accent would sound too suspicious, but resurrecting his Shakespearean lilt wouldn't have been too wise either. "My great uncle is a homesteader," he said, making it up on the fly.

Shielding his eyes from the taunting sun, the soldier squinted and tried to make him out. "Can't place yer accent. Where's it from?"

"Grew up near Flanders fields. My ancestors were lucky to flee before those *Pickelhaube Boches* took over their town during the last terrible war."

"*Pickelhaube…*" It took the soldier a moment to interpret Rudy's derogatory slang. "Ah, yes. I get it now. Like those funny pointy helmets the Krauts used to wear… But California is halfway around the world. What brought you out here?"

"Got me some work if I'm willing to brave it."

The steadfast soldier held his aim at Rudy. "Hope he's not a typical, stern and ruthless *Dutch uncle* and plans on workin' ya into the ground. Summers are scorchers, and I hear winters will cut right through you like a dagger. Lots of extremes. You'll find out soon enough that it's mighty harsh livin' in these Alabama Hills."

A sudden headwind picked up from out of nowhere, blowing dust and grit in Rudy's direction. Rudy wheezed and shielded his face inside his leather jacket. The soldier tucked inside the guard booth for protection.

"Is that what they call them?" Rudy asked, clearing his lungs. "Maybe I should check my map. I might've gotten lost."

The private cursed the climate and spat on the ground. Then he rinsed his mouth with cold black coffee. "Wouldn't want to raise sheep or cattle. Can't grow much of anythin', but some Hollywood folk like to make movies not far from here."

How interesting, Rudy thought. "Really? What kind?"

"Cowboy films, I reckon. Lots of shoot-'em-ups. Started with the silent pictures. Tom Mix… Fatty Arbuckle… Guess Hollywood thinks this is what the Wild West is supposed to look like. That *Maltese Falcon* fella did a film up here not too long ago."

"Humphrey Bogart? Which one?"

"My buddies told me it was *High Sierra.* You're in mountain country. Mount Whitney is the highest peak and ain't far from here."

"Ah…but this is nowhere near Alabama," Rudy interjected. "Why that name?"

"Named the hills after a Confederate battleship, not the state. Civil War stuff…in case foreigners like you aren't up on our history."

Rudy nodded but then noticed a handful of demoralized Japanese internees with their heads down, forming into a single file outside their barracks and marching toward another building. "Where are they going?"

"Headin' to the showers."

Despite the arid heat, Rudy felt a sudden chill and broke out in goosebumps. In Germany, that meant only one thing. He prayed the Americans had more humanity. Mr. Otake deserved so much better.

The sentry gave Rudy one last warning. "Anyway, you better head toward your destination, 'cause you ain't supposed to be here, and I have my orders to shoot any protesters."

Rudy took one last rueful look. "Maybe I should get on the Hollywood bandwagon should they come to town. Anything's got to be more exciting than tending the herd." He tipped his helmet to the soldier, mounted his motorcycle, and sped away.

Chapter Thirty-One

In Scene 227, Rick Blaine opened the door to his dark apartment. Inside, Ilsa waited for him. "Your unexpected visit isn't concerned, by any chance, with the letters of transit?" Rick asked, lighting a cigarette.

Ilsa pleaded, "You could ask any price you want, but you must give me those letters."

"No deal, sugar," he replied. "You—"

"Cut!" shouted Curtiz. "You forgot your dialogue! That sounded like a line from one of your old gangster films."

"What did I say that was wrong?" Bogie tried to apologize. "Maybe it just came to me, and I improvised. Is that a crime?"

The camera crew said they needed to reload. The assistant director gave the actors a fifteen-minute break, explaining Curtiz needed to examine his notes.

"We all know what that means," Bogie said to Ingrid.

"No, I don't."

"He calls his wife at home and asks for her opinion about our dialogue and how the scene should be going."

"Maybe it's because we've had so many rewrites and still don't have an ending," said Ingrid.

"What's more, his wife Bess used to be some muckety-muck screenwriter before she married him. He values her opinions more than the Ten Commandments. Since Warner keeps hiring him, I guess his old lady must be right on the money."

Ingrid excused herself to make a call. Today's scenes only involved her,

Bogie, and Henreid, and Claude had the day off. She needed to see if he had made any progress in the PI's absence. Bogie said he'd go outside for a smoke and find a payphone to call Peter and Sydney.

After making fun of Curtiz's idiosyncrasies, Claude asked her, "Have you exercised your charms on Henreid at all?"

"If you're asking whether he reconsidered and cooperated with us, I've failed miserably. He keeps repeating Rick Blaine's line, 'I stick my neck out for nobody.'"

"Too bad. I thought he'd make a turnaround."

"Claude, after interviewing many of those who played extras in *Casablanca*, have you come to any conclusions about who might've murdered Sauer?"

"If you had heard all the sob stories about how these unfortunate souls escaped Nazi-occupied territories, you could've written an Oscar-winning screenplay. Many hocked everything of value they owned, including their jewelry. Yet, no one, so far, seemed vindictive enough to steal from the set as compensation for their losses. Sorry to say, but I'm no further in recovering who might've taken your grandmother's earrings. Regarding Sauer, I've been stuck at square one."

Meanwhile, Bogie called Peter. During their time off, Peter admitted that he and Sydney had been inseparable and often conducted their inquiries together.

"We really make a great team," Peter snickered. "Sydney corners them, making them feel on the spot with his imposing presence. Then I come in for the kill, *heh, heh, heh*. Not literally, of course."

"Yeah, I gotcha. You can skip the comedy. Any conclusions?" Bogie dropped the remains of his cigarette and ground it out with the heel of his shoe, still bolstered on lifts.

"Most of the extras I spoke with confessed they were Jewish refugees," explained Peter. "Ilka Grüning, who played Mrs. Leuchtag, is a sixty-six-year-old Viennese actress and the oldest performer in the film. Believe it or not, she appeared with Conrad Veidt in a German silent film. After she fled Nazi Germany and came to the States, she was out of work for close to nine years before the director, Vincent Sherman, offered her a part in

Underground, filmed last year."

Bogie looked at his watch and reckoned he could pick Peter's brains for a few more minutes. "Anybody else of interest?"

"The actor who played her husband, Ludwig Stössel…he and I had a lot in common, except he's Austrian and I'm Hungarian. He's a former stage actor who made his way into films. Like me, he even worked with Fritz Lang. However, I believe he's in the clear. The two of us got together for beer and shared a few war stories."

Bogie continued his query. "Maybe you can save me a call. Any idea what Sydney uncovered?"

"I heard rumors that Curtiz wanted to keep some extras on salary, even when they were no longer needed."

"Why would he want to do that?"

"Wanted to be charitable, I guess. They needed the money, but Wallis caught wind of it and had a fit."

"I bet he did—" Cut short, Bogie spun around as a production assistant tapped him on the shoulder. "I guess they need me back on the set."

* * *

Reluctantly putting up the money for the rental deposit, Rudy smuggled Mr. Otake from Salka's basement and over to the Garden of Allah in Hollywood. Hammett agreed to put his signature on the lease and claimed his girlfriend, Lillian Hellman, wanted her own apartment, separate from his, when she went back and forth from New York.

He came up with the excuse, "She prefers the proletariat approach and takes the train when she's not in a rush, but it's an exhausting ride. For days afterward, she insists on being alone, and, when you have two writers working on separate projects, they can get in each other's hair, and nothing will get done."

The hotel management bought his cock-and-bull story.

Concerned about Otake's welfare, Guy brought him groceries. He became furious when he found him smelling of whiskey and being sloshed in the middle of the afternoon.

"Hammett and I, we became drinking buddies." He wobbled, unsteady on his feet.

Guy demanded he sit down, insisting he eat something. He double-checked the shades were pulled down so no one could look inside. Then he locked the door and stormed over to Hammett's and pounded on his door.

"What's this about being a bad influence?" Guy asked.

"I'm helping the poor fellow learn and practice his English," Hammett said in his defense. "If the radio is too loud, some passersby are liable to think there's someone here other than Lillian. It's too bad I can't get him to retype my manuscripts without errors. Otherwise, he could earn a little pocket change."

"Don't you have better things to do with your time?"

"Like what?"

"Scripts to write on deadline? Don't know how much more patience the studios will have with those flimsy excuses."

"What else can he do all day?" Dash asked.

"Didn't I mention that the studios have been clamoring for good war stories? Mr. Otake can provide you with an angle that will put you a cut above your competition."

"I'm sick of this damned war. We just got over the first one with the Krauts. Now, it feels like we're going through another Prohibition, but this time it makes German beer and Italian wine harder to get."

"Opportunity has stared you in the face the entire time, and you've failed to take advantage of that."

"Your Japanese friend teaches me the fine art of calligraphy. Something I bet you can't brag about."

Guy grunted and was at the end of his rope. "Won't help you win an Oscar anytime soon."

Unconcerned, Hammett replied, "You want me to show you how I can write the word liquor in Japanese characters?"

Chapter Thirty-Two

Even though the private detectives had, in essence, been fired, a great deal of activity continued to buzz over at Babs' residence. Guy made frequent runs to the Garden of Allah, dispatching books, clothes, food, and other personal effects for Mr. Otake. He shouldn't have had to supervise Hammett, but in the two years Guy had known him, he had encountered enough incidents of insobriety to give him cause for concern.

Proving not to be the best idea in the long run, the "newlyweds" corralled their pets from the office and transferred them to her cottage. When left alone and locked inside all day, they reacted to every outside noise. The bulldog was too short to reach the windowsills, but the wolfhound and the birds often poked their noses under the shades. Every so often, Sir Henry would cause them to roll up, giving Babs' nosy neighbor, Mrs. Dietz, the opportunity to spy on them if no one was home.

It didn't take long for Guy to open the back door to let out the dogs and have the parrots escape. They flew over the hedge into Dietz's backyard, targeting her terrier. As she scooped the pooch into her arms, Pedro and Petunia assaulted her with their sharp beaks and claws. Dietz ran back inside screaming and vowed to take revenge.

Realizing he needed to make a peace offering, Guy made another raid on Babs' liquor cabinet. Armed with a bottle of gin, when he knocked on Mrs. Dietz's door to make a goodwill gesture, she slammed it in his face.

Guy hurried back home and stole another bottle of booze for Hammett. Bribing Dash with bourbon seemed to buy his friendship and enough time, he hoped, to find a palatable solution for poor Mr. Otake. He couldn't imagine what it was like to be shuffled from one asylum to the next and under house arrest.

He climbed into Babs' attic and swiped a small ceramic cask of Otake's sake. Adding fruit from her backyard trees, Guy concealed everything inside a burlap sack, told the animals to behave before he locked up, and sped out of the driveway.

* * *

Dietz called the police, pleading, "I'm fed up with those birds threatening my baby."

Two beat cops, Officers Murphy and Gallagher, arrived on the scene and laughed in her face the moment they discovered her "baby" was a Yorkshire Terrier. They warned her not to waste their time and headed back to their squad car.

She wouldn't let this opportunity slide. Looking for other excuses to get her neighbors in trouble, she blathered about Otake. "Babs Norman had an older man as her tenant, and I'm positive he was Japanese. I swear I saw him after the internment order forced all of them to leave town."

Given more serious grounds, the officers broke into Babs' place without a warrant. Mrs. Dietz followed at their heels and asked, "Are you allowed to do that?"

"Don't tell us how to do our jobs, ma'am," Gallagher replied as he and his partner began a thorough search of the house. Meanwhile, Doris Dietz looked to cause even more damage and went so far as to steal a bottle of peppermint schnapps from Babs' liquor cabinet and stowed it in her purse.

Murphy lumbered his way to the second floor, and Gallagher discovered the trapdoor to her attic crawlspace unlatched and slightly ajar. After he pulled down its attached wooden ladder, he crawled into the attic, cleared a few cobwebs, and coughed from the dust.

"Well, I'll be darned," he said upon discovering Mr. Otake's personal collection of ceramic saké jars marked with Japanese calligraphy. He popped open the lid of one to confirm his suspicions. "If this were still Prohibition,

I'd say we found a fine stash."

"What is it, boss?" Murphy asked.

Leaning over to take a whiff, he said, "Smells like the rice wine that's popular in Japantown."

"Maybe we should take a sample for testing."

"Naw, tried it before. To me, it tastes like piss."

"Can't be that bad if so many Japs drink it. Maybe it's an acquired taste. I still say we should take a sample down to the boys in the lab. Could be some contraband substance. Imagine making a killing with this stuff on the black market. Free money would fall right into our hands."

Murphy cleared his throat. "Find anything else?"

Gallagher straightened up too fast and banged his head against the rafters. "A few kimonos. Framed photos. The rest of it either looks like tourist stuff from a junk shop, or I have no way of identifying it."

Descending the ladder, Officer Gallagher clutched onto one of the smaller saké jars. He asked Mrs. Dietz, "What time does the owner…this Babs Norman lady…get home?"

"She seems to have an unpredictable schedule. Now, she has another fella staying with her. His hours are just as hit and miss."

"Any idea who he is?"

Dietz shook her head. "Not sure, but he seems familiar with the place, as if he's been here many times before."

Heading out, the police left a summons on the front door.

* * *

During this time at Warner Brothers, thanks to the stage lighting, the set felt as hot as the desert in Morocco. A group of French police officers forced open the front door at Rick's Café. Rick and Victor rose to their feet.

"We have a warrant for your arrest," the chief officer said.

"On what charge?" Victor asked.

"Captain Renault will discuss that with you later," he said as his men took Laszlo into custody.

Curtiz yelled, "Cut!" and the cast took a break for the crew to set up for Scene 238 inside Renault's office. Bogie took advantage of their recess to head to the nearest payphone and touch base with Lorre and Greenstreet. Previously, they had told him to give them a ring over at Musso & Frank's Grill.

When one of the waiters summoned Bogie's fellow actors away from the bar, they took their unfinished martinis with them. Both huddled with their ears to the telephone receiver, but Sydney knocked Peter's arm, causing him to spill some of his drink on his jacket.

Peter pointed at the obvious wet stain. "Look, King Kong. If you hadn't crowded me—"

Bogie broke up their war of words. "Unless you want to pay me to be your referee, we've got business to discuss. But first, explain to me why you probed potential perps in a bar."

"Not every man on the street can afford to drink at Musso & Frank's," Sydney explained. "Therefore, we felt it a tantalizing incentive. I think you Americans call it dangling a carrot, so to speak. On busy nights, if I showed up without a reservation, I'd have to sweeten the deal with substantial tips."

"More like bribes," Bogie grumbled. "But in the middle of the afternoon? Shouldn't these actors…or extras be out scrounging for work?"

"Of course," Lorre said with a serpentine slur. "When someone else is buying, who can pass up an exotic cocktail costing as much as their weekly salary?"

Fanning his neck with pages from his script, Bogie opened the phone booth's door to let in a slight summer breeze. "Do you have anything newsworthy?"

"So far," Sydney said, "we've interviewed three actors. We're waiting for a fourth."

"Are you telling me you've been drinking with each of your suspects?"

Bogie looked at his watch. He had to wrap this up and get back to the set, or Curtiz would throw a fit. "Give me some names."

Peter started counting on his fingers. "Let's see… There's what's-his-face, and—"

CHAPTER THIRTY-TWO

"Did you bring Babs' list?" Bogie asked.

Peter fished it out of his pocket and had trouble making heads or tails of it.

"Well, I did but—"

Bogie rolled his eyes. "But what?"

"Remember that scene at the Paris train station? You…or Rick Blaine was waiting for Ilsa to arrive, but Sam handed you a note, saying she wouldn't be joining you in Marseille. Curtiz insisted you hold it up for the cameraman to take a closeup of its ink smearing from the rain."

"Peter, don't tell me—"

"I'm afraid King Kong's martini mishap got all over the list."

Chapter Thirty-Three

Babs, who had been organizing her office, had returned home to discover Guy's car gone and the summons on her front door. She also found it unlocked and with clear signs of a forced entry. Inside, she noticed everything in disarray. Except for her liquor cabinet, which appeared like someone had raided it, nothing else seemed missing. After feeding the pets, she dashed down to the police station. That's when Officers Gallagher and Murphy put her in handcuffs and had her wait in the women's detention area.

With a metallic clang, the door slammed shut. Babs gave a leery eye to her cellmate, who looked like she had once been a knockout. Now, she struck her as a has-been actress turned Hollywood Boulevard streetwalker, who reeked of perfume, perspiration, and cheap whiskey.

Babs asked, "How long are you going to keep me here?"

"That's up to the judge," said Murphy.

"If I have to go in front of a judge, I'll need a lawyer." The problem was that she was out of work and couldn't afford one. "Any chance you've got a public defender?"

The two cops left the room, ignoring her. She wasn't sure if they hadn't heard her, or they just didn't care.

* * *

A strange man hovered over Babs when she woke the following morning. He offered her coffee from his portable thermos, but the black brew sloshed over the sides as he clutched it with a shaky hand. She jerked upright and rubbed her scalded arm. "Who are you?"

This fellow reminded her of the stereotypical down-and-outer. Every fiber of his rumpled seersucker suit retained the smell of cheap cigars. Between his tufted hair like a Kewpie doll, yesterday's five o'clock shadow, and his tarnished wedding ring held in place with masking tape, he looked like his wife had ordered him to sleep on the couch.

"Aren't you the dame who requested the public defender?" He chomped on his unlit stogie with yellowed, uneven teeth.

His slapdash look alone made her question his credentials. "Does it mean anything to anyone around here that I'm a private investigator?"

The snipper-snapper cast his shadow over her. "Nada, mama. They suspended your license."

Babs glanced over at her jail mate. The floozy had passed out on a cot and snored like Babs' floundering Crosley, reminding her she needed to take her car to the mechanic's.

"Are you sure you can handle a federal case?" *I'm scared to think about where he went to law school.*

"I handle whatever they assign me, dollface."

"They're accusing me of harboring a fugitive—a violation of Executive Order 9066."

"The one demanding the Japs to evacuate the West Coast."

No mirror. No comb. The cops had confiscated her purse. Babs ran her fingers through her tangled hair, but to no avail.

He pulled a copy of her summons out of his jacket pocket. "According to this, cops discovered Japanese trinkets in your attic. Stuff only a native-born would possess. This could get bad. Really bad and fast."

Doris Dietz ratted me out!

Every time Babs addressed her court-appointed attorney, his attention went straight for her voluptuous cellmate, Lola Montana, with her hiked-up skirt and torn fishnet stockings.

"What is your name?" Babs asked, realizing he had never identified himself.

"Vinny Krackowski." He handed her his card. Under normal conditions, she would've stashed it in her wallet. After patting her hips and realizing her dress had no pockets, she slipped it inside her bra.

Later that afternoon, Lola used her God-given charms and convinced the prison guard to give Babs phone privileges. She insisted, "We ladies need to stick together." Babs mumbled that someone needed to pass a law where a prisoner had the right to make a phone call rather than beg or pretend to offer favors for one.

A prison guard placed Babs back in handcuffs and escorted her to a pay phone. Not only did she have to ask for change since they had confiscated her purse, but he had to dial the number and hold the receiver to her ear. The only lawyer she knew and felt she could gamble on was Leon Lewis.

He answered after three rings and warned Babs with harsh words, "Didn't I advise you I couldn't exempt your tenant from those edicts?"

The towering prison guard who had accompanied Babs kept staring at Krackowski's business card poking out of her cleavage. Every time she tried to turn away from his lecherous gaze, the receiver fell.

"How are the cops treating you?" Lewis asked.

"As much as expected." She didn't want to say anything in front of the prison guard that she'd regret, so she kept her more scathing opinions to herself. "Hate to admit, I'm unemployed and probably can't afford you, but my court-appointed attorney..."

"Doesn't seem he'll do you justice, correct?"

Babs grumbled.

"You could find yourself in a real pickle if the prosecutor assigned to your case wants to make an example of you."

"Why should he want to do that?"

"For any number of reasons. You're a female PI. How many gals are in that profession? You weren't carrying a firearm at the time of your arrest, I hope?"

"No, but they suspended my license. Despite Warner Brothers firing me, how do they expect me to find new clients and earn a living? What about Guy?"

"You might have to switch hats."

"And let Guy run my agency?"

"The standard term of probation is 'violate no law.' This would also include not associating with known criminals like your Japanese tenant."

Wait till they review my arrest records, including that raid at Ciro's lounge involving George Raft, Bugsy Siegel, and his girlfriend Virginia Hill, when I worked The Maltese Falcon case. "Leon, isn't there a law about police breaking and entering one's house without a search warrant?"

"This town is like the Wild West. Until someone steps in, lays down the law, and enforces it properly, they'll do as they damned well please. Whether seized evidence is admissible in court will be up to the judge, but something like this had better not happen again."

Chapter Thirty-Four

Production moved to scenes at the Black Market, using another revamped set from *The Desert Song*. Curtiz filmed the establishing shots first to set the feel of the location. Then he came in with cutaway shots showing Arabs in the busy Moroccan marketplace, selling merchandise, and with hints of illicit trade. Between the replicated costumes, sets, and props, one would never have realized they shot this on the Warner's lot rather than on location.

The assistant director announced, "Next up, Scenes 144 and 146 with Ilsa Lund and Victor Laszlo in the Black Market. Extras are to go to the holding area to stand by while we reset the camera."

* * *

Curtiz snuck out to have one of his not-so-secret story conferences with his wife, Bess. Often, she'd come up with a better solution.

Upon his return, he startled Ingrid as she was talking to an actor portraying an Arab, played by Babs and Guy's janitor, Abel Wiggins. After adding a turban and a caftan, the swarthy, bearded Black Irishman fit right in with the rest of the crowd. He had volunteered his services, taking vacation time from work, to help the absent PIs.

"Did I interrupt your little affair?" Curtiz asked.

In lieu of the discharged private detectives, the principal actors took their sleuthing duties seriously. Ingrid, trying to disguise her espionage activities, gave him a puzzled look.

"You're a fine actress." He gave her a mischievous smile. "Maybe you are more secretive than I am, but I think I know what you do in your spare time. Maybe that's a woman's way, and men are more open."

He left his starlet in the company of the Arab with whom she had been interrogating. She turned to Wiggins, bewildered. "Did he think we were making whoopee?"

She fanned her neck from the hot lights, trying to calm down. Paul Henreid busted up their exchange. "Is this man bothering you?"

She shook her head so hard, he knew she was covering up some kind of lie.

"Are you sure?" Paul asked.

Wiggins answered for her. "On the contrary. Our director was agitating her."

"Pardon my English if this is incorrect," said Paul, "but he seems to have a talent for ruffling everyone's feathers."

"Enough to drive one to drink, so I'm told," said Wiggins, letting some of his Hibernian accent slip by accident.

Paul laughed. "Did casting run out of Arabs and have to resort to other nationalities?"

Wiggins amplified his accent for effect. "Nary a soul or a rogue can match me with my brogue. If I can play a priest, I can play a swindler. Makes no difference where I get my paycheck."

Paul dismissed his remark with a wave of his hand and excused himself for a smoke. Once he had left, Ingrid pulled a note out of her purse. She explained, "It's the extras' call sheet. There are so many people we need to cross-examine."

"I also got a copy," said Wiggins. "But with all the turbans, fake beards, dark makeup, and caftans, it's hard to figger out who anybody is around here."

"We shouldn't let that stop us."

He eyed the crowd. "We got ourselves a large headcount today. Are you up to the task?"

* * *

Meanwhile, Babs would have her day in court. Leon Lewis requested time alone before her hearing, which was granted. Babs still couldn't believe she'd been arrested. Vouching for her good behavior, Leon met with her at a coffee shop a stone's throw from the courthouse.

"I tried to go by the rules." Babs strained to hold back her tears. "If only we had money and the influence of a friend, since Mr. Otake had no other relatives in the States. They could sponsor him and offer him work and a place to live far away from the West Coast, where he'd be away from everyone's radar. The longer this crisis dragged on, the greater the chance of one of us getting caught."

"That aside, we've got to agree on a strategy for getting you out of this."

"I appreciate you helping me on such short notice," said Babs, who stared at the menu as if she hadn't eaten in days.

"My dear, I insist you order breakfast."

Her head turned when a waitress brought out another customer's ham and eggs and a stack of pancakes from the kitchen. "I want to order everything in sight."

"Be my guest, and I'll help you eat what you can't finish." When the waitress asked for their order, he said, "Bring me another cup of coffee, an extra plate, and plenty of napkins."

Lewis reviewed his notes while sipping his coffee. "By the way, I couldn't reach your partner...your husband, or whatever you want to call him. When he wouldn't pick up the phone, I even went so far as to stop by your house. Several times, in fact."

"Oh, no! What about our animals?"

"Heard no barking dogs or animals in distress. After seeing the vandalism caused by those cops, Guy might've gone somewhere else and taken the pets with him. Especially when he couldn't get a hold of you and had no clue where you had gone."

He returned to his notes and continued, "This is not a jury trial. It's a hearing before Judge Horace Dunwell. The cops who served you the summons should be there, presenting evidence that you've been assisting Mr. Otake. However, you're telling me he wasn't at the house when they broke in and entered, correct?"

Babs nodded and shoveled more food into her mouth.

"Outside of Doris Dietz's eyewitness accounts, they have no evidence, including a copy of a lease, that he ever lived at your place. Yes?"

She chewed as fast as she could and swallowed. "Well…there's Mr. Otake's saké… Most Americans don't even know what it is, because it's stored in such unique containers. Someone might argue if I drank it on a regular basis, I would've stored it in my liquor cabinet. The other stuff in my attic? I could've found it at a flea market after the forced evacuation of Japanese families. There's nothing that could tie it to a specific person I knew or otherwise."

"You know the general rule is to tell the truth…the whole truth and nothing but. I shouldn't be encouraging you to stretch it to suit your situation. For the past few years, my role as an attorney has involved civil liberties."

"I know. I know," Babs sputtered through a mouthful of eggs. "The U.S. Constitution provides people with First Amendment rights, including Freedom of Speech, Freedom of the Press, and Freedom of Religion."

"And," Leon continued, "Freedom to Assemble, which, in my case, applied to the Jewish population in Los Angeles. However, antisemitic groups abused that privilege, claiming it was their First Amendment right to assemble and spread hatred and violence."

"Too bad the Japanese are being denied their rights," said Babs.

Leon hung his head. "War is horrific, no matter how you look at it."

"A few mementos in my attic don't prove I'm pro-Japanese or anti-American," said Babs.

"Correct, but we need to convince the judge you did nothing wrong and to sympathize with you rather than your neighbor." Lewis hailed the waitress and asked for the check. "Don't forget to touch up your lipstick before entering the courtroom. Even if you're guilty, and you are…you'll always want to give the best impression."

* * *

Despite the cracked-open windows with electric fans running, people grabbed whatever papers they had at hand to waft in a cool breeze on this sweltering day in July. Lewis kept fiddling with his watch and looking at the clock on the courtroom wall.

"Is something wrong?" Babs asked.

"It's probably a good thing our case is toward the bottom of the docket. My co-counsel either bailed at the last minute, or he got caught in traffic."

"Is my case so complicated that you'd need extra help?"

"I invited a friend. In all the years he's practiced law, he's almost never lost a case. But he's driving from Riverside County, which is rather far. Let's hope his car didn't break down."

* * *

The bailiff announced, "All rise," and the judge entered the courtroom and sat down on his bench between Old Glory and the California State Bear flag.

Babs gasped and whispered to Leon, "I know that man."

"Who? The bailiff or Judge Dunwell?"

"Dunwell lives down the street from me. We never knew each other until my dog, Sir Henry, rescued his Old English Sheepdog, Binkie, who got trapped in Mrs. Dietz's cactus garden. Of all people, she'd have a yard full of prickly plants to match her personality."

"This is no time for jokes," advised Lewis. "But we might be able to use that to our advantage."

In front of the judge, an Assistant U.S. Attorney pressured Babs for being unable to bring her Japanese tenant with her. In truth, she had no idea where he was but knew he was in excellent hands, thanks to Guy and Rudy.

"I had, and I emphasize *had*," Babs explained, "a Japanese gardener tending my yard until the mandate. It should be obvious he's no longer around since my grass is knee high and weeds have taken over the yard."

The cops, who had raided her house without a search warrant, presented her tenant's personal effects as evidence. Lewis kept giving her glances, which she interpreted that the case didn't seem to go well in her favor.

Finally, the courtroom doors burst open. A hefty man, clammy with sweat, straightened his tie and said, "Your Honor, I'm her Court of Last Resort," as he bustled toward the bench and apologized for his disruption and tardiness.

"Who's he?" Babs whispered to Lewis.

"The man who's written for countless pulp magazines and penned the Perry Mason stories and who also happens to be a formidable attorney—Erle Stanley Gardner."

Gardner took a seat on the other side of Babs. Lewis leaned over and asked, "What's this special *court* you're talking about?"

"Something I've been tossing around. Been thinking of teaming up with a few other lawyers and legal experts, and representing Chinese and Mexican migrants and those who never seem to get a fair shake. Prejudice can be a sharp needle, but I plan on stitching tough situations together."

Lewis turned to Gardner. "Babs just told me she's encountered Judge Dunwell before, and he's one of her neighbors. Maybe you can think of an angle where she can curry his favor."

Gardner asked Babs, "Honey, how do you know him?"

"One day, his dog got loose. I was out walking my Irish Wolfhound, Sir Henry. Yeah, I know. That's a funny name for a dog. It's short for Sir Henry of the Baskervilles. I named him after the Sherlock Holmes story. Well, he perked up his ears and sensed something was wrong. Took off like a rabbit and dragged me behind him."

"A giant dog like that probably weighs two-to-one compared to a tiny lady like you," Gardner said. "Tell me more."

"Sir Henry wouldn't stop until he found Judge Dunwell's Old English Sheepdog tangled—"

Gardner held up his hand. "Stop right there. I want you to tell that story to the judge." He approached the bench and said, "Your Honor, sorry for being late. I am Erle Stanley Gardner, co-counsel on the case, and I propose its dismissal without prejudice."

The judge raised his brow. "On what grounds?"

"Outside of an unauthorized raid on her house by the police, who found nothing but trinkets which she could've purchased secondhand, the defendant, Miss Barbara Ann Norman, known to most as Babs, tells me she's a former acquaintance of yours."

"How so?"

"Why don't we ask her to explain?" He motioned to Babs to stand by his side.

She rose, joined him, and the judge requested a statement.

"Sir… I'm sorry. Your Honor…" She tried to keep from trembling. "How can you forget the time when I…actually, my dog rescued yours from the spiky plants in Doris Dietz's backyard?"

"Hard to forget combing out all sorts of nasty things from Binkie's long fur. Those prickly pear spines buried themselves in my skin afterward. Hard as heck to find but hurt like the dickens. Not sure who felt it worse," said Judge Dunwell.

"If it weren't for my dog's remarkable search-and-rescue skills, which, by the way, helped rescue Asta from *The Thin Man* films, Toto from *The Wizard of Oz*, and a bunch of other celebrity dogs on a previous case—"

"Previous case?" asked the judge.

"I was a private investigator until my arrest. Then I lost my license. My dog can challenge the best K-9s at the Police Academy. He's proved it more than once."

"Odd for a female to get into private investigations. What prompted that choice?"

"I tried my luck with acting for a little while, but the real inspiration came when I solved my daddy's murder when I was a young girl, and no one dared to give me any credit."

Judge Dunwell scratched his chin as she explained the instance with his dog.

Gardner concluded, "Therefore, Your Honor, since the two of you have a history together, not only do I feel you can't be objective during this hearing, but I think she has proved that she's an upstanding citizen and—"

To the surprised look of the cops and Mrs. Dietz, Judge Dunwell banged his gavel on his desk. "Case dismissed!"

"On what grounds?" Officer Murphy asked.

"Breaking and entering and conducting a search without a warrant. Shame on you! None of your evidence is admissible in court. Your supervisor should take disciplinary action." Looking at his docket, he announced, "Next up. Rodriguez versus The Department of Sanitation." His voice lowered to a mumble. "Why do I always get the garbage cases?"

Lewis stuffed his notes inside his briefcase and told Babs to gather her belongings.

Gardner turned to Lewis. "You're going to owe me one after this is all over."

Chapter Thirty-Five

"Smells divine." Rudy took a deep whiff as a partygoer passed by with a platter of roasted bratwurst and tangy German potato salad. He took Guy by the hand and led him through the denser-than-normal Sunday afternoon crowd at Salka's salon.

"If you crave your native cuisine so much, I still can't understand why you won't let me take you to the *Risqué Café*," said Guy, trying to dodge someone toting more than they could carry. "I've always been curious to compare their cabaret review with the American ones."

Rudy ignored his remark and brought up a different topic. "I expect two important guests today."

Guy grabbed Rudy's shoulder so they wouldn't get separated. "Are you going to leave me guessing?"

"Greta Garbo will make one of her rare appearances."

This time, Guy gripped the fabric of Rudy's suit jacket, stopping Rudy in his tracks. "I thought she never came out in public."

"True, but she's contributed a significant amount to the film fund. Salka said that Garbo wanted to know how her money was being spent." Rudy peeled Guy's fingers from his blazer and pointed toward a staircase leading to the second floor, where he urged him to follow. "The second is Manfred Coblenz. Since Curtiz dismissed him, Salka has hired him to take over Sauer's bookkeeping."

"He couldn't be in a better position to siphon funds if that was his intention," Guy remarked. "For some time, Manfred has been on our list. It's interesting how he's always been one step ahead of us."

Rudy reprimanded Guy for making too much noise as they climbed the wooden staircase, covered with a thin layer of carpet.

After they made it to the landing, Rudy led him down a hall. "Where are we going?" Guy asked. "The party's downstairs and in the backyard."

Rudy interlaced his fingers with Guy's, something he would've never dared among Salka's guests. They heard footsteps.

"Quick!" Rudy said in a panicked whisper. He pointed to the nearest closet. "In here!"

They slipped inside, trying not to cause any noise. The forced proximity of their warm bodies, along with the scent of Rudy's aftershave, caused Guy's breathing to quicken. He shed his jacket, loosened his dampened collar, and dropped his suspenders. Leaning in, he seized the moment and stole a kiss.

With what little room they had, Rudy tried to pull back.

"Ever since you told me about your relationship with Sauer, you've withdrawn," Guy protested, "And yet, here you drag me upstairs…for what seemed to be an intimate moment. I'm confused."

"Ever since you married Babs—"

"Kiss me, Rudy." Guy raised the pitch of his voice to mimic Ingrid's. "Kiss me as if it were the last time."

Rudy pinched Guy's lips shut. Taking a chance since the hallway seemed quiet, he cracked open the door. "I think it's safe now." He smoothed Guy's hair back in place before leaving first.

That was quick, Guy thought, since nothing happened beyond a brief tease. He waited a minute, so as not to make it obvious they were in there together. *What had Rudy intended?*

Guy made his way downstairs, knowing the main cast from *Casablanca*, including the director and Paul Henreid, who up till now had been indifferent and uncooperative, had all come to Salka's party. Humphrey Bogart and Dooley Wilson were the only American-born among them. Having learned a few keyboard tips from Elliot Carpenter, who did most of the real piano playing on set, Dooley distracted the guests by plunking out a few simple tunes on Salka's piano.

* * *

Approaching the cast members individually, Guy spotted Bogie over by the self-serve bar.

"Was in the mood for a martini, but this place didn't seem to have any dry vermouth. Got creative." Bogie poured his homemade concoction into two glasses and offered one to Guy. "Try the Humphrey Humdinger!"

Hesitant to ask what poisons were in his glass, he cringed and forced down a sip. Bogie seemed unfazed, licked his lips, and made a satisfying, "*Ahhhh*," after gulping it down.

"I noticed you dragged Paul Henreid and our revered director into the game," said Guy, still trying not to grimace from that potent cocktail.

"I'll be glad when this is over," Bogie said. "It was bad enough when all of us on your…team of spies…got caught in the act by Curtiz. We made him swear to keep his trap shut and not rat us out to Warner or Wallis that we took over your job at Warner Brothers. In fact, we all threatened to quit the show if he didn't cooperate."

Guy asked, "Isn't the filming almost done?"

"It is, but our screenwriters still haven't come up with a story ending that will satisfy the top brass. Despite everything, Sydney and Peter, since they had time off, tried a few unconventional interrogation tactics. I've had to deal with the constraints of being on the set in most of the scheduled scenes."

"Bogie, remember the young man who helped Scheid in the sound department during the first few days, the one who got let go?"

"Yeah, what about him?"

"Rudy and I think we've pinpointed him as the prime suspect."

"I'd certainly have my daggers drawn if Curtiz made a spectacle of me."

"We would like to turn him over to the police. Flag me if you see him."

* * *

Rudy homed in on Conrad Veidt without making it obvious. "Welcome or not, you are like my shadow," Veidt said in German.

Rudy laughed and said, "But that's what they pay me to do." He remarked on how different Conrad looked, wearing a casual polo shirt and baggy trousers. "Out of uniform, I almost didn't recognize you. Are you teeing off later this afternoon? You look like you're ready for a game of golf."

"Why? Do you plan on standing in for that, too?"

Rudy had no time to waste. He gave Conrad a brief description of Coblenz, figuring if Conrad called for his attention by speaking in German, that might draw him out faster than anything else. Noticing Ingrid Bergman, Sydney Greenstreet, and Paul Henreid gathered at the buffet, Rudy excused himself and headed their way.

Ingrid, familiar with five languages, mentioned she had overheard a variety of tongues spoken the moment she arrived.

"I wonder if these people realize how lucky they are," said Paul. "A few years ago, a boat carrying almost one thousand refugees sailed from Europe to Havana. Authorities welcomed only the twenty-eight passengers who already had legitimate visas. The rest had to submit applications to enter the United States—"

"Because the Cuban government refused to admit them on grounds of antisemitism and accused them of being Communists, said Sydney. "I remember reading about that. Afterwards, the boat tried to dock in Florida but received a telegram from the State Department saying the asylum-seekers must wait their turn. Apparently, they had a long waiting list."

Ingrid weighed in. "Canada also rejected them. They ran low on food, and the sanitation on board became deplorable. Finally, the captain had no other choice but to sail back to Europe, where some faced dire consequences."

Rudy knew what it was like to feel unwanted. Rejected. Many of these émigrés were outspoken artists and writers who were being denied the freedom of speech and expression in Berlin or under the fascist Franco regime—something he could relate to, having escaped a similar type of persecution himself. Recently, he had heard from Leon Lewis that, as an alternative, many Jews escaping the Nazis in Western Europe were seeking refuge in Mexico. Could that be an option for Mr. Otake?

* * *

Peter Lorre slipped a letter-sized envelope into Guy's front jacket pocket.

"What's this?" Guy reached in to pull it out, but Peter stopped him and took a quick look in both directions.

"Shush! Don't tell anyone. These are your *letters of transit*. In your case, all-access studio passes for you and your lady partner. With Jack Warner's signature, no less. I went to great lengths to steal them." Peter cackled, "Except I didn't kill any couriers to get them."

* * *

Rudy volunteered to handle Michael Curtiz, who seemed to be less interested in sleuthing and more enthralled in flirting with the ladies.

"You're blocking my view," Curtiz said as he pushed Rudy aside. "I'm trying to find myself a Hungarian hot potato."

Unable to conjure a witty comeback, Rudy went straight to the point. He reminded Curtiz of the kid he fired in the sound department and told him to keep his eyes open.

* * *

Guy nearly collided with Claude Rains, who shielded the top of his glass. "Were you planning on covering my dry-cleaning bill?"

"If that were the case, Babs has a miracle worker in West Hollywood who's been known to be the Houdini of spots, blotches, or blemishes on any piece of fabric," Guy said, apologizing.

"I wonder if he could also remove any smears on one's reputation," Claude remarked.

"Glad I bumped into you, but not in this respect." Guy visually described the likes of Coblenz. "You wouldn't have been on the set that day, but we think he's our man. If anyone fits the bill, inform Bogie or Ingrid. We need to prevent his escape."

Claude tried to peer over Guy's shoulders. "Where's your attractive lady partner?"

Feeling guilty, Guy admitted he hadn't contacted Babs since her arrest. "Her place became a crime scene. I needed to stay clear since I had nothing to do with it."

"Arrest?" Claude's cigarette dropped from his mouth. "What else have I been missing out on?"

* * *

Guy worried whether a bunch of drunk actors would help or hinder their investigation. He snapped out of his thoughts only to become mesmerized by Greta Garbo. Dressed in loose, wide-legged trousers and a matching jacket, she flowed into the room as if stepping from a cloud. When he finally pushed his way past others, she surprised him by being the first to open their conversation.

Brushing her hair out of her eyes, she said, "No politics. No autographs. We're in a safe space, and don't ask me to help you find a job. In essence, I've retired from show business."

Guy felt like she had put him in his place. He desperately wanted to speak with her but was at a loss for words. What finally came out of his mouth sounded inappropriate and idiotic. "I'm not with the FBI."

Her response, almost condescending, as she made no effort to disguise her Swedish accent, "You don't look the type."

He asked why she had brought that up.

"They have files on everyone in the émigré community and assume if you're anti-Nazi, you must embrace the Communist agenda."

* * *

Feeling confident his team knew their objective, Rudy circulated around the party. Once again, he encountered Virginia Hill.

"I adore visiting Mexico City this time of year," she boasted to an interested male coterie.

Another admirer lit the cigarette she placed in her mouth. "It's a business arrangement, but believe me, I'm always one to take advantage of any festivities. So does Chick, my brother. He often accompanies me. I hate traveling alone. Besides, it's always advisable for a lady to have a male escort if she runs into trouble."

Some lady! Rudy thought she had the morals of a cheap whore but with mob money…and lots of it. Trying to eavesdrop, Rudy's brain chimed like the pinball machine he played at that hole-in-the-wall diner he went to with Guy after they saw the Charlie Chaplin film.

Ping! The last time he was here, against his better judgment, he consulted a Gypsy fortuneteller, but she wasn't a Gypsy. She was the *Filipino* woman from the Santa Monica Pier.

Boozy and brash, Virginia flung her arms in the air, clicking her fingers like castanets. She began stomping her feet, pretending to be a flamenco dancer, to a tune that she alone could hear. While she seduced her captive audience, Rudy tried to piece together these puzzling thoughts. The game going on in his head seemed to overshadow all else. *Ping!* Guy mentioned that one of his first cases as a private detective involved Gypsies. When it was all over, they paid him with *counterfeit cash.*

Cash! He needed cash. Rudy found Salka harvesting figs from a tree in her backyard. During a previous visit, he had hinted about borrowing money from the refugee film fund to help set up Mr. Otake at the Garden of Allah. She avoided the topic, giving him the impression he'd have to find other resources.

Lucky to catch her alone, he whispered, "Remember my friend, the Japanese gardener?"

"Of course. Did you find him a reliable alternative?"

"For now, but I've got to get him away from the coast and out of town. That'll take funding."

Salka tried to pass the buck. "I no longer concern myself with those money matters. My new accountant thinks I've been too lenient and will bankrupt our coffers."

Playing dumb, he asked, "Who might that be? Is he...or perhaps she...here this afternoon?"

Without mentioning his name, she said, "I gave him one of the spare rooms in my guesthouse. Instead of taking the day off to enjoy himself, he's probably going over the books and counting every penny." She excused herself and left Rudy contemplating his next move. He knew this accountant was Coblenz, and she just disclosed where to find him.

While Garbo captivated Guy's attention, the last people Rudy expected to run into were Billy Wilder and Birgit Müller, a towering Teutonic woman with short, cropped hair and at least six feet in stature. So tall and powerful. From the rear, in a packed crowd, she could've been mistaken for a man. They both knew the secrets of Rudy's past—too many secrets in too many places.

Birgit squinted, trying to recognize Rudy without her glasses, which she finally pulled out of her purse. Once she recognized him, the confrontation started. Rudy realized there was no getting out of this, but he could nail her for being his accomplice.

Wilder, not wanting to get in the middle of a Battle Royale, made up an excuse for a quick exit. With him out of the way, Rudy gripped Birgit's arm. "I know where *he's* staying, and don't ask me who." He herded her past the crowd and straight for Salka's guest house, smiling and acknowledging revelers along the way.

She protested at every step. "Maybe you should be abducting Billy. He was present at the Berlin nightclub. If he hadn't witnessed the incident firsthand, he was certainly aware of what was in the news afterward. If it weren't for me, you would've been shot after killing that Gestapo officer who harassed you and your queer playfellows."

Rudy snapped, "You're one to talk! Explain what you were doing in that club if you weren't left of center. My heart goes out to Levi Bernstein, or Leia, as he wished to be called in the cabarets that allowed him to doll himself up. Since childhood, I defended him every time a bully would taunt him for being different. Remember, it was you who helped me dump that bastard stormtrooper into the incinerator."

"True, but his gun belt got caught, forcing us to undress him. He smelled as if he hadn't bathed in over a week. Instead of disposing of his Gestapo uniform, you escaped by wearing it yourself. You'd blend right in and wouldn't look suspicious. You hoped, because you were so much taller, that no one noticed your sleeves and pants were too short!"

Rudy tried the back entrance to the guesthouse. "We're in luck. It's unlocked." He slipped inside, dragging her with him.

They started on the ground floor, listening for signs of occupancy. Off to the side of the kitchen was a small communal dining room, along with shared bathrooms on each floor. They noticed modest-sized bedrooms, both upstairs and down, almost like a dormitory. Then they tiptoed upstairs, where they overheard a male voice on the telephone.

"John Reilly, please," the man told the operator. "Yes, I know the INS reps are off on Sunday, but he said today would be an exception. Please switch me over to him."

Mouthing the word "*Coblenz*" without making a sound, Rudy held up his hand, signaling to Birgit they should wait to determine what the conversation was about before making their surprise entry.

Gesturing with a nod, Rudy entered first. Birgit followed, shutting the door and using her body to block anyone from coming in or out. Both noticed Manfred Coblenz's desk piled with paperwork and ledgers, along with neat stacks of American cash and an open leather briefcase.

"Do you plan on depositing those in the film fund account or plan on pocketing everything for yourself?" Rudy asked, interrupting.

Coblenz halted mid-sentence. "Got an emergency. Will call you back."

Their further conversations transpired in German. Rudy confronted him. "Did you think you'd get away with killing my lover?"

"I think you've got it wrong," Coblenz replied.

"You were the one who first pulled the knife," Rudy uttered through gritted teeth. "I was unarmed."

"Such a poor memory, *mein Freund*. Perhaps your spy pal caught me intruding on him. When I pulled out a pocketknife to defend myself, it was *you* who tried to wrestle it out of my hand. *You* shoved it into his neck and dealt the fatal blow."

"Only after you'd already stabbed Gerhard several times! I tried to stop you. I didn't mean to kill anyone. It was an accident."

"If you take me to the police, you'll have to confess your involvement. The American courts won't sympathize with a couple of ex-pat Krauts. Wouldn't be much different from Auschwitz. Here, we'll both go to the gas chamber for murder, and you know it."

Rudy vaulted over his desk, scattering pens, papers, and piles of cash onto the floor. The two grappled. Rudy dug his nails into his enemy's face. Birgit blocked the only viable exit other than leaping from the second-floor window.

Coblenz lost his footing, and they crashed to the floor. Having the advantage of being on top, Rudy grabbed a hunk of Coblenz's hair and slammed his head continuously against the unforgiving mahogany desk. Stunned and unable to fight back, Rudy delivered a final blow to his bloodied face and knocked him out. Birgit checked but couldn't tell whether he was breathing.

Sensing no movement from his adversary, Rudy said, "I never meant to hurt anyone, especially Gerry, but I couldn't have Coblenz blow the whistle on me."

The loose cash rustled like dried leaves from a breeze blowing from the open window. "Help yourself," Rudy said.

Birgit scooped a pile of cash into her purse, barely clasping it shut without a bill or two poking out. He grabbed just enough not to draw attention to his bulging pockets.

Avoiding the party, they exited behind the guesthouse, crawled under a hedge, and escaped through a neighbor's yard.

"Did you drive?" he asked.

"Came with a friend."

Rudy insisted she mount his motorcycle, which he had parked on the street. He handed her the spare helmet, and they sped off together.

He roared out of the posh Santa Monica beachside community, avoiding the scenic route by the ocean, and using back roads toward Hollywood.

He finally killed the motor in front of Birgit's apartment complex, set off from the street by a gate with twelve tiny off-white stucco bungalows with a colorful Spanish-tiled walkway in between.

Birgit straightened her dress and handed Rudy back his helmet. "How did you know where I live?"

"I keep tabs on any Berliner in Los Angeles who might've been a witness."

"Billy, too? We're thousands of miles away in another country."

"Those capable of having anything over me. I'm surprised you weren't worried. After all, you were my accomplice."

"More than once, and not by choice. Why do I seem to be fated to wind up with you in nightclubs or at parties, only to drag away bodies? First, it was after you killed the Gestapo officer in Berlin. Then at the *Risqué Café*, here in Hollywood, helping you transport Sauer to a Warner Brothers soundstage to make it look like somebody killed him there."

"It was your idea to carve a swastika on his neck. I'm sure you had your fingerprints all over him."

Her look was stern and serious. "Aren't you forgetting now we have another problem?"

Rudy sat silent for a moment. "You're right. It's July, and Coblenz's body won't take long to decompose. Other tenants might occupy Salka's guesthouse. We had no way of knowing, because they could've been at the party. Sooner or later, someone will discover the corpse."

Several twenty-dollar bills fell out of Birgit's pocketbook as she tried to find her keys. She ducked down and retrieved them. "Are you saying we have to go back there to get rid of it?"

"We'll do it tomorrow."

"*We?* I work on Mondays translating German documents into English for—I'd rather not say unless you've spied on me and already know."

"Call in sick. It'll go a lot quicker if I don't have to drag a body by myself."

"Just like last time," she lashed out.

"Besides, you have a car, and I don't. You can't expect me to ride through Los Angeles with a corpse strapped to my motorcycle! We're in this together."

* * *

While the *Casablanca* team mingled throughout the party, Guy broke the spell Garbo had cast upon him but couldn't figure out where Rudy had gone. Patting down his pockets and realizing he was out of cigarettes, Guy noticed Bogie, who'd always have a spare, hanging out with Dooley Wilson, who was still entertaining guests by singing and trying to play the piano.

He approached Bogie and asked for a smoke. "You haven't seen Rudy by any chance?"

Bogie shook his head. "Come to think of it, I haven't noticed him for a while. Hope you don't suspect he found another boyfriend and is cheating on you already."

Guy didn't know what to make of that remark. Getting anxious with every passing second, he made a quick surveillance of the main house and the backyard. Finally, he headed to where he thought Rudy had parked his motorcycle, but noticed it was gone. Confused about why he had left him stranded, Guy went back inside and asked around for a ride home.

When Bogie volunteered, he was surprised to hear that Guy wanted to be dropped off at the Garden of Allah. "You're staying with Hammett? How do either of you get any work done?"

"I felt guilty about abandoning Babs, but the police raid at her house had me worried. So, I gathered the animals and fled over to the Garden of Allah, seeking his help. Rather than getting a short-term rental, he insisted I stay with him since I was unemployed."

"Right! Big Jack fired you—both of you."

What Guy couldn't admit was that Dash felt it was unwise to share the same digs as Mr. Otake. None of the cast members were supposed to know he and Rudy conspired with Hammett to hide Otake at the Garden of Allah until they found a better alternative.

"When the issue arose about how he'd get any of his writing done, he told me he'd camp out at the studio, but I don't know for how much longer," said Guy, setting the record straight. "All I do here is steal his Lucky Strikes. I stay clear of his hooch."

"What are you doing now?" Bogie asked.

"Looking for work *is* work."

"Aren't you supposed to be a married man? If you're trying to fool your father…or anyone else, for that matter, it doesn't look too convincing if others know you're living in separate quarters."

He shrugged and thanked Bogie for the ride. The hotel manager had left a note with Guy's name on it and tacked it on Hammett's front door. It said, "Call me, Leon Lewis." He threw his jacket over the back of a chair, made himself a cup of black coffee, and took a few sips to get sober before picking up the phone.

Still a bit buzzed from the party and stunned by Rudy's disappearance, he skipped formalities. "Heya. It's Guy. What's going on?"

"Erle Stanley Gardner and I sprang your partner from jail."

"I wondered where Rudy had disappeared to."

"Always thought your partner was Babs."

Guy kept silent.

"Well, anyway, Gardner and I got her off on a technicality. She's back in the house since it's no longer a crime scene. I'd suggest you move back in. For moral support, if anything."

"I was actually starting to get comfortable over here," Guy joked, but in the back of his mind, he still wondered why Rudy hadn't taken advantage of an opportunity where they'd have privacy together.

"Consider your host," said Lewis. "Eventually, someone's going to catch Hammett drinking on the job. Heard he's got a big problem with that."

Lewis explained that late Friday afternoon, after the judge dismissed Babs' case, he and his wife invited her over for Shabbos dinner and to relax at their place over the weekend. "It's safe to say the coast is clear of any cops making any more surprise entries. Why don't you return with the pets and give her a proper homecoming?"

Not up for many more words, Guy thanked him for the quick rundown. He dumped his coffee in the sink, slipped off his tie, and passed out on the bed with his clothes on.

Chapter Thirty-Six

Long before Guy left the party, Rudy dropped off Birgit and went straight to the Garden of Allah. Having his own set of keys, he barged in on Mr. Otake.

"You're coming with me," he said, taking him by the arm and heading for the door.

Otake protested and wanted to gather his belongings. "What about Mr. Hammett? He will miss me."

"Worry about him later. You…you must leave everything," Rudy barked. Realizing he needed to make sure nobody recognized Otake as being Japanese, he looked around for an expedient disguise. Taking two *furoshikis*, or a traditional Japanese scarf-like cloth used to wrap gifts and carry packages, he tied them around his face and head like a bandit from a Western film and placed his driving goggles over his eyes.

"You remind me of Claude Rains from *The Invisible* Man. Between that and the helmet, no one will recognize you."

Otake remained unconvinced. "Don't you think I'd attract more attention like this?"

Rudy laughed. "This is Hollywood. Anything goes."

* * *

He parked his motorcycle in front of a cheap hooker hotel east of Vine, plunked down some of the cash he pocketed from Coblenz, and busied the front desk clerk long enough to smuggle Otake upstairs.

Rudy locked the door and removed Otake's disguise.

"Who's the Invisible Man?" Otake asked.

Rudy figured there hadn't been a version in the theaters with Japanese subtitles.

Otake examined his strange surroundings. "What about clothes?"

"Wear what you have for now. I'm more worried you have something to eat. Hope you like American food." Before Rudy left, he hung a Do Not Disturb sign on his door and instructed Otake to open it for no one.

Rudy sped through town seeking a Salvation Army. After two attempts, he realized it was Sunday, and stores would be closed. Heading downtown, he found a charity shop open in Chinatown and purchased small-sized Western-style business attire, a pair of eyeglasses with weak lenses, and a pair of scissors. When he returned, he ordered Mr. Otake to sit down on a chair and began cutting his hair. Otake popped to his feet, angry and alarmed.

Simplifying his words, Rudy explained, "We need to make you into a new man." After he finished, he showed how to slick it back. He perched the eyeglasses on the end of Otake's nose and gave him a few coaching lessons.

"Think of it like being cast in a film. You need to convince others of your new character," Rudy explained, recalling the fortuneteller who had posed as a Gypsy.

Puzzle pieces came together. "Imagine you are no longer Japanese. Now, you are Filipino. Your new name is Mr. Alon Flores. Better get used to it. Your last name translates to flowers, since you used to be a gardener—or still are, but not according to anyone else."

Otake looked at him, confused.

"For short, people will call you Mr. Alon or just Alon. It's not that far off from your real name—Aoi. Others might think you are Mexican or even Chinese. Perhaps you should further disguise your face by wearing a hat."

"Then what?"

Ping! Virginia Hill made frequent trips south of the border. These thoughts, which came out of nowhere, suddenly connected. "You'll be going to Mexico." Rudy tried to give him the impression he had planned everything down to the letter, but, in fact, he had no clue how he was going to pull this off. The ideas came to him as he spoke.

The poor old man looked tormented and demoralized. "Will you accompany me?"

"Still working it out, Mr. Alon." That was the best Rudy could tell him. He needed another one of those brilliant *pings*, a flash of insight, and a viable solution.

Rudy rode home and brooded over what had transpired in the past twenty-four hours. He counted the remaining cash he took from Coblenz, realizing it would never be enough to put Mr. Otake on a train and get him secured out of the country. Someone else would have to accompany him. The man hardly spoke English, much less Spanish, and if anyone challenged him to speak Tagalog, a Filipino's native tongue, he'd blow his cover.

Virginia Hill! He remembered overhearing her say she made frequent trips to Mexico, but why? She seemed untouchable, and she had the money so desperately needed to ensure Otake's well-being. Nobody wanted to mess with the mob if they valued their life, but under her protection, *Alon Flores* could be as immune to the law as she.

Rudy poured himself a whiskey. He realized this was a tall order to ask.

* * *

In case someone followed, Rudy took precautions and parked his motorcycle three blocks away from Birgit's. She waited for him in her black Bantam coupe.

"After Berlin, I had hoped never to run into you again," she said bitterly.

"Let's hope you won't ever have to after today."

"Have you figured out a plan to remove the body without being caught?" she asked as he hopped into the passenger seat.

She was full of questions. Rudy had been so preoccupied making sure Mr. Otake was out of harm's way that he hadn't had time to make proper plans. He'd think up the answers on the spur of the moment. When they arrived at Salka's, Rudy noticed the door to her front wooden gate was locked.

He jiggled it to see if the latch had rusted shut. "For as long as I've known her, she's always kept it open."

He boosted Birgit over the fence and climbed after her.

"What now?" she asked.

Peering through the ground-floor windows of the main house, they noticed sheets covering the furniture. "Nobody goes to that much trouble unless they expect to be gone a long time," she said.

Rudy suggested they should check the mailbox. "Maybe she left a note for the postman, so her mail won't pile up and alert thieves."

The note they found revealed little, except it instructed the postal carrier to leave her letters and packages with her next-door neighbor. When they knocked on the woman's door, she explained, "You say you know her well? Then you're aware that her husband spends most of his time in either New York or London. She flew to New York, where she booked passage on an ocean-bound vessel to London. If you ask my opinion, I'd say that was a daring move, considering all the threats from German U-boats."

"Are you sure?" Birgit asked.

The neighbor folded her arms across her chest. "As sure as the day is long."

Rudy and Birgit thanked the neighbor and headed back to the Viertel's house. "Maybe Salka discovered the body and didn't want authorities to think she did it," said Birgit. "Americans despise us. They'd be glad to see a few Germans deported." The tension was so high, Rudy tasted it.

He wouldn't let the obvious signs of Salka's absence deter them. "She always had several temporary tenants. This isn't Berlin. Over here, people aren't used to packing up and evacuating overnight." He warned her to keep a low profile.

Determining that all the windows were closed and the doors locked on the main house, they made their way to the guest house.

Birgit noted, "There aren't any cars in the driveway."

"I doubt if any of her tenants owns one," said Rudy. "If they did, they'd be out hustling for work."

Someone had drawn the blinds and secured the doors at the guesthouse.

"Looks abandoned," she remarked.

Rudy jimmied the front door open. He motioned for her to follow, but she stopped short.

"Where do you expect to bury the body?"

He put his finger to his lips. "Assume people might be listening."

They sprinted to the second floor to Coblenz's room, but when they opened the door, they noticed his body was no longer there. Both gave each other a look of horror and dashed back to her car.

Chapter Thirty-Seven

Everything turned into one big shuffle. Guy woke with a hangover and realized he hadn't checked on Mr. Otake since before he had left for the party. That was when he discovered the man had disappeared from his bungalow. He wasn't sure if he had snuck out and was tired of feeling like he was a prisoner, whether the immigration authorities got wise to their cat-and-mouse antics, or whether he had lost hope and turned himself in.

Following Lewis's advice, Guy left a message at the studio for Hammett that he was vacating the premises. Then he gathered the critters and moved back in with Babs. With the legal matters over and their PI licenses reinstated, both were eager to head back to the office and drum up new business since Jack Warner had terminated their contract.

Hammett phoned while they were trying to get the office back in order. Guy, acting as Babs' receptionist, picked up.

"Seems like this is a day for memos," Hammett said. "First, I get yours. Then some juvenile delinquent dropped off a message from your boyfriend."

"Rudy?" Guy asked.

"Yeah, but his delivery guy looked more like a barfly who'd been loitering on the street looking for spare change. Said that a tall German fella handed him round-trip bus fare and a buck to take it to my place, unaware you had already moved out. Figured if you weren't stopping by soon, maybe I could catch you at the office. Doesn't say a lot, but if you're okay with it not being private, I could read it over the phone."

Guy shooed Babs away from his desk and insisted she go into her office.

"The letter says, 'Mr. Otake is safe for now. Will approach Virginia Hill. Don't worry about me.'"

"That's all?" Guy caught Babs peeking under the privacy shades. He motioned for her to go away.

"Sorry. There's nothing more conclusive, but what's this about working with Siegel's gal? If your pal plans on hanging with his circle, maybe it's best he gives you the slip."

Seems like he's done that already, Guy thought. "Tell me. What do you know about the dame?"

Hammett laughed. "So, now you're talking tough like one of my private investigator characters? Should name him Guy Brandt—branded for life. How's that sound? Well, you know I don't play the Pinkerton detective game anymore, but for what it's worth, the word on the street is Hill's got the underworld wrapped up in a neat little package in Chicago, New York, New Jersey, and of course, Los Angeles, sometimes playing them against each other. One could consider her the mob's Mata Hari. How 'bout I model a character after her and have her be your nemesis? That might be just the inspiration I need to get productive and start some serious writing again."

Guy thanked him for the tips and for relaying Rudy's letter. After he hung up, he went to the file cabinets he kept on local celebrities. Pulling out a folder, he laid it on his desk.

"Between us, there are to be no secrets," Babs said, miffed, because she couldn't listen in on their conversation. She grabbed his folder to find out for herself. "Virginia Hill! I thought those files only contained stuff about those in the film world."

"I also keep clippings of anyone newsworthy. Anything to do with Bugsy Siegel, despite his failed attempts to get into the pictures, I consider relevant, but Hammett filled me in with a few tidbits that never made it in print."

Babs lost her composure. "I know Hill well enough to realize she spells trouble." Memories became front and center. Despite being rude and stand-offish to Babs at Ciro's during their *Maltese Falcon* case, it was hard not to separate her from her notorious boyfriend.

"Hill was a force to be reckoned with in the Chicago and East Coast mobs long before she aligned with the Bug," Guy explained. "Since she was a woman without a prior rap sheet, she started out as a carrier for a racketeer, Joe Epstein, in Chicago. Not to be confused with the twin screenwriters of *Casablanca*."

"Then who's this Joe fella?"

"He's got his eye on every dime that passes through the Capone syndicate. Joe Epstein's primary racket involved bookies, sports gambling, and running the wire services. But he needed to pay his winners and launder the profits without raising eyebrows. Remember, the Feds did everything they could to put Capone behind bars. They nailed him for tax evasion. He and his guys needed to guarantee that wouldn't happen again, so they developed ways where they could turn illegal profits and declare the money as legitimate income."

"How?" Babs asked, tapping her toes nervously on their linoleum floor.

"Investing in hotels…restaurants…nightclubs. For a while, Epstein had sent Miss Hill packages with cash or stolen jewelry. Together with her brother, Chick, she established business connections with the rich and powerful south of the border. By the time she made her mark in Hollywood, she concocted a story that she was an oil heiress with a tie-in to royalty."

Babs was skeptical. "Where's that article from? Stolen FBI files?"

Guy shook his head.

"Or was that another tidbit you got from being buddies with Hammett? Perhaps the special agents I dealt with were fans of his stories published in *Black Mask*, and they divulged classified information because they were star-struck."

"Don't be silly, Babs. Every member of gangland, whether friends or foes, puts up a false front. Jack Dragna, a kingpin in the LA mob, insisted to federal authorities he was a banana importer. Siegel claimed he had come to LA to be a movie star."

"So, that's why he wanted a screen test."

"Johnny Roselli, another one of those crooks, pretended to be a movie producer, but he was really trying to rub out Mickey Cohen."

"Who has cleverly set up a rival bookmaking operation behind a men's clothing store close to our office!" The phone rang again. "Let's hope this is a new client."

Guy picked up and exclaimed, "Hallelujah! At last, we've got the chance to get rid of the parrots! They'll be out of our office and our house and won't bother anyone."

Babs asked him how.

"That was an animal handler from the studio. They're finally shooting the scenes at the Blue Parrot Café. It's our lucky day. The ones he had flew away!"

* * *

Production on *Casablanca* moved to the Blue Parrot, also using refurbished scenery from *The Desert Song*. Guy contributed his share by donating his blue hyacinth macaws.

"We tried substituting a red one since the movie is being filmed in black-and-white," explained the handler, "but he made too much noise, infuriating the soundman. A screen test also showed a variance in the gray tones, and other markings made it obvious to experts this bird wasn't from one of the blue species."

Between those dressed as Moroccans, Vichy French, German military, and refugees from all over Europe, the stage was, once again, full of extras. Curtiz wanted more material to intercut with previously shot footage. He started out staging establishing shots of the Black Market and moved in for close-ups with traders dressed in native dress. The camera moved along a row of stalls toward a seedy-looking building with Guy and Babs' parrots perched outside. A faded sign over the entrance indicated the Blue Parrot Café.

Bogie emerged from his dressing room, surprised to find the detectives. Before anyone said a word, he put a finger to his lips and pointed to his wife, sleeping off a bender but far away from the camera. "It's always best not to disturb Sleeping Beauty…but I thought you weren't on the payroll any longer. Conrad's off today, but come to think of it, I haven't seen the likes of Rudy for several days now."

Interrupting their banter, Petunia cawed, "I'm shocked! I'm shocked!" Pedro finished her dialogue saying, "Gambling! Gambling here!"

"How did they know to say that?" Babs asked. "They weren't even on the set when you filmed that."

Bogie doubled over laughing. "I'm just as surprised as you are. Perhaps they overheard a crew member repeating it, especially since we've done a bit of gambling over my chess games. Hoped they paid you handsomely for giving up the bird…or giving them the bird…or in this case, the two birds."

"They were such a nuisance," Guy replied. "I was glad to donate them."

"You gave them away for free?" Babs was so furious that she stomped her foot and broke her heel. "We've been out of work!"

"Would you have wanted to risk eviction from our office, or another spat with Mrs. Dietz?"

"Guy, we need the money!"

The assistant director cut their argument short and yelled, "Quiet on the set! Roll sound."

Chapter Thirty-Eight

Rudy needed to align himself with Virginia Hill if his game plan with Otake was going to succeed. Using former connections from when he worked undercover for Leon Lewis, he persuaded a local print shop to allow him to operate one of their little-used presses. He'd learned as a teen when he worked for the Marxist bookseller, Herr Gutfreund in Berlin, how to create faked documents. Resurrecting those skills, he created a birth certificate and a Canadian passport under the name of Alon Flores.

On one of his trips to bring Mr. Otake his necessities, he caught him in the middle of hemming the pants from his new thrift shop wardrobe. Rudy asked him to put his work aside. He had the forged documents and was eager to show him his handiwork.

"Your father was Filipino," he explained. "After being offered a job in Vancouver, he married a mixed-race woman who was part-Chinese and partially from an indigenous Pacific Northwestern tribe, and you were their only child. While your mother was pregnant, he died suddenly, and she became widowed early on. Forced to find employment, she worked as a maid in the brothel where you were born. I conceived a complicated-enough lineage that no one would dare ask questions. Especially about the brothel. Owners of such places shut them down and move elsewhere all the time."

Rudy went into detail about his new identity. "Your mother only spoke English, and you were too young to learn Tagalog, the Filipino national language, when your father died."

"What about Spanish?"

"You'll also be mute but not deaf."

Still confused, Otake asked, "What's that?"

"Someone who can't speak, but that doesn't mean he can't hear what others say. You'll take your instructions from Miss Hill. That's what you'll call her. Never by Virginia. It'll be disrespectful if you call her by her first name."

Otake interrupted, "But you said I can't speak in public."

"Correct. You can only whisper in private, where you're sure no one is listening. She'll be employing you as her personal servant."

Otake said he yearned for a cup of tea. All Rudy had left him were a few bottles of warm Coca-Cola but forgot to leave him ice. Drinking it anyway, he stuck out his tongue and forced it down. "What'll I do for money?"

"I'll make sure Miss Hill gets you settled," said Rudy. "It's not like we're abandoning you. After all, I survived many hardships after leaving Berlin. You might have to break your moral code and learn to steal. Everyone else does. Think of it this way. Mexico isn't so bad. It's become home to many who fled Franco when he won the Spanish Civil War."

Otake crossed his arms over his chest and stood his ground. "No stealing. Japanese consider that very dishonorable."

The *pings* Rudy kept hearing the other day finally made sense. Perhaps he could get permission to use the printing press again and craft enough *counterfeit cash.* He'd keep it a secret the money wasn't real.

"Those exiles already speak Spanish," Otake argued. "I only know a phrase or two."

"If you learned English after only knowing Japanese, Spanish should be easier."

Otake had all sorts of worries. "Before everything shut down, I listened to Japanese radio and read our newspapers. I don't like the idea of trusting a woman, especially one with a criminal reputation. In my culture, men are in charge and make the major family decisions."

Rudy kneaded his fingers into the creases of his forehead. On every issue, Otake voiced opposition. "Consider her your new family. More like your mother rather than your employer," he warned him, "and a child is supposed to always obey his parents."

"If Miss Hill returns to the United States, nobody stays with me?"

"It will take a miracle to get you out of California, and the anti-Japanese American agents have outlawed miracles."

Rudy felt the pressure of always needing to have an answer. This time, he didn't have one.

* * *

Next, he needed to contact Virginia. Salka would've had her number, but she'd left to reunite with her husband, or so her neighbor said. Despite wanting to avoid further contact with Birgit Müller, especially since they never resolved what happened to Coblenz's body, she knew which bar was Chick Hill's favorite hangout. Rudy bought him a few drinks, and Chick gave Rudy his sister's number.

Reserved for a variety of reasons, Virginia insisted on meeting Otake. Rudy feared it was too dangerous. "We could all risk getting in trouble. As it stands, I won't permit him to leave his place on his own."

As much as she prodded him, Rudy refused to disclose where he had hidden him.

"I can tell you right now, if I'm affiliated with anything to do with your friend, Benny will want to have his say."

Meeting at her house was out of the question, so they tried to agree on a neutral location. "Benny's got a front in Boyle Heights, where middle-class and lower-income Jews still live," she said. "The cops figure anyone with money has already left the area and has gone to Hollywood or Beverly Hills.

"The place where we're to meet has a mishmash of signs, so confusing that it throws off the curious. On the one hand, it says it sells life insurance. *Ha! Ha!* You betcha it does, but not by one's normal definition. It also advertises Mexican immigration services and accounting for small businesses."

"I don't get it," Rudy confessed. "Why all the options?"

"It's a bookie joint—bookkeeping—get it? The Mexican deal is that a lot of immigrants reside in the neighborhood. During the Depression, many people knew others that the government forcibly repatriated or deported, even if they had never lived in Mexico."

"What if someone requests legitimate help?" Rudy asked.

"We tell them the person they need to talk to is out of the country, and we're not sure when or if he'll return. Then we apologize and say we forgot to remove the sign."

"Are you telling me the life insurance bit is—?"

"If they value their lives, they'd *¡vámonos!* in a hurry."

True to its description, the place looked like a jack-of-all-trades rundown storefront. Benny's guys had installed a secret door, which led to a smoky back room, reminding Rudy of a bare-bones speakeasy during Prohibition. A couch and upholstered chairs circled a coffee table. Behind those were a few card tables, and beyond the gambling area, they had a bank of five phones where the bookies received their bets. With no windows, they had several electric fans running.

Siegel had used too much of his pungent men's cologne, so Rudy was glad someone had cracked open the back door to a private alleyway to air the place out. The Bug had dressed in a starched black shirt with a gold tie pin and had his cream-colored pinstriped gabardine jacket draped over the back of his chair.

Pointing at Rudy, he ordered two of his thugs to pat him down. Once they cleared him for concealed weapons, Rudy introduced himself and pleaded his case.

"You've explained the benefits for your Oriental friend, but what's in it for me?" Siegel asked while shuffling a stiff deck of brand-new cards. "Are you offering us your services if the situation gets too hot?"

Tit for tat. He worried his silence meant yes, but to what?

After Virginia felt satisfied she could trust Rudy, she disclosed her plans. "I'm due to make my next run to Mexico City on July 27th. My brother won't be going. Therefore, it would be helpful if I had a valet or an attendant.

"Have Otake…I mean, Alon Flores, meet me at Union Station. Check which track has the 10:30 a.m. train bound for San Diego. Don't know it off the top of my head, but Benny will send one of his boys over ahead of time to give you my seat number.

"From the station in San Diego, we'll taxi to the harbor and take a boat along the coastline of Baja. Then we'll hop aboard another vessel at Cabo heading to Puerto Vallarta. From there, I'll hire a driver to take us to the inland capital. No one will follow us. My driver will carry a firearm."

Rudy returned to Otake's hotel hideout and relayed the rest of the story. "Hill's associates in Mexico City own a hotel. When she arrives, she'll be in a luxury suite. You'll stay in the hotel's servants' quarters. Her business partners will provide you with a temporary job and lodging until you get settled elsewhere." He handed Otake a small duffel and explained his personal items had to be kept at a minimum, and even less than what he had now.

The day arrived when Rudy transported the newly transformed Alon Flores to Union Station. The men sprinted to the train when they announced the track with only minutes to spare.

"Where's Miss Hill?" Flores whispered, concerned someone might've been watching them when he had to assume his new role as a mute. "Aren't I supposed to be carrying her luggage?"

"Shush! No one is to see you speaking!" Rudy looked at the station's clock. "She probably found a porter and boarded early. Worry about yourself."

Rudy saw him to the train car entrance. Flores boarded the first step but got the eleventh-hour jitters and refused to go any farther. "Maybe this is not a good idea," he said.

Rudy felt like Sam when Rick Blaine didn't want to board the last train from Paris, and he wanted to believe Ilsa was still on her way. Against his better judgment, he shoved Flores up the stairs and climbed on board with him, ensuring he wouldn't escape.

Suddenly, he remembered the *Death Card* when the *Filipino* fortune teller did his reading. She insisted, "You not die. Nobody dies, but there's no going back." He hated digging himself into a hole he couldn't get out of, but it seemed he had no other choice.

Chapter Thirty-Nine

The final farewell scenes of *Casablanca* required only a minimal cast. Being the last day, save for a few pickup shots with a skeleton crew at later dates, Warner and Wallis showed up to give everyone a proper sendoff. Everyone was glad the film would soon be over.

Ingrid swung over toward Bogie and his wife Mayo, who clung to him like a bear cub to its mama. Almost to the point of being spiteful and sarcastic, she said, "Can you believe me now when I said I never had an affair with your husband?"

Afterward, she whispered to Henreid, "Even if I had wanted to, how could I? She patrolled the set every day like a prison guard. I'm so glad I no longer need to worry about being a target."

Then she gathered her fellow actors. Once she got their attention, she shouted, "My agent just called. The first actress didn't work out. I landed the role of Maria in *For Whom the Bell Tolls!*"

Everyone gave her a round of applause, but Warner's excitement dimmed when he spotted Babs and Guy in the crowd. "What are they doing here?"

Ingrid lied to cover up for Lorre. "I got them studio passes and invited them."

Peter overheard and gave her a wink of acknowledgement.

The detectives decided it was best to distance themselves from the producers and checked out the new set. The film crew had previously filmed the plane takeoff and landing scenes at the Metropolitan Airport. This time, the art department transformed an empty soundstage into an airplane hangar. Instead of using a real plane, they built a scaled-down version using plywood because of wood shortages.

The director of photography planned on positioning his camera and the actors using a technique called *forced perspective*. The casting department found midgets to play airplane mechanics to make the visual illusion of size and distance even more believable.

"What's with the fog?" Guy asked a technician who prepared the effect. "Casablanca is in the desert."

He explained the fog would help conceal any glitches that might betray the plane's hasty construction.

First up, Curtiz shot the scenes showing the plane, the hangar, and the ones featuring Bogie, Henreid, Bergman, and Rains. Everything before the part when Captain Renault calls Strasser and reports that Ilsa and Laszlo are trying to escape.

The assistant director announced, "We'll do Conrad's scenes after lunch."

Curtiz was eager to restart, but his assistant informed him that one actor was missing. "Sir, Rudy Schmitz hasn't reported in yet."

"Why do we need a stuntman today?"

"In the scene when Major Strasser gets shot," his assistant explained. "It's too risky to use Conrad if something goes wrong. Plus, it's in his contract."

Guy, who'd been looking forward to seeing his friend, was at his wits' end. He didn't want to say anything, but he was sure something had detained Rudy while he was trying to help Mr. Otake escape.

Curtiz despised delays. Instead of throwing his typical tantrum, he excused himself for a smoke. "Call casting and replace him. If he slept late, that's his problem. Not mine. I can't wait any longer."

"If he's only stuck in traffic, it'll take longer to go through casting." His assistant tried to reason with him. "Then we've obligated ourselves to pay two actors."

"Why don't we find someone on set as a substitute?" Curtiz asked. "Even if we borrow a stagehand. They're already on the payroll."

"I'm sure that's a union or contractual violation."

"I don't care," Curtiz yammered. "Get on it!"

The director returned to the staging area, gave a quick glance, and shook his head. "No one is tall enough." Upon closer examination, he focused on one of the Vichy gendarmes. "Maybe him. He could work. When Strasser gets shot, he…what you say in English? Crumples…and falls to the ground."

Pointing at him, he said, "You! Go to wardrobe! Today, you'll double for Conrad. His stuntman probably had too much fun with the ladies."

"More like the boys," Guy said with sarcasm, jealous at the thought his boyfriend betrayed him.

* * *

After Curtiz filmed the scene and approved the final take, a messenger arrived on a bicycle.

He looked around and announced, "I have a package addressed to Guy Brandt." The assistant director handed Guy a pen, and he signed for it.

The young man explained, "I tried to deliver it to your office, but your janitor said you were at the studio." Guy tipped him, and he sped off.

Babs insisted on taking a closer look. "It's from Mexico. I wonder if it's from Mr. Otake."

They ducked inside the airplane hangar to find a flat surface. Taking special care, since he didn't know its contents, Guy said, "I feel like Sam Spade unwrapping the delivery by Captain Jacoby, but this isn't heavy enough to be the Maltese Falcon."

Removing the outer layer of the parcel, he discovered two neat little packages—one large and flat, bearing his name. Babs' name was on the bulkier, smaller one. She found a jewelry box inside hers, which said, "Return to Ingrid." Babs opened it and exclaimed, "Her grandmother's earrings!"

Inside was a more detailed note: *Virginia stole Ingrid's earrings the day she, Siegel, and George Raft crashed the set. She was going to fence them in Mexico for cash but got arrested.*

For safekeeping, Guy put the box with the earrings in his pocket. "If I forget, remind me later to give these to Ingrid," he said to Babs, who urged him to open his package. Inside, he discovered a letter from Rudy and read it out loud.

"Guy, I guess this is my goodbye letter, but with good reason. I had never intended to become a stowaway on the train from Los Angeles or on the two boats afterward…"

"Stowaway?" Babs couldn't believe her ears. "Go on."

He cleared his throat. "When we traveled by train from Union Station, I hid in the luggage car. It was hot and cramped and noisy, and it smelled like hay and manure, because I had to share the car with two horses. Considering the money Virginia always bragged about, the three of us hopped a mail boat to get to Cabo. The fishing boat to Puerto Vallarta wasn't much better. Virginia looked conspicuous wearing a mink coat and gaudy jewelry."

Babs tried to snatch the letter out of his hands. Risking having it torn in half, Guy stepped aside and continued reading but guarded it close to his chest. "Once we reached land, we rode with her hired chauffeur, as she called him, but he was more like a toothless villager who needed a handout but had wheels. For all I know, he stole the vehicle, but at that point, no one was going to think I was trying to get away with a free ride."

Out of the corner of his eye, Guy noticed Babs sneaking closer, attempting to steal the letter. "If you don't take three steps back, you're taking a taxi or walking home!"

She pouted but complied, and he continued reading.

"In an odd way, the streets of Mexico City reminded me of our sets from *Casablanca*, except everyone dressed differently. Instead of being shrouded like typical Muslim women, the Mexican women had exposed tan faces. Some wore wide-brimmed straw hats to keep off the sun. All wore their thick, dark hair long, either loose or in braids. They wore festive, colorful skirts, often with embroidered cotton blouses. On cooler evenings, men and women wore blanket-like ponchos or *serapes*. Never quite understood the difference. Despite the scorching pavement, many went barefoot. Those who had money wore sandals or woven leather shoes called *huaraches*.

"In my travels throughout Europe, I had never been to Spain, but Virginia told me the Spanish conquistadors influenced Mexico's architecture, especially its churches. We discovered dusty streets where old men played dice inside shady nooks or doorways. We found markets in larger piazzas with vendors selling bananas, mangoes, and pottery.

"Soon it became clear that Virginia had come to Mexico on business for the Chicago Syndicate. The Midwestern mobsters profited from pushing drugs after the repeal of Prohibition. She told me her Chicago contact sent her upwards of five grand a week, in cash, for bribes and to buy Mexican cocaine and marijuana."

Overwhelmed, Guy couldn't contain himself any longer. He relinquished the note to Babs, who read it out loud for him.

"Working on a movie, we're in a microcosm, protected in our own cocoon and exempt from the woes of the world," she said. "My number one concern was Mr. Otake, but I never intended to hop on board the train with him. Still, I couldn't have anticipated he would raise a fuss when it came time to disembark and catch the boat from San Diego to Cabo. He kept insisting that back in June, Mexico had declared war against the Axis powers after German submarines had destroyed several of its shipping vessels. He still didn't feel safe being Japanese, even with a forged Canadian passport and a new identity. Being German, he insisted I'd also be in danger.

"How could he have known? Except I seemed to recall Dashiell Hammett had lent him a radio when he stayed hidden at the Garden of Allah. Otherwise, he was no longer in communication with his friends in the Japanese community. I refused to believe him.

"Guess who was the fool and out of touch? I realized once I got to Mexico, if I didn't get out of there fast, authorities would either throw me in jail or send me to the equivalent of a detention center. I needed to find a neutral country. At first, I considered Brazil or Argentina. These countries provided sanctuaries for Germans, but for me, considering the reasons I left Berlin, being around Nazis wasn't safe, either. Finally, I took my chances and fled to El Salvador. Police detained Virginia in a Mexican jail for smuggling contraband, but I assure you, Mr. Otake is out of danger. Best wishes, Rudy. P.S. Before I end this note, there's something I must confess."

Babs became hoarse. She looked at Guy and asked, "Should I go on?"

Still unable to say a word, he signaled for her to resume.

"I disclosed to you earlier that before I met you, Gerhard Sauer was my former lover—" Babs paused to take it all in. This was news to her. "Both of us had also worked undercover for Lewis's organization, trying to expose antisemitic organizations threatening Jews in Los Angeles County.

"Even after disbanding our organization, there were still a few rogue extremists at large. We had always suspected that one of our agents, Manfred Coblenz, also worked for a pro-fascist fellowship, passing along information and undermining our efforts. One day, I expected to meet Sauer at a nightclub. I'm not sure what transpired before I arrived, but I discovered Coblenz strangling and stabbing him in a back alley. I rushed in to save my friend. While trying to wrestle the knife away from Coblenz, I killed Sauer by accident. A woman I had known from Berlin, Birgit Müller, had witnessed the entire thing. Coblenz got away, but I needed to make sure I wouldn't get blamed. Gerhard's death wasn't my fault.

"Birgit, who owned a car, helped me move the body to Warner Brothers. Since others, like Lewis and Roos, knew he worked undercover at the studio, it only made sense that someone would find him there. We had no trouble getting past the gate with the pass I had as an actor. It was unlikely we'd get caught, because the studio lot was massive. Even after hours, so many employees came in and out, and with all the wizardry of the film world, nothing was as it seemed.

"Of course, you and I were aware when Coblenz worked the first day as the boom operator on *Casablanca*, but you didn't know about any crimes he committed before then. Neither did Leon Lewis nor Joseph Roos, and I failed to speak up because of my involuntary role in the tragedy. I can't begin to tell you what it was like to look at Coblenz, to hold in my *angst* and…" Babs looked up at Guy. "I'm not sure how to pronounce this word. It looks like it's in German."

"*Weltschmerz*," he said, grabbing hold of the letter. This time, he ripped it in half.

"What's that supposed to mean?" she asked.

"It's like bearing the sorrow of the world and, in Rudy's case," Guy said with a sigh, "he had to pretend nothing happened."

He pocketed the part of the letter they had already read and continued reading, "When Coblenz resurfaced and started working for Salka, filling Sauer's shoes as her bookkeeper, I ran into Birgit, who witnessed the first murder—the accidental one. She and I found him at Salka's guesthouse. Coblenz threatened me. We got into a fight, and I left him for dead. Figuring we'd get caught if we tried to remove his body during the party, we had to disappear.

"The next day, when we tried to get rid of him, someone beat us to it. I still don't know who it was. It was probably best that I left town with Otake. The police could've accused me of two murders, and who knows if Birgit would tell the truth about her involvement in the matter? If you must find her to get her testimony, you can always reach her through Billy Wilder. If you don't know who he is, my friend, you have no business working in Hollywood. She and Wilder have been long-time friends."

Despite the devastating news, Babs blew out a deep breath and began to feel at ease. "Let's hope this provides enough proof for us to convince Warner to halt production, call the police, and arrest Coblenz. We might even get lucky and find Birgit." She put her arm around her brokenhearted partner and said, "Let's get back to the set."

* * *

Along the way, Guy had a disturbing thought. "Babs, I saw Coblenz's name on the call sheet, but I don't recollect seeing anyone who fit his description. I also hate to say, but when Rudy wrote that letter—"

"Oh, gosh! You're right," said Babs. "He didn't know Coblenz could still be alive and here right now!"

"Don't panic. If he knows something's up, we'll bungle it. We've known what he looks like since we were there the day he got fired. I'm going to head over to wardrobe and makeup to see what they can tell me."

Babs agreed with his plan and told him she'd warn the producers. They needed to keep this quiet until the police arrived, and the filming needed to stay on schedule.

CHAPTER THIRTY-NINE

Guy returned ten minutes later. Babs asked whether he had discovered anything.

"Makeup told me Coblenz had bruises in the process of healing, and it looked like he'd broken his nose in a fight."

"With Rudy, I bet. What else?"

"He played a gendarme earlier. They hid the discolorations with pancake makeup, a fake mustache, and a prosthetic nose, so he'd look more like a typical Frenchman. Between his makeover and his Vichy kepi and uniform, that's why no one, not even the soundman, identified him."

Curtiz was eager to start the rehearsal. When Babs saw the actors emerge from backstage, she couldn't believe her eyes. "Guy, look, but don't stare! Ingrid must've shown our wedding photos to the costume designer. He copied the outfits we wore at our wedding for Rick Blaine and Ilsa Lund."

Guy slapped his hand over his mouth to keep from laughing out loud. "Well, I'll be darned. Who looks better? Us or them?"

Even though they kept their voices low, Curtiz still got gruff. "Didn't I ask for quiet?" He looked around but only got a "not me" look on everyone's faces. "Continue your coffee break. In the meantime, I'll call my wife."

He marched off the set to make a last-minute call for advice. Guy approached Ingrid and pulled the box out of his pocket. "We found your earrings."

"How? Where?" Ingrid cried tears of joy. "You don't know how much this means to me."

Guy replied, "That's a story for later."

* * *

The various craftsmen removed Coblenz's makeup and switched his wardrobe. After they transformed him to play Conrad's new double, all those who had been on the lookout finally recognized him.

"Call the police!" Guy shouted. "That's our murderer!"

Not even thinking, Henreid rushed toward the dummy prop phone. Ingrid, knowing better that the phone was a fake, darted for the nearest working phone.

"Pin him down, Guy!" Bogie hollered as they charged in and tackled him. "Between the two of us, he won't be going anywhere."

Wallis rushed over to break them up, but Babs stopped him. "He's the one who murdered Sauer, the dead technician you found on the set of *Yankee Doodle Dandy*! Now, we have proof!"

Coblenz managed to free his arm enough to grab his prop gun. Bogie rolled aside just enough to clear when Coblenz pulled the trigger. The gun thundered, and Guy wailed. Babs screamed and dashed into the fray. No longer restrained, Coblenz made a mad dash for the nearest exit, only to get stopped by police who had already been on the lot for another matter. They immediately cuffed him and locked him in the back of their squad car while listening to testimonies from the producers.

Babs put pressure on Guy's wound. "Call an ambulance!" she cried. When the bleeding got out of hand, she shouted, "Can anyone find something to use as a bandage?"

Guy thrashed from side to side, delirious and in agony. "I'll be fine…" His voice was barely above a whisper. "There're only…blanks."

Suddenly, Babs remembered the conversation he had with Raoul Walsh when he recruited Guy as a last-minute extra on *Desperate Journey*. Walsh asked, "Do you mind getting shot? Not real bullets, of course. I'm not like some of my more careless contemporaries who've killed a horse or two to get the effect."

Babs strained to speak. "At close range, you can still get killed by blanks!" She knelt beside him, hesitant about whether to roll him over. His blood soaked her outfit.

"Even after the prop master assured me it didn't have live ammunition, I double-checked," he croaked. "I'll be all right." Guy's eyes rolled back in their sockets, and he passed out.

Babs jumped to her feet. "Isn't there a first-aid station somewhere around here?" Since the cops seemed more concerned with their detainee, one of the production assistants volunteered to fetch help.

* * *

She continued to watch over Guy. "You've quit my agency once or twice, but I'm not losing you now!"

The police left with Coblenz in custody. Warner said he'd follow them to the station to give a detailed account about discovering Sauer's corpse on the set of *Yankee Doodle Dandy*. Wallis was still worried sick about the film coming in over one week behind schedule. Despite the commotion, Curtiz insisted on filming the final farewell scenes, but without the part when Rick Blaine shoots Major Strasser, since they were minus one stuntman.

The cast's looks of disapproval built to a crescendo. Henreid broke the spell of silence. "Haven't we been through enough? Why don't you let us go home?"

When Curtiz refused to relent, Bogie stepped forward. "I'm no good at being noble, but it doesn't take much to see that the problems of two penny-pinching producers and an insensitive director, *or three little people*, don't amount to a hill 'o beans in this crazy world."

Everyone gave the director a mean stare. "Maybe we should take time off," Curtiz said. "We still don't have an ending."

Undaunted, Wallis argued, "What? Where are our screenwriters when you need them?"

"It's not like you can snap your fingers, and they'll magically appear," said the assistant director.

Wallis, who was always the eye of the hurricane compared to Warner, raised his voice. "Summon them here now and have them bring their typewriters with them! How many months have the Epstein twins been working on it? We need a good punch line for the ending at the airport when Rick and Renault walk off into the fog."

Medics finally came and stabilized Guy's bleeding. "You're a lucky guy, Guy," one said. "The bullet scratched the skin's surface, enough to cause significant bleeding, but you're still getting it checked by a doctor. He'll want to treat it with antiseptic, and you'll need stitches."

Two men lifted him onto a stretcher. Babs clasped his hand and insisted on coming along.

Dooley and Peter leaned over and gave Guy their well-wishes. Peter looked at Babs and said, "He's your husband. You love him. Aren't you going to kiss him?"

She pulled a face. *He knew their marriage was just a front.*

"Ah, come on, Babs. A kiss is just a kiss," Dooley said, giving her a wink. He gave Guy a firm squeeze on the shoulder and said, "Hang in there, son."

Everyone lined up to give their last goodbyes. Sydney made a joke, calling himself the Fat Man, as he was called in *The Maltese Falcon.* He called Guy the *Thin Man*, after the PI's first celebrity case. "Put some meat on those bones while you're in the hospital."

Claude's parody of "Don't be a stranger" backfired when he tried to use the analogy of "Don't be invisible," like the Invisible Man.

"Thanks once again for finding my earrings," said Ingrid, as she bent over and kissed Guy on the forehead. "*As Time Goes By*, you'll be good as new."

Bogie tipped his hat to Guy, saying, "First, it's the bird. Now, it's the ticket to freedom. Don't know what's on the horizon next, but…here's looking at you, kid."

Walking alongside him, Babs squeezed his hand even tighter. "After all we went through, between my arrests and you losing your lover…and getting shot, I hope this film turns out halfway decent."

Guy gave her a mournful sigh. "Think of it this way, Babs. No matter what happens…" Once again, he lost consciousness.

"Stay with me!" Babs shouted. "You're not leaving me now!"

"No matter what happens, we…" he said, opening his eyes, "we will always have Burbank."

Author's Note and Disclaimer

Readers should familiarize themselves with the film *Casablanca*. Being aware of the plot and the relationships between the characters is vital to the satisfactory understanding of this story. On that note, please know that *Round Up the Unusual Suspects* is a work of fiction. The author took artistic license and altered the historical timeline to fit the logical narrative, along with the blending of fictional characters with real-life people who, in reality, never met, and in situations that never happened.

Thank you for your understanding.

— Elizabeth Crowens

RESOURCES

The challenge Elizabeth Crowens had with writing *Round Up the Unusual Suspects* was to create a plausible situation within impossible constraints. Although much of this story has been fictionalized, and often the author had to write actual events out of order to suit the narrative, she wanted to give credit to the sources she used to create this unique tale.

Although it's next to impossible to list every documentary or fictional film, radio show, interview, or television program she watched from a variety of streaming sources, from Turner Classic Movies to YouTube to IMDb.com to *The Hollywood Reporter* and *Variety* magazines to research this novel, here is a list of resources she used for her research. Please note that often descriptions of celebrities' personalities, quirks, and idiosyncrasies were often gleaned not only from historians but from biographies of other prominent people who knew and worked with people like Michael Curtiz and Humphrey Bogart. Therefore, the author will categorize this bibliography and filmography according to subject.

History of California and Los Angeles during the 1940s

- *A Tragedy of Democracy, Japanese Confinement in North America*, by Greg Robinson
- *Boyle Heights, How A Los Angeles Neighborhood Became the Future of American Democracy*, by George J. Sanchez
- *City of Nets, A Portrait of Hollywood in the 1940s*, by Otto Friedrich
- *Coming Out Under Fire: The History of Gay Men and Women in World War Two*, by Allan Berube
- *Desert Exile: The Uprooting of a Japanese Family*, by Yoshiko Uchida
- *Evergreen* and *Clark and Division*, fictional interpretation in novels by Naomi Hirahara
- *Gay L.A., A History of Sexual Outlaws, Power Politics, and Lipstick Lesbians*, by Lillian Faderman and Stuart Timmons
- *Hitler in Los Angeles*, by Stephen J. Ross
- *Hollywood's Spies: The Undercover Surveillance of Nazis in Los Angeles*, by Laura B. Rosenzweig
- *Prisoners Without Trial, Japanese Americans in World War II*, by Roger Daniels
- *The Collaboration: Hollywood's Pact With Hitler*, by Ben Urwand

Relevant world history leading up to World War II

- *Destination Casablanca*, by Meredith Hinley
- *Eldorado: Everything the Nazis Hate* (2023 documentary film, directed by Benjamin Cantu)
- *Gay Berlin*, by Robert Beach
- *The Great Dictator* (1940 Film, directed by Charles Chaplin)
- *The Pink Triangle*: *The Nazi War Against Homosexuals*, by Richard Plant
- *Unexpected Routes: Refugee Writers in Mexico*, by Tabea Alexa Linhard
- *Voluptuous Panic: The Erotic World of Weimar Berlin*, by Mel Gordon

The making of and history behind the film of *Casablanca*

- *Casablanca*, the script by Julius Epstein, Phillip Epstein, and Howard Koch
- *Casablanca: As Time Goes By*, by Frank Miller
- *Casablanca: An Unlikely Classic* (2012 short video, directed by Gary Leva)
- *Casablanca: Script and Legend*, by Howard Koch
- *Round Up the Usual Suspects: The Making of Casablanca-Bogart, Bergman, and World War II*, by Aljean Harmetz
- *You Must Remember This: The Filming of Casablanca* by Charles Francisco

Ingrid Bergman

- *Ingrid: A Personal Biography*, by Charlotte Chandler
- *Ingrid Bergman: In Her Own Words* (2015 documentary film, directed by Stig Björkman)
- *Notorious: The Life of Ingrid Bergman,* by Donald Spoto
- (Cross-referenced with other biographies)

Humphrey Bogart

- *Bogart: Life Comes In Flashes* (2024 film, directed by Kathryn Ferguson)
- *Humphrey Bogart: The Man and His Films*, by Paul Michael
- *Bogart*, by A.M. Sperber and Eric Lax
- *Humphrey Bogart: The Greatest Icon of Classic Hollywood* (Biographics)
- *John Huston: Courage and Art*, by Jeffrey Meyers
- *John Huston: Maker of Magic*, by Stuart Kaminsky
- *The Bogey Man: Portrait of a Legend*, by Jonah Ruddy and Jonathan Hill
- *The Hustons*: by Lawrence Grobel
- *The Pictorial Treasury of Film Stars: Humphrey Bogart*, by Alan G. Barbour
- *Tough Without a Gun: The Life and Extraordinary Afterlife of Humphrey Bogart*, by Stefan Kanfer

- (Cross-referenced with other people's biographies who had worked with him.)

Michael Curtiz

- *Michael Curtiz: A Life in Film* (Screen Classics) by Alan K. Rode
- *Michael Curtiz: The Greatest Director You've Never Heard Of* (Film, directed by Gary Leva)
- (Cross-referenced with other people's biographies who had worked with him.)

Sydney Greenstreet

- *Sydney Greenstreet & Peter Lorre: A Retrospective,* (Date: unknown, short documentary film)
- *The Maltese Falcon* (1941 film, directed by John Huston)
- *Across the Pacific* (1941 film, directed by John Huston)
- *Background to Danger* (1943 film, directed by Raoul Walsh)
- *The Mask of Dimitrios* (1944 film, directed by Jean Negulesco)
- *Three Strangers* (1946 film, directed by Jean Negulesco)
- *The Life and Times of Sydney Greenstreet,* by Derek Sculthorpe
- (Clipping files at the Lincoln Center Library of Performing Arts in New York)

Paul Henreid

- *Ladies Man: An Autobiography*, by Paul Henreid with Julius Fast
- *Now, Voyager* (1942 film, directed by Irving Rapper)
- *The Conspirators* (1944 film, directed by Jean Negulesco)
- (Cross-referenced with other sources)

Peter Lorre

- *Arsenic and Old Lace* (1944 film, directed by Frank Capra)
- *Hotel Berlin* (1945 film, directed by Peter Godfrey)
- *M* (1931 film, directed by Fritz Lang)
- *Mad Love* (1935 film, directed by Karl Freund)
- *Stranger on the Third Floor* (1940 film, directed by Boris Ingster)
- *The Face Behind the Mask* (1941 film, directed by Robert Florey)
- *The Films of Peter Lorre*, by Stephen D. Youngkin, James Bigwood, and Raymond Cabana, Jr.
- *The Lost One: A Life of Peter Lorre*, by Stephen D. Youngkin
- *The Man Who Knew Too Much* (1934 film, directed by Alfred Hitchcock)
- *Think Fast, Mr. Moto!* (1937 film, directed by Norman Foster and other Mr. Moto films.)
- (Clippings files at the Lincoln Center Library of Performing Arts in New York and the Margaret Herrick Motion Picture Academy Library in Beverly Hills.)

Claude Rains

- *Claude Rains: A Comprehensive Illustrated Reference,* by John T. Soister
- *Claude Rains: An Actor's Voice*, by David J. Skal
- *Notorious* (1946 film, directed by Alfred Hitchcock)
- *Now, Voyager* (1942 film, directed by Irving Rapper)
- *Passage to Marseille* (1944 film, directed by Michael Curtiz)
- *The Adventures of Robin Hood* (1938 film, directed by Michael Curtiz and William Keighley)
- *The Invisible Man* (1933 film, directed by James Whale)

Conrad Veidt

- *Above Suspicion* (1943 film, directed by Richard Thorpe)
- *All Through the Night* (1942 film, directed by Vincent Sherman)

- *A Woman's Face* (1941 film, directed by George Cukor)
- *Conrad Veidt: Demon of the Silver Screen,* by Sabine Schwientek
- *Conrad Veidt On Screen: A Comprehensive Illustrated Filmography,* by John T. Soister
- *Different from the Others,* Original title: *Anders als die Andern* (1919 silent film, directed by Richard Oswald)
- *Nazi Agent* (1942 film, directed by Jules Dassin)
- *The Cabinet of Dr. Caligari* (1920 film, directed by Robert Wiene)

Mobsters and organized crime in Los Angeles

- *Bugsy* (1991 film, directed by Barry Levinson)
- *Bugsy's Baby: The Secret Life of Mob Queen Virginia Hill,* by Andy Edmonds
- *Bugsy Siegel: The Dark Side of the American Dream,* by Michael Shnayerson
- *Bugsy Siegel: The Mobster Who Built Las Vegas and Paid the Price (Rogues Gallery, Killer Crime and Wild Life Documentary)*
- *George Raft,* by Lewis Yablonsky
- *The George Raft File,* by James Robert Parish with Steven Whitney
- *Mobsters: Bugsy Siegel on Bio.com*
- *We Only Kill Each Other: The Life and Bad Times of Bugsy Siegel,* by Dean Jennings
- (Cross-referenced with other sources)

Salka Viertel

- *Exiled in Paradise,* by Anthony Heilbut
- *Strangers in Paradise: The Hollywood Émigrés, 1933-1950,* by John Russell Taylor
- *The Kindness of Strangers,* by Salka Viertel

Hal B. Wallis

- *Starmaker: The Autobiography of Hal Wallis*, by Hal Wallis and Charles Higham
- (Cross-referenced with other people's biographies who had worked with him.)

Jack L. Warner

- *Clown Prince of Hollywood: The Antic Life and Times of Jack L. Warner*, by Bob Thomas
- *Jack L. Warner: The Last Mogul* (2023 film, directed by Gregory Orr)
- *My First Hundred Years*, autobiography by Jack L. Warner
- *The Warner Brothers*, by Chris Yogerst
- *The Warner Brothers*, by Michael Freedland
- *Warner Brothers*, by Charles Higham
- *Warner Brothers: The Making of an American Movie Studio*, by David Thomson

Other films and books for research

- *Algiers* (1938 film, directed by John Cromwell)
- *Anna Karenina* (1935 film, directed by Clarence Brown, starring Greta Garbo)
- *Dashiell Hammett: A Daughter Remembers*, by Jo Hammett
- *Desperate Journey* (1942 film, directed by Raoul Walsh)
- *Erle Stanley Gardner: The Case of the Real Perry Mason, A Biography*, by Dorothy B. Hughes
- *For Whom the Bell Tolls* (1943 film, directed by Sam Wood)
- *Garbo* (2005 film, directed by Christopher Bird & Kevin Brownlow)
- *Garbo: Where Did You Go?* (2024 film, directed by Lorna Tucker)
- *Grand Hotel* (1932 film, directed by Edmund Goulding, starring Greta Garbo)

- *Hammett* (1982 film, directed by Wim Wenders and Francis Ford Coppola)
- *Hammett: A Life at the Edge*, by William F. Nolan
- *Julia* (1977 film directed by Fred Zinnemann)
- *Lillian Hellman*, by William Wright
- *Mata Hari* (1931 film, directed by George Fitzmaurice, starring Greta Garbo)
- *Memo from David O. Selznick*, edited by Rudy Behlmer
- *Ninotchka* (1939 film, directed by Ernst Lubitsch, starring Greta Garbo)
- *Shadow Man: The Life of Dashiell Hammett*, by Richard Layman
- *The Court of Last Resort: The True Story of a Team of Crime Experts Who Fought to Save the Wrongfully Convicted*, by Erle Stanley Gardner
- *The Desert Song* (1943 film, directed by Robert Florey)
- *Three Penny Opera* (1931 film, directed by Georg Wilhelm Pabst, written by Bertolt Brecht)
- *Yankee Doodle Dandy* (1942 film, directed by Michael Curtiz)

Acknowledgments

My agent, Elizabeth K. Kracht at Kimberley Cameron & Associates, Shawn Reilly Simmons, and Deb Well at Level Best Books, Bree Russell at the Warner Brothers USC Archives, Brian Weldon at the Access Services Division and his associates at The New York Public Library of the Performing Arts, Chris Arabadjis and Elizabeth Berg at the Pratt Institute Reference Library, David Kaye, Alan K. Rode, Ann Louise Bannon and Michael Holland, Bernd Willand, Richard Koreto, Grace Bradley, Dan White, Catalina Eagan, Shizuka Otake, Kevin Wetmore, Jennifer Morita, James L'Etoile, Daniel Stashower, Kenny Lane, Sue and Gary Baughman, Sonya Steele, and Lola, who inspired the character of Babs Norman.

Book Club Questions for Round Up the Unusual Suspects

1. What was your favorite part of the book?
2. What was your least favorite?
3. Which scene stuck with you the most?
4. Did you feel the book was educational? Did you learn something new from the book that you hadn't expected?
5. What surprised you the most about the book?
6. Does this book remind you of any other books or films?
7. Would you ever consider re-reading the book? Why or why not?
8. If this book were adapted to film, who would you like to see in the cast?
9. What characters did you like the best? Which did you like the least?
10. How did the setting impact the story? Would you want to read more books set in 1940s Hollywood?
11. Which twist surprised you the most?
12. Did you guess the ending? If so, at what point?
13. Would you definitely recommend this author and read other books that will come up in this series?
14. Are you curious about the other books this author has written, even if they are in a different genre?

About the Author

Elizabeth Crowens is bi-coastal between Los Angeles and New York. For over thirty years, she has worn many hats in the entertainment industry, contributed stories to *Black Belt, Black Gate, Sherlock Holmes Mystery Magazines, Hell's Heart,* and the Bram Stoker-nominated *A New York State of Fright*, and has a popular Caption Contest on Facebook.

Awards include: Agatha Awards nominee for *Hounds of the Hollywood Baskervilles*, Lefty Awards nominee for *Bye Bye Blackbird*, Leo B. Burstein Scholarship from the MWA-NY Chapter, New York Foundation of the Arts grant to publish the anthology *New York: Give Me Your Best or Your Worst*, Eric Hoffer Award, Glimmer Train Awards Honorable Mention, Killer Nashville Silver Falchion Top Picks, Killer Nashville Claymore Award Finalist, two Grand prize, six First prize, and multiple Finalist Chanticleer Awards. Crowens writes multi-genre alternate history and historical Hollywood mysteries.

AUTHOR WEBSITE:
  https://www.elizabethcrowens.com/

SOCIAL MEDIA HANDLES:
   https://facebook.com/thereel.elizabeth.crowens
   https://instagram.com/ElizabethCrowens
   https://x.com/ECrowens
   https://www.linkedin.com/in/elizabeth-crowens-5227804/
   https://www.goodreads.com/author/show/15173793.Elizabeth_Crowens

Also by Elizabeth Crowens

Hounds of the Hollywood Baskervilles, Book One in the Babs Norman Golden Age of Hollywood Mystery series. Agatha nominee. First Prize winner of the Chanticleer Review Mystery & Mayhem (M&M) and Mark Twain Awards, Finalist in Killer Nashville's Claymore Awards and Top Pick in Killer Nashville's Silver Falchion Awards

Bye Bye Blackbird, Book Two in the Babs Norman Golden Age of Hollywood Mystery series and Lefty Awards nominee for Best Humorous Mystery

New York: Give Me Your Best or Your Worst (photo-illustrated anthology), Grand Prize winner of the Chanticleer Review Shorts/Anthologies Award

Three novels in the Time Traveler Professor series (alternate history):
   Silent Meridian, First Prize winner of the Chanticleer Review Goethe Award
   A Pocketful of Lodestones, First Prize winner of the Chanticleer Review Mary Shelley / Paranormal Award
   A War in Too Many Worlds, Grand Prize winner of the Chanticleer Review Cygnus Award

www.ingramcontent.com/pod-product-compliance
Lightning Source LLC
Chambersburg PA
CBHW020741310726
48969CB00002B/355